SCOTT TUROW

PRESUMED
INNOCENT

PENGUIN BOOKS

PENGUIN BOOKS

Published by the Penguin Group
27 Wrights Lane, London W8 5TZ, England
Viking Penguin Inc., 40 West 23rd Street, New York, New York 10010, USA
Penguin Books Australia Ltd, Ringwood, Victoria, Australia
Penguin Books Canada Ltd, 2801 John Street, Markham, Ontario, Canada L3R 1B4
Penguin Books (NZ) Ltd, 182–190 Wairau Road, Auckland 10, New Zealand

Penguin Books Ltd, Registered Offices: Harmondsworth, Middlesex, England

First published in Great Britain by Bloomsbury 1987
Published in Penguin Books 1988
20

Made and printed in Great Britain by
Richard Clay Ltd, Bungay, Suffolk
Filmset in 9/11 pt Monophoto Times

PENGUIN BOOKS

PRESUMED INNOCENT

'A marvel of authenticity married to a beautifully original plot. Turow plays his cards like a poker player. Above all his work is original' – *Today*

'Impossible to put down' – *London Evening Standard*

'Spellbinding . . . a roller-coaster ride of moods for Rusty, and a crack-the-whip of surprising revelations for the reader. And when it is over, the sharpest twists and turns are still to come' – *The New York Times*

'The combination of violent crime and sleazy politics proves as volatile a cocktail as a wino's meths and floor-polish special' – *Independent*

'A riveting performance' – *Observer*

'A splendid piece of work . . . It snags both of your lapels and presses you down in your chair until you've finished it' – *Chicago Tribune Book World*

Scott Turow was Stegner Fellow in creative writing at Stanford before attending Harvard Law School. He served with distinction as an assistant US attorney in his native Chicago, winning a number of important cases involving corruption in the Illinois legal system. He is now a partner in the Chicago law firm of Sonnenschein Carlin Nath and Rosenthal. *Presumed Innocent* won the 1987 Silver Dagger Award.

FOR MY MOTHER

OPENING
STATEMENT

This is how I always start:

'I am the prosecutor.

'I represent the state. I am here to present to you the evidence of a crime. Together you will weigh this evidence. You will deliberate upon it. You will decide if it proves the defendant's guilt.

'This man –' And here I point.

You must always point, Rusty, I was told by John White. That was the day I started in the office. The sheriff took my fingerprints, the chief judge swore me in, and John White brought me up to watch the first jury trial I'd ever seen. Ned Halsey was making the opening statement for the state, and as he gestured across the courtroom, John, in his generous, avuncular way, with the humid scent of alcohol on his breath at ten in the morning, whispered my initial lesson. He was the chief deputy P A then, a hale Irishman with white hair wild as cornsilk. It was almost a dozen years ago, long before I had formed even the most secret ambition to hold John's job myself. If you don't have the courage to point, John White whispered, you can't expect them to have the courage to convict.

And so I point. I extend my hand across the courtroom. I hold one finger straight. I seek the defendant's eye. I say:

'This man has been accused.'

He turns away. Or blinks. Or shows nothing at all.

In the beginning, I was often preoccupied, imagining how it would feel to sit there, held at the focus of scrutiny, ardently denounced before all who cared to listen, knowing that the most ordinary

7

privileges of a decent life – common trust, personal respect, and even liberty – were now like some cloak you had checked at the door and might never retrieve. I could feel the fear, the hot frustration, the haunted separateness.

Now, like ore deposits, the harder stuff of duty and obligation has settled in the veins where those softer feelings moved. I have a job to do. It is not that I have grown uncaring. Believe me. But this business of accusing, judging, punishing has gone on always; it is one of the great wheels turning beneath everything we do. I play my part. I am a functionary of our only universally recognized system of telling wrong from right, a bureaucrat of good and evil. This must be prohibited; not that. One would expect that after all these years of making charges, trying cases, watching defendants come and go, it might have all become a jumble. Somehow, it has not.

I turn back to face the jury.

'Today you – all of you – have taken on one of the most solemn obligations of citizenship. Your job is to find the facts. The truth. It is not an easy task, I know. Memories may fail; recollections may be shaded. The evidence might point in differing directions. You may be forced to decide about things that no one seems to know, or to be willing to say. If you were at home, at work, anywhere in your daily life, you might be ready to throw up your hands, you might not want to make the effort. Here you must.

'You must. Let me remind you. There was a real crime. No one will dispute that. There was a real victim. Real pain. You do not have to tell us why it happened. People's motives, after all, may be forever locked inside them. But you must, at least, try to determine what actually occurred. If you cannot, we will not know if this man deserves to be freed – or punished. We will have no idea who to blame. If we cannot find the truth, what is our hope of justice?'

SPRING

1

'I should feel sorrier,' Raymond Horgan says.

I wonder at first if he is talking about the eulogy he is going to deliver. He has just looked over his notes again and is returning two index cards to the breast pocket of his blue serge suit. But when I catch his expression I recognize that his remark was personal. From the rear seat of the county's Buick, he stares through the auto window toward the traffic thickening as we approach the South End. His look has taken on a meditative cast. As I watch him, it strikes me that this pose would have been effective as The Picture for this year's campaign: Raymond's thick features fixed in an aspect of solemnity, courage, and a trace of sorrow. He shows something of the stoic air of this sometimes sad metropolis, like the soiled bricks and tarpaper roofs of this part of town.

It is a commonplace among those working around Raymond to say he does not look well. Twenty months ago he split with Ann, his wife of thirty years. He has picked up weight and a perpetual grimness of expression which suggests he has finally reached that time of life when he now believes that many painful things will not improve. A year ago the wagering was that Raymond did not have the stamina or interest to run again, and he waited until four months before the primary to finally announce. Some say it was addiction to power and public life that made him proceed. I believe the chief impulse was Raymond's outright hatred of his primary opponent, Nico Della Guardia, who was until last year another deputy prosecuting attorney in our office. Whatever the motivation, it has proved a difficult campaign. While the money lasted, there were agencies involved and media consultants. Three young men of dubious sexuality dictated as to matters such as The Picture, and saw to it that this image of Raymond was applied to the backside of one in every four buses in the city. In the picture he has a coaxed smile, meant to show a toughened whimsy. I think the photograph makes him look like a kind of sap. It is one more sign that Raymond has fallen out of step. That is probably what he means when he says he should feel sorrier. He means that events seem to be slipping past him again.

Raymond goes on talking about Carolyn Polhemus's death three nights ago, on the first of April.

'It's as if I can't reach it. I have Nico on one side making out like I'm the one who murdered her. And every jackass in the world with press credentials wants to know when we're going to find the killer. And the secretaries are crying in the johns. And in the end, you know, there's this woman to think about. Christ, I knew her as a probation officer before she graduated law school. She worked for me, I hired her. A smart, sexy gal. A helluva lawyer. And you think about it eventually, you know, the actual event – I think I'm jaded, but Jesus. Some cretin breaks in there. And that's how she ends up, that's her *au revoir*? With some demented slug cracking her skull and giving her a jump. Jesus,' Raymond says again. 'You can't feel sorry enough.'

'No one broke in,' I finally say. My sudden declarative tone surprises even me. Raymond, who has momentarily resumed his consideration of a lapful of papers brought along from the office, rears his head and fixes me with an astute gray eye.

'Where do you get that from?'

I am slow to answer.

'We find the lady raped and bound,' says Raymond. 'Off-hand, I wouldn't be starting off my investigation with her friends and admirers.'

'No broken windows,' I say, 'no forced doors.'

At this point Cody, the thirty-year copper who is living out his last days on the force by driving Raymond's county car, breaks into the conversation from the front seat. Cody has been unusually quiet today, sparing us the customary reverie about the bum deals and good pinches he has witnessed in gross on most city avenues.

Unlike Raymond – or, for that matter, me – he has no difficulty bringing himself to sorrow. He appears to have been without sleep, which gives his face an edge of roughened grief. My comment about the condition of Carolyn's apartment has stirred him for some reason.

'Every door and window in the joint was unlocked,' he says. 'She liked it that way. The broad was living in wonderland.'

'I think somebody was being clever,' I tell them both. 'I think that's misdirection.'

'Come on, Rusty,' Raymond says. 'We're looking for a bum. We don't need fucking Sherlock Holmes. Don't try to get ahead of the murder dicks. Keep your head down and walk in a straight line. Okay? Catch me a perpetrator and save my worthless ass.' He smiles at me then, a warm, savvy look. Raymond wants me to know he is bearing up. Besides, there is no need to further emphasize the implications of catching Carolyn's killer.

In his reported comments about Carolyn's death, Nico has been base and exploitative and relentless. 'The prosecuting attorney's lax approach to law enforcement for the last twelve years has made him the accomplice of the city's criminal elements. Even the members of his own staff are no longer safe, as this tragedy illustrates.' Nico has not explained how his own hiring by Raymond as a deputy P A more than a decade ago fit into Raymond's liaison with lawlessness. But it is not the politician's lot to explain. Besides, Nico has always been shameless in his public conduct. That is one thing that made him ripe for a political career.

Ripe or not, Nico is widely expected to lose the primary, now eighteen days away. Raymond Horgan has wowed Kindle County's one and a half million registered voters for better than a decade. This year he is yet to win the party endorsement, but that is largely due to an ancient factional dispute with the mayor. Raymond's political people – a group that has never included me – believe that when the first of the public polls are published in the next week and a half, other party leaders will be able to force the mayor to reverse field, and that Raymond will be safe for another quadrennium. In this one-party town, victory in the primary is tantamount to election.

Cody turns back from the front seat and mentions that it is getting close to one. Raymond nods absently. Cody takes this for assent and reaches below the dash to let the siren go. He uses it in two brief spells, almost like punctuation in the traffic, but the cars and trucks part neatly and the dark Buick noses ahead. The neighborhood here is still marginal – older shingle-sided houses, splintering porches. Kids with a kind of potatoey pallor play with balls and ropes at the edge of the street. I grew up about three blocks from here, in an apartment over my father's bakery. I recall them as dark years. During the day my mother and I, when I was not in school, helped my father in the shop. At night we stayed in one locked room while my father drank. There were no other children. The neighborhood today is not much different, still full of people like my father – Serbians, as he was, Ukrainians, Italians, Poles – ethnic types who keep their peace and their own dim outlook.

We are stopped dead in the heavy traffic of Friday afternoon. Cody has driven up the back end of a city bus, which emits its noxious fumes with an intestinal rumble. A Horgan campaign poster is right there, too, and Raymond looks out overhead, six feet wide, with the hapless expression of a TV talk-show host or the spokesman for some canned cat food. And I cannot help myself. Raymond Horgan is my future and my past. I have been a dozen years with him, years full of authentic loyalty and admiration. I am his second-in-command, and his fall would be my own. But there is no silencing the voice of discontent; it has its own imperatives. And it speaks now to the image overhead in a sudden forthright way. You sap, it says. You are, it says, a sap.

As we turn down Third Street, I can see that the funeral has become an important event for the police department. Half the parked cars are black-and-whites, and there are cops in pairs and threes moving up and down the walks. Killing a prosecutor is only one step short of killing a cop, and whatever the institutional interests, Carolyn had many friends on the force – the sort of loyal lieges a good PA develops by appreciating skilled police work and

14

making sure it is not squandered in court. Then, of course, there is the fact that she was a beautiful woman and one of modern temperament. Carolyn, we know, got around.

Nearer the chapel the traffic is hopelessly congested. We stutter only a few feet before waiting for the cars ahead to disgorge passengers. The vehicles of the very important – limousines with official plates, press people looking for spaces nearby – clog the way with bovine indifference. The broadcast reporters in particular obey neither local ordinance nor the rules of common civility. The Minicam van of one of the stations, complete with its rooftop radar dish, is parked on the sidewalk directly in front of the open oak doors of the chapel, and a number of reporters are working the crowd as if they were at a prizefight, thrusting microphones at arriving officials.

'Afterward,' Raymond says, as he bulls through the press horde that encircles the car as soon as we finally reach the curb. He explains that he is going to make some remarks in eulogy which he will repeat again outside. He pauses long enough to pet Stanley Rosenberg from Channel 5. Stanley, as usual, will get the first interview.

Paul Dry, from the mayor's staff, is motioning to me. His Honor, it seems, would like a word with Raymond before the service begins. I relay the message just as Horgan is pulling free of the reporters. He makes a face – unwisely, for Dry can certainly see it – before he walks off with Paul, disappearing into the gothic dark of the church. The mayor, Augustine Bolcarro, has the character of a tyrant. Ten years ago, when Raymond Horgan was the hot face in town, he almost ran Bolcarro out of office. Almost. Since losing that primary, Raymond has made all the appropriate gestures of fealty. But Bolcarro still feels the ache of his old wounds. Now that it is, at last, Raymond's turn to endure a contested primary, the mayor has claimed that his party role demands neutrality and he has designed to withhold the party's endorsement as well. Clearly he is enjoying watching Raymond struggle on his own toward shore. When Horgan finally hits the beach, Augie will be the first to greet him, saying he knew Raymond was a winner all along.

Inside, the pews are already largely occupied. At the front, the bier is ringed with flowers – lilies and white dahlias – and I imagine, notwithstanding all the bodies, a vague floral scent on the air. I make my way forward, nodding to various personages, and shaking hands. It is a heavyweight crowd: all the city and county pols. Most of the judges are here; most of the bright lights of the defense bar. A number of the leftish and feminist groups with whom Carolyn was sometimes aligned are also represented. The talk is appropriately low key, the expressions of shock and loss sincere.

I back into Della Guardia, who is also working the crowd.

'Nico!' I shake his hand. He has a flower in his lapel, a habit he has acquired since becoming a candidate. He asks after my wife and son, but he does not await my answer. Instead, he assumes a sudden look of tragical sobriety and begins to speak of Carolyn's sudden death.

'She was just –' He circles his hand for the word. I realize that the dashing candidate for prosecuting attorney aspires to poetry and I cut him off.

'She was splendid,' I say, and am momentarily amazed by my sudden rush of sentiment, and the force and speed with which it has wrenched itself from some hidden inner place.

' "Splendid" That's it. Very good.' Nico nods; then some mercurial shadow passes across his face. I know him well enough to recognize that he has found a thought which he believes is to his advantage. 'I imagine Raymond's pressing pretty hard on that case.'

'Raymond Horgan presses hard on every case. You know that.'

'Oh ho. I always thought you were the one who was nonpolitical, Rusty. You're picking up your lines now from Raymond's copywriters.'

'Better than yours, Delay.' Nico acquired that nickname while we were both new deputy PAs working in the appellate section. Nico never could complete a brief on time. John White, the old chief deputy, called him Unavoidable Delay Guardia.

'Oh, no,' he says. 'You fellas aren't angry with me, are you, for what I've been saying? Because I believe that. I believe that effective law enforcement starts right at the top. I believe that's true. Raymond's soft. He's tired. He doesn't have it left to be tough.'

I met Nico a dozen years ago, on my first day as a deputy PA, when we were assigned to share an office. Eleven years later I was the chief deputy and he was head of the Homicide Section and I fired him. By then he had begun overtly attempting to run Raymond out of office. There was a black physician, an abortionist, whom Nico wanted to prosecute for murder. His position made no sense as a matter of law, but it excited the passions of various interest groups whose support he sought. Nico planted news stories about his disagreements with Raymond; he made jury arguments – for which abundant press coverage always was arranged – that were little more than campaign speeches. Raymond left the final act to me. One morning I went to K Mart and bought the cheapest pair of running shoes they had. I centered them on Nico's desk with a note: 'Goodbye. Good luck. Rusty.'

I always knew campaigning was going to suit him. He looks good. Nico Della Guardia is about forty now, a man of medium height, fastidiously trim. He has been concerned about his weight, eating red meat, things like that, as long as I've known him. Although his skin is bad and his coloring peculiar – red hair and olive skin and light eyes – he has the sort of face whose imperfections are not detected by a camera or even across a courtroom and he is uniformly regarded as handsome. Certainly he has always dressed the part. Even in the days when it required half his paycheck, his suits were tailor-made.

But far beyond good looks, Nico's most arresting aspect has always been the brassy and indiscriminate sincerity he is displaying here, reciting the elements of his platform while conversing, in the midst of a funeral, with his opponent's chief assistant. After twelve years, including two in which we shared an office, I have learned that Delay can always summon up that kind of overeager and unreflective faith in himself. The morning that I fired him nine months ago, he strolled past my office on his way out, bright as a new penny, and said simply, I'll be back.

I try to let Nico down easy now.

'It's too late, Delay. I've promised my vote to Raymond Horgan.'

He is slow to get the joke, and when he does, he will not give the subject up. We go on playing a sort of lawyer's Dozens, dwelling on weaknesses. Nico admits his campaign is short of money but claims that the archbishop's unspoken support lends him 'moral capital.'

'That's where we're strong,' he says. 'Really. That's where we'll pick up votes. People have forgotten why they ever wanted to vote for Civil Rights Raymond. He's just a blur to them. A blob. I have a strong, clear message.' Nico's confidence is radiant, as ever, when he speaks about himself. 'You know what worried me?' Nico asks. 'You know who would have been hard to beat?' He has crept a foot closer and lowered his voice. 'You.'

I laugh out loud, but Nico goes on: 'I was relieved. I'm telling you the truth. I was relieved when Raymond announced. I'd seen it coming: Horgan holds a big press conference, says he's hanging it up, but he's asked his top assistant to carry on. Media is going to love Rusty Sabich. A non-political guy. A professional prosecutor. Stable. Mature. Somebody everyone can depend on. The man who broke up the Night Saints. They play all that stuff and Raymond brings Bolcarro in behind you. You'd've been tough, very tough.'

'Ridiculous,' I say, manfully pretending that like scenarios have not described themselves to my imagination on a hundred occasions in the last year. 'You're really something, Delay,' I tell him. 'Divide and conquer. You'll just never stop.'

'Hey listen, my friend,' he says, 'I am one of your true admirers. I mean that. There are no hard feelings here.' He touches his shirt above the vest. 'That is one of the few things that's going to stay the same when I get there. You'll still be in the chief deputy's office.'

I tell him, affably, that's a bunch of crap.

'You'll never be PA,' I say, 'and if you were, Tommy Molto would be your guy. Everybody knows you have Tommy in the woodshed now.' Tommy Molto is Nico's best friend, his former second-in-command in the Homicide Section. Molto has been a

18

no-show in the office for three days. He hasn't called in and his desk is clean. The common belief is that when the furor over Carolyn's death abates a bit next week, Nico will stage another media occasion and announce that Tommy has joined his campaign. It will provoke a few more headlines. DISAPPOINTED HORGAN DEPUTY BACKS NICO. Delay handles these things well. Raymond has a fit whenever he hears Tommy's name.

'Molto?' Nico asks me now. His look of innocence is entirely unconvincing, but I do not get the chance to respond. At the lectern, the reverend has asked the mourners to assume their seats. Instead I smile at Della Guardia – smirk, in fact – as we are parting, and begin buffeting my way toward the front of the chapel, where Raymond and I are supposed to sit as office representatives. But as I go, making restrained gestures of acknowledgment to the people that I know, the heat of all of Nico's forceful confidence is still upon me. It is like having come in out of the blazing sun: the skin tingles and remains tender to the touch. And it strikes me then abruptly, as I gain my first clear view of the pewter-colored casket, that Nico Della Guardia actually may win. This prophecy is announced by a small voice somewhere in my interior reaches, only loud enough, like some whining conscience, to tell me what I do not want to hear. Undeserving as Nico is, unqualified, a pygmy in his soul, something may be propelling him toward triumph. Here, in this region of the dead, I cannot help but recognize the carnal appeal of his vitality and how far it is bound to take him.

In keeping with the character of this public occasion, two rows of folding chairs have been positioned next to Carolyn's coffin. They are occupied, for the most part, by the dignitaries you would expect. The only unfamiliar figure is a boy in his late teens who is seated beside the mayor, directly at the foot of the bier. This young man has a poorly barbered tangle of blondish hair and a necktie drawn too tight, so that the collar points on his rayon shirt are lifted in the air. A cousin, I decide, perhaps a nephew, but definitely – and surprisingly – family. Carolyn's people, as I understood it, were all back East, where she meant to leave them long ago. Beside him in the front row there are more of the mayor's people than there should be, and no room is left for me. As I pass in the row behind Horgan, Raymond leans back. He has apparently observed my talk with Della Guardia.

'What did Delay have to say for himself?'

'Nothing. Bullshit. He's running out of money.'

'Who isn't?' Raymond asks.

I inquire about the meeting with the mayor, and Horgan rolls his eyes.

'He wanted to give me some advice, just in confidence, me and him, because he doesn't want to appear to be taking sides. He thinks it would help my chances a lot if we arrested Carolyn's murderer before Election Day. Can you believe that jagoff? And he said it with a straight face, too, so I couldn't walk out on him. He's having a great time.' Raymond points. 'Look at him up there. The chief mourner.'

Raymond as usual cannot contain himself about Bolcarro. I look around, hoping we have not been overheard. I chuck my face toward the young man seated beside the mayor.

'Who is the kid?' I ask.

I do not think I have understood Horgan's answer, and I lean closer. Raymond brings his face right to my ear.

'Her son,' he says again.

I stand up straight.

'Grew up with his father in New Jersey,' Raymond says, 'then came out here for college. He's over at the U.'

Surprise seems to drive me backward. I murmur something to Raymond and push down the row toward my seat at the end, between two sizable floral arrangements on pedestals. For an instant I am certain that this lightheaded moment of shock has passed, but as an unexpectedly bold tone forges from the organ immediately behind me, and the reverend speaks his first words of address, my amazement deepens, ripples, and somehow takes on the infected hurt of real sorrow. I did not know. I feel a sort of shimmering incomprehension. It does not seem plausible that she could have kept a fact like this to herself. The husband I had long ago surmised, but she never made mention of a child, let alone one

20

nearby, and I must stifle an immediate instinct to leave, to remove myself from this theater darkness for the sobering effect of strong light. As a matter of will, I urge myself, after a few moments, to attend to what is present.

Raymond has arrived at the podium; there has been no formal introduction. Others – the Reverend Mr Hiller, Rita Worth from the Women's Bar Association – have spoken briefly, but now a sudden gravity and portentousness comes into the air, a current strong enough to wrest me from my sense of grievance. The hundreds here grow stiller. Raymond Horgan has his shortcomings as a politician, but he is a consummate public man, a speaker, a presence. Balding, growing stout, standing there in his fine blue suit, he broadcasts his anguish and his power like a beaconed emission.

His remarks are anecdotal. He recalls Carolyn's hiring over the objections of more hard-bitten prosecutors who regarded probation officers as social workers. He celebrates her toughness and her flint. He remembers cases that she won, judges she defied, archaic rules she took pleasure in seeing broken. From Raymond, these stories have a soulful wit, a sweet melancholy for Carolyn and all of her lost courage. He really has no equal in a setting like this, just talking to people about what he thinks and feels.

For me, though, there is no quick recovery from the disorder of the moments before. I find all of it – the hurt, the shock, the piercing force of Raymond's words, my deep, my unspeakable sorrow – welling up, pushing at the limits of tolerance and a composure I desperately need to maintain. I bargain with myself. I will not go to the interment. There is work to do, and the office will be represented. The secretaries and clerks, the older ladies who always criticized Carolyn's airs and are here now, crying in the front rows, will be pressed close at the graveside, weeping over one more of life's endless desolations. I will let them observe Carolyn's disappearance into open ground.

Raymond finishes. The impressive register of his performance, witnessed by so many who regard him as beleaguered, sets a palpable stir in the auditorium as he strides toward his seat. The reverend recites the details of the burial, but I let that pass. I am resolved: I will go back to the office. As Raymond wishes, I will resume the search for Carolyn's killer. Nobody will mind – least of all, I think, Carolyn herself. I have already paid her my respects. Too much so, she might say. Too often. She knows, I know, that I have already done my grieving over Carolyn Polhemus.

2

The office has the bizarre air of calamity, of things badly out of place. The halls are empty, but the phones are pealing in wearying succession. Two secretaries, the only ones who stayed behind, are sprinting up and down the corridors putting callers on hold.

Even in the best of times, the Office of the Kindle County Prosecuting Attorney has a dismal aspect. Most deputies work two to an office in a space of Dickensian grimness. The Kindle County Building was erected in 1897 in the emerging institutional style of factories and high schools. It is a solid red-brick block dressed up with a few Doric columns to let everybody know it is a public place. Inside, there are transoms over the doors and dour casement windows. The walls are that mossy hospital green. Worst of all is the light, a kind of yellow fluid, like old shellac. So here we are, two hundred harried individuals attempting to deal with every crime committed in a city of one million, and the surrounding county, where two million people more reside. In the summer we labor in jungle humidity, with the old window units rattling over the constant clamor of the telephones. In the winter the radiators spit and clank while the hint of darkness never seems to leave the daylight. Justice in the Middle West.

In my office, Lipranzer is waiting for me like a bad guy in a Western, hidden as he sits behind the door.

'Everybody dead and gone?' he asks.

I comment on his sentimentality and throw my coat down on a chair. 'Where were you, by the way? Any copper with five years' service showed.'

'I'm no funeralgoer,' Lipranzer says dryly. There is, I decide, some significance in a homicide dick's distaste for funerals, but the connection does not come to me immediately and so I let the idea go. Life in the workplace: so many signs of the hidden world of meanings elude me in a day, bumps on the surface, shadows, like creatures darting by.

I attend to what is present. On my desk there are two items: a memo from MacDougall, the chief administrative deputy, and an envelope Lipranzer has placed there. Mac's memo simply says, 'Where is Tommy Molto?' It occurs to me that for all of our suspicions of political intrigue, we should not ignore the obvious: someone ought to check the hospitals and Tommy's apartment. One deputy PA is dead already. That is the reason for Lipranzer's envelope. It bears a label typed by the police lab: OFFENDER: UNKNOWN. VICTIM: C. POLHEMUS.

'Did you know that our decedent left an heir?' I ask as I'm looking for the letter opener.

'No shit,' says Lip.

'A kid. Looked to be eighteen, twenty. He was at the funeral.'

'No shit,' says Lip again, and considers his cigarette. 'You figure one thing about goin to a funeral is at least no surprises.'

'One of us ought to talk to him. He's at the U.'

'Get me an address, I'll see him. "Anything Horgan's guys want." Morano gave me that crock again this mornin.' Morano is the police chief, an ally of Bolcarro's. 'He's waitin to see Raymond fall on his ass.'

'Him and Nico. I bumped into Delay.' I tell Lip about our visit. 'Nico's really high on himself. He even made me believe it for a minute.'

'He'll do better than people say. Then you'll be kickin yourself in the ass, thinkin you should have run.'

I make a face: who knows? With Lip, I do not have to bother with more.

For my fifteenth college reunion I received a questionnaire which asked a lot of personal questions I found difficult to answer: What contemporary American do you admire most? What is your most important physical possession? Name your best friend and describe him. On this one, I puzzled for some time, but I finally wrote down Lipranzer's name. 'My best friend,' I wrote, 'is a cop. He is five foot eight inches tall, weighs 120 pounds after a full meal, and has a duckass hairdo and that look of lurking small-time viciousness that you've seen on every no-account kid hanging on a street corner. He smokes two packs of Camel cigarettes a day. I do not know what we have in common, but I admire him. He is very good at what he does.'

I first ran across Lip seven or eight years ago, when I was initially assigned to the Violence Section and he had just begun working Homicide. We have done a dozen cases since, but there are still ways in which I regard him as a mystery, even a danger. His father was a watch commander in a precinct in the West End, and when his old man died, Lip left college to take up a place that came to him by rights of a kind of departmental primogeniture. By now he has been placed in the P A's office on direct assignment, a so-called Special Command. On paper, his job is to act as police liaison, coordinating homicide investigations of special interest to our office. In practice, he is as solitary as a shooting star. He reports to a Captain Schmidt, who cares only that he has sixteen homicide collars to show at the end of every fiscal year. Lip spends most of his time alone, hanging out in bars and on loading docks, drinking shots with anybody who's got good information – hoods, reporters, queers, federal agents, anybody who can keep him up to speed on the world of big-time bad guys. Lipranzer is a scholar of the underlife. Eventually, I have come to recognize that it is the weird weight of that information that somehow accounts for his rheumy-eyed sulking look.

I still have the envelope in my hands.

'So what do we have here?' I ask.

'Path report. Three-sheet. Bunch of pictures of a naked dead lady.' The three-sheet is the prosecutor's copy of the arriving officers' reports – the third leaf in the carbon layers. I have talked to these cops directly. I go on to the report of the police pathologist, Dr Kumagai, a weird-looking little Japanese who seems to have come out of a forties propaganda piece. He is known as Painless, a notorious hack. No prosecutor calls him to the witness stand without crossing his fingers.

'And what's the scoop? Male fluids in every hole?'

'Just the main one. Lady is dead of a skull fracture and resulting hemorrhage. Pictures might make you think she was strangled, but Painless says there was air in her lungs. Anyway, the guy musta hit her with somethin. Painless has got no idea what. Heavy, he says. And real hard.'

'I take it we looked for a murder weapon in the apartment?'

'Turned the place upside down.'

'Anything obvious missing? Candlesticks? Bookends?'

'Nothin. I sent three separate teams through.'

'So,' I say, 'our man showed up already thinking he'd be doing some heavy hitting.'

'Could be. Or else he just took what he used with him. I'm not positive this guy came prepared. Seems like he was hittin to subdue her – didn't realize he cooled her. I figure – you can see when you look at the pictures – that the way the ropes were tied, that he put himself between her legs and was trying to let his weight strangle her. It's all slip-knotted. I mean,' Lipranzer says, 'that he was sort of tryin to fuck her to death.'

'Charming,' I say.

'Definitely charming,' says Lip. 'This was a very charming-type fellow.' We are both quiet a moment before he goes on. 'We got no bruises on the arms, hands, nothin like that,' Lip says. That would mean there was no struggle before Carolyn was bound. 'Contusion's rear right. It's got to be that he hit her from behind, then tied her up. Only it seems strange that he would knock her cold to start with. Most of these creeps like em to know what they're doin.'

I shrug. I'm not so sure of that.

The photos are the first thing I take out of the envelope. They are clean, full-colored shots. Carolyn lived in a place on the waterfront, a former warehouse parceled into 'loft condominiums'. She had divided the space with Chinese screens and heavy rugs. Her taste ran to the modern, with elegant touches of classical and antique. She had been killed in the space off the kitchen which she used as a living room. An overall shot of that area is first on the stack. The thick green-edged glass top of a coffee table has been tumbled off its brass props; a modular seating piece is upside down. But overall I agree with Lip that there is less sign of struggle than I have seen on other occasions, particularly if you ignore the bloodstain worked into the fiber of the flokati rug so that it has the shape of a large soft cloud. I look up. I do not feel I am ready yet to take on the photos of the corpse.

'What else does Painless tell us?' I ask.

'This guy was shootin blanks.'

'Blanks?'

'Oh yeah. You'll like this.' Lipranzer does his best to repeat Kumagai's analysis of the sperm deposit that was found. Little of it had seeped to the labia, which means that Carolyn could not have spent much time on her feet after sexual contact. This is another way we know that the rape and her death were roughly contemporaneous. On 1 April, she had left the office a little after seven. Kumagai puts the time of death at somewhere around nine.

'That's twelve hours before the body's found,' Lip says. 'Painless says normally, with that kinda time span, he'd still see some of the guy's little thingies swimmin upstream in the tubes and in the womb, when he looked under the microscope. Instead, this guy's wad's all dead. Nothin went nowhere. Painless figures this guy is sterile.' Lip pronounces the word so that it rhymes with pearl. 'Says you can get like that from mumps.'

'So we're looking for a rapist who has no children and once had the mumps.'

Lipranzer shrugs.

'Painless says he's gonna take the semen specimen and send it over to the forensic chemist. Maybe they can give him another idea of what's up.'

I groan a little bit at the thought of Painless exploring the realms of higher chemistry.

'Can't we get a decent pathologist?' I ask.

'You got Painless,' Lip says innocently.

I groan again, and leaf through a few more pages of Kumagai's report.

'Do we have a secreter?' I ask. People are divided not merely by blood type but by whether they secrete identifying agents into their body fluids.

Lip takes the report from me. 'Yep.'

'Blood type?'

'A.'

'Ah,' I say, 'my very own.'

'I thoughta that,' says Lip, 'but you got a kid.'

I again comment on Lipranzer's sentimentality. He does not bother to respond. Instead, he lights another cigarette and shakes his head.

'I'm just not grabbin it yet,' he says. 'The whole goddamn deal is too weird. We're missin somethin.'

So we begin again, the investigator's favorite parlor game, who and why. Lipranzer's number-one suspicion from the start has been that Carolyn was killed by someone she convicted. That is every prosecutor's worst fantasy, the long-nurtured vengeance of some dip you sent away. Shortly after I was first assigned to the jury trial section, a youth, as the papers would have it, by the name of Pancho Mercado, took exception to my closing argument, in which I had questioned the manliness of anyone who made his living by pistol-whipping seventy-seven-year-old men. Six foot four and well over 250 pounds. Pancho leaped the dock and thundered behind me through most of the courthouse before he was stopped cold in the PA's lunchroom by MacDougall, wheelchair and all. The whole thing ended up on page 3 of the *Tribune*, with a grotesque headline: PANICKED PROSECUTOR SAVED BY CRIPPLE. Something like that. Barbara, my wife, likes to refer to this as my first famous case.

Carolyn worked on stranger types than Pancho. For several years she had headed what is called the office's Rape Section. The name gives a good idea of what is involved, although all forms of sexual assault tend to be prosecuted there, including child abuse, and one case I can recall where an all-male *ménage à trois* had turned rough and the state's main witness had ended the evening with a light bulb up his rectum. It is Lipranzer's hypothesis, at moments, that one of the rapists Carolyn prosecuted got even.

Accordingly, we agree to go over Carolyn's docket to see if

there was anybody she tried – or investigated – for a crime resembling what took place three nights ago. I promise to look through the records in Carolyn's office. The state investigative agencies also maintain a computer run of sexual offenders, and Lip will see if we can cross-match there on Carolyn's name, or the stunt with the ropes.

'What kind of leads are we running?'

Lipranzer begins to tick it off for me. The neighbors were all seen on the day following the murder, but those interviews were probably hasty and Lip will arrange for homicide investigators to make another pass at everyone in a square block. This time they'll do it in the evening, so that the neighbors who are home at the hour when the murder took place will be in.

'One lady says she saw a guy in a raincoat on the stairs.' Lip looks at his notebook. 'Mrs Krapotnik. Says maybe he looked familiar, but she doesn't think he lives there.'

'The Hair and Fiber guys went through first, right?' I ask. 'When do we hear from them?' To these people falls the grotesque duty of vacuuming the corpse, picking over the crime scene with tweezers, in order to make microscopic examinations of any trace materials they discover. Often they can type hair, identify an offender's clothing.

'That should be a week, ten days,' Lip says. 'They'll try to come up with somethin on the rope. Only other interesting thing they tell me is they got a lot of floor fluff. There are few hairs around, but not what you'd find if there was any kinda fight.'

'How about fingerprints?' I ask.

'They dusted everything in the place.'

'Did they dust this glass table here?' I show Lip the picture.

'Yeah.'

'Did they get latents?'

'Yeah.'

'Report?'

'Preliminary.'

'Whose prints?'

'Carolyn Polhemus.'

'Super.'

'It ain't all bad,' says Lip. He takes the picture from me and points. 'See this bar here. See the glass?' One tall bar glass, standing undisturbed. 'There're latents on that. Three fingers. And the prints ain't the decedent's.'

'Do we have any idea whose prints they are?'

'No. Identification says three weeks. They got all kinda backlogs.' The police department identification division keeps a digit-by-digit record of every person who has ever been printed, classified by so-called points of comparison, the ridges and valleys on a fingertip to which numerical values are assigned. In the old days, they were unable to identify an unknown print unless the subject left behind latents of all ten fingers, so ID could search the existing catalogue. Now, in the computer era, the search can be done by machine. A laser mechanism reads the print and compares to every one in memory. The process takes only a few minutes, but the department, due to budgetary constraints, does not yet own all of the equipment and must borrow pieces from the state police for special cases. 'I told them to rush it up, but they're giving me all that shit about Zilogs and onloading. A call from the PA would really help. Tell them to compare to every known in the county. Anybody. Any dirtball who's ever been printed.'

I make a note to myself.

'We need MUDs, too,' Lipranzer says, and points to the pad. Although it is not well known, the telephone company keeps a computerized record of all local calls made from most exchanges: Message Unit Detail sheets. I begin writing out the grand-jury subpoena *duces tecum*, a request for documents. 'And ask them for MUDs on anybody she called in the last six months,' says Lip.

'They'll scream. You're probably talking about two hundred numbers.'

'Anybody she called three times. I'll get back to them with a list. But ask for it now, so I'm not runnin my ass around tryin to find you to do another subpoena.'

I nod. I'm thinking.

'If you're going back six months,' I tell him, 'you're probably going to hit this number.' I nod toward the phone on my desk.

Lipranzer looks at me levelly and says, 'I know.'

So he knows, I think. I take a minute with this, trying to figure how. People guess, I think. They gossip. Besides, Lip would notice things that anyone else would miss. I doubt that he approves. He is single, but he is no rover. There is a Polish woman a good ten years older than he, a widow with a grown kid, who cooks a meal and sleeps with Lipranzer two or three times a week. On the phone, he calls her Momma.

'You know,' I say, 'as long as we're on the subject, Carolyn always locked her doors and windows.' I tell him this with admirable evenness. 'I mean, always. She was a little soft, but Carolyn was a grownup. She knew she lived in the city.'

Lipranzer's look focuses gradually and his eyes take on a metallic gleam. He has not lost the significance of what I'm telling him or, it seems, of the fact that I delayed.

'So what do you figure?' he asks at last. 'Somebody walked around there openin the windows?'

'Could be.'

'So they'd make it look like a break-in? Somebody she let in the first place?'

'Doesn't that make sense? You're the one who's telling me there's a glass on the bar. She was entertaining. I wouldn't bet the ranch on the bad guy being some crazed parolee.'

Lip stares at his cigarette. Looking through the doorway, I see that Eugenia, my secretary, has returned. There are voices now in the hallway as people filter back in from the graveside. I detect a lot of the anxious laughter of release.

'Not necessarily,' he says finally. 'Not with Carolyn Polhemus. She was a funny lady.' He looks at me hard again.

'You mean, you think she'd open the door to some bum she sent to jail?'

'I think with Carolyn there's no tellin. Suppose she bumped into one of these characters in a bar. Or some guy called her up and said, Let's have a pop. You think there's no chance she'd say yes? We're talkin Carolyn now.'

I can see where Lip is going. Lady P A, Prosecutor of Perverts, Fucks Defendant and Lives Out Forbidden Fantasy. Lip has got her number pretty well. Carolyn Polhemus would not have minded at all the idea that some guy had dwelled with the thought of her for years. But, somehow, with this discussion a seasick misery begins to ebb through me.

'You didn't like her much, did you, Lip?'

'Not much.' We look at each other. Then Lipranzer reaches over and chucks me on the knee. 'At least we know one thing,' he says. 'She had piss-poor taste in men.'

That is his exit line. He tucks his Camels into his windbreaker and is gone. I call out to Eugenia to please hold anything else. With a moment's privacy I am now ready to examine the photographs. For a minute, after I begin sorting through them, my attention is mostly on myself. How well will I manage this? I urge myself to maintain professional composure.

But that, of course, begins to give way. It is like the network of crazing that sometimes seeps through glass in the wake of an impact. There is excitement at first, slow-entering and reluctant, but more than a little. In the top photographs the heavy glass of the table is canted over, compressing her shoulder, so that you might almost make the comparison to a laboratory slide. But soon it is removed. And here is Carolyn's spectacularly lithe body in a pose which, for all the agony there must have been, seems, initially, supple and athletic. Her legs are trim and graceful; her breasts are high and large. Even in death, she retains her erotic bearing. But, I slowly recognize, other experiences must influence this response. Because what is actually here is horrible. There are bruises on her face and neck, mulberry patches. A rope runs from her ankles to her knees, her waist, her wrists; then it is jerked tight around her neck, where the rim of the burn is visible. She is drawn back in an ugly tormented bow and her face is ghastly; her eyes, with the hyperthyroid look of the attempted strangulation, are enormous and protruding and her mouth is fixed in a silent scream. I watch, I study. Her look holds the same wild, disbelieving, desperate thing that so frightens me when I find the courage to let my glance fix on the wide black eye of a landed fish dying on a pier. I take it in now in the same reverential, awestruck, uncomprehending way. And then, worst of all, when all the dirt is scraped off the treasure box there is rising within, unhindered by shame, or even fear, a bubble of something light enough that I must eventually recognize it as satisfaction, and no lecture to myself about the baseness of my nature can quite discourage me. Carolyn Polhemus, that tower of grace and fortitude, lies here in my line of sight with a look she never had in life. I see it finally now. She wants my pity. She needs my help.

3

When it was all over, I went to see a psychiatrist. His name was Robinson.

'I would say she's the most exciting woman I've known,' I told him.

'Sexy?' he asked after a moment.

'Sexy, yes. Very sexy. Torrents of blond hair, and almost no behind, and this very full bosom. And long red fingernails, too. I mean, definitely, deliberately, almost ironically sexy. You notice. That's the idea with Carolyn. You're supposed to notice. And I did. She's worked around our office for years. She was a probation officer before she went to law school. But that's all she was to me originally. You know: this very good-looking blonde with big tits. Every copper who came in would roll his eyes and make like he was jerking off. That's all.

'Over time, people began to talk about her. Even while she was still in the branch courts. You know: high-powered. Capable. Then for a while she was dating this newsman on Channel 3. Chet whatever his name is. And she showed up a lot of places. Very active in the bar organizations. An officer for a while in the local NOW chapter. And shrewd. She asked to be assigned out to the Rape Section when it was considered a crappy place to work. All these impossible one-on-ones where you could never figure out if it was the victim or the defendant who was closer to the truth. Hard cases. Just to find the ones that deserved to be prosecuted, let alone to win them. And she did very well out there. Eventually Raymond put her in charge of all those trials. He liked to send her on those Sunday-morning public service TV programs. Show his concern on women's issues. And Carolyn liked to go and carry the banner. She enjoyed the limelight. But she was a good prosecutor. And damn tough. The defense lawyers used to complain that she had a complex, that she was trying to prove that she had balls. But the coppers loved her.

'I'm not sure what I thought of her then. I suppose I thought she was just a little bit too much.'

Robinson looked at me.

'Too much everything,' I said. 'You know. Too bold. Too self-impressed. Always running one gear too high. She didn't have the right sense of proportion.'

'And,' said Robinson, proceeding to the obvious, 'You fell in love with her.'

I went silent, still. When are words enough?

'I fell in love with her,' I said.

Raymond felt she needed a partner and so she asked me. It was September of last year.

'Could you have said no?' asked Robinson.

'I suppose. The chief deputy isn't expected to try a lot of cases. I could have said no.'

'But?'

But I said yes.

Because, I told myself, the case was interesting. The case was strange. Darryl McGaffen was a banker. He worked for his brother, Joey, who was a gangster, a florid personality, a hotshot type who enjoyed being the target of every law-enforcement agency in town. Joey used the bank, out in McCrary, to wash a river of dirty money, mostly mob dough. But that was Joey's action. Darryl kept his head down and the accounts straight. Darryl was as mild as Joey was flamboyant. An ordinary guy. He lived out west, near McCrary. He had a wife. And a somewhat tragic life. His first child, a little girl, had died at the age of three. I knew all about that, because Joey had once testified before the grand jury about his niece's fall from a second-floor terrace at his brother's home. Joey had explained, almost convincingly, that the girl's resulting skull fracture and immediate death were large in his mind and had obstructed his judgment when four mysterious fellows delivered to his bank certain bonds which, to Joey's great chagrin, turned out to be hot. Joey wrung his hands when he talked about the girl. He touched his silk pocket hankie to both his eyes.

Darryl and his wife had another child, a boy named Wendell. When Wendell was five, his mother arrived with him at the West End Pavilion Hospital emergency room. The boy was unconscious and his mother was hysterical, for her child had taken a terrible fall, sustaining severe head injuries. The mother claimed that he had never been at the hospital before, but the emergency room physician – a young Indian woman, Dr Narajee – had a memory of treating Wendell a year earlier, and when a medical record was summoned she found he had been there twice, once with a broken collarbone, once with a broken arm, both the results, his mother had said, of falls. The child was unconscious now and not likely in most events to speak, and so Dr Narajee studied his injuries. When she testified later, Dr Narajee said she realized initially that the wounds were too symmetrical and too evenly positioned laterally to be the result of a fall. She repeatedly examined the gashes, two inches by one inch on each side of the head, over more than a day, before she had it all figured out, and then she called Carolyn Polhemus at the prosecuting attorney's office to report that she was treating a child whose skull appeared to have been fractured when his mother placed his head in a vise.

Carolyn obtained a search warrant at once. They recovered the grip with skin fragments still on it from the basement of the McGaffen home. They examined the unconscious child and found healed wounds which appeared to have been cigarette burns in his anus. And then they waited to see what would happen with the boy. He lived.

By then he was in court custody. And the PA's office was under siege. Darryl McGaffen came to his wife's defense. She was a loving and devoted mother. It was insanity, he said, to claim she'd hurt her child. He had seen the boy fall, McGaffen said, a terrible accident, a tragedy, marred by this nightmarish experience of doctors and lawyers madly conspiring to take their sick child away. Very emotional. Very well staged. Joey made sure the cameras were there when the brother got to the courthouse and that Darryl claimed a vendetta by Raymond Horgan against his family. In order to show forthrightness, Raymond was going to try the case himself at first. But the campaign was beginning to heat up. Raymond sent the case back to Carolyn and recommended, given the press attention, that she try it with another senior deputy, someone like me, whose presence would show the office's commitment. So she asked. And I agreed. I told myself I was doing it for Raymond.

The physicists call it Brownian movement, the action of molecules coursing against one another in the air. This activity produces a kind of hum, a high-pitched, almost screeching sound at a frequency level on the margins of human audibility. As a child I could hear this tone, if I chose to, at virtually any moment. Most often, I would ignore it, but every now and then my will eroded and I would let the pitch rise inside my ears to the point where it was almost blaring.

Apparently at puberty the bones in the inner ear harden so that the Brownian ringing can no longer be heard. Which is just as well. Because by then there are other distractions. For me, during most of my married life, the allure of other women has been like that daily hum which I willfully ignored, and when I started working around Carolyn that resolve went weak, and the pitch rose, vibrated, *sang*.

'And I can't really tell you why,' I said to Robinson.

I consider myself a person of values. I had always despised my father for his philandering. On Friday nights he was emitted from the household like a wandering cat, headed for a tavern and, later, the Hotel Delaney over on Western Avenue, only a little better than a flop, with its old woolen carpets worn to the backing over the stairs, and the naphtha scent of some chemical agent used to control the infestation of pests. There he would pursue his passion with various soiled women – barroom chippies, horny divorcées, wives out on the sneak. Before he left on these outings, he had dinner with my mother and me. We both knew where he was going. He would hum, the only sound anything like music which came from him all week.

But somehow as I worked around Carolyn, with her jangling jewelry and her light perfume, her silk blouses, her red lipstick and painted nails, that large heaving bosom and her long legs, that splash of bright hair, I became overwhelmed by her – and in just that fashion, detail by detail, so that I would become excited when I smelled her scent on another woman who passed me in the hall.

'And I can't really tell you why. Maybe that's why I am here. Some frequency is heard and everything begins to shatter. A vibration sets in, a fundamental tone, and the whole interior is shaking. We'd talk about the trial, our lives, whatever, and she seemed such a remarkable mix of things. Symphonic. A symphonic personality. Disciplined and glamorous. This musical laugh. And an orthodontic wonder of a smile. She was much wittier than I expected; tough, as they said, but she did not seem hard.'

I was affected particularly by her offhand remarks, the way her eyes, hooded with shadow and liner, would take on this tone of level assessment. Analysing politics or witnesses or cops, she showed you just how firm a purchase she had on what was going on. And that was very exciting to me, to meet a woman who seemed to really have the lowdown, who was moving through the world at Carolyn's speed, and who was so many different things to different people. Maybe it was the contrast to Barbara, who is so deliberately none of that.

'There was this bold, bright, handsome woman, much celebrated, with a kind of spotlight radiance. And I find I am going down to her office – which is itself a minor wonder in a place as stark as ours. Carolyn having taken the trouble to add a small Oriental rug, plants, an antique bookcase, and an Empire desk she snagged through a connection with Central Services – I'm going down there with nothing to say. There is this heat, this parched sensation – all the old crappy metaphors – and I start thinking, Jesus Christ, this can't be happening. And maybe it still wouldn't have, but about this time I begin to notice, I begin to think she is

38

paying attention to me. She is *looking* at me. Oh, I know, this sounds like high school. No, worse, junior high school. But there is this thing, people don't *look* at one another.'

And when we're interviewing witnesses, I turn and Carolyn is staring at me, watching with this placid, almost rueful smile, as I do my stuff – or in a meeting with Raymond, all the top felony people, I'll glance up, I'll feel the weight of her eyes on me, and she continues watching me in such an unwavering fashion that I do something, a wink, a smile, as a form of acknowledgment, and she responds, usually that little cat's grin, and if I'm speaking I stop, everything washes out of my mind, it is just Carolyn, things are unraveling right from the center of the skein.

'That was the worst part, this incredible domination of my feelings. I get in the shower, I drive down the street – it's Carolyn. Fantasies. Conversations with her. An uninterrupted movie. I see her full of relaxed amusement and appreciation – of me. Of me. I can't finish a phone call; I can't read a prosecution memo or a brief.'

And all of it, this whole grand obsession, carried on in the face of a racing heart, a turning gut, a frantic sense of resistance and disbelief. I shudder at random moments. I tell myself that this has not happened. This is a juvenile episode, a mind trick like *déjà vu*. I grope around inside myself for the old reality. I say to myself that I will get up in the morning feeling unaffected, feeling right again and sane.

But I do not, of course, and the moments when I am with her, the anticipation, the appreciation is exquisite. I feel short of breath and giddy. I laugh too easily, too much. I do what I can to stay near her, show her a paper over her shoulder while she's at her desk, so that I can linger with the details of her person: her hammered golden earrings, the odors of her bathwater and her breath, the soft bluish color of her nape when her hair falls away. And then, when I'm by myself, I feel desperate and ashamed. This raging, mad obsession! Where is my world? I am departing. I am gone already.

4

In the dark, the red-and-blue figure of Spider-Man can be made out on the wall above my son's bed. Life-size, he is poised in a wrestler's crouch, prepared to take on all invaders.

I did not grow up reading the comics – it was too lighthearted an activity for the home I was raised in. But when Nat was two or three we began, each Sunday, to explore the funny papers together. While Barbara slept, I made Nat breakfast. Then, with my son very close beside me, we sat on the sofa in the sunroom as we discussed and recollected the weekly progress in each strip. All the random little-boy fury of that age would leave him, and he was reduced to a more essential self, small and full of a transport I could feel through his body. So it was that I came to establish my rapport with the Web Slinger. Now Nat, in second grade and almost brittlely self-sufficient, reads the funnies by himself. I must await a moment when I will not be noticed to check on Peter Parker's fate. They really are funny, I explained to Barbara a few weeks ago when I was observed with the comics in my hands. Oh, for crying out loud, muttered my wife, the almost Ph.D.

Now I touch the fine hair, so thin against Nat's scalp. If I fuss long enough, Nat, accustomed by the years to my late arrivals, will probably rouse himself to murmur some gentle appreciation. I stop here first each evening. I have an almost physical craving for the reassurance. Right before Nat's birth we moved out here, to Nearing, a former ferry port to which the city dwellers fled long enough ago that it is called a town rather than a suburb. Although it was Barbara who initially favored this move, by now she would eagerly forsake Nearing, which she sometimes blames for her isolation. I'm the one who needs the distance from the city, the gap in time and space, to manufacture in myself a sense that some perimeter protects us against what I see each day. I suppose that is another reason I was happy to see Spider-Man assume his place here. I take comfort in Spidey's agile vigilance.

I find Barbara face-down on our bed, largely unclothed. She is breathless, the tight muscles of her narrow back lustrous with sweat. The VCR hums in rewind. On the set, the news has just begun.

'Exercise?' I ask.

'Masturbation,' Barbara answers. 'Refuge of the lonely house-wife.'

She does not bother a backward glance. Instead, I advance and kiss her quickly on the neck.

'I called from the bus station when I missed the 8:35. You weren't here. I left a message on the tape.'

'I got it,' she says. 'I was picking up Nat. He had dinner with Mom. I tried to get in some extra time on the mainframe.'

'Productive?'

'A waste.' She rolls over and back, breasts girdled in her sports bra.

As I undress, I receive a laconic report from Barbara on the day's occurrences. A neighbor's illness. The bill from the mechanic. The latest with her mother. Barbara delivers all this information lying face-down on the coverlet in a tone of weariness. This her drear offensive, a bitterness too tired even to be regret, against which I defend in the simplest fashion, by seeming not to notice. I show interest in each remark, enthusiasm for every detail. And in the meantime, an inner density gathers, a known sensation, as if my veins have become clogged with lead. I am home.

About five years ago, just when I thought we were getting ready to have another child, Barbara announced that she was going back to school, entering a Ph.D. program in mathematics. She had filed the application and taken the exams without a word to me. My surprise was taken as disapproval, and my protests to the contrary have always been disparaged. But I did not disapprove. I never thought Barbara was obligated to be homebound. My reaction was to something else. Not so much that I was not consulted, but that I really never could have guessed. In college, Barbara had been a math whiz, taking graduate division classes of two or three students with renowned professors, all of them hermit-like creatures with wild-grown beards. But she had been cavalier about her abilities. Now, I learned, mathematics was a calling. A consuming interest. About which I had not heard a word in more than half a decade.

At the moment Barbara is facing her dissertation. When she started, she told me that projects like hers – I could not possibly explain it – are sometimes set out in a space as small as a dozen pages. Whether those were words of hope or illusion, the dissertation has lingered like a chronic disease, one more source of her painful melancholy. Whenever I pass by the study, she is looking pitifully over her desk, out the window toward a single dwarf cherry tree that has failed to thrive in the clay landfill in our back yard.

Waiting for inspiration, she reads. Nothing so much of this world as newspapers and magazines. Instead, she carts in from the university library armloads of heavy texts on arcane subjects. Psycholinguistics. Semiotics. Braille and sign language for the deaf. She is a devotee of facts. She reclines at night on her brocade living-room sofa, eating Belgian chocolates, and finds out about the operation of the world she never visits. She reads, literally, about life on Mars, the biographies of men and women whom most people would find boring, and certainly obscure. Then there will be a spate of medical reading. Last month she spent with books that seemed to be about cryogenics, artificial insemination, and the history of lenses. What is occurring on these galaxian visits to other planets of human learning is unknown to me. No doubt she would share her newfound knowledge if I asked. But over time I have lost the ability even to pretend high interest, and Barbara regards my dullness to these matters as a failing. It is easier to maintain my own counsel, while Barbara roams the far-off realms.

Not long ago it occurred to me that my wife, with her abrupt social mannerisms, her general aversion to most human beings, her dark taciturn side, and her virtual armory of private and largely uncommunicated passions could be described only as weird. She has virtually no serious friendships aside from her relationship with her mother, to whom, when I met her, Barbara barely spoke, and whom she still regards with cynicism and suspicion. Like my own mother, when she was alive, Barbara seems largely a willing captive within the walls of her own home, flawlessly keeping our house, tending our child, and toiling endlessly with her formulae and computer algorithms.

Without really noticing at first, I become aware that both of us have ceased comment, even motion, and are facing the television set, where the screen has filled with images of today's service for Carolyn. Raymond's car arrives and the back of my head is briefly shown. The son is escorted up to the doors of the chapel. The newsreader is doing a voice-over: eight hundred persons, including many city leaders, gathered at First Presbyterian Church for final rites for Carolyn Polhemus, a deputy prosecuting attorney slain three nights ago in a brutal rape-murder. Now people are emerging. The mayor and Raymond are both depicted speaking to reporters, but only Nico gets audio. He employs the quietest voice he knows and deflects questions about the investigation of the murder. 'I came to remember a colleague,' he tells the camera, with one foot in his car.

It is Barbara who speaks first.

'How was it?' She has wrapped herself now in a red silk robe.

'Gala,' I answer. 'In a way. A meeting of all the luminaries.'

'Did you cry?'

'Come on, Barbara.'

'I'm serious.' She is leaning forward. Her jaw is set and there is a savage deadness in her eye. I always marvel that Barbara's anger remains so near at hand. Over the years, her superior access has become a source of intimidation. She knows I am slower to respond, restrained by archaic fears, the dark weight of memory. My parents often fell into robust shouting matches, even occasional brawls. I have such a vivid recollection of one night when I awoke to their disturbance and found that my mother had taken hold of a handful of my father's Brillo-y red hair while she slapped

43

him with a rolled-up newspaper, as if he were a dog. The aftermath of these quarrels would send my mother to bed for days, where she would lie spent, dwelling with the sensational pain of enormous migraine headaches that required her to remain in a darkened room and left me under an injunction to make no sound.

Lacking that kind of refuge now, I move over to a basket of clean laundry Barbara has brought up and begin matching the socks. For a moment we are silent, left to the burbling of the TV and the nighttime noises of the house. A tiny finger of the river runs behind the homes half a block away, and without the traffic you can hear it licking. The furnace kicks in two floors below. On for the first time today, it will spill up through the ducts a kind of oily effluvium.

'Nico was trying hard enough to look unhappy,' Barbara finally tells me.

'He wasn't very successful if you saw him up close. He was positively radiant. He thinks he's got a shot at Raymond now.'

'Is that possible?'

I sort the socks and shrug. 'He's gained a lot of ground with this thing.'

Barbara, a witness all these years to Raymond's invincibility, is obviously surprised, but the mathematician in her shows, for I can see that she is quickly factoring the new possibilities. She grabs at her hair, gray-flecked and curly, worn in a fashionable shag, and her pretty face takes on the light of curiosity.

'What would you do, Rusty, if that happened? If Raymond lost?'

'Accept it. What else could I do?'

'I mean for a living.'

Blue with blue. Black with black. It is not easy with only incandescent light. Some years ago I used to talk about leaving the office. That was when I could still imagine myself as a defense lawyer. But I never got around to making that move, and it has been some time since we have spoken at all about my future.

'I don't know what I'd do,' I tell her honestly. 'I'm a lawyer. I'd practice law. Teach. I don't know. Delay says he's going to keep me on as chief deputy.'

'Do you believe that?'

'No.' I take my stockings to my drawer. 'He was a river of bullshit today. Told me, in a very serious tone, that the only real primary opponent he had been afraid of was me. You know, as if I would talk Raymond into stepping aside and anointing me successor.'

'You should have,' Barbara says.

I look back at her.

'Really.' Her enthusiasm, in a way, is not surprising. Barbara has always felt a spouse's disdain for the boss. And besides, all of this comes, somewhat, at my expense. I'm the one who lacked the nerve to do what everybody else could see was obvious.

'I am not a politician.'

'Oh, you'd make do,' says Barbara. 'You'd love to be P A.' As I figured: I am tweaked by wife's superior knowledge of my nature. I decide to sidestep and tell Barbara that this is all academic. Raymond will pull through.

'Bolcarro will finally endorse him. Or we'll catch the killer' – I nod toward the T V set – 'and he'll ride into Election Day with all the media murmuring his name.'

'How's he going to do that?' asks Barbara. 'Do they have a suspect?'

'We have shit.'

'So?'

'So Dan Lipranzer and Rusty Sabich will work day and night for the next two weeks and catch Raymond a killer. That's the strategy. Carefully devised.'

The remote snaps and the T V shrinks to a star. Behind me, I hear from Barbara a whinny, a snort. It is not a pleasant sound. When I look back, her eyes, fixed upon me, are stilled to a zero point, an absolute in hatred.

'You are so predictable,' she says, low and mean. 'You're in charge of this investigation?'

'Of course.'

'"Of course"?'

'Barbara, I'm the chief deputy prosecuting attorney and Raymond's running for his life. Who else would handle the investigation? Raymond would do it himself if he weren't campaigning fourteen hours a day.'

It was the prospect of a moment just like this that left me in a state of excruciating unease a couple of days ago when I realized that I would have to phone Barbara to tell her what had happened. I could not ignore it; that would pretend too much. My call was for the announced purpose of telling Barbara I would be late. The office, I explained, was in an uproar.

Carolyn Polhemus is dead, I added.

Huh, said Barbara. Her tone was one of detached wonder. An overdose? she asked.

I stared at the receiver in my hand, marveling at the depth of this misunderstanding.

But I cannot divert her now. Barbara's rage is gathering.

'Tell me the truth,' she says. 'Isn't that a conflict of interest or something?'

'Barbara –'

'No,' she says, standing now. 'Answer me. Is that professional – for you to be doing this? There are 120 lawyers down there. Can't they find anybody who didn't sleep with her?'

I am familiar with this rise in pitch and descent in tactics. I strive to remain even.

'Barbara, Raymond asked me to do it.'

'Oh, spare me, Rusty. Spare me the high-purpose, noble crap. You could explain to Raymond why you shouldn't do this.'

'I don't care to. I would be letting him down. And it happens to be none of his business.'

At this evidence of my embarrassment, Barbara hoots. That I realize was poor strategy, a bad moment to tell the truth. Barbara has little sympathy for my secret; if it would not pain her equally, she would put it all on billboards. During the short time that I was actually seeing Carolyn, I did not have whatever it is – the courage or the decency or the willingness to be disturbed – to confess anything to Barbara. That awaited the end, a week or two after I had become resolved it all was past. I was home for an early dinner, atoning for the month before when I had been absent almost every evening, my liberty procured with the phony excuse

46

of preparation for a trial, which I ultimately claimed had been continued. Nat had just gone off to his permitted half hour with the television set. And I, somehow, became unglued. The moon. The mood. A drink. The psychologists would say a fugue state. I drifted, staring at the dinner table. I took my highball tumbler in my hand, just like one of Carolyn's. And I was reminded of her so powerfully that I was suddenly beyond control. I cried – wept with stormy passion as I sat there – and Barbara knew immediately. She did not think that I was ill; she did not think that it was fatigue, or trial stress, or tear-duct disease. She knew; and she knew that I was crying out of loss, not shame.

There was nothing tender about her inquisition, but it was not prolonged. Who? I told her. Was I leaving? It was over, I said. It was short, I said, it barely happened.

Oh, I was heroic. I sat there at my own dining-room table with both arms over my face, crying, almost howling, into my shirt-sleeves. I heard the dishes clank as Barbara stood and began clearing her place. 'At least I don't have to ask,' she said, 'who dropped who.'

Later, after I got Nat into bed, I wandered up, shipwrecked and still pathetic, to see her in the bedroom, where she had taken refuge. Barbara was exercising again, with the insipid music on the tape thumping loudly. I watched her bend, do her double-jointed extensions, while I was still in deep disorder, so ravaged, beaten, that my skin seemed the only thing holding me together, a tender husk. I had come in to say something prosaic, that I wanted to go on. But that never emerged. The unhindered anger with which she slammed her own body about made it obvious to me, even in my undefended state, that the effort would be wasted. I just watched, perhaps as long as five minutes. Barbara never glanced at me, but finally in the midst of some contortion she uttered an opinion. 'You could have. Done better.' There was a little more which I did not hear. The final word was 'Bimbo.'

We have gone on from there. In a way my affair with Carolyn has provided an odd kind of relief. There is a cause now for the effect, an occasion for Barbara's black anger, a reason we do not get along. There is now something to get over and, as a result, a shadowy hope that things may improve.

That is, I realize, the issue now: whether we will give up whatever progress has been made. For months Carolyn has been a demon, a spirit slowly being exorcised from this home. And death has brought her back to life. I understand Barbara's complaint. But I cannot – *cannot* – give up what she wants me to; and my reasons are sufficiently personal as to lie within the realm of the unspoken, even the unspeakable.

I try a plain and quiet appeal.

'Barbara, what difference does it make? You're talking about two and a half weeks. Until the primary. That's all. Then it's another routine police case. Unsolved homicide.'

'Don't you see what you're doing? To yourself? To me?'

'Barbara,' I say again.

'I knew it,' she says. 'I knew you'd do something like this. When you called the other day. I could hear it in your voice. You're going to go through everything again, Rusty. You want to, that's the truth, isn't it? You want to. She's dead. And you're still obsessing.'

'Barbara.'

'Rusty, I have had more than I can take. I won't put up with this.' Barbara does not cry on these occasions. She recedes instead into the fiery pit of a volcanic anger. She hurls herself back now to gather her will, bound, as she sits on the bed, within her wide satin sleeves. She grabs a book, the remote control, two pillows. Mount Saint Helens rumbles. And I decide to leave. I go to the closet and grope for my robe.

As I reach the threshold, she speaks behind me.

'Can I ask a question?' she says.

'Sure.'

'That I always wanted to ask?'

'Sure.'

'Why did she stop seeing you?'

'Carolyn?'

'No, the man in the moon.' The words have so much bitterness that I wonder if she might spit. I would have thought Barbara's

48

question would be why did I start, but she apparently decided on her own answers to that long ago.

'I don't know,' I say. 'I tend to think I wasn't very important to her.'

She closes her eyes and opens them. Barbara shakes her head.

'You are an asshole,' my wife tells me solemnly. 'Just get out.'

I do. Quickly. She has been known to throw things. Having nowhere else to go, and craving some form of company, I cross the hall to check once more on Nat. His breath is husky and uninterrupted in the deepest phase of sleep, and I sit down on the bed, safe in the dark beneath the protecting arms of Spider-Man.

5

Monday morning: a day in the life. The commuter coach unleashes
the gray-flannel flock on the east side of the river. The terminal
plaza is surrounded by willows, their skirts greening in the spring.
I am in the office before 9:00. From my secretary, Eugenia Martinez, I receive the usual: mail, telephone-message slips, and a
dark look. Eugenia is obese, single, middle-aged, and, it often
seems, determined to get even for it all. She types reluctantly,
refuses dictation, and many times of day I will find her staring
with immobile droopy-eyed irritation at the telephone as it rings.
Of course, she cannot be fired, or even demoted, because civil
service, like concrete, has set. She remains, a curse to a decade of
chief deputies, having first been stationed here by John White,
who did so in order to avoid the carping that would have followed
if he'd assigned her to anybody else.

On the top of what Eugenia has given me is a leave slip for
Tommy Molto, whose absence remains unaccounted for. Personnel wants to dock him as Away without Leave. I make a note
to talk to Mac about this and graze through my communications.
The docket room has provided me with a printout naming thirteen
individuals released from state custody in the last two years whose
cases had been prosecuted by Carolyn. A handwritten note says
that the underlying case files have been delivered to her office. I
position the computer run in the center of my desk, so that I will
not forget.

With Raymond out most of the day on campaign appearances,
I resolve much of what the PA would ordinarily be faced with. I
call the shots on case prosecutions, immunities, plea bargains, and

deal with the investigative agencies. This morning I will preside over a charging conference in which we will decide on the phrasing and merits of all of this week's indictments. This afternoon I have a meeting about last week's fiasco, in which a police undercover bought from a Drug Enforcement Administration agent in disguise; the two drew guns and badges on each other and demanded surrender. Their backups became involved, too, so that in the end eleven law enforcement officers were standing on opposite corners, shouting obscenities and waving their pistols. Now we are having meetings. The coppers will tell me the feds do everything in secret; the DEA agent in charge will insinuate that any confidence the police department learns is up for sale. In the meantime, I am supposed to find somebody to prosecute for killing Carolyn Polhemus.

Someone else may be looking, too. Near 9:30 I get a call from Stew Dubinsky from the *Trib*. During the campaign, Raymond answers most press calls himself; he does not want to miss the free ink or draw criticisms that he is losing his hold on the office. But Stew is probably the best courthouse reporter we have. He gets most of his facts straight and he knows the boundaries. I can talk to him.

'So what's new on Carolyn?' he asks. The way he shorthands the murder with her name disconcerts me. Carolyn's death is already receding from the ranks of tragedy to become one more ugly historic event.

I cannot, of course, tell Stew that nothing is doing. Word could trail back to Nico, who would use the occasion to blast us again.

'Prosecuting Attorney Raymond Horgan had no comment,' I say.

'Would the PA care to comment on another piece of information?' This, whatever it is, is the real motive for Stew's call. 'I hear something about a high-level defection. From the Homicide Section? Sound familiar?'

That would be Molto. After Nico left, Tommy, his second-in-command, became acting head of the section. Horgan refused to give him the job permanently, suspecting that sooner or later something like this would come to pass. I contemplate for a moment the fact that the press is already sniffing. No good. Not at all. I see, from the way Dubinsky has lined up the questions, how this will run. One high-ranking deputy is killed; another, who should be in charge of the investigation, quits. It will sound as if the office is on the verge of chaos.

'Same response,' I tell him. 'Quote the PA.'

Stew makes a sound. He is bored.

'Off the record?' I ask.

'Sure.'

'How good is your information?' I want to know how close we are to reading about this.

'So-so. Guy who always thinks he knows more than he does. I figure this has got to be Tommy Molto. He and Nico are hand-and-glove, right?'

Stew clearly does not have enough to run. I avoid his question. 'What does Della Guardia tell you?' I ask.

'He says he has no comment. Come on, Rusty,' Dubinsky says, 'what gives?'

'Stew, off the record, I do not have the most fucked-up idea where Tommy Molto is. But if he's holding hands with Nico, why won't the candidate tell you that?'

'You want a theory?'

'Sure.'

'Maybe Nico has him out there investigating the case on his own. Think about that one. DELLA GUARDIA CATCHES KILLER. How's that for a headline?'

The notion is absurd. A private murder investigation could too easily end up an impediment to the police. Obstruction of justice is bad politics. But as ridiculous as it is, the sheer flare of the idea makes it sound like Nico. And Stew is not the kind to float loony notions. He works off information.

'Do I take it,' I ask, 'that this is part of your rumor, too?'

'No comment,' says Stew.

We laugh at each other, before I hang up the phone. Immediately I make some calls. I leave a message with Loretta, Raymond's secretary, that I have to speak with him whenever he phones in. I try to find Mac, the administrative deputy, to talk about Molto. Not in, I'm told. I leave another message.

Then, with a few minutes before the charging conference, I venture down the hall to Carolyn's office. This place already has a desolate air. The Empire desk which Carolyn commandeered from Central Services has been swept clean, and the contents of the drawers – two old compacts, soup mix, a package of napkins, a cableknit sweater, a pint bottle of peppermint schnapps – have been pitched into a cardboard box, along with Carolyn's diplomas and bar certificates, which were formerly clustered on the walls. Cartons called in from the warehouse are pyramided in the middle of the room, giving the office an air of obvious disuse, and the dust gathered in a week's inactivity has its own faintly corrupt smell. I pour a glass of water in the wilting greenery and dust some of the leaves.

Carolyn's caseload was made up primarily of sexual assaults. According to the codes on the file jackets, there are, by my count, twenty-two such cases awaiting indictment or trial which I find in the top drawers of her old oak file cabinet. Carolyn claimed a special sympathy with the victims of these crimes, and over time, I found that her commitment was more genuine than at first I had believed. When she talked about the reviving terrors these women experienced, the glittery surfaces receded from Carolyn and revealed alternating moods of tenderness and rage. But there is in these cases also an element of the bizarre: an intern at U. Hospital who gave a number of female patients a physical which ended with insertion of his own instrument; one victim received this treatment on three separate occasions before she was moved to complain. The girlfriend of a suspect who, on her second day of questioning, admitted that she had met him when he cut through the screen door to her apartment and forced himself on her. When he put the knife down, she said, he had seemed like such a nice young man.

Like many others, I suspected Carolyn of more than a passing fascination with this aspect of her work, as well, and I examine the case files with the hope that there will be a pattern I can seize on – we will be able to charge that it was actually some cultish ceremony that was duplicated six days ago in Carolyn's loft apartment, or a brutal mimicry of an offense in which Carolyn somehow displayed too obvious a voyeuristic interest. But there is none of that; the thirteen names lead nowhere. The new files disgorge no clues.

It is now time for the charging conference, but something is nagging at me. When I look again at the computer printout, I recognize that there is one case I have not come across yet – a B file, as we call it, referring to the subsection of the state criminal code addressed to bribery of law enforcement officials. Carolyn seldom handled anything outside her domain, and B files, which are so-called Special Investigation cases, were directly under my supervision when this case was assigned. At first, I assumed the B designation was the usual computer mess-up, maybe an included charge. But there is no companion case; in fact, this one is listed as an UnSub – unknown subject – which usually means a non-arrest investigation. I go through her drawers quickly, one more time, and check down in my office. I have my own printout of B cases, but this one isn't there. In fact, it seems to have been generally obliterated from the computer docketing system, except for Carolyn's call.

I make a note on my pad: B file? Polhemus?

Eugenia is standing in the doorway.

'Oh men,' she says. 'Where you been? I been lookin for you. Mr Big Cheese called back.' Mr Big Cheese, of course, is Raymond Horgan. 'I was lookin all over. He left a message to meet him at the Delancey Club, 1:30.' Raymond and I have many of these meetings during the campaign. I catch him after a luncheon, before a speech, to bring him up to speed on the office.

'How about Mac? Did we hear anything?'

Eugenia reads the message. ' "Be cross the street all morning." ' Observing, no doubt, watching some of the newer deputies do their stuff during the morning call in the Central Branch.

I ask Eugenia to set back the charging conference half an hour; then I head over to the courthouse to find Mac. On the second floor, the Central Branch session is held. The branch courts are where arrested persons make their first formal court appearance to set bail, where misdemeanors are tried and preliminary evidentiary hearings are held in felony cases. An assignment to one of the branches is usually the second or third stopping-off place for a deputy, after time in Appeals or the Complaint and Warrant Section. I worked this courtroom for nineteen months before I was sent to Felony Review, and I try to come back as little as possible. It is here that crime always seemed most real, the air quivering with a struggling agony at the brink of finding voice.

In the hallway outside two enormous central courtrooms, there is a churning mass, like my imaginings of the crushed poor in the steerage bowels of the old oceangoing vessels. Mothers and girl-friends and brothers are here weeping and crying out over the young men detained in the granite lockup that abuts the courtroom. Lawyers of a kind move about hustling clients in the subverted tones of scalpers, while the state defenders shout out the names of persons whom they have never met and whom they will be defending in a moment. The prosecutors are shouting, too, searching for each of the arresting officers on a dozen cases, hoping to enhance the slender knowledge provided by police reports prepared in a deliberately elliptical fashion, the better to hinder cross-examination.

Inside the vaulted courtroom, with its red marble pillars and oaken buttresses and straight-backed pews, the tumult continues, a persistent din. Situated closer to the front so they will not fail to hear their cases called, prosecutors and defense lawyers haggle amiably over prospective plea bargains. Beside the judge's bench, six or seven attorneys are clustered around the docket clerk, handing in appearance forms, examining court files, and urging the clerk to pass their case forward to be called next. The cops, most of them, are lined up in pairs against the grimy walls – many of them in from the 12-to-8 shift for the bail hearings on their nighttime collars – sipping coffee and rolling on the balls of their feet to keep themselves awake. And far to one side of the courtroom, there is a continuing clamor from the lockup, where defendants in custody await their appearance, one or two of them inevitably shouting obscenities at the bailiffs or their attorneys, complaining about the cramped conditions back there and the indecent odors from the commode. The rest moan occasionally or bang on the bars.

Now at the dead end of the morning call, the streetwalkers in their halter tops and shorts are being arraigned, tried, fined, and sent back out on the street in time for sleep and another night's work. Usually they are represented in groups by two or three lawyers, but every now and then a pimp, to economize, will take on the assignment himself. That is occurring right now as some jerk in a flamingo-colored suit goes on about police brutality.

Mac takes me into the cloakroom, where no coats are hung. No visitor would be so cavalier as to leave a valuable garment unguarded in this company. The room is completely empty, except for a court reporter's shorthand typewriter and a huge dining-room chandelier in a plastic bag which is evidence, undoubtedly, in a case that is going to be called.

She asks me what is up.

'Tell me what Carolyn Polhemus was doing with a B file,' I say.

'I had no idea that Carolyn was interested in crimes above the waist,' says Mac. An old line. She beams up from her wheelchair, everybody's favorite smart-ass, brassy and irreverent. She makes a number of suggestions concerning the B file, all of which I've already tried. 'It doesn't figure,' she finally admits.

As chief administrative deputy, Lydia MacDougall is in charge of personnel, procurement, and the deployment of staff. It is a lousy, thankless job with a nice-sounding title, but Lydia is accustomed to adversity. She has been a paraplegic since shortly after we started in this office together, nearly twelve years ago. It was one of those early winter nights where the mist is half snow. Lydia was driving. Her first husband, Tom, was killed in the plunge into the river.

In the general run of things, I would say Mac is probably the finest lawyer in this office, organized, shrewd, gifted in court. Over the years she has even learned to use the chair to advantage before a jury. There are some tragedies that run so deep that our comprehension of them is evolutionary at best. As the jurors get a couple of days to think about what it would be like to have their legs flapping around, loose as flags, as they listen to this woman, handsome, forceful, good-humored, absorb the wedding ring, the casual mention of her baby, observe the fact that she is – impossibly – normal, they are full of admiration and, as we all should be, hope.

56

Next September, Mac will become a judge. She already has party slating and will run in the primary unopposed. The general election will be an automatic. There are not, apparently, a lot of people who feel they can beat a lawyer with support from women's groups, the handicapped, law-and-order types, and the city's three major bar associations.

'Why don't you ask Raymond about the file?' she finally suggests.

I make a noise. Horgan is not a detail man. He is unlikely to know anything about an individual case. And these days I am reluctant to advise him of problems. He is always looking for someone to blame.

Going down the corridor to the next courtroom, where Mac is scheduled to observe, I talk to her about Tommy Molto and the problem of his unaccounted-for-status. If we fire Molto, Nico will make capital, alleging that Horgan is on a witch-hunt for Delay's friends. If we keep Tommy on the staff, we increase Nico's profit from the defection. We decide, at last, that he will be placed on Unauthorized Leave, an employment category which previously did not exist. I tell Mac I would feel more comfortable about this if somebody I trusted had seen Molto alive.

'Let's get a posse out. We have one deputy P A dead already. If some lady finds little pieces of Molto in her trash tomorrow morning, I'd like to be able to say we'd been searching high and low.'

It is Mac's turn. She makes a note.

His Honor, Larren Lyttle, his large dark face full of wiliness and majesty, is the first to notice me. A black man in a club in which only whites were members until three years ago, the judge shows no sign of yielding to the atmosphere. He is at ease among the leather club chairs and the servers in green livery.

Larren is Raymond's former law partner. In those days, they were agitators, defending draft dodgers and possessors of marijuana, and most of the local black militants, as well as a paying clientele. I tried one case against Larren before he took the bench – really just a juvenile proceeding against a very rich kid from the West Shore suburbs who liked to break into the homes of his parents' friends. Larren was an imposing figure of robust stature, shrewd and bullying with witnesses, and possessed of a rhetorical range of operatic dimension. He could adopt a refined demeanor and then move with the next utterance into the round oratory of a pork-chop preacher, or squealing ghettoese. The jury rarely noticed there was another lawyer in the courtroom.

Raymond made the break for politics first. Larren managed the campaign, quite visibly, and brought out black voters in substantial numbers. Two years later, when Raymond thought he could be mayor, Larren joined him on the ticket as a candidate for judge. Larren won and Raymond lost, and Judge Lyttle suffered for his loyalties. Bolcarro kept him quarantined in the North Branch, where Larren heard traffic cases and rumdum misdemeanors, usually the job of the appointed magistrates, until Raymond bought his freedom four years later with his early and enthusiastic endorsement of Mayor Bolcarro's re-election campaign. Larren has been a downtown felony judge ever since, a ruthless autocrat in his courtroom and, notwithstanding his friendship with Raymond, the sworn enemy of the deputy prosecuting attorneys. The saying is that there are two defense lawyers in the courtroom, and the one who's hard to beat is wearing a robe.

In spite of that, Larren remains an active force in Raymond's campaigns. The Code of Judicial Conduct now prohibits him from taking any official role. But he is still a member of Raymond's inner group, the men from Horgan's years in law school and his early time in practice whose intimacy with Raymond has filled me at moments with a kind of adolescent pining. Larren; Mike Duke, the managing partner at a massive firm downtown; Joe Reilly from the First – these are the people Raymond falls back on at these times.

To Mike Duke goes the duty of overseeing campaign financing. It has proved a more daunting task this year than in the past, when Raymond was without significant opponents. Then Raymond would not take part in a campaign solicitation of any kind, for fear that it might compromise his independence. But those scruples this year have been laid aside. Raymond has been through a number of these meetings of late, preening for the checkbook liberals, elegant-looking gentlemen like the group assembled here today, showing them that he is still the same sleek instrument of justice that he was a decade ago. Raymond delivers his campaign speech in conversational tones, awaiting the moment that first he, and then the judge, can be called away so that Mike, in their absence, can apply the squeeze.

That is my function here today. I will be Raymond's excuse to leave. He introduces me and explains that he has to catch up with the office. In this atmosphere, I am pure flunky – no one even thinks of asking me to sit down, and only Judge Lyttle bothers to stand to shake my hand. I remain behind the table and the cigar smoke, while there is a final round of handshakes and bluff jokes, then head out behind Raymond as he grabs a mint by the doorway.

'What's going on?' he asks me as soon as we are past the doorman and beneath the club's green awning. You can feel, just since the morning, that the air is starting to soften. My blood stirs. It is going to be spring.

When I tell him about Dubinsky's call, he makes no effort to hide his irritation.

'Let me just catch either one of them fucking around like that.' He means Nico and Molto. We are walking briskly down the street now toward the County Building. 'What kind of crap is this? An independent investigation.'

'Raymond, this is a reporter thinking out loud. There is probably nothing to it.'

'There better not be,' he says.

I start to tell Raymond about the debacle between the police and DEA, but he does not let me finish.

'Where are we on Carolyn ourselves?' he asks. I can see that the speculation on Molto's activities has reheated Raymond's desire for results in our own investigation. He machine-guns questions. Do we have a Hair and Fiber report? How long will it be? Have we gotten any better news on fingerprints? How about a report from the state index on sexual offenders Carolyn prosecuted?

When I tell Raymond that all of this is in the offing, but that I spent the last three hours in the charging conference, he stops dead in the street. He is furious.

'Damnit, Rusty!' His color is high and his brow flexed down angrily over his eyes. 'I told you the other day: Give this investigation *top* priority. That's what it deserves. Della Guardia is eating me alive with this thing. And we owe Carolyn as much. Let Mac run the office. She's more than capable. She can watch DEA and the coppers urinate all over each other. She can second-guess indictments. You stay on this. I want you to run out every ground ball, and do it in a goddamn orderly fashion. Do it! Act like a fucking professional.'

I look down the street, both ways. I do not see anyone I know. I am thirty-nine years old, I think. I have been a lawyer thirteen years.

Raymond walks ahead in silence. Finally, he looks back at me, shaking his head. I expect a further complaint about my performance, but instead he says, 'Man, those guys were assholes.' Raymond, I see, did not enjoy lunch.

In the County Building, Goldie, the little white-haired elevator operator who sits all day with an empty car, waiting to take Raymond and the county commissioners up and down, tosses his stool inside and folds his paper. I have begun to broach the subject of the missing B file, but I hold off while we are in the elevator. Goldie and Nico were the best of pals. I even saw Goldie break with protocol and hie Nico up and down on one or two occasions: that was the kind of touch Nico adored – the official elevator. His destiny. Nico maintained a noble poker face as Goldie scanned the lobby to be sure the coast was clear.

Once we are in the office, I trail behind. Various deputies come forward to get a word or two with Raymond, some with problems, a number who simply want the news from the campaign front. On a couple of occasions, I explain that I have been through Carolyn's docket. I do this in a desultory fashion, since I have no desire to confess to further failures, and Raymond loses the thread of what I am telling him as he moves between conversations.

'There's a file missing,' I say again. 'She had a case we can't account for.'

This finally catches Raymond's attention. We have come through the side door to his office.

'What kind of case? Do we know anything about it?'

'We know it was logged in as a bribe case – a B. Nobody seems to know what happened to it. I asked Mac. I checked my own records.'

Raymond studies me for a second; then his look becomes absent.

'Where am I supposed to be at two o'clock?' he asks me.

When I tell him that I have no idea, he shouts for Loretta, his secretary, calling her name until she appears. Raymond, it turns out, is due at a Bar Committee meeting on criminal procedure. He is supposed to outline various reforms in the state sentencing scheme that he has been calling for as part of his campaign. A press release has been issued; reporters and TV crews will be there – and he is already late.

'Shit,' says Raymond. 'Shit.' He stomps around the office saying 'Shit.'

I try again.

'Anyway, the case is still in the computer system.'

'Did she call Cody?' he asks me.

'Carolyn?'

'No. Loretta.'

'I don't know, Raymond.'

He screams again for Loretta. 'Call Cody. Did you call him? For Chrissake, call him. Well, get somebody to go down there.' Raymond looks at me. 'Sot sits on the car phone and you can never get through. Who the hell does he talk to?'

'I thought maybe you had heard something about this case. Maybe you remember something.'

Raymond is not listening. He has fallen into an easy chair, angled against what the deputies irreverently refer to as Raymond's Wall of Respect, a stretch of plaster solid with plaques and pictures and other mementos of great triumphs or honors: bar associations' awards, courtroom artists' sketches, political cartoons. Raymond has that aging look again, wandering, pensive, a man who has seen things unravel.

'God, what a fucking disaster this is. Every campaign Larren has told me to ask a deputy to take a leave so that I have somebody running things full-time, and we've always been able to scrape by without it. But this is out of control. There's too goddamn much to do and nobody in charge. Do you know that we haven't taken a poll in two months? Two weeks to the election and we have no idea where we are, with who.' He folds his hand against his mouth and shakes his head. It is not anxiety he shows so much as distress. Raymond Horgan, Kindle County Prosecuting Attorney, has lost his ability to cope.

A moment passes between us, completely silent. I am not inclined, however, after the pasting I took out on the street, to be reverential. After thirteen years in government, I know how to be a bureaucrat and I want to be sure my butt is covered with Raymond on the subject of the missing file.

'Anyway,' I say yet again, 'I don't know what significance to attach to it. I don't know if its misfiled or something's sinister.'

Raymond stares. 'Are you talking about that file again?'

I do not get a chance to answer. Loretta announces a phone call and Raymond takes it. Alejandro Stern, the defense lawyer who is the chairman of the Bar Committee, is on the line. Raymond begs apologies, says he's been wrapped up in discussions of that bizarre episode between DEA and the local police, and is on the way. When he puts the phone down he screams again for Cody.

'I'm right here,' Cody announces. He has come in the side door.

'Great.' Raymond starts in one direction, then the other. 'Where the hell is my coat?'

Cody already has it.

I wish Raymond luck.

Cody opens the door. Raymond goes through it and comes right back.

'Loretta! Where's my speech?'

Cody, it turns out, has that, too. None the less, Raymond continues to his desk. He opens a drawer and hands me a folder on his way out again.

It is the B file.

'We'll talk,' he promises me and, with Cody hard behind him, goes running down the hall.

6

'Somehow, the boy, Wendell, became important,' I said to Robinson. 'To us, I mean. To me, at least. It's hard to explain. But somehow he was part of this thing with Carolyn.'

He was an unusual child, big for his age, and he had the ambling clumsiness of some big children, a thick, almost oafish appearance. He was not so much slow as dulled. I asked one of the psychiatrists for an explanation, as if one is needed, and he said of this five-year-old, 'He's depressed.'

Wendell McGaffen, during the pendency of his mother's case, had been moved from the County Shelter to a foster home. He saw his father every day, but never his mother. After the usual disputes in court, Carolyn and I were given permission to speak with him. Actually, at first we did not talk to him at all. We sat in on sessions he had with the psychiatrists, who introduced us to Wendell. Wendell would play with the toys and figures that the shrink had around the room, and the shrink would ask Wendell whether he had any thoughts on different topics, which, almost inevitably, Wendell did not. The shrink, named Mattingly, said that Wendell had not in his weeks there asked once about his mother. And as a result they had not raised the subject.

Wendell liked Carolyn right from the start. He brought her the dolls. He made remarks to her. He directed her attention to birds, trucks, objects passing outside the window. On our third or fourth visit Carolyn told Wendell that she wanted to talk to him about his mother. The shrink appeared alarmed, but Wendell gripped his doll with both hands and asked, 'What about?'

So it progressed, twenty, thirty minutes a day. The shrink was openly impressed and eventually asked Carolyn's permission to remain during their interviews, and over a period of weeks the story was told, in snatches and mumbled remarks, disordered offhand answers to questions Carolyn had asked, often days before. Wendell showed no real emotion other than his hesitation. Usually he would stand in front of Carolyn, with both his hands gripped hard around the midsection of a doll, at which he stared unflinchingly. Carolyn would repeat what he had told her and ask him more. Wendell would nod or shake his head or not answer at all. Now and then there were his explanations. 'It hurt.' 'I criet.' 'She set I shouldn't be quiet.'

'She wanted you to be quiet?'

'Yes. She set I shouldn't be quiet.'

From another person the repetition, particularly, might have seemed cruel, but Carolyn somehow seemed to have a need to know that was in some measure selfless. Not long before the trial, Carolyn and the shrink decided that the county would not call Wendell to the witness stand unless it was an absolute necessity. The confrontation with his mother, she said, would be too much. But even with that decision made, Carolyn continued to meet with Wendell, to draw more and more from him.

'It's hard to explain,' I told Robinson, 'the way she looked at this kid. Into him almost. That intense. That earnest. I never figured her to be the type to have any kind of rapport with children. And when she did, I was astounded.'

It made her mystery so much larger. She seemed like some Hindu goddess, containing all feelings in creation. Whatever wild, surging, libidinal rivers Carolyn undammed in me by her manner and appearance, there was something about the tender attention she showed this needy child that drew me over the brink, that gave my emotions a melting, yearning quality that I took to be far more significant than all my priapic heat. When she took on the quiet, earnest tone and leaned toward dear, slow, hurting Wendell, I was, whatever my regrets, full of love for her.

A wild love. Desperate and obsessive and willfully blind. Love, as love at its truest is, with no sense of the future, love beguiled by the present and unable to derive the meaning of signs.

One day I talked to Mattingly about the way Carolyn had worked with the boy. It was extraordinary, wasn't it? I asked. Amazing. Inexplicable. I wanted to hear him praise her. But Mattingly took my comments instead as a clinical inquiry, as if I was asking what could account for this phenomenon. He drew meditatively on his pipe. 'I've thought about that,' he said. Then his look became troubled, recognizing, I suppose, that he was liable to give offense or be misjudged himself. But he went on, 'And I believe,' he said, 'that in some small way she must remind him of his mother.'

The trial went well. Mrs McGaffen was represented by Alejandro Stern – Sandy, outside the courtroom – an Argentinian Jew, a Spanish gentleman, courtly combed and perfect with his soft accent and his manicure. He is a mannerly, fastidious trial lawyer, and we decided to follow his low-key approach. We put in our physical evidence, the doctors' testimony and their test results; then we offered the fruits of the search. With that, the county rested. Sandy called a psychiatrist who described Colleen McGaffen's gentle nature. Then he showed how good a lawyer he was by reversing the usual order of presentation. The defendant testified first, denying everything; then her husband came to the stand, weeping unbearably as he described the death of his first child; Wendell's fall, which he insisted he had witnessed; and his wife's devotion to their son. A fine trial lawyer always has a latent message to the jury, too prejudicial or improper to speak aloud, whether it's a racist appeal when black victims identify white defendants or the no-big-deal manner that a lawyer like Stern takes when the crime is only an attempt. In this case, Sandy wanted the jury to know that her husband forgave Colleen McGaffen, and if *he* could, why couldn't *they* do that, too?

In a kind of professional salvation, I found that in the courtroom I could almost wall myself to Carolyn; I enjoyed extended periods of concentration and would wake to her presence beside me, and to the grip of my obsession, almost with surprise. But this work of will came at a heavy price. Outside, I was largely useless. To perform the most routine tasks – talking to witnesses, gathering exhibits – required that all my energies be directed to a frozen inattention: Do not think about her, please do not think about her now. I did. I moved about in a spaced-out reality, vacillating among various lurid fantasies and moments of intense self-rebuke and instants when she was present in which I simply helplessly gawked.

'Finally,' I told Robinson, 'we were there one night, working in her office.' The defense case was nearly over. Darryl had begun his testimony, and the pathos of this man's feckless inability to deal with anything that had happened was, in truth, terribly moving. Carolyn was going to do the cross-examination, and she was high. The courtroom was full of reporters; there were stories about the case on a couple of the TV stations most nights. And the cross itself was exciting because it required a kind of surgical skill: Darryl had to be destroyed as a witness but not as a human being. The jury's sympathy would never leave him, for he was, in the end, not doing anything less than most of us would do, trying to save what was left of his family. So Carolyn was lingering over this cross, practicing it, modulating it, talking it out, flashing in front of me like a coin turning in the air. She was in her stocking feet, and a full skirt that twirled slightly around her whenever she pivoted in the narrow space; she was pacing briskly as she worked through the tone and the questions.

'And there are wrappers from our fast-food dinner on the desk, and a scatter of various records: Darryl's time and attendance sheets from work to show that he's too busy to know what is up at home; medical reports on the child; statements from his teachers and an aunt. And we are setting up each question. "No, no, softer, softer. 'Mr McGaffen, you couldn't know that Wendell showed his bruises at school?' Like that. Maybe three questions: 'Do you know Beverley Morrison? Well, would it refresh your recollection to know that she was Wendell's teacher? Did you know that Ms Morrison discussed Wendell's physical condition with your wife on the evening of 7 November of last year?'

'"Softly," she says.

'"Softly, right," I say. "Don't come too close to him. And

don't move too much in the courtroom. You don't want to seem angry."

'And Carolyn is excited and she reaches across the desk, very high, and grabs both my hands.

'It's going to be so good,' she says, and then her eyes, which are quite green, stay on me a little longer, just enough so that I know we've suddenly left the trial, and I say – and I have never said a word out loud up to that moment – I just say, as hollow and pathetic as I feel, "What the hell is going on, Carolyn?" and she smiles, for the fleetest instant, but with a stunning radiance, and says, "Not now," and goes right back to talking out the cross.'

'Not now.' Not now. I caught the last bus back to Nearing that night and sat in the dark pondering as we flashed under the streetlights. Not now. I haven't decided? I have. It's good. It's bad. I'm uncertain. I want to let you down easy.

But at least there was something. I gradually recognized the significance of our communication. I was not mad. I was not caught up with something imaginary; something was happening. We had been talking about *something*. And that turbulent, lost unease of mine began to change. There in the bus, as I sat in the rear, in a pit of darkness, my obsessions now took on a sabering quality, and knowing that I had entered the region of the real, I began to feel, simply, fear.

7

Studio B, it says outside the door. I enter a large open space the size of a small gymnasium. There is a mustardy quality to the light in here; the walls are yellow tile and they seem vaguely luminescent. The feeling is very much like Nat's grade school: a row of sinks, floor-to-ceiling compartments of white birch that are apparently student lockers. One young man is working at his easel by the windows. I spent, of course, many years around the U. – probably, if I had to get down to this kind of dismal estimate, the happiest time of my life – but I doubt that I ever entered the Art Center before, especially if you do not count the adjacent auditorium, where Barbara, on occasion, brought me to attend some plays. For an instant, I am perplexed that I am here. Better to send Lipranzer, I think clearly. Then I speak.

'Marty Polhemus?'

The boy turns from the easel, some anxious sign working through his expression.

'Are you from the police?'

'PA's office.' I offer my hand and give my name. Marty tosses his brush down on a table where tubes of acrylic paint and round white bottles of gesso are randomly set; he picks up his shirttail to wipe his hand before he shakes. Marty is an art student, all right, a pimply kid, with lots and lots of hair, loose brass-colored ringlets; he has spots of paint all over his clothing and a gruel of paint and just plain dirt under his long fingernails.

'They said somebody else might like come to see me,' Marty tells me. He is a nervous sort, eager to please. He asks if I want coffee and we go to a drip pot back near the door. Marty pours two foam cups full, then has to put them down to grope in his pockets for change. I, finally, toss two quarters in the kitty.

'Who was it,' I ask, as we both stand blowing into our coffee cups, 'who said someone else might see you? Mac?'

'Raymond. Mr Horgan. He said.'

'Ah.' An awkward silence – although Marty is the kind of kid with whom it seems there would be many. I explain that I am the deputy PA assigned to the investigation of his mother's murder, and that I received his class schedule from the registrar. Tuesday, 1–4 p.m., Independent Art Studio.

'I just wanted to touch base in case there's something you might be able to add.'

'Sure. Right. Whatever you want,' Marty says. We drift back toward his easel, and he ends up sitting on the broad ledge beneath the windows. From here, beyond the university, you can see the railroad lines, dug out and gathered over the belly of the city like a large and tangible scar. The boy is looking in that direction, and I stare for a moment, too.

'I didn't know her very well,' he tells me. 'You heard the story, didn't you?' As he asks this, his eyes are quick, and I am not certain if he would prefer that I say yes or no. When I admit my ignorance, he nods and looks away.

'I didn't see her for like a long time,' he says simply. 'My father can tell you the whole thing, if you want. Just call him. He said he'd do what he could to help.'

'He's in New Jersey?'

'Right. I'll give you the phone.'

'I take it they were divorced.'

At that Marty laughs. 'God, I hope so. He's been married to my mother – I mean Muriel, but I always call her my mother. They've been married fifteen years.'

He brings his legs up onto the window ledge and looks out over the clustered campus structures as he speaks. After suggesting that I call his father, the boy, in a moment, tells me himself about what's behind him. He has no particular ease about this; his hands are wound about each other in an almost crippled fashion. But he continues without prodding. The story which Marty tells in fits and starts is one of the contemporary era. His father, Kenneth, was a high school English teacher in a small town in New Jersey, and Carolyn was his pupil.

'My father said she was, you know, like real attractive. I think he started going out with her while she was still in school. I mean, they were sneaking around or something. Which isn't Dad. At all. He's real quiet. I bet he didn't know two girls when he met her. He never said that, but I'd bet. I think it was like some big passionate thing. You know. Real romantic. On his end, anyway.' Here the boy appears confounded. His estimate of Carolyn is clouded. He clearly does not know enough to even guess at her emotions.

'Her,' he says. 'Carolyn. You know, my mother. My *real* mother,' says the boy, screwing up his face. 'My father called her Carrie. She had all these brothers. And her father. Her mother was dead. I guess she hated all of them. I don't know. They all hated each other. Dad said her father was always beating the tar out of her. She was real happy to get away from them.'

The boy abruptly leaves the ledge and approaches his painting, a swirling eye of red. He squints at it, reaches out for one of the tubes. He intends to work while we speak.

He does not, he says, know exactly how his parents broke up. When he was born, Carolyn was trying to go to college and was unhappy that she had to quit. His father just says that all hell was breaking loose in those days and Carrie got caught up in it. She had a boyfriend, Marty says, he is pretty sure of that from the way his father talks. But the father apparently does not dwell on that. The way his father puts it is that because of other dissatisfactions she stopped liking the town, his father, the life she had.

'My father says she was too young when they got married, and she grew up and wanted to be something else, and just like decided to be it. Dad says it was a big mess. One day she took off. And my father, you know, says it was probably for the best. He's that kind of person. He says stuff like that and means it.'

This father emerges in his son's words as a kind of Norman Rockwell figure, wise and gentle, with spectacles in his hand and the paper – the kind of man to spend long nights in thought in the parlor, a teacher who always took his students to heart. I have a son, I almost tell this boy. I would like to think that someday he would feel this way about me.

'I don't have any idea who killed her,' Marty Polhemus tells me suddenly. 'I mean, I assume that's why you came.'

Why did I come? I wonder. To see what she was hiding, I suppose, or did not care to tell. To diminish a little further my idea of what I had thought was intimacy.

'Do you think it was somebody she knew?' he asks. 'I mean, do you have like leads, or whatever you call it. Clues?'

The answer, I tell him, is no. I describe the equivocal state of the evidence: the unlocked windows, the glass. I spare him the description of the cords, the non-viable condition of the seminal fluid. This is, after all, his mother. Although my sense is that there is little need for care or solicitude. I doubt that Marty's look of nervous bewilderment has anything to do with recent events. Indeed, there is something that makes it seem as if he regards himself, largely, as an outsider to all of this.

'Carolyn tried a lot of rape cases,' I say. 'Some people think it might be someone like that.'

'You don't?'

'Murders aren't usually mysterious. In this city these days, half of them are gang-related. In almost all the other cases, the victim and the killer knew each other well. About half of them are broken love affairs: marriage on the rocks, unhappy lovers, that kind of thing. Usually there's been some kind of breakup in the last six months. Generally, the motivation is pretty obvious.'

'She had a lot of boyfriends,' Marty volunteers.

'Did she?'

'I guess. I mean, there were lots of times she didn't want me around. I'd call, you know, and I could tell somebody else was there. I couldn't always figure out what was going on with her. I think she liked having secrets, you know?' He shrugs. 'I mean, I thought I'd get to know her. That's why I came out here. My dad kept trying to discourage me, but I thought it would be neat. I'm not so interested in school right now, anyway. I figured, you go to college, one place is as good as another. It turns out that I'm like flunking everything anyhow.'

'Really?'

'Not everything. I can't understand physics, though. I really can't. I honestly am flunking that.'

A girl with a T-shirt from the world tour of a rock group and a smart-looking set comes through the door and asks if he's seen somebody named Harley. Marty says he hasn't. You can hear a stereo on down the hallway when she goes in and out the door. The boy changes brushes and comes within inches of the canvas as he works. His strokes are achingly small.

He goes on talking about Carolyn.

'I knew she was out here for years. I started writing her letters. Then when I could really get my courage up, I got her on the phone. It wasn't the first time I ever like talked to her or anything. She'd call up once in a while. Right after the first of the year a lot. Like she wanted to call over the holidays but she knew better than to do that. Anyway, she was nice about it. Real nice. "Oh, well that would be lovely." La la, ta ta. Real polite,' he says, and nods to himself. 'Civil. That's a word, right?'

'Right,' I say.

'I'd see her. Sundays I saw her a lot. Once or twice, I met people – I guess, when it seemed to her like the right thing to do. You know, that's how she introduced me to Mr Horgan.'

The emotional currents are strong here. It is best just to let the boy go, it seems, whatever my impulse to ask questions.

'I mean, she was real busy. She had her career and all. She wanted to run for prosecuting attorney someday. Did you know that?'

I hesitate longer than I should, even in this ungainly conversation. Perhaps my own expression discloses some reflex of distress, for the boy looks at me oddly. I tell him, finally, that the PA's office is full of people who see that in their future. But that does not put him off.

'Did you like know her real good? I mean, did you work with her or something?'

'Now and then,' I say, but I can tell from the way his glance lingers that I have failed in my effort to be oblique. 'You were telling me what happened when you saw her.'

He waits a moment, but he is accustomed to cooperating with grownups, and he turns his attention to his brush, rubbing it around inside a little plastic tray. His shoulders move before he speaks.

'Not much happened,' he says, then rears his head of tangled brass-colored hair and looks back at me directly. 'I mean she never talked about back then,' he tells me, 'about when I was a kid. I suppose I expected her to. But I guess she just didn't feature that part of her life. You know? She like said nothing.'

I nod, and for a moment we are silent, still looking at one another. His eyes again take on that quickened light.

'I didn't make any difference to her. You know? She was as nice as pie. Now. But like she didn't care. That's why my old man didn't want me to come out here. I mean, he spent all those years making up for her, saying that it was a time in her life, all that. He never wanted me to feel like she left because of me. But he knew what was going on.' He throws his brush down. 'If you want to know the truth, Mr Horgan had to like talk me into going to the funeral. I wasn't gonna. I just really didn't feel like it. My own mother. That's pretty terrible, isn't it?'

'I don't know,' I say. He takes his canvas down and stares at it, near his feet. He seems to recognize – and welcome – my close observation of him. Young, I think. There is such a tender quality to this boy's discomfort. I speak quietly.

'My mother died while I was in law school,' I say. 'The next week I stopped by to see my father. I never did that, but I figured under the circumstances –' I motion. 'Anyway, he was packing. Half the household was in boxes. I said, "Pa, where you going?" He says, "Arizona." Turned out he'd bought a piece of land, a trailer. And he never said word one to me about it. If I hadn't come by that day, I'm sure he'd have left town without even saying goodbye. And it was always like that with us. Sometimes that's the way things are between parents and kids.'

The boy looks toward me for a long moment, mystified by my candor or the things of which we speak.

'And what do you do about that, huh? Anything?'

'You try to grow up,' I say. 'In your own way. I have this son and he's the world to me.'

'What's his name?'

'My son?'

'Right.'

'Nat.'

'Nat,' says Carolyn's son. He looks at me again. 'What was she to you, anyhow? I mean, this isn't just work, right? Was she like your girlfriend, too?'

I am sure that he has seen my wedding band. His gesture toward me with his chin as he asks this question seems almost to point in that direction, but I do not feel capable of further devices with this soft, decent boy.

'I'm afraid at one point she was my girlfriend, too. Late last year.' I say. 'Just a little while.'

'Yeah,' says the kid, and shakes his head with real disgust. He's waiting to meet somebody she didn't gull, and there is nobody here who can make that claim.

'When I flunk out,' he says to me, 'I'm going home.' This declaration has sufficient weight that it seems to me, perhaps, this matter has just now been decided. But I do not respond. He does not need me to tell him he is correct. I smile, warmly enough, I hope, to show how much I like him. Then I leave.

8

'In the Hall, you know,' says Lip, referring to McGrath Hall, the police department headquarters, 'they are calling this thing Mission Impossible.' He means our investigation of Carolyn's murder. 'That's how the dicks are talkin. You know, "What's new with Mission Impossible?" Like nobody'll ever figure this fuckin thing out. Not in time for Horgan. He never shoulda let the press think we could come up with somethin fast. He shoulda downplayed it, instead of givin forty fuckin interviews about how hard we're workin.'

Lip's mouth is full of torn bread and red sauce, but that does not stop him from complaining. His irritation is extreme. We are standing before a vacant lot, a dump of sorts beneath the highway viaduct. Broken pieces of stressed concrete, with the snaky rusted coils of reinforcement sticking from them, litter the uneven ground, along with more ordinary refuse: bottles, newspapers, abandoned auto parts. There is also a snowfall of white wax-paper balls and crushed cups left by the many customers who have preceded us in taking a sandwich from Giaccalone's across the street. It is one of Lip's favorite places, an Italian stand where they insert an entire veal chop, laden with marinara, into a Vienna roll. Lipranzer likes heavy fare at lunchtime, the single man's answer to the anomie of dinner. Our soft drinks rest on the backless remains of a public bench on which each of us has perched one foot. Various street gangs and adolescent lovers have inscribed their names in the planks of the bench's punky seat.

Walking back to Lip's car, we trade information. I talk about my visit with the kid, and the fact that he provided no meaningful

75

leads. Lip discusses his own recent activities. He interviewed the neighbor who said she thought she saw a stranger.

'Mrs Krapotnik,' Lip says. 'She's a winner. Talk some? I'm tellin you.' He shakes his head. 'She'll look at mug books, but first I gotta get some earplugs.'

'How about the Index?' The Index is the state file on sex offenders.

'Nothin,' Lip says.

'Nothing like the ropes?'

'This lady I'm talkin to tells me she read somethin like that once in a book. No one she knows of ever done it. Christ, can you imagine that's what she's readin? You'd think she gets enough on the job.'

Lip has his customary OPV – official police vehicle – a gold Aries, unmarked but for the blackwall tires and the license plates, which, like those on every other OPV, begin with ZF, thus forming a code recognized by every minor hoodlum in the city. Lip guns away from the curb. Coppers, cabbies, people who live in their cars always drive so fast. He swings through one of his many shortcuts back downtown and, because of a detour, is forced onto Kinbark, main drag of my old neighborhood. The diverted traffic is thick and we move with processional slowness down the avenue. There it is, I think, there it is. His cousin Milos, who bought the bakery when my father left, never even changed the sign. It still says SABICH'S in a heavy sea-blue script.

Even though I worked there every day, I remember only certain details of the interior – the summertime screen door that transfigured the moving shapes of the street, the racks of blue metal trays behind the counter, the heavy steel cash register with its round clang. When I was six, my presence was first demanded. I was a pair of hands, unemployed, and not requiring pay. I was taught to break and stack the smooth, white-sided cake boxes. I made them a dozen at a time and brought them from the cobwebbed basement to the store. Because the boxes were so slick and substantial, their edges had, at certain angles, the lacerating power of the finest cutlery; my knuckles and fingertips were often cut. I learned to dread this, for my father regarded a trace of blood on the outside of a cake box as a scandal. 'Is not here a butcher shop.' This remark would come with a look that mixed loathing and disgust in fearsome proportions. In my dreams of those times, it is always summer, when the air of this valley is as stilted as a swamp's, and the added dry heat of the ovens made it labor just to walk about the shop. I dream that my skin is slick with sweat, my father is calling, a cake has fallen, and my fear is like an acid that is corroding my veins and bones.

If I were to paint my father, he would have a gargoyle's face and a dragon's scaled heart. The channels of his emotions were too intricately wound upon themselves, too clotted, strangulated, crowded with spite to admit any feeling for a child. There was never any question of picking sides for me. Like the apartment, its walls and pictures, the furniture he broke, it was clear that my father regarded me as a possession of my mother's. And I grew up with what seemed a simple understanding: my mother loved me; my father did not.

He took his satisfaction, if you could call so arid a feeling by that name, from opening the shop, firing the oven, raising the shade, pushing the whitened dust out the back door at the end of the day. His family had been bakers for four generations and he simply did as he had been taught. His standards were unyielding and his procedures were exact. He never tried to charm his customers; he was far too humorless and insular for that. In fact, he saw every person who entered as a potential enemy, someone who would complain, chisel, wheedle, and finally settle for day-old bread. But his income was always steady: he was known to be reliable; he distrusted employees and did the work of two, at least, himself, and he did not file a tax return for more than twenty years.

He had come to this country in 1946. I was named for the town in which he had been raised, a village two hundred miles from Belgrade. Almost everyone there was a partisan. When the Nazis came through in 1941, all the adults were lined up against the schoolhouse and shot. The children were left, abandoned. My father, then barely eighteen, and soft-faced enough to have been spared, roamed with a band in the mountains for almost six months before they were captured. He spent the rest of the war in camps – first the Nazi labor camps, and the Allied DP camps after the liberation. His relatives here arranged his passage, hectoring their congressman and the congressman's local staff in a ceaseless and eccentric way. My father was one of the first of the Displaced Persons allowed to enter the United States. And after a year here, he no longer spoke to my great-aunt and my cousins who had worked so hard to save him.

Hearing the rough chorus of auto horns, I look back to make out the problem. A white man in the car behind us pounds on his steering wheel and makes a belligerent gesture in my direction, and I finally realize that Lip has stopped dead in the traffic. I take it that he has surveyed my line of sight and let the other cars move on, but when I turn to catch his expression, his eyes have shifted and he is making a determined effort to study the traffic.

'Hair and Fiber come in,' Lip says finally. His gray eyes, his lined, high-cheeked face betray nothing, quiet as a pond.

'Tell me,' I say, and Lip dutifully recounts the contents of the report. On Carolyn's clothes and body were minute fibers of a carpeting not found in her apartment – Zorak V is its name. It is a synthetic, milled domestically. The color is called Scottish Malt, the most popular shade. The dye lot cannot be identified and the fiber could be from either an industrial or a domestic weave. In all there are probably fifty thousand homes and offices in Kindle County from which the carpet fibers could have come. There are no hair or skin fragments in Carolyn's fingers or under her nails, confirming that there was no struggle before she was bound, and the only human hair not Carolyn's shade found anywhere near the corpse has been made as female and, thus, insignificant. The cord with which she was bound is regular clothesline, American-made, sold in every K Mart, Sears, and Walgreen's.

'That didn't get us very far,' I tell Lipranzer.

'Not very,' he answers. 'At least we know she didn't grab anybody.'

'I wonder,' I say. 'I keep thinking about what we said last week. How maybe this was some guy she knew. I remember when I was in law school, everyone used to pass around this case about a guy whose life insurer refused to pay out. His widow was bringing the suit, which was a real stitch, because it turned out this character had bought it whacking off while he was hanging himself. Literally. Head through a noose and everything. He cashed in when he knocked over the stool he was supposed to land on.'

'No shit.' Lipranzer laughs out loud. 'Who won the case?'

'The insurance company, as far as I remember. The court didn't think it was a covered risk. Anyway, maybe that's what this was all about. You know, big-time kinkiness? I'm thinking that more and more. Apparently it's some weird high, coming while you're passing out.'

'How does she end up dead from gettin hit?'

'Maybe her stud gets scared. *Thinks* he's cooled her. Figures it's John Belushi all over again, and starts to make it look like it was something else.'

Lip shakes his head. He doesn't like it.

'You're stretchin,' he says. 'I don't think the path report supports it.'

'I'm gonna run it by Painless, anyway.'

This reminds Lipranzer of something else.

'Painless called me a couple days ago. Says he's got a report back from the forensic chemist. From the way he sounded, I take it we didn't get much, but maybe you can pick up whenever you get there. I gotta get out west today. Show Mrs Krapotnik some pictures.' He closes his eyes and shimmies his head, like maybe, if he tries, he can stand the thought.

We are back downtown now. Lip eases into the first open space in the police lot, and we trek back through the noontime crowds toward the County Building. Out on the street, our spring, as so often happens, is turning fast to summer. You can feel some of the balminess that is a month or two away. It has inspired some of the ladies passing on the avenue to summer fashions, sleeveless tops, and those light, clingy fabrics of the season.

'Brother,' I tell Lip suddenly, 'we are really nowhere.'

He makes a sound. 'You ever get the fingerprint lab?'

I swear. 'I knew I forgot something.'

'You are a class A fuck-up,' he says. 'They ain't gonna do it for me. I asked twice already.'

I promise I will do that, as well as see Painless, today or tomorrow.

When we get back to my office, I ask Eugenia to hold my calls and I close the door. I pull the B file that Horgan gave me out of my drawer.

Lip studies it a moment.

The B file, as I received it from Raymond, consists, in its entirety, of a log-in slip, produced when the case was entered in our computer system; a single sheet of sparse notes in Carolyn's hand; and a xerox of a long letter. There is nothing in the file to indicate whether an original of this letter was received or this copy is all that came in. The letter is typewritten and clean – but it still does not look professional. The margins are narrow and there is only a single paragraph. The author is someone who knows how to type but seemingly does not do it often – a housewife, perhaps, or a professional man.

I have read the letter four or five times by now, but I read it one more time, taking each page from Lip as he finishes.

Dear Mr Horgan:

I am writing to you because I have been a fan of yours for many years. I am sure that you didn't know anything about the things that are making me write this letter. In fact, I think you would want to do something about them. Probably there is nothing you can do, since all this happened a long time ago. But I thought you would like to know. It happened while you were P A and it's kind of about somebody who worked for you, a deputy prosecuting attorney who I think was taking bribes. Nine years ago this summer a person I will call Noel got arrested. Noel was not this person's real name, but if I told you his real name you would go to him first to talk about a lot of the things I am saying in this letter and he would think about it and know I turned him in. Then he would hurt me to get even. Believe me, I know him real well and I know what I am talking about. He would make me very sorry. Anyway, Noel got arrested. I happen to think that what it was for isn't real important but I will tell you that it was something which he was very embarrassed about, because that is the kind of person he is. Noel thought that if the people he worked with and hung out with found out, they wouldn't have anything to do with him. Great friends. But that's Noel. The lawyer he got told him he should just admit it in court because nothing was going to happen and nobody would ever know about it. But Noel is a very paranoid-type person and he ran all over the place fussing about what would happen if anybody ever found out. Pretty soon he started saying how he was going to pay somebody off. I thought he was joking around at first. Noel would stoop to anything, but it just didn't sound right for him. If you knew him you would understand why. But he kept telling me he was going to do this. And it would cost $1500. I know all this because, to make a long story short, I'm the one who gave him the money. Since Noel is like he is, I thought I better be sure it was going where he said. We went all the way out to the North Branch at Runyon and 111th. Out there, we didn't wait even a minute, when a secretary who seemed to know Noel walked up and took us downstairs to the PA's office. Your name, *RAYMOND HORGAN*, was written right on the door, I remember. Noel told me to wait outside. I was too scared by then to fight about it, which was pretty dumb since I came all the way out there to see him give somebody the money. But anyway, he wasn't inside two minutes and he's back out. He had put all of this money in a sock (*I'm not kidding!*) and when he came out he showed me the sock and it was empty. I just about ran out of there, but Noel was very cool. I asked him later what happened. Noel never liked to talk about this thing. He said he was protecting me, which is a laugh. I'm sure he just figured that if I didn't forget about it, sooner or later I'd want the money back. Anyway, he did say that the girl took him into an office and told him to wait at a desk there. Then a man talked behind him. He told Noel just to put what he brought in the center drawer of the desk and to leave. Noel said he never looked back or anything. Ten days later, Noel had to go to court. He was just about crazy again. He kept saying he knew he was going to get screwed over and everything, but when we got there, *the lawyer from the prosecuting attorney told the judge that the case was dismissed. I have tried and tried to remember this lawyer's name, but I can't. Once or twice I asked Noel the name of the guy he bribed, but like I said, he really never liked to talk about this and just told me to mind my own business. So I am writing this letter to you. I haven't seen Noel in about two years. Frankly, this is not the worst thing he ever did, by a long shot, if you believe him, but it's really the only thing I ever saw him do myself. I'm not really out to get Noel, but I thought that this P A was really wrong for taking this money and taking advantage of people that way, and I wanted to write to you so that you could do something about it. A couple of people who I have told this story to without using any names said that you couldn't do anything about something so old since the statute of limitations is past, but I figure this couldn't have been the only time something like this ever happened and maybe even they're still doing the same thing. Actually, I think that what I just wrote isn't true. I hope you get Noel too. But I don't want him to know you got him from me. And if you do get him from someone else, I beg you please (Please!) not to show him this letter. I am TRUSTING YOU.*

The letter, of course, is unsigned. Our office gets letters like this every day. Two paralegals are assigned to do pretty much nothing but answer this kind of correspondence, and talk to the various cranks who wander into the reception area in person. The more serious complaints tend to get passed along, which, presumably, is how this one found its way to Raymond. Even at that point, a lot of what comes in is junk. But this one, for all its funny twitches, has the ring of the real thing. It is more than possible, of course, that our tipster was simply scammed by his friend Noel. But the guy who wrote the letter was in the best position to judge, and he doesn't seem to think that was the case.

Scam or not, it is easy to figure out why Raymond Horgan would not want this file floating around in an election year. Nico would love to have evidence of any kind of undiscovered crimes committed during Raymond's regime. As the letter writer surmises, it is not likely that friend Noel's case was an isolated episode. What we have in hand is a first-class scandal: an unnoticed – worse – unapprehended bribery ring operating in one of the branch courts.

Lipranzer has lit a cigarette. He has been quite a long time.

'You think it's bull?' I ask.

'Neh,' he says. 'Somethin's there. Maybe not what this jamoche thinks, but it's somethin.'

'Do you think it's worth looking at?'

'Can't hurt. We ain't exactly buried in leads.'

'That's what I thought. Carolyn figured these guys were gay,' I say. 'I think she was probably on the right track.' I point to her notes. She has the section number of various provisions of what is still titled the Morals chapter of the state criminal code written down, a question mark beside them. 'Remember the panty raids out in the Public Forest? That would have been right about then. We were busting those guys in carloads. And the cases went to the North Branch, didn't they?'

Lip is nodding: it all fits. The embarrassing nature of the crime, the mania to conceal it. And the timing is right. Sexual crimes, involving consenting adults, were ignored as a matter of policy in Raymond's first administration. The cops brought in the cases, but we gave them the shuffle. By the time Raymond began to campaign for re-election, certain groups, prostitutes and gays particularly, were, in their more florid segments, largely beyond control. With the gays, the problem was acute in the public forests which ring the city. Families would not go there at midday on the weekends for fear of what their children would be exposed to. There were some fairly graphic complaints about what was taking place in broad daylight on the picnic tables, where, Mom tended to point out, people were supposed to eat. With the election nine months away, we made a large show of a concerted clean-up. Dozens of men were arrested every night, often *in flagrante delicto*. Their cases were usually disposed of with court supervision – a kind of expungeable guilty plea – and the defendants then disappeared.

That is the problem. Both Lip and I recognize it will be difficult to find Noel. There were probably four hundred of these cases that summer, and we don't even know his name. If Carolyn made much progress, the file does not seem to show it. The jacket date indicates she got the case about five months before her murder. Her notes reflect little investigation. 'Noel' is written in an upper corner and underlined countless times. A little farther down the page she has written 'Leon.' The significance of this eluded me at first, then I realized that she had assumed that, like many aliases, the name chosen by the letter writer was the product of some meaningful association. Maybe the name was a rebus. Carolyn was going to suppose that she was looking for somebody named Leon. Finally, she has another name, 'Kenneally,' at the foot of the page, and his assignment. This is Lionel Kenneally, a good copper, now a commander. We worked the Night Saints cases together. He runs the watch in the 32nd Police District, whose cases are heard in the North Branch.

'I still don't understand why I never heard about this case,' I tell Lip. I can't imagine a procedural reason for not informing me – or for the case to have ended up in the hands of Carolyn, who did not work in our public corruption unit. I have spent more than a few moments with that puzzle, full as it is with sorrowful implications about my fading romance with Raymond Horgan, and his with me.

Lip shrugs. 'What's Horgan tell you?'

'I haven't been able to corner him. It's twelve days to the election. They're on a twenty-four-hour operation now.'

'How about Kenneally. What'd he say?'

'He's been on leave.'

'Well, you better talk to him. He ain't tellin shit to me. We ain't in each other's fan clubs.'

The police department is full of people with whom Lipranzer does not get along, but I would have guessed Lip would take to Kenneally. He likes good cops. But there is something between them. He's hinted at it before.

Lip starts to leave, then steps back in the office. I am already headed out to see Eugenia, but Lip takes me by the elbow to detain me. He closes the door I just opened.

'One thing,' he says. He looks right at me. 'We got her MUDs back.'

'And?'

'Nothin great. Only we wanted to get MUDs on any number she called more than three times in the last six months.'

'Yeah?'

'I noticed as I'm goin through there, one of the numbers that comes up that way is yours.'

'Here?' I ask.

An especially narrow look emerges from Lip's narrow, Slavic face.

'Home,' he says. 'Last October. Thereabouts.'

I am about to tell him this could not possibly be right. Carolyn never tried to reach me at home. Then I realize what it is. *I* made those calls from Carolyn's place. Lying to my wife. Late again, kid. This trial's gonna be a bitch. I'll catch dinner down here.

Lip watches me calculate. His eyes are flat and gray.

'I'd just as soon you let it go,' I say at last. 'If Barbara sees a subpoena notice from the phone company, she'll blow a gut. Under the circumstances. If you don't mind, Lip, I'd appreciate it.'

He nods, but I can see that it is still not right with him. If nothing else, we have always depended on each other to be above certain base kinds of stupidity, and Dan Lipranzer would be unfaithful to that compact if he did not take one more moment to cast his gray eyes on me harshly, so that I know I've let him down.

9

'In the end,' I told Robinson, 'we had to put Wendell McGaffen on the witness stand.' His testimony was the only effective response to his father, and so we called the boy in rebuttal. Carolyn was splendid. She wore a dark blue suit and a beige blouse with a huge satin bow, and she stood beside Wendell, whose feet did not reach the floor from the hard oak chair in the witness box. You could not hear a thing in the courtroom.

And then what did your mother do, Wendell?

He asked for water.

When your mother took you in the basement, Wendell, what did she do?

It was bad, he said.

Was it this? Carolyn went to the vise, which had sat throughout, like an omen, at the edge of the prosecution table, grease-smeared and black, thicker in all its parts than any of Wendell's limbs

Uh huh.

Did she hurt you?

Uh huh.

And did you cry?

Uh huh. Wendell drank some more water and then added. A lot.

Tell how it happened, said Carolyn finally, softly, and Wendell did. She said to lie down. He said he screamed and cried. He cried, Mommy don't. He begged her.

But he finally laid himself down.

And she told him not to scream.

Wendell swung his feet as he talked. He gripped his doll. And as

Carolyn and Mattingly had instructed him, he never looked over at his mother. On cross Stern did what little he could, asked Wendell how many times he'd met with Carolyn and whether he loved his mother, which caused Wendell to ask for more water. There was no disputing, really. Every person there knew the child was telling the truth, not because he was practiced or particularly emotional, but because somehow in every syllable Wendell spoke there was a tone, a knowledge, a bone-hard instinct that what he was describing was wrong. Wendell convinced with his moral courage.

I delivered the closing argument for the county. My state of personal disturbance was such that when I approached the podium I had no idea of what I was going to say, and for one moment I was full of panic, convinced that I would be speechless. Instead, I found the well of all my passionate turmoil and I spoke fervently for this boy, who must have lived, I said, desperate and uncertain every moment, wanting, as we all wanted, love, and receiving instead, not just indifference or harshness, but torture.

Then we waited. Having a jury out is the closest thing in life to suspended animation. Even the simplest tasks, cleaning my desk, returning phone calls, reading prosecution reports, are beyond my attention, and I end up walking the halls, talking over the evidence and the arguments with anyone unlucky enough to ask me how the case went. About 4:00, Carolyn came by to say she was going to return something to Morton's and I volunteered to walk along. As we left the building, it began raining hard, a cold downpour driven almost sideways by the wind, which was full of winter. People dashed down the street, covering their heads. Carolyn returned her merchandise, a glass bowl whose source she did not identify, and then we headed back into the rain. She more or less shouted out as the wind came up, and I put an arm around her protectively, and she leaned against me beneath my umbrella. It was like something coming loose, and we went on that way for a few blocks, saying nothing, until I finally followed my impulse to speak.

Listen, I said. I started again. Listen.

In her heels, Carolyn was about six feet, an inch or so taller

87

than me, so it was almost an embrace when she turned her face in my direction. In the natural light, you could see what Carolyn, with her devotion to lotions and gyms and spectacular fashions, tried to obscure – that it was an older face, past forty, the makeup clinging to the lines radiating from her eyes, a haggard roughness now part of the skin. But somehow that made her more real to me. This was my life and this was happening.

I've been wondering, I told her, about something you said. What you meant the other night when you told me, Not now.

She looked at me. She shook her head as if she did not know, but her face was full of caprice, her lips sealed to hold back her laughter.

The wind came up again then, and I drew her into the shelter of a recessed storefront. We were on Grayson Boulevard, where the shops face the stately elms of the Midway.

I mean, I said, hopeless and pitiable and small, there seems to be something going on between us. I mean, am I crazy? To think that?

I don't think so.

You don't.

No.

Ah, I said.

Still smiling wonderfully, she put her arm through mine and moved me back down the street.

The jury returned a little before 7:00. Guilty on all counts. Raymond had remained in the office awaiting the verdict, and he came downstairs with us to meet the press, cameras not being allowed above the lobby of the County Building. Then he took us out for a drink. He had a date, and so around 8:30 he left us in a back booth at Caballero's, where Carolyn and I talked and became drunk and moony. I told her that she had been magnificent. Magnificent. I don't know how many times I said that.

TV and the movies have spoiled the most intimate moments of our lives. They have given us conventions which dominate our expectations in instants whose intensity would ordinarily make them spontaneous and unique. We have conventions of grief, which we learned from the Kennedys, and ordained gestures for victory by which we imitate the athletes we see on the tube, who in turn have learned the same things from other jocks they saw on TV. Seduction, too, has got its standards now, its sloe-eyed moments, its breathless repartee.

And so we both ended up coming on smooth and wry and bravely composed, like all those gorgeous, poised movietime couples, probably because we had no other idea of how to behave. And even so, there was a gathering in the air, a racing current that made it difficult to sit in place, to move my mouth or lift my glass to drink. I don't believe we ordered dinner, but we had the menus, something to stare at, like coquettes with their silk fans. Beneath the table Carolyn's hand was laid out casually, very close to my hip.

I didn't know you when this started.

What? she asks. We are close on the plush bench, but she must lean a bit nearer because I am speaking so softly. I can smell the liquor on her breath.

I didn't know you before this case, before this started. That amazes me.

Because?

Because it just doesn't seem that way now – that I didn't know you.

Do you know me now?

Better. I think so. Don't I?

Maybe, she says. Maybe what it is, is that now you know you want to get to know me.

That's possible, I say, and she repeats it:

That's possible.

And will I get to know you?

That's possible, too, she says. If that's what you want.

I think that is, I say.

I think that's one thing, she says, that you want.

One thing?

One thing, she says. She brings her glass up to drink without looking away from me. Our faces are not very far apart at all. When she puts her glass down, the large bow on her blouse almost brushes my chin. Her face seems coarse with too much makeup, but her eyes are deep and spectacularly bright, and the air is wild with cosmetic scents, perfume, and body emanations from our closeness. It seems as if our talk has been drifting like this, circling languorously, like a hawk over the hills, for hours.

What else do I want? I ask.

I think you know, she says.

I do?

I think you do.

I think I do, I say. But there's one thing I still don't know.

There is?

I don't quite know how to get it – what I want.

You don't?

Not quite.

Not quite?

I really don't.

Her smile, so arch and delicately contained, now broadens, and she says, Just reach.

Reach?

Just reach, she says.

Right now?

Just reach.

The air between us seems so full of feeling that it is almost like a haze. Slowly I extend my hand and find the smooth edge of her bright satin bow. I do not quite touch her breast in doing that. And then, without turning my eyes away from hers, I gradually tug on that wide ribbon. It slides perfectly, and the knot breaks open so that the button at her blouse collar is exposed, and at just that moment, I feel Carolyn's hand fluttering up beneath the table like some bird and one long fingernail skates for an instant down my aching bulge. I almost scream, but instead, it all comes down to a shudder, and Carolyn says quietly that we should get a cab.

'So', I said to Robinson, 'that was how my affair began. I took her back to her fashionable loft and made love to her on the soft Greek rugs. I just grabbed her the minute she set the bolt in her front door, hiked her skirt up with one hand, and put the other down her blouse. Very suave. I came like lightning. And afterward, I lay on top of her, surveying the room, the teak and walnut and the crystal figurines, thinking how much it looked like the show window of some tony shop downtown and wondering in this idle way what in the fuck I was doing with my life, or even in a life where the culmination of a long-cultivated passion passed so quickly that I could hardly believe it had happened at all. But there was not a lot of time to think about that, because we had a drink, and then went to her bedroom to watch the story about our case on the late news, and by then I was capable again, and then, that time, when I reared up over her, I knew I was lost.'

10

'Whatever I can do for you, Rusty. Anything you need.'

So says Lou Balistrieri, the police department's Commander of Special Services. I am sitting in his office in McGrath Hall, where the PD's central operating sections are housed. I can't tell you how many Lous there are over here, fifty-five-year-old guys with gray hair and guts that hang on them like saddlebags, phlegmy voices from smoking. A gifted bureacrat, ruthless with any person in his employ and a shameless toady to anyone, like me, who has sufficient power to harm him. He is on the phone now, calling down to the crime lab, which is under his control.

'Morris, this is Balistrieri. Get me Dickerman. Yeah, now. If he's in the can, go in there and get him off. Yeah.' Balistrieri winks at me. He was a street cop for twenty years, but he works now without a uniform. His rayon shirt is sweated through under the arms. 'Dickerman, yeah. On this Polhemus thing. Rusty Sabich is over here with me. Yeah. Sabich. Sabich, for Chrissake. Right, Horgan's guy. Chief deputy. We got a glass or something. Yeah, I know there're latents, I know, that's why I'm calling you. Whatta you think? Right, I'm a big dumb gumba. Right, and don't fuckin forget it. This big dumb gumba can send you home with your nuts in a paper bag. Right. Right. But why I'm calling is this. Can't we do a computer scan with that laser thing against our knowns? Yeah, you got three good prints there, right? So get what you need and run them through the computer and let's figure out if they're anyone we know. I hear the cop on the case has been asking for ten days now you should do this. Murphy? Yeah, which one? Leo or Henry? Because Henry is a horse's ass. Good. Well, tell him to un-onload it. Don't give me the computer crap, I don't understand that shit anyway. No. No. Not good enough. All right. Call me back. Ten minutes. Ten. Let's figure this thing out.'

The problem, as it gradually emerges, is not equipment but the fact that the computer is under another section's jurisdiction. The department owns only one machine, and the people who do things like payroll believe it should be regarded as theirs alone.

'Right. I'll ask. I'll ask,' says Balistrieri when he gets the return call. He covers the receiver. 'They want to know how big a field you want to run against. We can do all felons or all knowns in the county. You know, everybody who's ever been printed. County employees. Shit like that.'

I pause. 'Felons is probably enough. I can do the rest later if we ever need it.'

Balistrieri makes a face. 'Do it all. God knows if I can get back on.' He takes his hand away before I get a chance to answer. 'Do all of it. Yeah. How soon? What the fuck is gonna take a week? This man's runnin the biggest murder case in the city and he's got to kiss your ring? Well, fuck Murphy's statistical analysis. Yeah. Tell him I said so. Right.' He puts the phone down. 'A week, probably ten days. They gotta get the payroll out, then the chief needs some statistics for the LEAA' – Law Enforcement Assistance Administration. 'I'll push, but I doubt you'll see it any sooner. And have your copper get the glass back out of evidence and bring it to the lab, case they need it for anything.'

I thank Lou for his help and head down to the Pathology Lab. This building looks more or less like an old high school, with varnished oak trim and worn hallways. It is coppers wall to wall, men – and more than a few women these days – in deep blue shirts and black ties, bustling around and making jokes with one another. People of my generation and social stratum do not like cops. They were always beating our heads and sniffing for dope. They were unenlightened. So when I became a prosecutor I started from some distance behind which, in truth, I have never made up. I've worked with policemen for years. Some I like; more I don't. Most of them have two failings. They're hard. And they're crazy. They see too much; they live with their nose in the gutter.

Three or four weeks ago, I stayed longer than I should have on a Friday night at Gil's, and began buying rounds with a street copper named Palucci. He did a beer and a shot a couple of times, and started talking about a heart he had found that morning in a Ziploc bag. That was all. Just the organ, and the major vessels, lying right next to a garbage can at the end of an alley. He picked it up; he looked at it; he drove away. But then he made himself come back. He lifted the lid of the can and stirred the rubbish. No body parts. 'That was it. I done my duty. I dropped it off downtown and told them to mark it goat.'

Crazy. They are our paid paranoids. A copper sees a conspiracy in a cloudy day; he suspects treachery when you say good morning. A grim fellowship, nurtured in our midst, thinking ill about us all.

The elevator takes me to the basement.

'Dr Kumagai.' I greet him. His office is right outside the morgue, which lies beyond, with its stainless-steel tables and the ghastly odors of open peritoneal cavities. Through the walls, I can hear a surgical saw screaming. Painless's desk is a mess, papers and journals in ramparts, overflowing wooden trays. Set at one corner, a small TV is on, the volume low, with an afternoon baseball game.

'Mr Savage. Real important stuff, huh? We got chief deputy with us.' Painless is every kind of weird, a five-foot, five-inch Japanese, with heavy brows and a small mustache divided over the middle of his lip. A kinetic type, always dodging and twisting, talking with his hands in the air. The mad scientist, except there is nothing benevolent about him. Whoever got the idea that Painless would be best off working with stiffs pushed him in the right direction. I can't imagine his bedside manner. He is the kind to throw things at you, cuss you out. Whatever bitter little notion is in his brain will find expression. He is one of those people of whom the globe at moments seems so full. I do not understand him. If I try very hard, in that sort of instinctive effort we all make at pseudo-telepathy, my screen comes up full of fuzz. I cannot imagine what is passing through his mind when he does his job, or watches TV, or turns after a woman. I know I could lose a bet even if I had ten chances to guess what he did last Saturday night.

'Actually, I just came in to pick up a report. You called Lip-ranzer.'

'Oh yeah, oh yeah,' says Painless. 'Right here somewhere. That fuckin Lipranzer. He wants you call right away with everything.' Painless works two-handed, transporting the stacks of paper across his desk as he seeks the new report. 'So you won't be chief deputy too much longer, huh? Della Guardia, I think, gonna kick Raymond Horgan in the ass. Huh?' He looks to me to respond. Painless is smiling, as is his custom when dealing with something that others find unpleasant.

'We'll see,' I say: then I decide to be a bit more aggressive. 'Delay a pal of yours, Doctor?'

'Nico's hell of a guy, *hell* of a guy. Oh yeah. We work on all kinda big murder case together. He's good, too, real good. Yeah, he get up there, he really kick those defense lawyers in the ass. This is this thing.' He tosses a file folder in my direction and bends toward the TV. 'That fuckin Dave Parker. Now he only got dope in one nostril, really hittin the goddamn ball.'

The association between Nico and Painless had eluded me before, but it's a natural, the big-time homicide prosecutor and the police pathologist. They would need each other badly from time to time. I ask Painless if I can sit down for a minute.

'Sure sit, sit.' He moves a stack of files and looks back to the television.

'Lipranzer and I have been kicking over this theory lately. Well, let's say idea. Maybe this was some weird bondage thing that got out of hand. Maybe Carolyn was living dangerously, and when her beau thought she had expired, he gave her a whack in the head to make it look like something else. Does that sound possible?'

Painless in his white lab coat rests his elbows on the turrets of papers.

'No fuckin way.'

'No?'

'No fuckin way. Coppers dumb,' says Painless, the police department pathologist. 'Somethin hard, they make easy. Somethin easy, they make hard. Read the fuckin report. I write a report, fuckin read it. Lipranzer wants me hurry up, hurry up. Then he don't read the fuckin report.'

'This report?'

'Not that report.' He swipes at the new report when I hold it up. 'My report. Autopsy. You see anything with bruises on wrists? Bruises on ankles? Bruises on knees? This lady is dead from gettin hit, not strangled. Read the fuckin report.'

'She was tied up pretty good. You can see the rope burn on the neck in the pictures.'

'Oh sure, oh sure. She was tied up real tight, real good. Looked like a fuckin bow and arrow when they brought her in. But you got one mark on the neck. Somebody jerkin that rope tighter and tighter, rope's gonna move. Get a wide bruise. She got one skinny little mark on her neck.'

'Meaning?' I ask.

Painless smiles. He loves to hold the cards. He pushes his face close enough to the TV that the gray gleam of the screen is reflected on his brow. 'First and third,' he says.

'What does it mean that there's a narrow mark?' I ask again. I wait. The TV announcer declaims over a line drive.

'Do I need a subpoena?' I ask quietly. I try to smile, but my voice has some edge.

'What?' asks Painless.

'What do you make of the bruises on her neck?'

'I make that rope was tightened there first. Okay?'

I take a moment to gather this in. As Painless knows, I'm lost.

'Time out,' I say. 'I thought the working theory was that somebody hit her to subdue her. The blow was lethal, but our guy doesn't realize that or care. He ties her up, and rapes her, with this bizarre slipknotting, so he's strangling her at the same time. Have I got it right or have you changed your mind?'

'Me change? Look at fuckin report. Don't say nothin like that. I'm not sayin that. *Looks* like that, maybe. Maybe that's what coppers think. Not me.'

'Well, what do you think?'

Painless smiles. Painless shrugs.

I close my eyes an instant.

'Look,' I say, 'we're ten days into a big-deal murder investigation and I hear right now for the first time that you think the rope went around her neck first. I would have appreciated knowing that a while ago.'

'Ask. Lipranzer call me up. "Hurry up. Need a report." Okay, he got a report. Nobody ask me what I think.'

'I just did.'

Painless sits back in his chair. 'Maybe I don't think nothin,' he says.

Either this guy is a bigger douche bag than I even remember or something is way out of line. I deliberate for a moment, working backward.

'Are you telling me you think she was raped and then tied up?'

'Tied up last, yeah. I think that. Raped? Now I'm thinkin no.'

'Now?'

'Now,' says Painless. We stare at each other. 'Read the report,' he says.

'The autopsy?'

'This report. This fuckin report.' He hits the folder I'm holding. So I read the report. It is from the forensic chemist's office. Another substance in the vagina of Carolyn Polhemus has been identified. It is known as nonoxynol 9. From the concentrations, the chemist concludes that it derived from spermicidal jelly. That is why there were no viable spermatozoa.

Painless is smiling hugely, and without generosity, when I look up again.

'We're saying this woman used contraception?' I ask.

'Not sayin. She did. Contraceptive jelly. Two percent concentration. Cellulose gum base. Used with diaphragm.'

'Diaphragm?' I am extremely slow. 'You missed a diaphragm during an autopsy.'

'Fuckin no!' Painless hits his desk. He laughs at me out loud. 'You been in autopsy, Savage. Slice her right open. No diaphragm in that lady.'

More time. Painless smiles and I watch him. I'll bite.

'Where'd it go?'

'My guess?'

'Please.'

'Somebody took it.'

'The cops?'

'Coppers ain't that dumb.'

'Who?'

'Look, Mr Savage. Ain't coppers. Ain't me. Gotta be the guy.'

'The killer?'

'Fuckin-A right.'

I pick up the report to read it again. When I do, I notice something else, and our conversation suddenly comes clear. I try to steady myself, but my temper is rising. I can feel the heat all the way to my ears. Perhaps Painless can see that, because after baiting me for ten minutes, he finally levels. He probably figures that sooner or later I would get it anyway.

'You want to know what I think? I think it's a setup. This man who kills her is her lover. He comes over. Has drinks. This lady has intercourse with man, okay? Real nice. But he's angry guy. Picks up somethin, kills her, tries to make it look like rape. Ties her up. Pulls out diaphragm. That's what I think.'

'What does Tommy Molto think?' I ask him.

Painless Kumagai, the sadistic little shit, has finally been cornered. He smiles insipidly and tries to laugh. 'Laugh' is actually not the right word. He wheezes. His mouth moves but he does not speak.

I hand him the report back, which, I notice in passing, is dated five days ago. I point out his own handwritten note at the top. It says 'Molto 762-2225.'

'Don't you want to copy this down, make sure you can reach Molto when you need him?'

Painless is gaining speed again. 'Oh, Tommy.' He does better at seeming genial. 'Good guy. Good guy.'

'How's he doing?'

'Oh, good, good.'

'Tell him to give us a call sometime. Maybe I can find out what's happening in my own fucking investigation.' I stand up. I point at Kumagai. I call him by the name I knew he detested. 'Painless, you tell Molto and Nico, too, that this is cheap. Cheap politics. And cheap police department bullshit. God better help them and you, that I can't make a case for tampering.'

I snatch the report from Painless's hand and leave without waiting for an answer. My heart is hammering and my arms are weak with rage. Raymond, of course, is not in when I get back to the County Building, but I tell Loretta to have him reach me, it is urgent. I look for Mac, but she, too, is elsewhere. I sit in my office and brood. Oh, how fucking clever. Everything we asked for. And nothing more. Give the results – but not the opinion. Call when the forensic chemist reports, but don't mention what it says. Let us run as long as possible in the wrong direction. And in the meantime, leak every goddamn thing you know to Molto. That's the part that gets me worst. God, I think politics is dirty. And the police department is dirtier. The Medici did not live in a world fuller of intrigue. Every secret allegiance in the community comes to bear there. To the alderman and your bookie and your girl-friend. To in-laws, your no-account brother, the guy from the hardware store who has always cut you a deal on screws. To the rookie you have to look out for, the junkie whose base sincerity gets to you, or the snitch you've got to watch. To the licensing inspector who helped out your uncle, or to the lieutenant who you figure has got an in with Bolcarro and is going to make captain soon and maybe more. Your lodge brother, your neighbor, the guy on the beat who's just a plain good sod. Every one of them needs a break. And you give it. In a big-city police department, at least in Kindle County, there is no such thing as playing by the book. The book got trashed many years ago. Instead, all two thousand guys in blue play it for their own team. Painless was simply playing it like everybody else. Maybe Nico told him he could make him coroner.

My phone rings. Mac. I go through the connecting door.

'Well,' I tell her, 'we finally know what Tommy Molto is up to.'

11

As I am leaving for the evening, I see lights on in Raymond's office. It is nearly 9 p.m. and my first thought is that someone is visiting who should not be. My encounter with Kumagai three days ago has left me edgy and suspicious, and I am actually somewhat surprised when I see Raymond at his desk, staring at what seems to be a computer run, and looking uncharacteristically at ease behind the wastrel fog of his pipe. At this point in the campaign this is a rare sight. Raymond is a hardworking lawyer and there have always been late nights when he was here with the stacks of prosecution reports, or indictments, or at least an upcoming speech; but with his job up for sale, most of his evenings lately are spent on the stump. When he's here, Larren and the other moguls of his campaign are with him, plotting. This moment is sufficiently unusual to be taken as private, and so I let two knuckles graze the old oak door as I am passing in.

'Tea leaves?' I ask.

'Sort of,' he says, 'but a lot more accurate. Unfortunately.' He adopts a public tone: 'The Channel 3–*Tribune* poll shows challenger Nico Della Guardia leading incumbent Raymond Horgan, with eight days remaining in the campaign.'

My reaction is succinct: 'Bullshit.'

'Read it and weep.' He shoves the computer run in my direction.

I can't make anything of the grid of figures.

'The bottom line,' says Raymond.

'"U" is undecided?' I ask. 'Forty-three, thirty-nine. Eighteen percent undecided. You're still in it.'

'I'm the incumbent. Once the public realizes that Delay's got a chance, they'll head his way. The new face is a showstopper in a primary.' Raymond's political wisdom is usually Delphic, particularly since it represents not only his insights but Mike's and Larren's as well. Nonetheless, I try to remain upbeat.

'You've had a bad couple of weeks. Nico's played Carolyn's murder real well. You'll come back. You've just gotta let him have it. What's the margin of error on this thing, anyway?'

'Well, fortunately or unfortunately for me, it's 4 percent.' Mike Duke, he tells me, is over at the TV station trying to convince them that their story should pitch the poll as reflecting a neck-and-neck race. Larren, dispatched to do the same job with the newspaper, has already gotten an agreement from the editors there, contingent on Channel 3's position. 'The paper's not contradicting the TV station on the interpretation of a joint poll,' Raymond explains. He puffs his pipe. 'And my bet is that's the way it'll run. They'll throw me the bone. But what's the point? The numbers are the numbers. Everybody in town will smell the odor of dead meat.'

'What do your own numbers look like?'

'They're crap,' Raymond tells me. The campaign hasn't had the money to do a decent job. This poll is the work of a national outfit. Everybody – Larren, Mike, Raymond himself – had the impression that the situation wasn't quite this bad, but nobody can dispute it.

'You're probably right on Carolyn,' he says. 'It hurt. But it's the whole loss of momentum.' Raymond Horgan puts down his pipe and looks straight at me. 'We're gonna lose, Rusty. You heard it here first.'

I look at the worn face of Raymond Horgan, my old idol, my leader. His hands are folded. He is in repose. Twelve and a half years after he got started talking about revolutionizing the idea of law enforcement, and a year too late for the best interests of us both, Raymond Horgan has finally pulled the plug. It is now all someone else's problem. And to the little incubus that argues that principles and issues are involved, there is, after twelve years, an exhausted man's reply. Ideas and principles are not foremost here.

Not when you do not have the jails to hold the crooks you catch, or enough courtrooms to try them; not when the judge who hears the case is too often some hack who went to night law school because his brother already had filled the one slot available in their father's insurance agency, and who achieved his appointment by virtue of thirty years' loyal precinct work. In the administration of Nico Della Guardia there will be the same imperatives, no matter what he's saying on his TV spots: too many crimes and no sensible way to deal with them, too few lawyers, too many calls for political favors, too much misery, and too much evil that will keep on happening no matter what the ideals and principles of the prosecuting attorney. He can have his turn. Raymond's ease at the abyss becomes my own.

'What the fuck,' I say.

'Right,' says Raymond after he gets done laughing. He goes to the conference table in a corner of the office and pulls out the pint bottle that's always in the pencil drawer. He pours two in the little folded cups from the water cooler and I come over and join him.

'You know, when I started here I didn't drink,' I say. 'I mean, I don't have a bottle problem, I'm not complaining, but twelve years ago, I just never drank. Not beer, not wine, not rum-and-Coca-Cola. And now I sit here and knock back Scotches neat.' I do just that; my esophagus contracts and tears come to my eyes. Raymond pours another. 'Ain't time a bitch.'

'You're getting middle-aged, Rusty. All this fucking looking back. One thing about getting divorced, it stopped that crap for me. You know, I leave this job, I'm not going to spend four months crying in my beer and talking about all the good times.'

'You'll be sitting in one of those glass cages on the fortieth floor of the IBM building, with hot-and-cold-running secretaries and a bunch of megabuck partners asking you if thirty hours a week is too much time for the privilege of having your name on the door.'

'Bullshit,' says Raymond.

'Sure,' I answer. In wistful moments in the last few years I have heard Raymond conjure just such a fantasy for himself – a few years to build a bankroll, then get on the bench himself, probably at the appellate level on his way to the state supreme court.

'Well, maybe,' says Raymond, and we share a laugh. 'Will you go?' he asks.

'I doubt I'll have much choice. Delay's going to make Tommy Molto his chief deputy. That's clearer than ever.'

Raymond moves his heavy shoulders. 'You can never tell with Della Guardia.'

'It's about time for me to head on, anyway,' I say.

'Can we get you on the bench, Rusty?'

This is a golden moment for me: here at last is loyalty's reward. Do I want to be a judge? Does a bus have wheels? Do the Yankees play baseball in the Bronx? I sip my whiskey, with sudden judiciousness.

'I would sure think about it,' I answer. 'I'd have to consider practice. I'd have to figure out the money. But I'd sure think about it.'

'We'll see how things turn out, then. Those guys'll owe me something. They'll want me to go out smiling. Party loyalty. All that shit. I should have the swag to look after a few people.'

'I appreciate that.'

Raymond gives himself another.

'How are things going with my favorite unsolved murder case?'

'Badly,' I say. 'In general. We know a little more about what seems to have happened. That is, if you can believe the pathologist. Did Mac tell you about Molto?'

'I heard,' he says. 'I heard. What is this crap?'

'Looks like Dubinsky had it right. Nico's got Tommy out there shadowing our investigation.'

'Shadowing,' asks Raymond, 'or subverting?'

'Probably a little of both. I'd guess, for the most part, Molto's just picking up information. You know, calling up old buddies in the department, getting them to bootleg reports. Maybe they've slowed some of the lab work down, but how would you prove it? I'm still not positive what the hell they're up to. Maybe they really think I'm a clown, and they're trying to solve the murder on their own. You know: come up with the whopper before Election Day '

'Nah,' says Raymond, 'that's just what they'll say. I blast them between the eyes for fucking around with our investigation and they come back with Molto, acting head of my Homicide Section, saying he was worried we would screw things up. Nah,' Raymond says again, 'I'll tell you why Nico has Tommy out there digging up information. It's surveillance. Very clever. He watches how we're doing and knows exactly how hard he can hit the issue, with very little risk. Every time he sees us stumble, he can turn the knob a little higher on his volume control.'

We talk a moment about Kumagai. We both agree it is unlikely that he changed results. He was just holding back. We could have his assistant assigned to go over his work, but it does not seem to make much difference now. When this poll hits tomorrow, we'll be done commanding loyalty in the police department. Any cop who ever called Nico by his first name will be feeding him information, investing in the future.

'So where does this path stuff leave us?' Raymond wants to know. 'Who's our bad guy?'

'Maybe it's a boyfriend, maybe it's a guy she picked up. Seems like it's somebody who knew enough about her to realize what to make it look like, but that could be coincidence. Who knows?' I stare at the moon of light on the surface of my whiskey. 'Can I ask a question?'

'I guess.' It is the natural moment for me to find out what the hell Raymond was doing with the B file in his desk drawer. No doubt that is what he expects. But there is something else I've wanted to put to him. This is bushwhacking, two drinks along, and enjoying the nicest moment that I've had with Raymond Horgan since the last case we tried together, one of the Night Saints conspiracies, years ago. And I know it is unfair to use the investigator's pose to explore my own obsessions. I know all of that, but I ask anyway.

'Were you fucking Carolyn?'

Raymond laughs, a big beefy laugh, so that all of him shakes, making it seem that he's feeling more whiskey than he is. I recognize a practiced barroom gesture, a way to stall when you're getting loaded and you need time to think: the wrong bimbo who wants to go home with you, an assistant ward committeeman whose name you can't recall, a reporter joshing but trying to get a little too close to the bone. If there was any ice in his glass he'd chew the cubes now, so that there'd be something in his mouth.

'Listen,' he says, 'I gotta tell you something about your technique as an interrogator, Rusty. You beat around the bush too much. You have to learn to be direct.'

We laugh. But I say nothing. If he wants off the hook, he'll have to wriggle.

'Let's say that the decedent and I were both single and both adults,' he says finally, looking down into his cup. 'That isn't any kind of problem, is it?'

'Not if it doesn't give you any better idea who killed her.'

'No,' he says, 'it wasn't that kind of thing. Who knew that dame's secrets? Frankly, it was short and sweet between us. It's been history, I'd say, four months.'

There's a lot of chess here, many poses. But if Carolyn caught Raymond at the quick, he doesn't show it. He seems to have been let down easy. Better than I can say. I look again into my drink. The B file, some of her son's comments, all were hints, but the truth is that I'd guessed at Carolyn's relationship with Raymond a long time ago, just watching the telltale signs, how often she trotted down to the office, the hours the two of them left. Of course, by then I was familiar with the local customs. I'd made my own journey to Carolyn's quaint country – and an abrupt departure. I had watched their doings with my own burning mix of tourist nostalgia, and a yearning far harsher. Now I wonder why I risked the offense of even bothering to hear it all confirmed.

'You knew some of her secrets,' I say. 'You met the kid.'

'That's true. You've talked to him?'

'Last week.'

'And he blew Mommy's cover?'

I say yes. I know how much a man in Raymond's shoes wants to believe he was inscrutable.

'An unhappy kid,' Raymond observes.

'You know, he told me that she wanted to be P A.'

'I heard that from her. I told her she had to work the vineyards a little. Either you got to have professional standing or political connections. You can't just walk into it.' Raymond's tone is casual, but he gives me a penetrating look: I'm not as dumb as you think, he is saying. I can see the forest for the trees. A dozen years of power and flattery have not dulled him that much. I feel, with pleasure, a gust of pride and respect again for Raymond. Good for you, I think.

So that's the way it worked. Four months ago they ended, Raymond said. Well, the arithmetic fits: Raymond announced and Carolyn went her own way. She had figured, like everybody else, that Raymond wasn't running, that he could hand the mantle to anyone he chose. Maybe he could be persuaded to make it a woman – depart with one final gesture in the direction of progress. The only puzzle is why Carolyn's train to glory had stopped first with me. Why tarry with the local when you're ready to hop the express? Unless it was all a little less calculating than it now seems.

'She was one tough cookie, that one,' Horgan says. 'A good kid, you know. But tough. Tough.'

'Yeah,' I say, 'good and tough and dead.'

Raymond stands.

'Can I ask one more?' I ask.

'Now you want to get personal, huh?' Raymond smiles, all Irish charm and teeth. 'Let me guess: What the fuck was I doing with that file?'

'Close,' I say. 'But I understand why you didn't want it floating around. Why'd you give it to her in the first place?'

'Shit,' he says, 'she asked. You wanna be cynical? She asked *and* I was sleeping with her. I guess she heard about it from Linda Perez.' One of the paralegals who read the crank mail. 'You know Carolyn. Hot case. I suppose she thought it would be good for her. I considered it bullshit all along. What's the guy's name?'

'Noel?'

'Noel, right. He rainmade this guy.' Swindled. Kept the money. 'That's my take. Don't you think?'

'I don't know.'

'She looked at it, went out, and shoveled through the records in the 32nd District. There was nothing there. That's what she told me.'

'I would like to have heard about the case,' I say, with the lightning tongue of a quick drunk.

Raymond nods. He drinks more of his whiskey.

'You know how it is, Rusty. You do one dumb thing, you do another dumb thing. She didn't want me to talk about it. Somebody asks why I gave her the case and pretty soon everyone knows she's balling the boss. The boss didn't mind keeping that one to himself, either. You understand. Who'd it hurt?'

'Me,' I say, as I have meant to do for many years.

He nods at that one, too.

'I'm sorry, Rusty. I really am. Shit, I'm the sorriest son of a bitch in town.' He goes to a sideboard and looks at a picture of his kids. There are five of them. Then he goes to put on his coat. His arms and hands move unevenly; he has a hard time smoothing down the collar. 'You know, if I really do lose this fucking election, I'm just gonna quit. Let Nico run the show, he wants to so bad.' He stops. 'Or maybe you. You wanna do this job for a little while?'

Thanks, Raymond, I think. Thanks a lot. In the end, maybe Carolyn had the right approach.

But I cannot help myself. I get up, too. I turn down Raymond's collar. I shut off the lights and lock his office and point him down the hall in the right direction. I make sure that he will take a cab. The last thing I say to him is 'Your shoes are too big to fill.' And, of course, old habits being what they are, when the words come out of me, I mean them.

12

Somehow the dizzy, mad hunger I felt for Carolyn showed itself in a revived addiction to rock music.

'This had nothing to do with Carolyn's tastes,' I explained to Robinson. Even in the madhouse of the PA's office, she kept a symphonic station on in her office. And it wasn't some kind of adolescent nostalgia. I did not crave the vintage sixties soul and rock, which had sound-tracked my late teens and early twenties. This was New Wave junk: screechy, whiny music with perverse lyrics and rhythms mindless as rain. I began driving to work, telling Barbara I was going through my annual phobic reaction to the bus. The car, of course, made my evening escapes to Carolyn's apartment easier, but those, in any event, could have been arranged. What I wanted was the chance to drive for fifty minutes with the windows cranked tight while Rock Radio, WNOF, screamed from the wagon's speakers, the volume so high that the windshield rattled when the bass line became prominent on certain songs.

'I was messed up, all strung out.' When I walked down the street after parking the car, I was half-tumescent because I was starting a day which was, I felt, a tantalizing sweet crawl toward my secret plunder of Carolyn. I sweated all day, my pulse raced. And every hour or so, in the midst of a phone call or a conference, I was visited by visions, so palpable and immediate, of Carolyn in passionate repose, that I would become lost in space and time.

Carolyn, for her part, was chilling in her command. The weekend after our initial night together, I spent hours – dazed, unrooted hours – pondering our next encounter. I had no idea what was to follow. At the door to her apartment, she had kissed my hand and said, simply, See you. For me, there was no thought of resistance. I would take whatever was allowed.

On Monday morning, I appeared at her office door with a file in my hand. My pose, my pace, had already been endlessly planned. Nothing urgent. I leaned against the doorjamb. I smiled, hip and calm. Carolyn was at her desk. The Jupiter Symphony was surging.

About the Nagel case, I say.

The Nalges were another visit to the dark side of surburbia: a husband-and-wife rape-and-sodomy team. She would approach women on the street, assist in the abduction, engage in imaginative uses of a dildo. Carolyn wanted to plead the case out, with the wife taking a lesser charge.

I can live with the plea, I tell her, but I think we need two counts.

Only now does Carolyn look up from her work. Impassive. Her eyes do not quiver. In a mild collegial way she smiles.

Who's got her? I ask, meaning who is her defense lawyer.

Sandy. Carolyn answers, referring to Alejandro Stern, who seems to represent every person of genteel upbringing who is charged with a crime in this state.

Tell Sandy, I say, that she has to plead to an Agg Battery, too. We don't want the judge to think we're trying to tie his hands.

Or the press to think we're pushing probation for female sex violators, says she.

That too, I say. We're equal-opportunity prosecutors.

I smile. She smiles. I linger. I have gotten through this, but my heart is knocking, and I fear that there is something fluttering and insipid in my expression.

Okay. I flap the file against my thigh. I turn.

We should have a drink, she says.

I nod with buttoned-up lips. Gil's? I ask.

How about, she says, the place we ended up on Friday?

Her apartment. My soul expands. She has the barest inkling of a smile, but she has looked back to her work, even before I have departed.

'In reflection, I see myself on that threshold with immense pity. I was so full of hope. So grateful. And I should have known the future from the past.'

There was great passion in my love for Carolyn, but seldom joy. From that instant forward, when I realized this would go on, I was like the mandrake in the old poems I read in college, pulled screaming from the earth. I was devastated by my passion. I was shattered. Riven. Decimated. Torn to bits. Every moment was turmoil. What I'd struck upon was old and dark and deep. I had no vision of myself. I was like a blind ghost groping about a castle and moaning for love. The idea of Carolyn, more even that the image, was upon me every moment. I wanted in a way I could not recall – and the desire was insistent, obsessive, and, because of that, somehow debased. Now I think of Pandora, whom as a child I always confused with Peter Pan, opening her box and finding that torrent of miseries unloosed.

'There was something so real in the flesh of another woman,' I told the shrink.

After almost twenty years of sleeping with Barbara, I no longer went to bed with only her. I lay down with five thousand other fucks; with the recollection of younger bodies; with the worries for the million things that supported and surrounded our life: the corroding rain gutters, Nat's unwillingness to study mathematics, the way Raymond, over the years, had come to greet my work with an eye to its defects rather than successes, the particular arrogant glint that came into my mother-in-law's eye when she discussed any person outside her immediate family, including me. In our bed, I reached for Barbara through the spectral intervention of all these visitors, all that time.

But Carolyn was pure phenomenon. I was dizzy. I was disoriented. After seventeen years of faithful marriage, of wandering impulse suppressed for the sake of tranquil domestic life, I could not believe that I was here, with fantasy made real. Real. I studied her naked body. The gorgeous large areolas, her long nipples, the sheen of her flesh running from her belly to her thighs. I was lost and high, here in the land beyond restraint, rescued from the diligent, slowly moving circles of my life. Each time I entered her, I felt I divided the world.

'I was with her three or four nights a week. We tended toward a routine. She left the door unlocked for me and the news was on when I arrived.' Carolyn was cleaning, drinking, opening her mail. A bottle of white wine, cool and wet like some river-bottom stone, was uncorked on the kitchen table. She never rushed to greet me. Her business, whatever it was, preoccupied her. Usually her comments to me as she traveled between rooms were about the office or local political events. The rumors were thick by then that Raymond would not be running, and Carolyn followed this possibility with great interest. She seemed to gather scuttlebutt from everywhere – the office, the police force, the bar association.

And then, sometime, finally, she would find her way to me. Open her arms. Embrace me. Welcome me. I found her bathing once and made love to her there. I caught her once while she was dressing. But usually we would go through that wandering toward one another, time passing until she was finally ready to lead me to the bedroom, where my hour of worship would begin.

My approach to her was prayerful. Most often, I found myself on my knees. I would unpeel her skirt, her slip, her pants, so that her perfect thighs, that lovely triangle, were exposed as she stood before me; even before I began to push my face in her, that heavy female aroma overpowered the atmosphere. Perfect mad wild moments. On my knees, straining and blind, driving my face inside her, my tongue at work in fevered, silent ululation, while I stretched my hands upward, probing in her garments for her breasts. My passion at those moments was as pure as music.

Then, slowly, Carolyn would take control. She liked it rough, and in time, I would be called upon to slam myself inside her. I stood beside the bed. I dug my hands into her behind and shook her.

'She did not stop speaking.'

'Saying what?' Robinson asked.

'You know: Mumbles. Words.' 'Good.' 'More.' 'Yes, yes. Oh yes.' 'Oh, hard.' 'Hold on, hold on, hold on, oh, please, baby, yes.'

111

We were not, I realized later, lovers who fulfilled each other's needs. As time went on, Carolyn's mood with me seemed to become more confrontational. For all her pretense to sophistication, I found that she could border on the gross. She liked to talk dirty. She boasted. She liked to talk about my parts: I'm going to suck your cock, your hard hairy cock. These outbursts would astound me. One time I laughed, but her look revealed such obvious displeasure, almost fury, that I learned to absorb these predatory remarks. I let her have her way. For her, over days, I realized there was a progression. This lovemaking seemed to have for her a destiny, a goal. She was to be given her own dominion. She would roam, take my penis in her mouth, let it go, and slide her hand past my scrotum, probing in that hole. One night she spoke to me. 'Does Barbara do this for you?' Working there. And looking up to ask again, serene, commanding. 'Does Barbara do this for you?' She showed no reluctance, no fear. By now, Carolyn knew there would be no wilting paroxysm of shame from me at the mention of Barbara's name. She knew. She could bring my wife into our bed and make her one more witness to how much I was willing to abandon.

Most nights we ordered out for Chinese food. The same kid always brought it, squint-eyed and looking greedily at Carolyn in her orange silk robe. Then we would lie in bed, passing the cartons back and forth. The TV was on. Always, wherever she was, a TV or a radio was going, a habit, I realized, of her many years alone. In bed, we would gossip. Carolyn was an acute observer of the maelstrom of local politics and its endless crabbed quests for private aggrandizement and power. She viewed it in those terms, but with more excitement than I did and less amusement. She was not as willing as I to disown the quest for personal glory. She viewed it as the natural right of everyone, including her.

While I was seeing Carolyn, Nico was in the initial phases of his campaign. At that point I did not take him seriously. None of us, including Carolyn, gave him any chance to win. Carolyn, however, saw a different potential, which she explained one night not long

112

before our little paradise came to an end. I was telling her my latest analysis of Nico's motives.

He wants a sop, I told Carolyn. He's waiting for Raymond's friends to find something for him. It's not good party politics in Kindle County to begin a primary fight. Look at Horgan. Bolcarro's never let him forget that Raymond ran against him for mayor.

What if Bolcarro wants to get even?

Bolcarro's not the party. Someday he'll be gone. Nico is too much of a sheep to set out on his own.

Carolyn disagreed. She saw, much more clearly than I, how determined Nico was.

Nico thinks Raymond is tired, she said. Or that he can convince him that he should be tired. A lot of people think Raymond shouldn't run again.

Party people? I asked her.

At that point, I had never heard that. Many people had said Raymond wouldn't run, but not that he was unwelcome.

Party people. The mayor's people. Nico hurt him just by announcing. They're saying Raymond should move over.

She reached for another carton, and a breast fetchingly swung free when the sheet fell away.

Does Raymond talk about it? she asked.

Not to me.

If he starts getting the wrong kind of vibes, will he think about it?

I made a face. The truth was that I did not have much idea about what Raymond thought these days. In the time since his divorce, he had grown increasingly insular. Although he had made me his chief deputy, he probably confided in me less.

If he agrees to step aside, said Carolyn, the party would probably let him decide who should be slated. He could bargain for that. They know he's not going to just hand it all to Nico.

That's for sure.

Who would he choose? she asked.

Probably someone from the office. Carry on his traditions.

You? she asked.

Maybe Mac. She'd make a hell of a candidate in her wheelchair.

No way, said Carolyn, elevating moo shu in her chopsticks. Not these days. That chair is not very telegenic. I think he'd pick you. You're the natural.

I shook my head. It was a reflex. Perhaps, at that moment, I even meant it. I was in Carolyn's bed and felt I had already indulged one temptation too many.

Carolyn put the food down. She grasped my arm and looked at me levelly.

Rusty, if you let him know you want it, it'll be you.

I watched her a moment.

You mean you think I should go to Raymond and tell him his time is up?

You could be tactful, said Carolyn. She was looking at me quite directly.

No way, I said.

Why not?

I'm not gonna bite that hand. If he wants out, he has to make up his own mind. I don't even think if he asked my advice I'd tell him to quit. He's still the strongest candidate around against Della Guardia.

She shook her head.

Without Raymond, Nico doesn't have an issue. You pull the party people and Raymond's people together behind somebody else, that person would walk into the PA's office. It wouldn't be close.

You've really thought about this, I told her.

He needs a push, she said to me.

Push him yourself, I told her. It's not in me.

Carolyn stood up naked from the bed. Standing barefoot, she looked limber and strong. She put on her robe. I realized then she was upset.

Why are you unhappy? I asked. Were you ready to become chief deputy?

She did not answer that.

*

114

'The last time I slept with Carolyn she pushed me off her in the midst of our lovemaking and turned away from me.'

At first I did not understand what it was she wanted. But she bumped her behind against me until I realized that was what I was being offered, a marble peach.

No, I said.

Try it. She looked over her shoulder. Please.

I came up close behind her.

Just easy, she said. Just a little.

I went in too fast.

Not that much, she said.

She said, Oh.

I pressed in, remained, pumped. She arched, clearly in some pain.

And I found, suddenly, that I was thrilled.

Her head lolled back. Her eyes held tears. Then she opened them and looked back at me directly. Her face was radiant.

Does Barbara? she whispered, does Barbara do this for you?

13

In the 32nd District the normal turmoil of a police station is concealed. About seven years ago now, while we were in the midst of our investigation, one of the Night Saints entered the station with a sawed-off in his windbreaker. It was nuzzled against his chest like a baby protected from a chilly breeze, and as a result, he merely had to lower the zipper slightly before placing the muzzle beneath the chin of the unfortunate desk officer, a twenty-eight-year-old guy named Jack Lansing, who had continued writing some report. The young man with the shotgun, who was never identified, is reported to have smiled and then blown off Jack Lansing's face.

Since then, the cops of this station house have dealt with the public from behind six inches of bulletproof glass, carrying on conversations through a radio system which sounds as if the signal must have been bounced first off the moon. There are public areas where the complainants, the victims, the police groupies loiter, but once you pass beyond the four-inch-thick metal door, with its electronic bolt, there is almost sterility. Prisoners are in a block downstairs, and are never permitted, for any purpose, above that level. Upstairs so much of the usual turbulence has been removed that it feels a little like an insurance agency. The working cops' desks are in an open area that could pass for any other large office, the guys with rank in partitioned areas along the back wall. In one of the larger offices, I find Lionel Kenneally. We have not seen much of each other since the Night Saints cases ended.

'Fucking Savage,' he says, 'fucking Savage.' He puts out his cigarette and claps me on the back.

Lionel Kenneally is everything a sensible person does not like about police. He is tough-talking, opinionated, downright mean, an unabashed racist. I have yet to see the situation in which I'd bet even an hour's wages on his scruples. But I like him, in part because he is a pure form, unalloyed and unapologetic, a coppers' cop, dedicated to the shadowy loyalties and mysteries of life out on the street. He can make out the riffs and scams of the inner city like a dog picking up a scent by lifting his muzzle to the breeze. During the Night Saints investigation, Lionel was the guy I went to when I needed someone found. He never faltered – he'd pull them out of shooting galleries or go into the Grace Street projects at four in the morning, the only hour that a police officer can safely move about there. I saw him at it once or twice, six foot three or thereabouts, pounding on a door so hard you could see it buckle in its frame.

Who that?

Open up, Tyrone. It's your fairy godmother.

We reminisce; he tells me about Maurice Dudley. I have already heard the story, but I do not interrupt. Maurice, a 250-pound brick, a killer, a cur, is deep in Bible studies down at Rudyard. He is going to be ordained. 'Harukan' – the Night Saints' leader – 'is so pissed, they say, he don't even talk to him. Can you imagine?'

'Who said there's no such thing as rehabilitation?' This strikes both of us as unbearably funny. Maybe we're each thinking of the woman on whose arm Maurice, with a kitchen knife, once wrote his name. Or the coppers from this station house who swore, in the inflated lore of cop and courthouse stories, that he had misspelled it.

'Are you passing through or what?' Kenneally asks me finally.

'I'm not really sure,' I say. 'I'm trying to figure something out.'

'On what now? Carolyn?'

I nod.

'What's the story there?' Kenneally asks. 'Latest thing I'm hearing from downtown is they're sayin it's not really rape.'

I give Lionel two minutes' worth on the state of our evidence.

'So you're figurin what?' he asks. 'The guy she's having cocktails with is the one who done her?'

'That seems obvious. But I keep wondering. Didn't we have a Peeping Tom, maybe ten years ago, who'd watch couples and then go in later and take a piece of the lady himself at gunpoint?'

'Christ,' says Kenneally. 'You really are lost. You're lookin for a law enforcement type – a cop, a PA, a private dick – somebody who knew what he wanted to make it look like when he cooled her. That's what I'd figure. She had any boyfriend who was with her that night, and left her alive, you'd have heard from him by now. He'd *want* to help.'

'If he doesn't have a wife to explain things to.'

Kenneally considers that. I get something like a shrug. I might be right.

'When's the last time you saw her?' I ask.

'Four months or so. She come out here.'

'Doing what?'

'Same shit you're doin: investigatin somethin and tryin not to let on what.'

I laugh. A coppers' cop. Kenneally gets up. He goes to a pile of transfer cases in the corner.

'She got some rookie to look through all this crap for her, so she didn't chip her nails or run her nylons.'

'Let me guess,' I say: 'booking sheets on cases from nine summers ago.'

'Right you are,' he says.

'Did she have a name she was looking for?'

Kenneally considers this. 'I think she did, and I'll be fucked if I remember. Something was wrong with it, too.'

'Leon?' I ask.

Lionel snaps his fingers. 'La Noo,' he says. L-N-U: Last Name Unknown. 'That's what was wrong. She was playin in the dark.'

'What'd she come up with?'

'Spit.'

'You sure?'

'Fuck yes. Not that she'd much notice. She was most of the time tryin to keep track of everybody who was watchin her ass. Which was everybody in the house, as she well knows. She was havin a good time bein back here, let's say.'

'Back?'

'She worked the North Branch when she was a PO. She didn't know what the fuck she was doin then, either. A real social-worker type. I never could figure Horgan hiring her as a PA.'

I had forgotten that. I probably knew it, but I did not remember. Carolyn worked the North Branch as a probation officer. I think about the secretary that Noel's boyfriend mentioned. He didn't say white or black, fat or skinny. But he did say Girl. Would anybody hang 'Girl' on Carolyn, even nine years ago?

'You didn't like her much.'

'She was a cunt,' says Kenneally, to the point. 'You know,' he says, 'out for herself. She was sleepin her way to the top, right from the git-go. Anybody coulda seen that.'

I look around a moment. Our conversation seems to have come to an end. I ask one more time if he's sure she did not find anything.

'Not a fuckin thing. You can talk with the kid that helped her if you want.'

'If you wouldn't mind, Lionel.'

'What the fuck do I care?' He reaches for the intercom and summons a cop named Guerash. 'Why you still botherin with this thing?' he asks me, while we wait. 'It'll be somebody else's problem pretty soon, don't you think?'

'You mean Delay?'

'I think he's got it in the bag.' In the last week, that is all you hear from coppers. They've never pretended to like Raymond.

'You can never tell. Maybe I'll crack this thing and save Raymond's ass.'

'God come down from Sinai ain't gonna save him, the way I hear it. Downtown they say Bolcarro's comin out for Nico this afternoon.'

I chew on that one. If Bolcarro endorses Nico six days before the election, then Raymond will be no more than a political memory.

Guerash enters. He looks like half the young men on the force, handsome in an old-fashioned way, with an erect bearing and a military order to his person. His shoes are spit-shined and the buttons on his jersey gleam. His hair is cleanly parted.

Kenneally addresses him.

'You remember this lady P A was out here – Polhemus?'

'Nice set of lungs,' says Guerash.

Kenneally turns to me. 'See, this kid's gonna make a copper. Never forgets a bra size.'

'She the one that got it over by the riverside?' Guerash asks me.

I tell him she is. Kenneally continues with Guerash.

'Okay, Rusty here is the chief deputy P A. He wants to know if she took anything when she come out here?'

'Not that I know of,' says Guerash.

'What'd she look at?' I ask.

'She had one day where she wanted to see the bookings. She told me there'd be like sixty, seventy people booked on public indecency. We're talking back forever, eight, nine years ago, or something. Anyway, I hauled up the boxes, right here.'

'How'd she come up with one day?'

'Beats me. She seemed to know what she was looking for. She just told me look for the day when there were the most arrests. So that's what I did. I mean, it must have took me a week to go through that crap. There were like five hundred arrests for 42s.' A 42 is a public-indecency violation.

One day. I think again about the letter. There was nothing in the file I saw that narrowed the time frame like that. Maybe Carolyn gave up before she started, figured she'd just do a sample.

'Did you find what she wanted?'

'I thought so. I called her back and she came out to see it. I left her with the stuff right here. She told me she didn't find nothin.'

'Do you remember anything about what you showed her? Anything common about the arrests?'

'All in the Public Forest. All guys. I thought it was probably some demonstration or something. I don't know.'

'Jesus,' says Kenneally to Guerash in disgust. 'For public indecency? This is the faggots, isn't it?' he asks me. 'Back when Raymond got some balls for about a day and a half.'

'Did she tell you anything about what she was looking for? A name? Anything?'

'She didn't even have a last name. Just a first. I wasn't real clear on whether she knew this guy or what.' Guerash pauses. 'Why do I think it had something to do with Christmas?'

'Noel? She gave you that name?'

Guerash snaps his fingers. 'That's it.'

'Not Leon?'

'No way. Noel. She told me she's looking for Noel LNU. I remember that because she wrote it down for me, and the Christmas thing went through my head.'

'Can you show me what she saw?'

'Boy, I don't know. I think I put it away.'

'Fat fuckin chance of that,' says Kenneally. 'I fuckin asked you three times. Here, help yourself.'

He points us to the transfer cases in the corner.

When Guerash opens the first case he swears. He picks up a clutch of loose sheets lying on the top of the file folders.

'She wasn't real neat, I'll say that. These records were in nice order when I gave them to her.' I would ask Guerash if he's sure, but there's no point. It's the kind of thing he would remember, and I can see the orderly ranks of the remaining records. Besides, that would be like Carolyn, to take records that other people have spent years maintaining and treat them like debris.

Guerash out of instinct begins to sort the booking sheets and bond slips, and I help. Kenneally pitches in, too. We stand around his desk, cursing Carolyn. Each booking jacket should contain a police report, an arrest card bearing the defendant's photo and fingerprints, a complaint, and a bond slip, but none of these sixty or seventy files is complete. Papers are missing from each and the sheets inside have been turned back to front, and at angles. The numerical order is gone.

Kenneally keeps saying cunt.

We are about five minutes along before the obvious strikes me – this disorder is not accidental. These papers have been shuffled.

'Who the hell has been at these boxes since Carolyn?' I ask Kenneally.

'Nobody. They been sittin in the corner for four months, waitin for fuckhead here to put em back. Nobody but him and me even know they're here. Right?' he asks Guerash. Guerash agrees.

'Lionel,' I ask, 'do you know Tommy Molto?'

'Fuck yes, I know Tommy Molto. About half my life. Little fuck was a PA out here.'

I knew that, if I had thought about it. Molto was notorious for his battles with the North Branch judges.

'Was he out here at the same time Carolyn was with probation?'

'Probably. Lemme think. Shit, Rusty, I don't keep a duty roster on these guys.'

'When was the last time you saw him?'

Lionel ponders. 'Three, four years. Maybe I run into him at a dinner or something. You know, he's all right. I see him, I talk. You know me.'

'But he hasn't been looking at these records?'

'Hey,' says Lionel, 'watch my lips. You. Me. Guerash. Her. That's it.'

When we are done sorting. Guerash goes through the files twice.

'One's missing, right?' I ask.

'We're missing a number,' he says. 'Could have been a mistake.'

'You book sixty faggots, you don't exactly worry about keeping a perfect count,' says Kenneally.

I ask Lionel, 'But it could be that the file is gone?'

'That too.'

'There would still be a court file, wouldn't there?' I ask. Kenneally looks at Guerash. Guerash looks at me. I write down the number. It should be on microfilm. Lipranzer will love doing this.

When Guerash is gone, I spend one more moment with Kenneally.

'You don't want to say what this is about maybe?' he asks.

'I can't, Lionel.'

He nods. But I can tell it grates.

'Oh yeah,' says Lionel, 'those were funny old days around here. Lots of stories.' His look lingers casually, just so I know that we both have our secrets.

Outside. there is real heat, 80 degrees. Pushing a record for April. In the car, I turn the radio to the news station. It's a live feed from the mayor's office. I just catch the tail end, but I hear enough of His Honor's blarney to get the drift. The PA's office needs new blood, a new direction. The people want that. The people deserve that.

I am going to have to start looking for work.

14

Tee ball. In the waning light of the spring evening, play commences in the second-grade Fathers/Students League. The sky hangs low across the open field, a meadow of landfill laid over what was once a marsh, while Mrs Strongmeyer's Stingers idly occupy the diamond, boys and girls sporting windbreakers zipped to the collars and baseball gloves. Dads creep along the baselines calling instructions as the dusk gathers in. At the plate, a behemoth of an eight-year-old named Rocky circles his bat two or three times in the vicinity of the rag ball perched atop the long-necked rubber tee. Then, with an astounding concentration of power, he smashes the ball into outer space. It lands in left center, beyond the perimeter of the Stingers' shaky defense.

'Nathaniel!' I yell, along with many others. 'Nat!' Only now he wakes. He reaches the ball a step ahead of an agile sprite named Molly, whose ponytail flows behind her baseball cap. Nat grabs it, whirls, and wings it in a single motion. The ball travels in a tremendous arc back toward the infield and lands with a dead thump between shortstop and third, just as Rocky lopes across the plate. Following the local etiquette, I alone may scold my son, and so I stroll along the foul line, clapping my hands. 'Wake up! Wake up out there.' For Nat, I hold no fear. He shrugs, throws up his gloved hand, and displays the full range of his gap-toothed jack-o'-lantern smile, his new ragged-edged teeth still looking a little like candles stuck into a cake.

'Dad, I just lost it,' he yells, 'I really did.' The pack of fathers on the side join me in sudden laughter. We all repeat the remark among ourselves. He lost it. Cliff Nudelman pats me on the back. At least the boy has learned the lingo.

Did other men, as boys, dream about their sons? I looked twenty years ahead with passion and with hope. As I always saw him, my son was a gentle, obedient soul. He was good; he was full of virtue and skill.

Nat is not like that. He is not a bad boy. That's a song around our house. Barbara and I have been telling each other that since he was two. Nat is not, we say, actually, we say, a bad boy. And I believe that. Fervently. And with a heart engorged with love. He is sensitive. He is kind. And he is wild and distracted. He has been on his own schedule since the time of his birth. When I read to him, he flips the pages in my hand to see what lies just ahead. He does not listen, or at least does not seem to care to. In school, he has always been a problem.

He is saved by his insouciant charm and his physical gifts. My son is beautiful. I am talking about more than the usual child-beauty, the soft features, the floral glow of being new. This boy has dark, acute eyes, a prepossessing look. These fine, regular features do not come from me. I am larger and squat. I have a bulky nose; a kind of Neanderthal ridge over the eyes. Barbara's people are all smaller and good-looking, and it is to them we routinely give the credit. Privately, however, I have often thought at moments, with discomfort, about my father and his piercing, somber, Slavic handsomeness. Perhaps because I suspect that source, I pray all the time, at my own inner altar, that this blessing should not lead Nat astray, into arrogance, or even cruelty – traits the beautiful people I have encountered have sometimes seemed to regard in themselves as natural afflictions, or worse, a sign of right.

With the end of the ball game, we disperse in pairs toward the herd of station wagons corraled in the gravel parking lot. In May, when the time changes and the weather mellows, the team will stay after the games to picnic. Sometimes a pizza delivery will be arranged. The fathers will rotate the weekly responsibility of bringing beer. After dinner, the boys and girls will renew their baseball game, and the dads will recline in the grass, talking casually about our lives. I look forward to these outings. Amid this group of men I do not know well, there seems a gentle compact, something like the way worshippers must feel about one another as they leave church. Fathers with their kids, beyond the weekly preoccupations of professional life, or even the pleasures and responsibilities of marriage. Fathers mildly lit on Friday nights, at ease with these immeasurable obligations.

In this cooler, darker season, I have promised Barbara that we will meet for a quick dinner at a local pancake house. She is waiting on the red vinyl bench when we arrive, and even while she is kissing Nat and receiving a report on the Stingers' near-triumph, she gazes beyond him to greet me with a look of cold reproof. We are in the midst of a dismal period. Barbara's fury with me for my role in the investigation of Carolyn's murder has not abated, and tonight I perceive at once that there is some new edge to her displeasure. My first thought is that we must be very late, but when I check the restaurant clock I find we are even a minute early. I can only guess at what I have done to provoke her.

For Barbara, though, it has become so easy over the years to disappear into the black forests of her moods. The elements of the outside world that might have once detained her by now have been relegated to the past. Six years of teaching in the North End struck at her faith in social reform. When Nat was born, she gave up being other-seeking. Suburban life, with its tight boundaries and peculiar values, has quieted her and exaggerated her willingness to be alone. Her father's death, three years ago, was taken as an act of desertion, part of his lifelong pattern of ignoring Barbara's and her mother's needs, and whetted her sense of deprivation. And our soulless moments of marital disconnection have robbed her of the outright gaiety that once counterpointed these darker spells. During these periods, her disappointments with virtually everyone are often worn so openly that at instants I believe the taste would be bitter if I were to grasp her hand and lick her skin.

And then the weather breaks. In the past it always has. Although this disruption, caused by my infidelity, is naturally the most prolonged one of our married life, I still maintain some expectation of improvement. Even now Barbara does not speak of lawyers and divorce, as she did in late November. She is here. Set out so plainly, this fact inspires some calm. I am like a shipwrecked survivor holding fast to the debris, awaiting the arrival of the scheduled liner. Sooner or later, I believe, I will see a woman of good humor, of blazing intelligence, full of quirky insight and sly wit, who is keenly interested in me. That is the person I still think of as my wife.

Now that same woman wears a look of diamond hardness as we wait in line to be seated. Nat has slipped away and gazes adoringly into the candy counter. His baseball pants have drooped almost to his shoe tops, and he stands with one knee and both hands against the glass case, staring with fixed appreciation at the forbidden rows of sugared gum and chocolate bars. He jiggles a bit, of course – the object in motion. As ever, Barbara and I both watch him.

'So?' she suddenly asks me. This is a challenge. I am supposed to entertain her.

'"So" what?'

'So how's work? The big investigation still going gangbusters?'

'No leads,' I tell her, 'and no results. It's mass confusion. Frankly, the whole place is sagging. It's like they let the air out of a balloon. You know – now that Bolcarro has come out for Delay.'

With the mention of this event, Barbara winces, then once more turns an acid eye on me. At last, I recognize my latest outrage. Yesterday I came home very late and stayed downstairs, thinking she was asleep. Barbara descended in her nightgown. From the staircase she asked what I was doing. When I told her I was working on my résumé, she turned directly and went back up.

'Raymond didn't mention making you a judge today?' she asks.

I wince myself, lanced with regret at the foolish vanity that led me to mention this prospect. My chances now are dim. Bolcarro showed two days ago how concerned he is about making Raymond Horgan happy.

'What do you want me to do, Barbara?'

'I don't want you to do anything, Rusty. I've stopped wanting you to do anything. Isn't that what you prefer?'

126

'Barbara, he did a good job.'

'And what did he do for you? You're thirty-nine years old. You have a family. And now you're looking forward to unemployment compensation. He let you carry his bags and solve his problems, and when he should have quit, he took you with him down the drain.'

'We did good things.'

'He used you. People have always used you. And you don't just let them do it. You like it. You actually like it. You'd rather be abused than pay attention to the people who have tried to care about you.'

'Is that supposed to mean you?'

'Me. Your mother. Nat. It's a lifelong pattern. It's hopeless.'

Not Nat, I nearly answer, but a sense of diplomacy or self-preservation intervenes. The restaurant hostess, a tiny younger woman with the trimmed-up figure of the health-club set, leads us to our table. Barbara negotiates his meal with Nat. French fries yes, but milk, not Coke. And he must eat some salad. Nat whines and flops around. I cuff him gently and recommend sitting up straight. Barbara remains aloof behind the barrier of her menu.

Was she happier when I met her? That must have been the case, although I have no clear recollection. She tutored me when I connived – insanely – to beat the university science requirement by taking calculus. She never got the chance to collect her fee. She fell for me; I fell for her. I loved her ferocious intellect, her teen-queen beauty, her suburban clothes, the fact that she was a doctor's daughter, and thus, I thought, someone 'normal.' I even loved the rocky currents of her personality, her ability to express so many things which, to me, remained remote. Most of all, I loved her omnivorous passion for me. No one in my life had been so openly desirous of my company, so alight with manifest appreciation of every angle of my being. I met half a dozen men who coveted Barbara. She wanted only me, pursued me, in fact, with an ardor that I at first found embarrassing. I supposed it was the spirit of the era that made her want to soothe this awkward boy, dark and full of secret woe, whom she knew her parents would regard as less than she deserved.

Like me, like Nat, she was an only child, and she felt oppressed by her upbringing. Her parents' attentions had been suffocating and, she felt, in some ways false. She claimed to have been directed, used at all times as an instrument of their wishes, not her own. She told me often that I was the only person she had met who was like her – not just lonely, but always, previously, alone. Is it the sad reciprocity of love that you always want what you think you are giving? Barbara hoped I would be like some fairy-tale prince, a toad she had transformed with her caresses, who could enter the gloomy woods where she was held captive and lead her away from the encircling demons. Over the years I have so often failed in that assignment.

The atomized life of the restaurant spins on about us. At separate tables, couples talk; the late-shift workers dine alone; the waitresses pour coffee. And here sits Rusty Sabich, thirty-nine years old, full of lifelong burdens and workaday fatigue. I tell my son to drink his milk. I nibble at my burger. Three feet away is the woman whom I have said I've loved for nearly twenty years, making her best efforts to ignore me. I understand that at moments she feels disappointed. I understand at times she is bereft. I understand. I understand. That is my gift. But I have no ability to do anything about it. It is not simply the routines of adult life which sap my strength. In me, some human commodity is lacking. And we can only be who we can be. I have my own history; memories; the unsolved maze of my own self, where I am so often lost. I hear Barbara's inner clamor; I understand her need. But I can answer only with stillness and lament. Too much of me – too much! – must be preserved for the monumental task of being Rusty.

15

Election Day the weather is bright. Last night, when I sat in Raymond's office, with Mike Duke and Larren and Horgan, they thought that good weather would help. Now that the party belongs to Della Guardia, Raymond needs the voters who are inspired by their candidate rather than the precinct captain's wishes. The last week has been an odd lesson. Every time there's a negative development, you say it's hopeless. Then you look ahead. In Raymond's office last night, they were still talking about winning. The last poll, sponsored again by the paper and Channel 3, was taken the day of Bolcarro's endorsement and showed Raymond only five points back. Duke said that he believes things have improved since then, that Raymond seems to have gained some of his old momentum by being the underdog. We sat there, four grown men, acting as if it could be true.

At work, as ever, Election Day brings a loose feeling, all at ends. The employees of the prosecuting attorney's office, once a group of wardheelers and hacks, have been discouraged throughout Raymond's tenure from active political involvement. Gone are the days of deputies selling tickets in the courtrooms to the PA's campaign outings; in twelve years, Raymond Horgan has never solicited a dime in donations, or even a minute of campaign help, from the members of his staff. Nonetheless, many of the administrative employees who came on before Raymond was elected have continuing political obligations to the party sponsors who secured employment for them. As part of the uneasy compact struck a decade ago with Bolcarro, Raymond agreed to give most of the PA's staff Election Day off. That way the party types can do the party thing: knock on doors, distribute leaflets, drive the elderly, watch the polls. This year they will be doing that for Nico Della Guardia.

For the rest of us, there are no established obligations. I am in the office most of the day, first mate at the helm of this sinking ship. A few others are around, mostly lawyers working on briefs or trials, or clearing up their desks. About two dozen younger deputies have been delegated to work with the US Attorney's office on a vote-fraud patrol. This generally involves responding to junk complaints: a voting machine won't work; someone's got a gun in the polling place; an election judge is wearing a campaign button, or overcounseling elderly voters. I receive occasional updates by phone and answer press calls in which I dutifully report that there is no sign of tampering with the democratic process.

Around 4:30, I get a call from Lipranzer. Somebody's propped up a TV set in the hallway, right outside my door, but there is nothing to report. The polls won't close for another hour and a half. The early news is just happy-talk stuff about the heavy turnout.

'He lost,' Lip tells me. 'My guy at Channel 3 saw their exit polls. He says Nico's gonna win by eight, ten points, if the pattern holds.'

Again my heart plunges, my gut constricts. Funny, but this time I really believe it. I look out the window towards the columns of the courthouse, the flat tarred roofs of the other downtown buildings, the rippled black waters of the river, which turns, like an elbow, two blocks away. My office has been on the same side of this building for almost seven years now, yet the sight does not quite seem familiar.

'All right,' I finally announce solemnly. 'What else?'

'Nothing,' Lip says. 'Just thought I'd let you know.' He waits. 'We still workin on Polhemus?'

'You have something better to do?'

'No,' he says, 'no. They come down here today to get all my reports. For Morano.' The police chief. 'He wants to look em over.'

'So?'

'Struck me strange. You know. His mother-in-law got stuck up at gunpoint three years ago, I don't think he looked at the reports.'

'You'd understand that,' I say, 'if you had a mother-in-law.' Lip takes my humor as intended: an offering, an apology for my impatience a moment before. 'They're just trying to make sure Nico's briefed. Which is a joke,' I say, 'Molto's probably been getting copies of the police reports from the steno pool.'

'Probably. I don't know. Somethin didn't sit right. Schmidt come in here himself. Real serious. You know. Like someone shot the President.'

'They just want to look good.'

'I guess. I'm goin over to the North Branch courthouse to finish up on those court files,' Lip says, referring to the records we have been looking for since my visit to the 32nd District. 'They promised they'd have the microfilm from the warehouse before five. I want to get there before they send it back. Where are you tonight in case I come up with somethin?'

I tell him I'll be around Raymond's party, somewhere in the hotel. It's beside the point by now to rush back with investigative results, but Lip says he'll be stopping in anyway, more or less to pay his respects.

'The Irish,' Lip says, 'always run a real fine wake.'

Lipranzer's estimate proves accurate. The band plays loud. The young girls who are always here are still full of that soft glow of eventfulness, with banners across their chests and campaign boaters balanced neatly on their hairdos. HORGAN! everything says in limegreen Gaelic script. In the front, at either side of the unoccupied speakers' platform, two ten-foot enlargements of The Picture stand. I drift around the ballroom, spearing meatballs and feeling bad.

Around 7:30, I go up to Raymond's suite on the fifth floor. Various people from the campaign are moving through the rooms. There are three trays of cold cuts and some liquor bottles on one of the dressers, but I decline the invitation to consume. There must be ten phones in these three rooms, all of them ringing.

All three local TV stations have projected Della Guardia the winner by now. Larren – Judge Lyttle – comes by with a tumbler of bourbon in his hand, grumbling about the exit polls.

'First time,' he says, 'I've seen a body pronounced dead before it hit the floor.'

Raymond, however, is sanguine. He is seated in one of the interior bedrooms, watching television and talking on the phone. When he sees me he puts the phone down and comes to hug me. 'Rožat,' he says, my given name. I know that this gesture has probably been repeated with a dozen other people this evening, but I find myself deeply grateful and stirred to be included in the grieving family.

I sit by Raymond on the footstool of the easy chair he is occupying. An open bottle of Jack Daniel's is on the candle table at the chair side, as well as a half-eaten sandwich. Raymond goes on taking phone calls, conferring with Larren and Mike and Joe Reilly. I do not move. I recall the nights I used to sit beside my father while he watched a ball game on TV or listened to the radio. I always asked his permission before taking a place next to him on the divan. They were the warmest moments that we had. As I became older, my father would drink his beer and occasionally pass the bottle to me. At moments he would even make a remark aloud about the game.

Eventually the conversation begins to turn to the protocol of concession. Does Raymond communicate with Della Guardia first, or does he go downstairs to address the faithful? Della Guardia, they decide. Mike says Raymond should call him. Joe says send a telegram.

'Screw that,' Raymond says, 'the man's across the street. I'm going over there to shake his hand.' He asks Larren to make arrangements. He'll see Nico, make his speech, then come back up here to do one-on-one interviews with print and media reporters. No point in spite with them. He tells Mac she should start scheduling those meetings about 9:30. He'll go live at 10:00 with Rosenberg. I have not noticed Mac until now, and when she turns her chair around she says one word to me: 'Sad.'

Raymond asks to see me alone. We go into a dressing room, between the two bedrooms in the suite, nothing more than a large closet with a lavatory.

'How are you?' I ask.

'There've been things that hurt worse. Tomorrow will be bad. The day after. We'll survive. Listen,' Raymond says. 'About what I mentioned the other night: when I see Nico, I'm going to offer to resign. I don't want any lame-duck crap. I don't want to appear to be playing around with the office. I'd like to make a clean break. If Nico wants to run in the general election as an incumbent, let him. I'll tell him he's free to assume office, if the county executive approves.' This is humor. Bolcarro is the county executive. Party chairman. Mayor. The guy has more titles than the leader of a banana republic.

I tell Raymond he's made a wise decision. We look at each other.

'I feel like I should apologize to you, Rusty,' Raymond says. 'If there was any deputy I would have wanted to take over, you know it would be you. I should have tried to make that happen, instead of running. The guys just pushed me so damn hard to give it one more shot.'

I wave my hand, I shake my head. I prohibit his apology.

Larren sticks his head in.

'I was just telling Rusty,' Raymond tells him, 'I never should have run again, I should have given him the shot. New face. Career prosecutor. Apolitical. Really could have revved things up. Wouldn't you say?'

'Shit,' says the judge, 'pretty soon you'll have me believing it.'

We all laugh.

Larren reports on his conversation with Della Guardia's people. He talked to Tommy Molto, who has emerged tonight as the primary aide-de-camp. They'd rather not have a face-to-face this evening. Instead, Molto and Nico want to see Raymond in the morning.

'Ten o'clock,' says Larren. 'He told me, didn't ask. And says, Please make sure it's with Raymond alone. How do you like that?

Bossy little shit.' Larren takes a private moment with his discontent. 'I said you'd call Nico to make a formal concession. When you're ready.'

Raymond takes Larren's bourbon from him and has a belt.

'I am ready,' he says.

Loyalty goes only so far. I do not want to listen. I head back to the ballroom.

Near the bar, I run into George Mason, an old friend of Raymond's. He is already drunk. We both are being jostled.

'Pretty good crowd,' he tells me.

Only near the bar, I think. But I save the thought.

'He had a good run,' George says. 'He did a good job. You guys should all be proud.'

'We are,' I say. 'I am.'

'So what's with you? Private practice?'

'For a while, I guess.'

'Gonna do criminal stuff?'

How many times have I had this conversation tonight? I tell George probably, I'll see, who can tell. I'm going to go on a vacation, that's for sure. George gives me his card and tells me to call. He may know some people I might want to talk to.

Horgan arrives in the ballroom twenty minutes later. The assholes from TV shove their way to the front, hold up their cameras and lights and boom mikes so that you cannot see much. Raymond is smiling and waving. Two of his daughters are with him on the platform. The band is playing an Irish jig. Raymond has said 'Thank you' for the third time, about halfway along to quieting the crowd, when somebody grabs my arm. Lipranzer. He looks harried from having had to push his way through to reach me. There is too much noise in here to speak: stamping, hooting, whistling. Some folks in the back have even started to dance. Lipranzer motions me outside and I follow him beneath an exit sign. We end up, unexpectedly, in an alley outside the hotel, and Lip walks down toward a street lamp. When I see him now, I can tell that something's wrong. He looks almost caved-in, compressed by some kind of worry. The sweat shines near his temple. From here, I can hear Raymond's voice inside but not what he's saying.

'This is too strange,' Lip says. 'Something's fucked-up over in the Hall. It's way wrong.'

'Why?'

'I don't know,' he says. 'But I'm gettin vibes like I haven't had in years. I got a message I'm supposed to be in Morano's office, 8:00 tomorrow morning to be interviewed. By Molto. That's the message. Not talk. Not discuss. Interview. Like they're after me. And here's another one. When I come back in tonight they tell me that Schmidt took all the receipts for the evidence I've inventoried on Polhemus. Any questions, see him.'

'Sounds to me like you're off this case.'

'Sure,' he says. 'Fine. But figure this in. I'm out in the North Branch before 5:00. All of this hits by 6:00, 6:30. And look at what I picked up out there.'

He reaches inside his windbreaker to his shirt pocket. He has four or five sheets of foolscap, xeroxes, I see, of court documents. The case number I recognize: it matches the complaint number missing from the 32nd District. The first sheet is a copy of the case jacket. *People versus Leon Wells*. A public-indecency complaint. Dismissed by court order a day in July nine years ago.

'Bingo,' I say out loud.

'This page,' Lip tells me. It is the bond order. In our state, a defendant is permitted to satisfy bail in minor cases merely with his signature on a promissory note, promising to pay a sum – by law less than $5,000 – in the event of his default. The only conditions are that he refrain from other crimes and report once weekly by phone to a member of the court's probation department. Leon's assigned probation officer according to his bond slip was Carolyn Polhemus. Her name and telephone number are right there.

'Wait. Here's the best.' He pulls the last sheet out. It is a copy of the court half-sheet, a form dismissing the case. Motion to Dismiss Without Prejudice, it is captioned. The attorney presenting the motion is the prosecutor. 'Raymond Horgan, Kindle County Prosecuting Attorney, By' is printed at the bottom of the form. The deputy handling the case is supposed to sign the blank. I cannot read the signature at first. Then I get it.

'Molto?'

Lipranzer and I stand a moment in the street lamps, looking at the papers again. Neither one of us says much. From inside there's an enormous roar; then you can hear the band striking up again, 'When Irish Eyes Are Smiling.' Raymond, I take it, has admitted defeat.

I try to pacify Lipranzer. Hang tight, I tell him. We're not sure of anything.

'You take this.' He gives me the copies from the court file.

I move back toward the ballroom. Lip heads off alone, past the dumpsters and debris, into the darkness of the alley.

16

'So we ended,' I told Robinson, 'and we ended badly. One week she saw me less. The next week not at all. No lunches, no calls, no visits to my office. No "drinks," as we so quaintly put it. She was gone.'

I knew she valued independence. And at first I tried to stanch my panic by telling myself it was only that: a show of freedom. Best not to resist. But each day the silence worked on me – and my pathetic longing. I knew she was only one floor down. I wanted nothing so much as simply to be in the same room. I went three days running to Morton's Third Floor, where I knew she liked to go for lunch. On the third day, she appeared – with Raymond. I thought nothing of that. I was blind then. I did not imagine rivals. I sat for half an hour, by myself, shifting lettuce leaves across my salad bowl and gazing at a table two hundred feet away. Her coloring! Her hair! When the feel of her skin came over me, I sat alone in a public dining room and groaned.

By the third week, I had passed the edge. I did not have to gather strength; I merely let myself go to impulse. I walked directly to her office, eleven o'clock one morning. I did not bring a file, a memo, any item for excuse.

She was not in.

I stood there on her threshold with my eyes closed, burning in humiliation and sadness, feeling I would die from being thwarted.

While I stood there, in that pose, she returned.

Rusty, she said brightly. A chipper greeting. She pushed past me. I watched her bend to pull a file from her drawer. A parched arrow of sensation ran through me, at the way her tweed skirt pulled across her bottom, the smoothness of her calves flexing in her hose. She was busy. She stood over her desk, reading the notations on the jacket, tapping a pencil on a pad.

I'd like to see you again, I said.

She looked up. Her face was solemn. She stepped around her desk and reached past me with one hand to close the door.

She spoke immediately.

I don't think that's a very good idea. Not now. It's not right for me now, Rusty. Then she opened up the door.

She went back behind her desk. She worked. She turned to flip on the radio. She did not glance toward the place where I remained another moment.

I do not think I believed at any time that Carolyn Polhemus loved me. I thought only that I pleased her. My passion, my obsession flattered and enlarged her. And so I did not suffer rejection; I was not ravaged by grief. When it finally occurred to me that I might have a successor, I did not have fantasies of his destruction. I would have agreed to share. I was devastated by denial, by longing, I wanted, simply, what it was I'd had. I craved Carolyn and my release in her in a way that did not end.

For me it never ended. There was nothing to make it end. Her willingness had always been only secondary, convenient. I wanted my passion, in its great exultant moments, the burning achievement of my worship, of my thrall. To be without it was to be in some way dead. I longed. I longed! I sat up nights in my rocking chair, imagining Carolyn, overcome by pity for myself.

In those weeks, my life seemed to have exploded. My sense of proportion left me; my judgment took on the grotesque exaggerations of a cruel cartoon. A fourteen-year-old girl was abducted, stored like merchandise in the defendant's trunk, sodomized in one manner or another every hour or two for three days, and then was beaten by him, blinded (so she could make no identification), and left for dead. I read reports about this case, attended meetings where the evidence was discussed. To myself I thought, I hurt for Carolyn.

At home I made my absurd confession to Barbara, weeping at the dinner table, crying in my highball. Do I have the guts to say it? I wanted her sympathy. That mad egoistic instant naturally went to make my suffering worse. Barbara would not endure the sight of me in any visible pain. Now there was no place left. At work, I did nothing. I watched the hallways for some glimpse of Carolyn passing by. At home, my wife was now my warden, daring me, with the threat of the imminent end of family life, to wear any sign of any neediness. I took to walks. December turned to January. The temperature sunk near zero and stayed that way for weeks. I trudged hours through our little town, with my scarf across my face, the fur trimming of my parka burning when it touched the exposed portion of my forehead and my cheeks. My own tundra. My Siberia. When would it end? I wanted simply to have – or if not to have, to find some peace.

Carolyn avoided me. She was as artful at that as at so many other things. She sent me memos, left Eugenia phone messages. She did not go to meetings I was scheduled to attend. I'm sure I drove her to it, that in the moments when we caught sight of each other, she could see my pathetic, hungering expression.

In March, I called her from home. It happened a few times. She had drafted an indictment in a recidivist case, complex charges with allegations going back to the 1960s. I told myself it would be easier to discuss involved legal problems without the interruptions of the office. I waited until Nat was asleep and Barbara was stowed in the closed womb of her study, from where I knew she could never hear me calling downstairs. Then I paged to Carolyn's listing in the little mimeographed directory Mac put out, containing all the deputies' home phones. I hardly needed to look to recall the number, but I suppose that in those moments of compulsion I took some strange satisfaction from seeing her name in print. It prolonged, in a way, the communication; it meant my fantasy was real. As soon as I heard Carolyn's voice, I knew how false my excuses had been. I could not bring myself to utter a sound. 'Hello? Hello?' I melted when I heard her speak in a tone without reproach. Who was it she was awaiting now?

Each time I did it, I was sure that pride would bear my saying a word or two. I intricately plotted the conversations beforehand. Humorous cracks to dislodge her from indifference or chagrin.

139

Sincere declarations for the instant when I was given half a chance. I could not make any of it take place. She answered, and I waited in a fiery pit of shame. Tears came to my eyes. My heart felt squeezed. 'Hello? Hello?' I was relieved when she slammed down the phone, when I quickly tucked the office directory into the hallway bureau.

She knew, of course, that it was me. There was probably something forlorn and beseeching in my breathing. One Friday night, late in March, I sat in Gil's, finishing a drink I had started with Lipranzer before he headed home. I saw her staring at me in the long beveled mirror behind the bar. Her face was there above the whiskey bottles; her hair was newly done, shining and stiff beneath the spray. The anger in her look was cruel.

Pretense was so much easier. I moved my glance from hers and told the bartender to give her an Old-Fashioned. She said no, but he did not hear her, and she waited until he brought the drink. She was standing. I was sitting. The burly Friday-evening tumult of Gil's went on around us. The juke was screaming and the laughter was wild. The atmosphere had the beefy smell of Fridays, the musk of sexuality unlimbering from the week's restraint. I finished my beer, and finally, thank God, found the strength to speak.

I'm like a kid, I told her. I was talking without looking her way. I'm so uncomfortable right now, just sitting here, I want to walk away. And most of the time, the only thing I think I want in life is to talk to you.

I looked up to see how she was taking this and found her expression largely abstracted.

That's what I've been doing for months now, walking past you. That's not cool, is it?

It's safe, she said.

It's not cool, I repeated. But I'm inexperienced. I mean, I want to have this war-weary, so-what thing about it all, but I'm not making it, Carolyn. I got engaged when I was twenty-two years old. And right before the wedding I did my time in the Reserves, and I got drunk and screwed some woman in a station wagon behind a bar. That's it, I said, that's the history of my infidelities, my life of wild amours. I'm dying, I said. Right this minute.

Sitting on this fucking bar stool, I am just about dead. You like that? I'm shaking. My heart is hammering. In a minute, I'll need air. That's not very cool, is it?

And what do you want from me, Rusty? It was her turn now, looking dead into the mirror.

Something, I said.

Advice?

If that's all I can get.

She put her drink down on the bar. She put her hand down on my shoulder. She looked straight at me for the first time.

Grow up, she said, and walked away.

'And for a minute then,' I said to Robinson, 'I felt the most desperate wish that she were dead.'

17

Around the office, Tommy Molto was nicknamed the Mad Monk. He is a former seminarian; five foot six inches if he is lucky, forty or fifty pounds overweight, badly pockmarked, nails bitten to the quick. A driven personality. The kind to stay up all night working on a brief, to go three months without taking off a weekend. A capable attorney, but he is burdened by a zealot's poverty of judgment. As a prosecutor, he always seemed to me to be trying to make facts rather than to understand them. He burns at too high a temperature to be worth much before a jury, but he made a good assistant to Nico – he has qualities of discipline that Della Guardia lacks. He and Delay go all the way back to grade school at St Joe's. Dago society. Molto's one of the guys who were included before they were old enough to worry about who was cool. Tommy's personal life is a cipher. He is single and I've never seen him with a woman, which inspires the usual conjecture, but if I were to guess, I'd imagine he's still celibate. That singular intensity seems to have a subterranean source.

Tommy, as usual, is whispering to Nico hotly when I come through the reception room. There's been a lot of rubbernecking in the office, file clerks and secretaries rushing to the receptionist's window to see what the new boss looks like. As if they could have forgotten in nine months. The TV crews followed Nico up here and did their takes of Nico and Tommy sitting in hard wooden chairs, waiting to meet with Horgan, but that is over now. The reporters have dispersed, and the two of them actually look somewhat forlorn when I come by. Nico does not even have his flower. I cannot resist giving it to Molto.

'Tommy Molto,' I say. 'We once had a guy of that name who

worked here, but we think he might be dead. Keep those calls and letters coming, Tom.'

This joshing, which I intend in all good humor, seems not merely to fall flat but to inspire a look of horror. Molto's heavy brows knit and he actually appears to recoil when I offer my hand. I try to ease the moment by turning to Delay. He takes my hand, although he, too, seems somewhat reluctant to accept my congratulations.

'I will never say you did not tell me so,' I admit.

Nico does not smile. In fact, he looks the other way. He is extremely ill at ease. I do not know if the campaign has left a wake of bitterness or if Delay, like so many of us, is simply scared to death now that he finally has what he so long wanted.

One thing I am certain of after this encounter: Nico will not be bidding to retain my services. I go so far as to call the file room and ask them to begin putting together some boxes. Late in the morning, I call Lipranzer's number at McGrath Hall. His phone, which is never answered when he's out, is picked up by someone whose voice I do not recognize.

'34068.'

'Dan Lipranzer?'

'Not in. Who is this, please?'

'When do you expect him?'

'Who is this?'

'No message,' I say, before hanging up.

I knock on the adjoining door to see what Mac makes of all this. She's gone. When I ask Eugenia where, she tells me that Mac is in Raymond's office, meeting, as she puts it, 'with Mr Della Guardia.' She has been there almost an hour. I stand next to Eugenia's desk, battling my own bitterness. All in all, this has not worked out. Nico is now Mr Della Guardia. Mac is on his staff, until she takes the bench. Raymond is going to get rich. Tommy Molto has my job. And I'll be lucky if next month I can pay the mortgage.

I'm still standing by Eugenia, when the phone rings.

'Mr Horgan wants to see you,' she says.

*

143

In the face of all the stern rebukes I have given to myself while I was marching down the hallway, the juvenile rush of sensation I feel when I see Nico in the PA's chair astonishes me. I am immobilized by anger, jealousy, and revulsion. Nico has assumed a perfect proprietary air. He has removed his suit coat and his face is gravely composed, an expression which I know Nico well enough to realize is completely affected. Tommy Molto is sitting beside him, his chair somehow dropped a few inches back into the room. It strikes me that Tommy has already mastered the art of being a toady.

Raymond motions for me to sit. He says that this is really Nico's meeting now, so he offered him the chair. Raymond himself is standing up beside his sofa. Mac has her chair wheeled up to the window and is looking out. She still has not greeted me, and I realize now, from her demeanor, that Mac wants to be nowhere near this scene. The old saw: harder for her than for me

'We've made some decisions here,' Raymond says. He turns to Della Guardia. Silence. Delay, in his first assignment as PA, is wordstruck. 'Well, perhaps I should explain this first part,' Raymond says. He is extremely grim. I know his forced expression well enough to realize that he is angry and laboring to remain composed. You can tell, just from the atmosphere, that there were bruises raised during the preceding meeting.

'I spoke last night with the mayor and told him that I had no desire to remain in office in light of the voters' preferences. He suggested to me that as long as I felt that way that I ought to talk it over with Nico to see if he wants to come on early. He does – and so that's what's going to happen. With the County Board's concurrence, I'll be leaving Friday.'

I can't help myself. 'Friday!'

'It's a little faster than I would have thought myself, but there are certain factors – ' Raymond stops. Something is precarious in his manner. He is struggling. Horgan straightens the papers on the coffee table. He drifts to the sideboard and looks for something else. He is having a miserable time. I decide to make it easy for everybody.

'I'll be taking off then, too,' I say. Nico starts to speak and I interrupt. 'You'll be better off with a fresh start, Delay,'

'That's not what I was going to say.' He stands. 'I want you to know why Raymond is leaving so soon. There's going to be a criminal investigation of his staff. We have information – some of it came to us during the campaign, but we didn't want to get into that kind of gutter stuff. But we have information and we think there's a serious problem.'

I am confused by Nico's apparent anger. I wonder if he is talking about the B file. Perhaps there's a reason for Molto's connection to that case.

'Here, let me butt in,' Raymond says. 'Rusty, I think the best way to deal with this is to be direct. Nico and Tom have raised some questions with me about the Polhemus investigation. They're not confident in the way you've handled it. And I've agreed now to step aside. They can examine that question in any way they think is best. That's a matter for their professional judgment. But Mac suggested – well, we all agreed to make you aware of the situation.'

I wait. The sense of alarm spreads through me before the instant of comprehension.

'I am under criminal investigation?' I laugh out loud.

From across the room Mac finally speaks. ''Tain't funny, McGee,' she says. There is no humor in her voice.

'This,' I say, 'is a crock. What did I supposedly do?'

'Rusty,' Raymond says, 'we do not need that kind of discussion now. Nico and Tom think that there are some things you should have spoken up about. That's all.'

'That is not all,' Molto says suddenly. His look is piercing. 'I think you've been engaged in misdirection, hide the ball, ring around the rosy for almost a month now. You've been covering your ass.'

'I think you're sick,' I tell Tommy Molto.

Mac has wheeled her chair about.

'We don't need this,' she says. 'This discussion should take place somewhere else, with somebody else.'

'The hell with that,' I say. 'I want to know what this is about.'

'It's about,' says Molto, 'the fact that you were in Carolyn's apartment the night she was killed.'

My heart beats so hard that my vision shifts, jumps. I was waiting for someone to chastise me because I had an affair with the decedent. This is incomprehensible. And I say so. Ludicrous. Bullshit.

'What was that? A Tuesday night? Barbara's at the U. and I was babysitting.'

'Rusty,' says Raymond, 'my advice to you is to shut your fucking mouth.'

Molto is on his feet. He is approaching me, stalking. He is enraged.

'We've got the print results. The ones you never could remember to ask for. And they're your prints on the glass. Yours. Rožat K. Sabich. Right on that glass on the bar. Five feet from where the woman was found dead. Maybe you didn't remember at first that all county employees get printed.'

I stand. 'This is absurd.'

'And the M U Ds you told Lipranzer not to get? The ones from your house? We had the phone company pull them this morning. They're on the way down here right now. You were calling her all month. There's a call from your house to hers that *night*.'

'I think I've had enough of this,' I say. 'If I can be excused.'

I have gotten as far as Loretta's little office outside Raymond's when Molto calls out behind me. He follows me into the anteroom. I can hear Della Guardia yelling Molto's name.

'I want you to know one thing, Sabich.' He points his finger at me. 'I know.'

'Sure you do,' I say.

'We're going to have a warrant for your butt the first day we're here. You better get yourself a lawyer, man, a damn good one.'

'For your bullshit theory of an obstruction case?'

Molto's eyes are burning.

'Don't pretend that you don't get it. I know. You killed her. You're the guy.'

Rage; as if my blood had quickened; as if my veins were filled only with that black poison. How old and familiar, how close to my being it seems. I come near Tommy Molto. I whisper, 'Yeah, you're right,' before I walk away.

SUMMER

IN THE SUPERIOR COURT OF KINDLE COUNTY

)	
)	
PEOPLE)	_____
vs.)	VIOLATION:
ROŽAT K. SABICH)	Section 76610 R.S.S.
)	
)	

THE KINDLE COUNTY GRAND JURY, JUNE SESSION, charges as follows:

On or about April 1 of this year, within the venue of Kindle County,

ROŽAT K. SABICH

defendant herein, did commit murder in the first degree in that he did knowingly, intentionally, and with malice aforethought trespass with force and arms upon the person of Carolyn Polhemus, thereby taking the life of the aforementioned Carolyn Polhemus;

In violation of Section 76610 of the Revised State Statutes.

A TRUE BILL:

————————————————/s
Joseph Doherty, Foreperson
Kindle County Grand Jury
June Session

————————————————/s
Nico Della Guardia
Kindle County Prosecuting Attorney

Done this Twenty—third day of June

[SEAL]

18

'The documents and reports are in the front. The witness statements are in the back,' says Jamie Kemp as he sets a heavy cardboard box on the faultless finish of the walnut meeting table. We are in the small conference room in the offices of his employer, Alejandro Stern, my attorney. Kemp is sweating. He walked two blocks in the July sun from the County Building with these papers. His navy tie has been pulled away from his collar and some of his fancy blond Prince Valiant hairdo, an affectation left over from his younger days, is matted to his temples.

'I'm going to check my phone messages,' Kemp says, 'then I'll be back to look at this stuff with you. And remember – ' Kemp points. 'Don't panic. Defense lawyers have a name for what you're feeling. They call it clong.'

'What's clong?'

'Clong is the rush of shit to your heart when you see the state's evidence.' Kemp smiles. I am glad he thinks I can still take a joke. 'It is not fatal.'

It is 14 July, three weeks since my indictment for murdering Carolyn Polhemus. Later this afternoon I will appear before Chief Superior Court Judge Edgar Mumphrey for my arraignment. Under state statutes governing discovery in criminal cases, the prosecution is required, prior to arraignment, to make available to the defense all physical evidence they intend to introduce, and a list of witnesses, including copies of their statements. Thus, this box. I stare at the familiar label applied to the cardboard: PEOPLE V. ROŽAT K. SABICH. I am full of that feeling again: This hasn't happened. Alone in this comfortable room,

151

with its dark wainscoting and rows of crimson-jacketed law books, I wait for this now familiar adhesion of dread and longing to pass.

There is another copy of the indictment in the front of the box. I always focus on the same words. Trespass with force and arms. Trespass *vi et armis*, a term of the common law. With these same words for centuries persons in the English-speaking countries were accused of acts of violence. The phrase is archaic, long abandoned in most jurisdictions, but it is part of the text of our state statute, and reading it here always leaves me with the sense of a bizarre heritage. I have made league with the all-stars of crime, John Dillinger, Bluebeard, Jack the Ripper, and the million lesser lights, the half-mad, the abused, the idly evil, and the many who surrendered to a moment's terrible temptation, to an instant when they found themselves well acquainted with our wilder elements, our darker side.

After two months of daily press leaks, of rumor, innuendo, cruel gossip, I said resolutely that it would be a relief if an indictment finally came down. I was wrong. The day before, Delay sent Stern what is called the defendant's 'courtesy copy.' I first read the charges about forty feet from here, down the hall in Sandy's tasteful cream-colored office, and my heart and all my other organs were at once all stalled and so full of pain that I was certain that something in those regions must have burst. I could feel the blood gone from my face and I knew that my panic was visible. I tried to sound composed, not to show courage but because I suddenly realized it was simply the only alternative.

Sandy was sitting beside me on the sofa, and to him I mentioned Kafka.

'Does it sound horrible and trite to say that I can't believe this?' I asked, 'That I am full of incomprehension and rage?'

'Of course you cannot,' said Sandy, 'of course not. I, who have practiced at the criminal bar for thirty years in this city, am not able to believe it, and by now I thought I had seen everything. *Everything!* And I do not say that loosely. I had a client, Rusty, I cannot use a name, of course, who once placed $25 million in gold bullion in exactly the place that you are sitting. Just the ingots, two feet high. And I, who have seen such things, I sit at

152

home at night and think to myself, Truly, this is remarkable and frightening.'

From Sandy these words had a kind of reach, the span of authentic wisdom. There is, with his soft Spanish accent, an elegance to the sound of even his ordinary speech. His dignity is soothing. Over time, I have found that I hover, like a lover, on every courtly gesture.

'Rusty,' Sandy said to me, touching the page I held in my hand, 'you make no mention of the only thing' – he searched for a word – 'which is encouraging.'

'What's that?'

'No notice. No Section 5 notice.'

'Ah,' I said, and a shiver passed through me. In our state the prosecution must give notice at the time of indictment if it is seeking the death penalty. With all my finely calibrated calculations of Delay's intentions over the months, some zealous internal defense had prevented my mind from even lighting on that possibility. My look, I believe, revealed some of my embarrassment, even humiliation, that I was already so detached from routine professional perspectives. 'I assumed,' I said weakly.

'Ah well.' Sandy smiled gently. 'We have these habits,' he said.

At Sandy's advice, we were not in town when the indictment was returned. Barbara and Nat and I went to a cabin owned by friends of her parents, up near Skageon. At night, you could hear the rushing of Crown Falls, a mile away, and the trout fishing proved better than at any time I can recall.

But, of course, the calamity four hundred miles south was never out of mind. The day after, George Leonard from the *Trib* somehow got the number of the cabin and asked me for a comment. I referred him to Stern. Later, I came in to hear Barbara in conference with her mother. After she put down the phone I asked, somehow feeling that I should:

'It's all over?'

'Everywhere. T.V. Both papers. Front page. Pictures. Your old officemate Delay handed out every scummy detail.'

153

This proved to be an understatement. My case is the stuff of supermarket tabloids: CHIEF PROSECUTOR CHARGED WITH MURDER – HAD AFFAIR WITH VICTIM. Sex, politics, and violence mix in Kindle County. Not only was the local press full of this for days, but the national media, too. Out of curiosity, I began to read these accounts myself. The library in Nearing has an excellent periodical section, and I have little to do now during the days. On Stern's advice I refused to resign as a deputy PA and was placed on an indefinite administrative leave, with pay. As a result I have spent more time in the library than I would have expected. I join the old men and the bag ladies in enjoying the silence and the air conditioning as I inspect these national reports of my misconduct. *The New York Times* was, as usual, dryly factual, referring to everyone as Mr and laying out the entire antic circumstance. It was, surprisingly, the national news magazines, *Time* and *Newsweek*, that did their best to make it all seem lurid. Each article was accompanied by the same photo, taken by some asshole I saw lurking in the bushes for a couple of days. Stern finally advised me to walk outside and let him take his picture, on the condition that he promise to beat it. That worked. The Minicam units which, according to the neighbors, were camped before the house for a week, while we were hiding out near Skageon, are yet to return.

That makes little practical difference. After twelve years in which I sometimes prosecuted the biggest cases in town, the papers and TV stations had enough footage of me on file to put my face everywhere. I cannot walk around Nearing without enduring endless staring. There is now a permanent hesitation in everybody's manner, a few portions of a second lost before a greeting. The comments of solace that are made, which are few, are ludicrous and inept – my cleaner telling me, 'Tough break,' or the teenage gas-station attendant asking if that's really me he's been reading about in the paper. Another thing I like about the library is that no one is allowed to talk.

And how do I feel, so instantly struck low, brought down from my station as model citizen and become a pariah instead? To say that there are no words is inaccurate. There are words, but they would be so many. My spirits keel about wildly. The anxiety is corrosive and I spend much time in a tumult of anger and disbelief. For the most part there is a numbness – a sense of idle refuge. Even in my concern for Nat, and how all of this will warp his future, the dawning thought is that it has happened, ultimately, just to me. I alone am the foremost victim. And to some extent, I can endure that. I acquired more of my father's fatalism than I expected; a side of me has always been without faith in reason or in order. Life is simply experience; for reasons not readily discerned, we attempt to go on. At instants I am amazed that I am here. I have taken to watching my shoes as I cross the pavement, for the fact that I am moving, that I am going anywhere, doing anything, strikes me, at odd moments, as amazing. That in the midst of this misfortune life continues seems bizarre.

And mostly I am like this, floating and remote. Of course, a great deal of the time is also spent wondering why this has occurred. But I find that at some point along the way my ability to assay ceases. My speculation seems to lead to a dark and frightening periphery, the edge of a black vortex of paranoia and rage from which, thus far, I have instantly withdrawn. I know that on some levels I cannot take much more, and I simply do not. I worry instead about when it will be over, and what the result will be. I want, with a desperation whose size cannot be encompassed by metaphor, I want all of this never to have taken place; I want things to be as they were before, before I allowed my life to be ransacked by Carolyn, and everything that followed. And then there is my consuming anxiety for Nat: What will happen to him? How can he be sheltered? How can I protect him from shame? How can I have brought him to the brink of being, for all purposes, half an orphan? These are in some ways my worst moments: this raging, lashing frustration, this sense of incompetence, these tears. And then, once or twice, in the last weeks, an extraordinary feeling, lighter than air, more soothing than a breeze, a hope that seems to settle in without accounting, and which leaves me with the sense that I have mounted some high rampart and have the courage simply to look ahead.

*

The case against me, as I assess it from the contents of the cardboard box, is straightforward. Nico has listed about a dozen witnesses of substance, more than half of them related to the physical and scientific evidence he plans to introduce. Lipranzer will be called, apparently to say I instructed him not to subpoena my home phone tolls. Mrs Krapotnik has identified me as someone she saw in Carolyn's building, although she is not positive I am the stranger she observed on the night of the murder. Also listed is a maid from Nearing whose somewhat cryptic statement suggests that she saw me on the Nearing–City bus one night close to the time Carolyn was killed. Raymond Horgan is named; Tommy Molto; Eugenia, my secretary; Robinson, the psychiatrist I saw on a few occasions; and a number of scientific experts, including Painless Kumagai.

None the less, this is clearly a circumstantial case. No one will say they saw me kill Carolyn Polhemus. No one will testify to my confession (if you do not consider Molto, whose file memorandum pretends to treat my last remark to him that Wednesday in April as if it was not rendered in a get-screwed tone). The heart of this case is the physical evidence: the glass with two of my fingerprints, identified from the knowns I gave a dozen years ago when I became a deputy PA; the telephone MUD records showing a call from my house to Carolyn's about an hour and a half before her murder; the vaginal smear, revealing the presence within Carolyn's genitalia of spermatozoa of my blood type, thwarted in their urgent blind migration by a contraceptive compound whose presence implies a consensual sex act; and finally, the malt-colored Zorak V fibers found on Carolyn's clothing, and her corpse, and strewn about the living area, which match samples taken from the carpeting in my home.

These last two pieces of evidence were developed as the result of a visit to my house by three state troopers, which took place a day or two after the Black Wednesday meeting, as Barbara and I now refer to it, in Raymond's office. The doorbell rang and there was Tom Nyslenski, who has served subpoenas for the PA's office for at least six years. I was still sufficiently unfocused that my initial reaction was to be mildly pleased to see him.

156

I don't like to be here, he said. He then handed me two grand-jury subpoenas, one to produce physical evidence – a blood specimen – and one to testify. He also had a search warrant, narrowly drawn, which authorized the troopers to take samples of the carpeting throughout my home, as well as every piece of exterior clothing I owned. Barbara and I sat there in our living room as three men in brown uniforms walked from room to room with plastic bags and scissors. They spent an hour in my closet, cutting tiny swatches from the seams. Nico and Molto had been clever enough not to search for the murder weapon, too. A law enforcement professional would know better than to keep the thing around. And if the troopers searched for it, the prosecutors would have to admit in court that it could not be found.

Is the stuff in here called Zorak V? I asked Barbara quietly while the troopers were upstairs.

I don't know what it is, Rusty. Barbara, as usual, seemed to be placing a premium on maintaining her composure. She had a little pursed-up expression, peeved but no worse. As if they were fourteen-year-olds setting off firecrackers too late at night.

Is it synthetic? I asked.

Do you think we could afford wool? she replied.

I called Stern, who had me make an inventory of what they took. The next day I voluntarily provided a blood sample downtown. But I never testified. Stern and I had our one serious dispute about that. Sandy repeated the accepted wisdom that an investigation target accomplishes nothing by pre-trial statements except to prepare the prosecutor for the defense. In his own gentle way, Stern reminded me of the damage I had already done with my outburst in Raymond's office. But in late April, unindicted, and convinced I never would be charged, my goal was to prevent this mad episode from damaging my reputation. If I took five and refused to testify, as I had the right to do, it would probably never reach the papers, but every lawyer in the PA's office would know, and through them half the others on the street. Sandy prevailed when the results of the blood test came back and identified me as a secreter – that is, someone who produced A-type antibodies, just like the man who had last been with Carolyn. The chances of this being a coincidence were about one in ten. I realized then that my last opportunity for quick exoneration had passed. Tommy Molto refused to accept any substitute for my assertion of the privilege and so one bleak afternoon in May, I, like so many others I had often ridiculed, snuck into the grand-jury room, a little windowless chamber that looks something like a small theater, and repeated in response to thirty-six different questions, 'On the advice of my attorney, I will decline to answer because it may tend to incriminate me.'

'So,' says Sandy Stern. 'How do you enjoy seeing the world from the other side?' Engrossed in mysteries of the cardboard box, I did not notice him enter the conference room. He stands, with one hand on the door handle, a short, roundish man, in a flawless suit. There are just a few stray hairs that cross his shining pale scalp, emanating from what was once a widow's peak. Tucked between the fingers is a cigar. This is a habit which Stern indulges only in the office. It would be uncivil in a public place and Clara, his wife, forbids it at home.

'I didn't expect you back so soon,' I tell him.

'Judge Magnuson's calendar is dreadful. Naturally, the sentencing will be called last.' He is referring to another case on which he has been engaged. Apparently he has spent a good deal of time waiting in court and the matter is not yet concluded. 'Rusty, would you mind terribly if Jamie appears with you at the arraignment?' He begins to explain at length, but I interrupt.

'No problem.'

'You're very kind. Perhaps then we can take a few moments with what your friend Della Guardia has sent over. What is it you call him?'

'Delay.'

Sandy's consternation is apparent. He cannot figure out the reason for the nickname and he is too gentlemanly to ask me to reveal even the most trivial confidence of the PA's office, with which he is so often a contestant. He removes his coat and calls

158

for coffee. His secretary brings it and a large crystal ashtray for his cigar.

'So,' he says. 'Do we now understand Della Guardia's case?'

'I think I do.'

'Fine, then. Let me hear it. Thirty-second summation, if you please, of Nico's opening statement.'

When I retained Sandy, within three or four hours of that bizarre meeting in Raymond's office, we spent thirty minutes together. He told me what it would cost – a $25,000 retainer, against a fee to be billed at $150 an hour for time out of court and $300 an hour in, the balance, strictly as a courtesy to me, to be returned if there was no indictment; he told me not to talk to anyone about the charges and, in particular, to make no more outraged speeches to prosecutors; he told me to avoid reporters and not to quit my job; he told me this was frightening, reminiscent of the scenes of his childhood in Latin America; he told me that he was confident that with my extraordinary background this entire matter would be favorably resolved. But Sandy Stern, with whom I have done business for better than a decade, against whom I have tried half a dozen cases, and who on matters of gravity, or of little consequence, has always known that he could accept my word – Sandy Stern has never asked me if I did it. He has inquired from time to time about details. He asked me once, quite unceremoniously, whether I'd had 'a physical relationship' with Carolyn, and I told him, without flinching, yes. But Stern has remained far clear of ever putting the ultimate question. In that he is like everybody else. Even Barbara, who evinces by various proclamations a belief in my innocence, has never asked me directly. People tell you it's tough. They cling or, more often, seem visibly repulsed. But nobody has sufficient sand to come out with the only question you know they have in mind.

From Sandy this indirection seems more of his classical manner, the formal presence that lies over him like brocaded drapes. But I know it serves for more. Perhaps he does not ask because he is not certain of the verity of the answer he may get. It is a given of the criminal justice system, an axiom as certain as the laws of gravity, that defendants rarely tell the truth. Cops and prosecutors, defense

lawyers and judges – everybody knows they lie. They lie solemnly;
with sweaty palms and shifty eyes; or, more often, with a look of
schoolboy innocence and an incensed disbelief when their credulity
is assailed. They lie to protect themselves; they lie to protect their
friends. They lie for the fun of it, or because that is the way they
have always been. They lie about big details and small ones, about
who started it, who thought of it, who did it, and who was sorry.
But they lie. It is the defendant's credo. Lie to the cops. Lie to
your lawyer. Lie to the jury that tries your case. If convicted, lie to
your probation officer. Lie to your bunkmate in the pen. Trumpet
your innocence. Leave the dirty bastards out there with a grain of
doubt. Something can always change.

Thus it would be an act contrary to his professional acumen
were Sandy Stern to commit himself to an unreserved faith in
everything I say. Instead, he does not ask. This procedure has one
further virtue. If I were to meet any new evidence by frontally
contradicting what I had told Sandy in the past, legal ethics might
require him to withhold me from the witness stand, where I almost
certainly intend to go. Better to see everything the prosecution
has, to be certain that my recollection, as the lawyers put it, has
been fully 'refreshed,' before Sandy inquires about my version.
Caught in a system where the client is inclined to lie and the
lawyer who seeks his client's confidence may not help him do
that, Stern works in the small open spaces which remain. Most
of all, he desires to make an intelligent presentation. He does
not wish to be misled, or to have his options curbed by rash
declarations that prove to be untrue. As the trial approaches, he
will need to know more. He may ask the question then; and I
certainly will tell him the answer. For the time being, Stern has
found, as usual, the most artful and indefinite means by which
to probe.

'Della Guardia's theory is something like this,' I say. 'Sabich is
obsessed with Polhemus. He's calling her house. Can't let go. He
has to see her. One night, knowing that his wife will be going out
and that he can get to Carolyn on the sneak, he calls up, begs to
see her, and Polhemus finally agrees. She rolls around with him
for auld lang syne, but then something goes wrong. Maybe Sabich

160

is jealous of another relationship. Maybe Carolyn says that this was merely the grand finale. Whatever it is, Sabich wants more than she will give. He blows a gasket. He gives her what-for with some heavy instrument. And decides to make it look like rape. Sabich is a prosecutor. He knows that this way there will be dozens of other suspects. So he ties her up, opens the latches to make it look like somebody slipped in, and then – this is the diabolical part – pulls her diaphragm out of her, so there won't be any evidence of consent. Like all bad guys, of course, he makes a few mistakes. He forgets the drink he had when he came in, the glass he left on the bar. And he does not think – maybe even realize – that the forensic chemist will be able to i.d. the spermicide. But we know he did evil to this woman, because he never revealed – he lied – about his presence on the night of the murder, which is established by all the physical evidence.'

This exposition is eerily comforting to me. The heartless hip analysis of crime is so much a part of my life and my mentation that I cannot make myself sound ruffled or even feel a fragment of concern. The world of crime has its argot, as ruthless as the jazzman's is sweet, and speaking it again I feel I am back among the living, among those who see evil as a familiar if odious phenomenon with which they have to deal, like the scientist studying diseases through his microscope.

I go on.

'That's Nico's theory, something like that. He has to straddle a little bit on the question of premeditation. He might argue that Sabich had it in mind to do her in from minute one, that he chose this night so he had an alibi, in case she refused to build the old fire anew. Maybe Sabich was on a different trip: You can't live if you won't be mine. That'll depend on evidentiary nuances. Probably Nico will give an opening that won't lock him in. But he'll be close to this. How does it sound?'

Sandy looks over his cigar. They are Cuban, he told me a few weeks ago. A former client gets them, he does not ask how. The wrapper, deep brown, burns so cleanly that you can see the leaf veins etched within the ash.

'Plausible,' he says at last. 'Evidence of motive is not strong here. And it is usually critical in a circumstantial case. Nothing ties you to any instrument of violence. The state is further disadvantaged because you were, in essence, a political opponent of Della Guardia – never mind that you did not consider yourself a political employee, a jury will not believe that, and for our purposes should not be told that. There is additional evidence of bad feeling between you and the prosecuting attorney inasmuch as you personally fired him from his post. The importance of these matters, however, could be greatly reduced if the prosecuting attorney himself did not try this case.'

'Forget that,' I say. 'Nico would never move out of the spotlight.'

Stern seems to smile as he draws on the cigar.

'I quite agree. So we will have those advantages. And these factors, which would raise questions in the mind of any reasonable person, will take on large importance in a circumstantial case, from which you and I both know juries are disinclined. Nevertheless, Rusty, we must be honest enough to tell ourselves that the evidence overall is very damaging.'

Sandy does not pause long, but the words, even though I probably would have said as much myself, feel like something driven against my heart. The evidence is very damaging.

'We must probe. It is difficult, of course, and I am sure painful, but now is the time that you must put your fine mind to work on this case, Rusty. You must tell me every flaw, every defect. We must look scrupulously at each piece of evidence, each witness, again and again. Let us not say that any of this hard work will be done tomorrow. Best to begin right now, today. The more deficiencies we find in this circumstantial case, the better our chances, the more Nico must explain, and explain with difficulty. Do not be afraid to be technical. Every point for which Della Guardia cannot account increases your opportunities for acquittal.'

Although I have hardened myself, one word catches me like a blow. Opportunities, I think.

Sandy summons Jamie Kemp to take part in our discussion, as it is bound to suggest various motions for discovery that we will soon be called upon to file. To hold down my expenses, Stern has agreed to allow me to assist in research and investigation, but I must act under his direction. With Kemp, I share the work of the junior lawyer, and I have enjoyed this collaboration more than I had counted on. Kemp has been Stern's associate about a year now. As I get the story, quite some time ago Jamie was a guitarist in a medium-popular rock-and-roll band. They say he went through the whole shot, records and groupies and road shows, and when things went downhill he decamped for Yale Law School. I dealt with him in the PA's office on two or three occasions without incident, but he had a reputation there for being preppie and stuck-up, impressed by his own blond good looks and a lifetime of good fortune. I like him, though he sometimes cannot suppress a little of that Waspy amusement with a world by which, he is convinced, he will never quite be touched.

'First,' says Stern, 'we must file a notice of alibi.' This is a declaration, no questions. We will formally notify the prosecution of our intention to stand by my statement in Raymond's office that I was at home the night Carolyn was murdered. This position deprives me of what, in theory, is probably the best defense – conceding that I saw Carolyn that night for an unrelated reason. That posture would dampen the force of the physical evidence and focus instead on the lack of any proof tying me to the murder. For weeks, I have been expecting some artful effort by Stern to discourage the alibi, and I find myself relieved. Whatever Sandy thinks of what I said, he apparently recognizes that to reverse field now would be too difficult. We would have to conceive an innocent explanation for my eruption on Black Wednesday – why I went out of my way to lie, in outraged tones, to my boss, my friend, and the two top lawyers from the new administration.

Stern pulls the box to him and begins sorting through the documents. He starts from the front, the physical evidence.

'Let us go to the heart of the matter,' says Stern. 'The glass.' Kemp goes out to make copies of the fingerprint report, and the three of us read. The computer people made their findings the day before the election. By then Bolcarro was playing ball with Nico, and so Morano, the police chief, surely was as well. This report must have gone straight to the top and right out to Nico. So Delay probably told the truth himself when he claimed that Wednesday in Horgan's office that he had acquired significant evidence against me during the campaign and chose not to publicize it. Too much of a last-minute mess, I would suppose.

As for the report, it says, in brief, that my right thumb and middle finger have been identified. The other latent present remains unknown. It is not mine; it is not Carolyn's. In all likelihood it belongs to one of the initial onlookers at the scene: the street cops who responded to the call, who always seem to run around touching everything before the homicide dicks arrive; the building manager, who found the body; the paramedics; maybe even a reporter. None the less, it will be one of the difficult stray details for Della Guardia to cope with.

'I would like to look at that glass,' I say. 'It might help me figure some things out.'

Stern points at Kemp and tells him to list a motion for production of physical evidence.

'Also,' I say, 'we want them to produce all the fingerprint reports. They dusted everything in the apartment.'

This one Stern assigns to me. He hands me a pad:

'Motion for production of all scientific examinations: all underlying reports, spectographs, charts, chemical analyses, et cetera, et cetera, you know it better than I do.'

I make the note. Stern has a question.

'You had drinks in Carolyn's apartment, of course, when you were there in the past?'

'Sure,' I say. 'And she wasn't much of a housekeeper. But I think she'd wash a glass once in six months.'

'Yes,' Stern says simply.

We are both grim.

Kemp has another idea.

'I'd like to get a complete inventory of everything in that apartment. Every physical object. Where's the contraceptive jelly or whatever it is that this chemist is saying he finds present? Wouldn't that have been in her medicine cabinet?' He looks to me for confirmation, but I shake my head.

'I don't even remember discussing birth control with Carolyn. I may be male chauvinist of the year, but I never asked her what she was doing.'

Stern is ruminating, temporizing in the air with his cigar.

'Caution here,' he says. 'These are productive thoughts, but we do not want to lead Della Guardia to evidence he has not thought to obtain. Our requests, whatever they are, must be unobtrusive. Remember that everything that the prosecution discovers which favors the defense must be turned over to us. Anything we discuss which might be useful to them will be better left forgotten.' Sandy gives me a sidewise look, quite amused. He enjoys being so candid with a former opponent. Perhaps he is thinking of some specific piece of evidence he kept from me in the past. 'Best we conduct this search ourselves without disclosing our intentions.' He points at Kemp; it is his turn. 'Another motion, then: for an inventory of all items seized from the apartment of the decedent and for an opportunity to conduct a view and inspection of our own. The apartment remains under seal?' he asks me.

'I presume.'

'Also,' says Stern, 'your mention of Carolyn's personal habits leads to this thought. We should subpoena her doctors. No privileges survive her death. Who knows what we might discover? Drugs?'

'Rope burns in the past,' says Kemp.

We all laugh, a grisly moment.

Sandy, decorous as ever, asks if the name of one of Carolyn's doctors is 'known to me.' It is not, but all county employees are covered by Blue Cross. A subpoena to them, I suggest, is bound to uncover a good deal of information, including doctors' names. Stern is pleased by my contribution.

The next group of documents we look at are the phone records from Carolyn's home number and my own, an inch-thick bundle of xeroxed pages with an endless train of 14-digit numbers. I hand the sheets one by one to Stern. From my phone, there are one-minute calls to Carolyn's recorded on 5, 10, and

20 March. When I get to 1 April, I spend a long time looking. I just lay my finger on the number that is recorded there at 7:32 p.m. A two-minute call.

'Carolyn's,' I tell him.

'Ah,' says Stern. 'There must be a commonsense explanation for all of this.' Observing Stern work is like tracking smoke, watching a shadow lengthen. Is it the accent that allows him to lay that perfect subtle stress on the word 'must'? I know my assignment.

He smokes.

'You do what at home, when you babysit?' he asks.

'Work. Read memos, indictments, prosecution packages, briefs.'

'Must you confer with other deputy prosecuting attorneys?'

'Occasionally.'

'Of course,' says Stern. 'Now and then, there is the need to ask a brief question, schedule an appointment. No doubt in all these months of records' – Stern taps them – 'there are a number of such calls to deputy prosecuting attorneys other than Carolyn.'

I nod with each suggestion.

'There are a lot of possibilities,' I say. 'I think Carolyn was working on a big indictment that month. I'll look over some things.'

'Good,' says Stern. He looks back to my MUD sheets for the murder night. His lips are rumpled, his look disturbed.

'No further calls after 7:32,' he says finally, and points.

In other words, no proof that I was home, where I say I was.

'Bad,' I say.

'Bad,' Stern finally says aloud. 'Perhaps someone called you that evening?'

I shake my head. None that I remember. But I know my lines now.

'I'll think about it,' I say. I take back the MUD sheet for 1 April, studying it a moment.

'Can those things be dummied up?' asks Kemp. 'The MUDs?'

I nod.

'I was thinking about that,' I say. 'The PA gets a bunch of

166

xeroxes of the phone company's printouts. If a deputy, or some-body else, wanted to do a job on a defendant, he could make a great cut-and-paste and nobody would know the difference.' I nod again and look at Kemp. 'These things could be faked.'

'And should we pursue that possibility?' asks Stern. Is there some hint of rebuke in his voice? He is studying a thread pulled on his shirt-sleeve, but when his eyes light on mine for the briefest instant, they are penetrating as lasers.

'We might think about that,' I say at last.

'Mmm hmm,' says Stern to himself. He is quite solemn. He points at Kemp to make a note. 'I do not believe we should explore this before the conclusion of the state's evidence. I would not want to see them introduce the fact that we made efforts to challenge the accuracy of these records and failed.' He directs this remark to Kemp, but it is clear to me who is meant to catch its import.

Stern reaches resolutely for another file. He checks his watch, a slim golden Swiss piece. The arraignment is in forty-five minutes. Sandy himself is due back in court sooner. He suggests we talk about the witnesses. I summarize what I have read thus far. I mention that Molto and Della Guardia provided no statements from two of the listed witnesses: my secretary, Eugenia, and Raymond. Sandy absently tells Kemp to list another motion for production. He has put his glasses back on, tortoiseshell half-frames, and continues studying the witness list.

'The secretary,' he says, 'does not trouble me, for reasons I will explain. Horgan, candidly, does.'

I start when Sandy says this.

'Certain witnesses,' Sandy explains, 'Della Guardia must bring to the stand, whatever their disadvantages to him. You know this, of course, Rusty, far better than I. Detective Lipranzer is an example. He was quite candid in his interview with Molto the day after the election and acknowledged that you asked him not to order your home telephone records. That is sufficiently helpful to the prosecution that Lipranzer will be called, notwithstanding the many fine things he will say about you personally. Horgan, on the other hand, is not a witness whom I would think a good prosecutor would ordinarily be eager to see. He will be known to all the jurors, and his credibility is such that it would seem quite risky to call him unless – ' Sandy waits. He picks up his cigar again.

'Unless what?' I ask. 'Unless he is going to be hostile to the defense? I don't believe Raymond Horgan will put the bricks to me. Not after twelve years. Besides, what can he say?'

'It is a matter of tone, not so much as content. I take it that he is going to testify to your statement in his office on the day after the election. One would think that Nico would be better off putting on Ms MacDougall, if he had to accept an unfriendly witness. She at least has not been a local personality for more than a decade. On the other hand, if it appears that Horgan, Della Guardia's political opponent, and your friend and employer for a dozen years, is sympathetic to the prosecution – that could be extremely damaging. That is the kind of courtroom nuance on which you and I both know close cases often turn.'

I look at him squarely, 'I don't believe that.'

'I understand,' he says. 'And you are probably correct. Probably there is something we have missed that will seem obvious when we know Horgan's prospective testimony. None the less –' Sandy thinks. 'Raymond would meet with you?'

'I can't imagine why not.'

'I will call him and see. Where is he now?' Kemp remembers the law firm. About six names. The League of Nations. Every ethnic group is mentioned. O'Grady, Steinberg, Marconi, Slibovich, Jackson, and Jones. Something like that. 'We should plan a meeting for Horgan, you, and me as soon as possible.'

Strangely, this is the first thing Sandy has said that is both entirely unexpected, and whose effect I cannot seem to shake. It is true that I have not heard from Raymond since that day in April that I walked out of his office, but he has had his own concerns: new job, new office. More particularly, he is an experienced criminal defense lawyer and knows how circumscribed our talks would necessarily have to be. His silence I had taken as a professional accommodation. Until now. I wonder if this is not simply some malicious effort by the prosecutors to unsettle me. That would be like Molto.

168

'Why does he need Raymond to testify, if he intends to call Molto?' I ask.

Principally, says Stern, because Molto is, in all likelihood, not going to testify. Della Guardia has referred a number of times to Tommy trying the case. A lawyer is prohibited from being a witness and advocate in the same proceeding. None the less, Sandy reminds Jamie that we ought to file a motion to disqualify Molto, since he is on the witness list. If nothing else, this will promote consternation in the P A's office. And it will force Nico to forswear any use of my statement to Molto. Like me, Sandy considers it unlikely that Nico would really want to offer this in the prosecution's case. As Della Guardia's best friend and chief assistant, Molto would be too easy to impeach. But on the other hand, the statement could be used effectively in cross-examining me. It is best, therefore, to file the motion and force Nico's hand.

Sandy moves ahead. 'This I do not understand.' he says. He holds aloft the statement of the maid who says she saw me on a bus into the city from Nearing on a night near the time Carolyn was murdered. 'What is Della Guardia up to?'

'We only have one car,' I explain. 'I'm sure Molto checked the registrations. Barbara took it that night. So I had to have another way to get to Carolyn. I bet they had a trooper standing out at the bus station in Nearing for a week, looking for someone who could make my picture.'

'This interests me,' Stern says. 'They apparently accept that Barbara indeed left you at home that night. I understand why they would concede that she took the car. There have been too many unfortunate episodes with women around the university for anyone to believe she would be using public transportation at night. But why agree she left at all? No prosecutor would want to argue that the defendant rode a bus to a murder. It does not sound authentic. They must have found nothing with the taxi companies and rent-a-car. I take it that they are looking at records of some kind which confirm Barbara's absence.'

'Probably the log-in sheet at the U.' I say. Nat and I have gone to watch his mother work on the computer on occasion. 'It'll show she used the machine. She signs in when she gets there.'

'Ah,' says Stern.

'What time would that be?' Jamie asks. 'Not late, right? She'll know you were home at the time of the murder – or at least that she left you there, won't she?'

'Absolutely. Her computer time's at eight. She leaves for the U. seven-thirty, twenty-to the latest.'

'And Nat?' asks Sandy. 'When is he in bed?'

'Around then. Most of the time, Barbara gets him down before she goes.'

Kemp asks, 'Does Nat get up a lot or does he sleep soundly?'

'Like a coma,' I say, 'But I'd never leave him alone in the house.'

Stern makes a sound. That is not the kind of thing we will be able to prove.

'None the less,' says Stern, 'these facts are helpful. We are entitled to whatever records they have. That is *Brady* material' – evidence favorable to the defense. 'We must make another motion. Fiery and outraged. A good assignment for you, Rusty.' He smiles, kindly.

I make the note. I tell Sandy there is only one more witness I want to talk about. I point to Robinson's name.

'He's a shrink,' I say. 'I saw him a few times.' Molto, I'm sure, is behind the ugly gesture of naming my former psychiatrist as a potential witness. Tommy is pulling my chain. I used to do things like that to defendants. Make sure they knew I'd been all over their lives. Last month Molto subpoenaed my bank account in Nearing. The president, an old friend of Barbara's deceased father, Dr Bernstein, will not look at me now when I come in. From my checks, no doubt, Molto got Robinson's name.

I am surprised by Stern's reaction to my disclosure.

'Yes, Dr Robinson,' Sandy says. 'He called me right after the return of the indictment. I neglected to mention that.' He was too decorous is what Stern means. 'He had seen my name in the paper as your lawyer. He merely wanted me to know he had been identified and that the police had attempted an interview. He was reluctant to trouble you with this information. At any rate, he told me he refused to make any statement on the grounds of privilege. I reaffirmed that and said we would not waive.'

'We can waive. I don't care,' I say. I don't either. It seems like a minor intrusion, compared to what has taken place in the last few months.

'Your attorney is ordering you to care. Della Guardia and Molto are no doubt hoping we will make a waiver, in the belief that this doctor will testify to your general mental health and the unlikeliness of criminal behaviour.'

'I bet he will.'

'I see I did not make my point,' says Stern. 'I commented before. Evidence of motive here is weak. You summarized Della Guardia's theory very ably, I think. Sabich is obsessed, you said. Sabich is unwilling to let go. Tell me, Rusty. You have looked over Della Guardia's case. Where is the proof here of any prior amorous relationship between the defendant and the decedent? A few telephone calls that can be accounted for by business needs? There is no diary here. No note that came with flowers. No lovers' correspondence. That, I take it, is what your secretary will be called for, to add what she can, which I assume is not very much.'

'Very little,' I say. Sandy is right. I did not see this hole. As a prosecutor, I would never have missed it. But it is harder when you have all the facts. Still, I battle back a lightheaded sensation of hope. I cannot believe that Nico could be weak on this essential. I point at the MUD sheets. 'There are calls to my home from Carolyn's in late October, last year.'

'Yes? And who is to say they are not from Ms Polhemus to you? You had been lawyers on an important case that was tried the month preceding. No doubt there were continuing developments. Bond questions. As I recall, there was a substantial dispute surrounding custody of the boy. What was his name?'

'Wendell McGaffen.'

'Yes Wendell. These are matters to which the chief deputy might have difficulty giving attention in the office.'

'And why did I tell Lipranzer not to get my home phone tolls?'

'More difficult.' Sandy nods. 'But I take it for granted that a person of innocent state of mind would rule himself out as a

171

suspect and prevent a busy detective from wasting his time.' The way he puts things. I take it for granted. Like sleight of hand.

'Mrs Krapotnik?' I ask, alluding to her expected testimony that I was seen around Carolyn's apartment.

'You were on trial together. Matters needed to be discussed. Certainly, if you want to get away from the Kindle County PA's office, a *most* dreary environment, you are not going to go out to Nearing, where you live. No one denies you were in the apartment on occasion. We agree. Your fingerprints are on the glass,' Sandy's smile is Latin, complex. His defense is taking shape, and he is quite persuasive. 'No,' Sandy says. 'Della Guardia cannot call you, of course, or, presumably, your wife. And so he faces difficulties. Tongues no doubt have wagged, Rusty. I am sure half the attorneys in Kindle County now believe that they suspected your affair. But gossip will not be admitted. The prosecution has no witnesses. And thus no proof of motive. I would be more hopeful,' Sandy says, 'were it not for the problem of your testimony.' His eyes, large and dark, deep and serious, briefly cross my own. The problem of my testimony. The problem, he means, of telling the truth. 'But these are questions for the future. Our job, after all, is merely to raise a doubt. And it may be that when Della Guardia concludes his case the jury will be led to wonder if you are not the victim of a miserable coincidence.'

'Or if I was set up.'

Sandy is a reasonable man and judicious. He again acquires his grave look in response to my proposal. He would obviously prefer that there be no illusions between client and counsel. He glances at his watch. It is getting close to show time. I touch his wrist.

'What would you say if I told you that Carolyn seems to have had something to do with a case on which a deputy PA was bribed? And the PA on the case was Tommy Molto?'

Sandy takes a very long time with this, his look tightly drawn.

'Please explain.'

I tell him in a few moments about the B file. These are, I explain, grand-jury secrets. Until now, I have preferred to keep them to myself.

'And your investigation led where?'

'Nowhere. It stopped the day I left.'

'We must find some way to continue. I would suggest an in-vestigator ordinarily. Perhaps you have some other idea.' Sandy puts out his cigar. He grinds the stub down carefully and looks at it an instant reverentially. He sighs, before he stands to put on his coat. 'To attack the prosecutor, Rusty, is a tactic that is almost always pleasing to the client, and seldom convincing to a jury. These matters I mentioned before – your political opposition to Della Guardia, your firing of him – are items that will tarnish him, diminish his credibility. They will help us explain the prosecutor's zeal to accuse on insufficient evidence. But before we venture down the road to actual accusation, we must consider the matter very carefully. Successes by suggesting sinister motives in the state are, as you well know, quite rare.'

'I understand,' I say. 'I wanted you to know.' I tell him.

'Of course. And I appreciate that.'

'It's just,' I tell him, 'that's the way I feel. That it isn't a coincid-ence it lays out this way. I mean,' and now, on sudden impulse, I finally bring myself to say what vestigial pride has so long pre-vented: 'Sandy, I'm innocent.'

Stern reaches over and, as only he could do, pats me on the hand. He has a look of deep, if practiced, sadness. And as I meet this brown-eyed spaniel expression I realize that Alejandro Stern, one of this town's finest defense lawyers, has heard these ardent proclamations of innocence too many times before.

19

At ten minutes to two Jamie and I meet Barbara at the corner of Grand and Filer and advance with her to the courthouse. The press horde is waiting for us on the steps beneath the columns. I know a back entrance through the heating and cooling plant, but I figure I can use that trick only once, and I have had the dismal thought that there may come another day when I am particularly eager to avoid this clawing mass, with their halogen lights, their boom mikes, their shoving and their shouting. For the moment, I am content to push my way through, saying, No comment.

Stanley Rosenberg from Channel 5, splendidly handsome except for particularly prominent front teeth, is the first to reach us. He has left his camera person and sound crew behind and approached me alone, walking beside us. We address each other by first names.

'Any chance you'll do something on camera?'

'None,' I answer.

Kemp already is trying to intervene, but I hold him off as we continue walking.

'If you change your mind, will you promise to call me first?'

'Not now,' Jamie says, and lays his hand on Stanley's sleeve. Stanley to his credit maintains his good humor. He introduces himself and makes his pitch to Kemp instead. Right before the trial, Rosenberg says, a broadcast interview with Rusty would be good for everybody. Stern will never let me make statements to anyone, but Kemp, as we approach the steps and the waiting crowd of cameras, lights, and microphones, says merely, 'We'll think about it.' Stanley remains behind as we start up, Kemp and

I flanking Barbara, more or less boosting her by the elbows as we shove our way through.

'What do you think about the fact that Raymond Horgan is going to testify against you?' Stanley shouts as we are parting.

I pivot quickly. Stanley's bad teeth are fully revealed. He knew he'd get me with that one. Where does that come from, I wonder. Stanley may have made assumptions upon reading the court file where Nico's witness list was filed. But Rosenberg has long-term connections to Raymond, and instinct tells me that he would not use Horgan's name loosely.

The cameras are barred by judicial order inside the courthouse, and as we swing through the brass revolving doors, it is only the print and radio reporters who follow us in a pack, thrusting out their tape recorders and shouting questions to which none of us respond. As we hurry down the corridor toward the elevators, I reach for Barbara's hand, which is around my arm.

'How are you doing?' I ask.

Her look is strained, but she tells me she is fine. Stanley Rosenberg is not as good-looking as he appears on TV, she adds. None of them is, I tell her.

My arraignment is before the Honorable Edgar Mumphrey, chief judge of the Kindle County Superior Court. Ed Mumphrey was leaving the PA's office just about the time that I began. He was regarded with a kind of awe even then, for one reason: he is very rich. His father opened a chain of movie theaters in this town, which he eventually parlayed into hotels and radio stations. Ed naturally has labored to appear immune to his fortune's influence. He was a deputy for almost a decade; then he entered private practice, where he remained for only a year or two before the call came to the bench. He has proved a straight, capable judge, short just enough candlepower to keep him from being regarded as brilliant. He became chief judge last year, an assignment which is primarily administrative, although he hears all arraignments, and negotiates and takes guilty pleas when they are offered in the early stages of proceedings.

I take a seat in Judge Mumphrey's dark, rococo courtroom, in the front row. Barbara is beside me in a fine blue suit. For reasons that baffle me, she has also chosen to wear a hat, from which descends a coarse black mesh, presumably intended to suggest a veil. I think of telling her that the funeral is not yet, but Barbara has never shared the blacker side of my sense of humor. Beside me, sketching madly, are three artists from the local TV stations drawing my profile. Behind them are the reporters and the court buffs, all awaiting my reactions upon first being called a murderer in public.

At two o'clock Nico enters from the cloakroom, with Molto close behind. Delay is without restraint and goes on answering the questions of reporters who followed him into the little side ante-room. He talks to them through the open door. The prosecuting attorney, I think to myself. The fucking PA. Barbara has taken my hand, and with Nico's appearance she grips it a little tighter.

When I first met Nico, a dozen years ago, I recognized him instantly as a smart-ass ethnic kid, familiar to me from high school and the streets, the kind who, over the years, I had self-consciously chosen not to be: savvier than he was smart, boastful, always talking. But with few others to look to, I formed with Nico the sort of fast association of fresh recruits. We went to lunch together. We helped each other with briefs. After our first few years, we drifted, a result of our native differences. Having clerked for the Chief Justice of the State Supreme Court, I was perceived as lawyerly. Nico, like dozens of deputy PA's for decades past, arrived in the office with his political network already thick. I would listen to him on the telephone. He had been a precinct captain in the organization of his cousin, Emilio Tonnetti, a county commissioner who had secured Nico's position, one of the last political hirings Raymond agreed to. Nico knew half the hacks and functionaries in the County Building, and he never stopped buying tickets to the political golf outings and dinners, and making the rounds.

In truth, he proved a better lawyer than was expected. He can write, although he hates to spend time in the library; and he is effective before a jury. His courtroom persona, as I have observed it over the years, is typical of many prosecutors: humorless, relentless, blandly mean. He has a unique intensity which I always illustrate by telling what is known as the Climax story. I told it last week to Sandy and Kemp, when they asked about the last case I tried with Della Guardia.

That was almost eight years ago, right after we had been assigned to the felony courts. We were both hungry for jury work, and therefore we agreed to try a dead-bang loser of a rape case on reassignment from somebody smarter.

'Delay had the complaining witness, Lucille Fallon, on the witness stand,' I told Sandy and Kemp. Lucille, a dark-skinned lady, had been in a bar at four in the afternoon, when she met the defendant. Her husband, on unemployment, was home with the four kids. Lucille got to talking with the defendant, Freddy Mack, and agreed to accept a ride home. Freddy was a four-time loser, with a prior rape and an assault – which the jury of course never heard anything about – and he got a little overeager and took a straight edge from his pocket, thereby helping himself to what by all appearances was already going to come his way. Hal Lerner had the defendant, and he knocked every black out of the box, so there were a dozen middle-aged white people looking over this Negro lady who'd gotten a little rougher treatment than she wanted when she went out to wander.

Nico and I had spent hours attempting to prepare Lucille for the testimony, with no visible result. She looked terrible, a frumpy fat lady in a tight dress, rambling on about this awful thing that happened to her. Her husband was in the front row and she laid it on thick, making up an entirely new version of events right in the courtroom. Now she had met Freddy as he was emerging from the tavern and asked her for directions. She was already heading for devastation on cross when Nico finally began to elicit testimony about The Act.

And what did Mr Mack do then, Mrs Fallon?
He done it.
What was that, ma'am?
What he been sayin he do.
Did he have intercourse with you, Mrs Fallon?
Yes, sir, he done.
Did he place his sex organ inside yours?

Uh huh.

And where was the razor?

Right here. Right here on my throat. Pressin right there, I thought every time I breathe he goin to slice me open.

All right. ma'am. Nico was about to move on, when I, seated at counsel table, handed him a note. That's right, said Nico, I forgot. Did he have a climax, ma'am?

Sir?

Did he have a climax?

No, sir. He be drivin a Ford Fairlane.

Delay never smiled. Judge Farragut was laughing so hard that he hid under the bench, and one of the jurors, literally, rolled out of his seat. Nico never even quivered. 'And after they came back NG,' I told Jamie and Sandy, 'he swore he would never try a case with me again. He said that because I had not managed to keep a straight face, I gave the jury the feeling it wasn't a serious case.'

Nico is looking happy enough today. The radiance of power hangs around him. He is wearing his carnation again, and he could not possibly carry himself more erect. He looks trim and well turned out in a new dark suit. There is an attractive vitality to him, as he moves back and forth, trading shots with the reporters, mixing answers to serious questions with personal remarks. One thing is for sure, I think, the son of a bitch is enjoying himself at my expense. He is this season's media hero, the man who solved the murder of the year. You cannot pick up a local paper without seeing his face. Twice last week I saw columns suggesting that Nico might try out for the mayoral race, two years down the line. Nico responded by pledging his fealty to Bolcarro, but you wonder where those columns came from.

None the less, Stern has insisted that Nico has endeavoured to handle the case fairly. He has talked to the press far more than either of us believes is appropriate, but not all of the leaks have come from him, or even Tommy Molto. The police department is beyond its meager capacities for restraint with a case like this. Nico has been candid with Stern about the progress of the investigation; he shared the physical evidence as it developed, and he gave me notice of the indictment. He agreed that I was not a flight risk, and will consent to entry of a signature bond. Most important, perhaps, he has thus far done me the favor of not adding an additional charge of obstruction of justice.

It was Stern, during one of our early conferences, who first pointed out the jeopardy I was in were I to be indicted for willfully concealing facts material to the investigation.

'A jury, Rusty, is very likely to believe you were in that apartment that night, and that at the very least you should have spoken up about it and certainly not lied in your meeting with Horgan and Molto and Della Guardia and MacDougall. Your conversation with Detective Lipranzer concerning the MUD sheets from your home is also very damaging.'

Stern was matter-of-fact about all this. His cigar was stuck in the corner of his mouth as he spoke. Did his eye flicker up for just an instant? He is the most subtle man I've met. Somehow I knew why the topic had been raised. Should he go to Nico with that deal? That was what he was asking. I could not get more than three years for obstruction of justice. I would be out in eighteen months. I would have my son again before he's grown. In five years I could probably regain my license to practice law.

I have not lost my power to reason. But I cannot overcome the emotional inertia. I want back the life I had. No less. I want this not to be. I do not want to be marked as long as I live. To plead would be the same as conceding to an unneeded amputation. Worse.

No plea, I told Sandy.

No, of course not. Of course. He looked at me with disbelief. He had not raised the subject.

In the weeks that followed, we assumed that Della Guardia would include this surer count in the indictment. In moments of weird buoyancy, particularly in the last weeks, when it became clear that charges were being readied, I fantasized that the indictment might be for obstruction alone. Instead, the indictment charged only murder. There are tactical reasons that a prosecutor might make that choice. An obstruction count would offer a tempting – and to a prosecutor, unsatisfying – compromise for a jury inclined to find me guilty but uneasy with the circumstantial nature of Nico's case. But on the day the indictment was returned, Sandy gave me what I found a surprising account of Nico's decision.

'I have spent a good deal of time, of course, speaking with Nico lately,' Sandy told me. 'He speaks of you and Barbara with some feeling. He has told me on two or three occasions stories of your early days together in the office. Briefs he says you wrote for him. Evenings that he enjoyed with the two of you while he was married. I must say, Rusty, that he seems sincere. Molto is a zealot. He hates every person he prosecutes. But about Nico I am not so sure. I believe, Rusty, that he has been deeply affected by this case and that he made this choice as a matter of fairness. He has decided that it would be irresponsible to put an end to your professional life simply because you were indiscreet, for whatever reason, and to whatever degree. If you are guilty of this murder, then you must be punished, he thinks. Otherwise, he is content to let you go. And I for one applaud him for that. I believe,' said the lawyer whom I have thus far paid $25,000 to defend me, 'that is the correct approach.'

'Criminal Case 86-1246,' calls out Alvin, Judge Mumphrey's handsome black docket clerk. My stomach sinks and I head up toward the podium. Jamie is behind me. Judge Mumphrey, who entered only a moment ago, is getting settled on the bench. The cynics sometimes explain Ed's ascension to chief judge as a function of his good looks. He was an elected judiciary's concession to the media age, someone whom voters would think of with comfort when they faced the judge's retention ballot. Ed's appearance is wonderfully judicial, with fine silver hair drawn straight back from the brow and features regular and yet sharp enough to be stern. He is asked a couple times each year to pose for one of the bar journals in some piece of advertising.

Della Guardia ends up standing beside me. Molto is a few feet behind. As good as Nico looks, Tommy is a disheveled mess. His vest, absurd by itself in July, has ridden up on his substantial belly and his shirt-sleeves stick too far out of his jacket. His hair had not been combed. Now that I've seen Molto, the impulse to call him a twerp, which I thought I would have to stifle, has passed. Instead, I seek to look Nico in the eye. He nods.

'Rusty,' he says simply.

'Delay,' I answer. When I look down toward his waist, I see that he has covertly offered his hand.

I do not have a chance to test the full extent of my charity. Kemp has caught hold of my coat sleeve and jerks it violently to pull me aside. He comes to stand between Della Guardia and me. We both know that I do not have to be told not to talk to the prosecutors.

Judge Mumphrey from the walnut bench looks down and smiles at me circumspectly before he speaks. I appreciate the recognition.

'This is Criminal Case 86-1246. Let me ask counsel to identify themselves for the record.'

'Your Honor, I am Nico Della Guardia, on behalf of the people of the state. With me is Chief Deputy District Attorney Thomas Molto.'

Funny, the things that get you. I cannot suppress the briefest sound when I hear my title with Molto's name. Kemp jerks my sleeve again.

'Quentin Kemp, Your Honor, of Alejandro Stern, PC, on behalf of the defendant, Rožat K. Sabich. I would request leave, Your Honor, to file our appearance.'

Jamie's motion is allowed, and the court records now officially indicate that Stern and Co are my lawyers. Jamie then moves on.

'Your Honor, the defendant is present in court. We would acknowledge receipt of Indictment 86-1246 and waive formal reading. In behalf of Mr Sabich, Your Honor, we would ask the court to enter a plea of not guilty to the charge.'

'Plea of not guilty to the indictment,' repeats Judge Mumphrey, making a note on the court record. Bail is set by agreement as a $50,000 signature bond. 'Is there a request from either party for a pre-trial conference?' This is the plea-bargaining session, usually an automatic, since it helps both sides buy time. Delay starts to speak, but Kemp interrupts.

'Your Honor, such a meeting would be an unnecessary waste of the court's time.' He looks down at his legal pad for the words that Sandy wrote. When Kemp gets outside, he will read the same speech again live for the TV Minicam teams. 'The charges in this case are very grave, and they are entirely false. The reputation of one of the city's finest public servants and attorneys has been impugned and, perhaps, destroyed with no basis in fact. In the truest sense of the words, justice in this case must be swift, and we ask the court therefore to set an immediate trial date.'

The rhetoric is splendid, but tactics of course govern this demand. Sandy has emphasized to me that a quick disposition will avoid interminable strain on my shattered emotions. But disordered though I may be, I recognize the fundamental rationale. Time is with the prosecutor in this case. Delay's principal evidence will not deteriorate. My fingerprints will not lose their memory. The MUD records will not die. With time the PA's case can only become stronger. A witness from the scene might appear. There may be some account of what happened to the murder weapon.

Kemp's request is a significant departure from form, since most defendants view delay as a second-best alternative to acquittal. Our demand seems to catch Nico and Molto short. Again, Della Guardia starts to speak, but Judge Mumphrey interrupts. For whatever reason, he has heard enough.

'The defendant has waived pre-trial conference. The matter will therefore be set over immediately for trial. Mr Clerk,' he says, 'please draw a name.' About five years ago, after a scandal in the clerk's office, the last chief judge, Foley, solicited suggestions on a method to ensure that the selection of a trial judge for a lawsuit was completely random. I came up with the idea that the draw be made in court, in front of everybody. The proposal – put forth of course in Horgan's name – was immediately adopted, and I believe was the touchstone for Raymond's belief that I had executive ability. Now wooden plaques, each bearing the name of a judge, are spun inside a closed cage, borrowed from a bingo game. Alvin, the clerk, rolls the bones, as they are known. He pulls the first into the opening.

'Judge Lyttle,' he says. Larren Lyttle. Raymond's old partner, the defense lawyer's dream. I am lightheaded. Kemp reaches back and with no other movement squeezes my hand. Molto actually groans. I am pleased to see that up on the bench Judge Mumphrey for an instant seems to smile.

'The case will be set down to Judge Lyttle's docket for motions and trial. Defendant's motions to be filed in fourteen days, the prosecuting attorney to respond according to Judge Lyttle's order.' Judge Mumphrey picks up his gavel. He is about to move on, but looks down at Nico for a moment. 'Mr Della Guardia, I should have interrupted Mr Kemp, but I suppose this case is likely to inspire many speeches by the time that it concludes. I do not mean to endorse what he said. But he is correct when he observes that these are very serious charges. Against a lawyer who I think we all know has served this court with distinction for many years. Let me say to you, sir, simply that I, like all other citizens of this county, hope that in this case that justice will be done – and has been done.' Ed Mumphrey nods again to me, and the next case is called.

Della Guardia leaves as he came, through the cloakroom exit. Kemp is straining to maintain a straight face. Jamie puts his pad in his briefcase and watches Nico go.

'He walks pretty well, doesn't he,' asks Jamie, 'with all that sticking out his behind?'

20

'I take it,' Barbara says, 'that you're very pleased about Larren.'
We are on the highway now, finally free of the downtown traffic.
Barbara is behind the wheel. We have learned in recent weeks that
my distraction is such that the world is not safe when I drive.
There is a primitive relief with the cameras and the clamor behind
us. The press pack followed us from the courthouse, down the
street, snapping pictures, the huge video cameras lurching toward
us like some monster's eyes. We walked slowly. Try, Stern urged
us earlier, to look relaxed. We left Kemp at a corner two blocks
on. If every day goes like this one, he said, Nico won't get past
opening statement. Jamie by nature is a cheerful soul, but
somehow his bonhomie conjured a shadow. Every day will not be
like this one. Grimmer moments are ahead. I shook his hand and
told him he was a pro. Barbara kissed him on the cheek.

'Larren is a good draw,' I say, 'the best probably.' I hesitate
only because of Raymond. Neither he nor Judge Lyttle would
ever communicate outside of court about the case, but the presence
of the judge's best friend as a witness is bound to have some
impact, one way or the other, depending on the balance of
Raymond's sympathies. I touch Barbara's hand, on the wheel. 'I
appreciate your being there.'

'I don't mind,' she says, 'Really. It was very interesting,' she
adds, sincere as ever in her curiosity, 'if you don't consider the
circumstances.'

Mine is what the lawyers call a 'high-profile case' – the press
attention will continue to be intense. In that situation, communication with the eventual jurors begins long before they come

to court for jury service. Nico has been winning the press battles so far. I have to do what I can to project a positive image. Since I am charged, in essence, with murder and adultery, it is important that the public believe that my wife has not lost faith in me. Barbara's attendance at every event the media will cover is critical. Stern insisted that she come downtown so that he could explain this to her face to face. Given her distaste for public occasions, her narrow suspicions of outsiders, I expected her to regard this as a taxing assignment. But she has not resisted. Her support in the last two months has been unfailing. While she continues to view me as the victim of my own follies – this time for having ever been enamored of public life and cutthroat politics – she recognizes that things have passed well beyond the stage where I am being served right. She regularly expresses confidence in my vindication and, without a word from me, presented me with a $50,000 cashier's check to cover Sandy's retainer and the later fees, which was drawn from a trust which her father left exclusively in her control. She has listened with fast attention to hours of table conversation in which I lambaste Nico and Molto or describe the intricacies of little strategies that Stern has devised. In the evenings, when I am apt to recede to a withdrawn vacancy, she will come to stroke my hand. She has taken on some of my suffering. Although she evinces bravery, I know that there are moments, alone, when she has cried.

Not only the stress of these extraordinary events, but the radical alteration of my schedule has added a new tempo to our relations. I journey to the library; draft notes for my defense; root pointlessly in the garden. But we are alone together now, much of the time. With the summer, Barbara has few responsibilities at the U. and we linger over breakfast after I drop Nat off for camp. At lunch, I go out and pick greens for our salad. And a new sexual languor has moved softly into our relationship. 'I was thinking we should do it,' she announced one afternoon from the sofa, where she was reclining with obscure reading material and Belgian chocolates. Thus, an afternoon encounter has become part of our new routine. It is easiest for her to come crouched over me, hunkered down. The birds sing outside the windows; the daylight seeps beyond the edges of the bedroom blinds. Barbara rolls around with my pin driven deep inside her, that muscular vortex at work, her eyes closed but rolling, her face otherwise serene as her hue increases and she works toward the point of release.

Barbara is an imaginative, athletic lover; it was not sensual deprivation which drove me to Carolyn. I cannot complain about hang-ups or fetishes or what Barbara will not do. Even in the worst of our times, even amid the upheaval that followed my idiotic confessions last winter, sex was not abandoned. We are of the revolutionary generation. We spoke openly of sexuality. When we were young we tended it like a magic lantern, and we continue to find its place. We have become expert in the physiognomy of pleasure, the nodes to press, the points to massage. Barbara, a woman of the eighties, would find it a further insult to do without.

For the time being, the clinical aspect which inhabited our relations for months is gone. But even now I find something desperate and sad in Barbara's loving. There are distances yet left to cross. I lie in bed in the sweet afternoons while Barbara dozes, the midday suburban quiet soothing and beguiling after years of downtown racket, and consider the mystery to me that is my wife.

Even at the zenith of my passion for Carolyn, I gave no thought to leaving. If my marriage to Barbara at times has been equivocal, our family life has not. We both dote relentlessly on Nat. I grew up knowing that other families lived differently from mine. They spoke across the dinner table; they went together to the movies and soda fountains. I saw them running, playing ball in the open fields of the Public Forest. I yearned. They shared a life. Our existence as a family, as parents and child, is the single aspiration of my childhood that I feel I have fulfilled, the only wound of that time I have healed.

And yet to pretend that Nathaniel is our sole salvation is too cynical. Pessimistic. False. Even in the grimmest period, we both respond to the inner commandments that find some value here. My wife is an attractive woman – extremely so. She minds the mirror carefully, assuming certain predetermined angles to be sure she remains intact; her bustline still peaked; the waist, notwithstanding pregnancy, still girlish; her dark, precise features not yet losing fineness in any gathering of adipose, or slackening from beneath the jaw. She could certainly find suitors; she chooses not to. She is an able woman. And on her father's death, $100,000 was placed in trust for her, so that it is not need which keeps her from departing. For better or for worse, there must be truth in the bitter words that she will sometimes hurl at me in the heat of quarrels: that I am the only one, the one person, save Nat, whom she has ever loved.

In the clement periods, as now, Barbara's devotion is apt to be extreme. She is eager to have me absorb her attentions. I become her ambassador to the outside world, bringing back to Nearing observations and stories. When I am on trial, I will frequently arrive home at 11 p.m. or midnight to find Barbara waiting in her housecoat, my dinner warm. We sit together and she listens with her intense, abstracted curiosity to what has taken place that day, much like a thirties child before the radio. The dishes clank; I speak with my mouth full, and Barbara laughs and marvels about the witnesses, the cops, the lawyers whom she sees only through me.

And for me? What is there? Certainly I value loyalty and commitment, kindness and attention, when they are shown. Her instants of selfless love, so focused upon me, are balm for my abraded ego. But it would be phony and hollow if I were to claim that there are not also moments when I despise her. The injured son of an angry man, I cannot fully master my vulnerabilities to her blackish moods. In her fits of lacerating sarcasm, I feel my hands twitch with the impulse toward strangulation. In response to these periods, I have taught myself to manifest an indifference, which, over time, has begun to become real. We stumble into a sickening cycle, a tug of war in which we are each maneuvering for position by forever stepping back.

But those times are far off now, and almost forgiven. We wait instead on the brink of discovery. What is it that holds me? Some yearning. In the languid afternoons, I seem almost to seize it, even while the doors and windows of my soul are thrown open to a fundamental gratitude. We have never been without momentary eruptions; Barbara is incapable of long-term serenity. But we have also made our trips to the brightest spots and highest places; with Barbara Bernstein I certainly have known the finest moments of my life. The first years were innocent, spirited, full of that clamorous passion and a sense of mystery that exceeds what can be described: I *long* at times, in transported recollection I pine, I perish with a groping sensation – I am like some misbegotten thing left at the end of science-fiction adventures which reels about with stumps out-stretched, beckoning toward the creatures of which it was once one: Let me in again! Unwork time.

When I was in the law school at the U., Barbara was teaching. We lived in a two-and-a-half-room apartment, ancient, vermin-ridden, in scandalous disrepair. The radiators shot out streams of boiling water in the middle of the winter; the mice and roaches claimed as their own domain any cabinet space below the level of the sink. Only because it was considered student quarters did this home escape categorization as what was then called slum housing. Our landlords were two Greeks, a husband and a wife, one sicker than the other. They lived a floor above and across the courtyard. We could hear his emphysemic eruptions in any season. Her problem was arthritis and degenerative diseases of the heart. I dreaded bringing up the rent each month, because of the odor of decay, a dense, foreign, rotting smell, something like cabbage, that came into the air as soon as their door opened. But it was all that we could afford. With my tuition deducted from a starting teacher's salary, we approached the bureaucratic standards for recognized poverty.

We had a standing joke, that we were so poor that the only form of entertainment we could afford was fucking. This humor was more in the nature of shared embarrassment, for we knew that we verged on the excessive. Those were sensuous years. The end of the week was something I would drag myself toward. We made our own kind of Sabbath: dinner alone, a bottle of wine, and then lovely, long, ambling amours. We could start anywhere around the apartment, and move, in growing deshabille, across the rug and toward the bedroom. This would sometimes go on for more than an hour, me aching and priapic, and my dark little beauty, her breasts tipped in ecstasy, as we lolled and meandered over one another. And it was one night like this, as I led Barbara toward the final steps into the bedroom, that I saw our blind was open and, above, our two elderly neighbors, their faces toward the window, were watching. There was something so starstruck and innocent about their expressions that in recollection they appear to me like startled animals: does, rabbits: a look of uncomprehending, roundeyed wonder. I never suspected them of having spied for long, a feeling which in no way eased my shame. I stood there with my erect member at that instant in Barbara's palm, which was wet with almond oil. Barbara saw them, too, I know. Because as I drew back and started toward the blind she stopped me. She touched my hand; and then she took hold of me again. 'Don't look,' she said, 'don't look,' she murmured, her breath sweet and warm on my face. 'They're almost gone.'

21

One week after my arraignment, Sandy and I stand together in the reception area of the law firm in which Raymond Horgan has been a partner since May. A very classy affair. The floor is parquet, covered by one of the largest Persian rugs I have ever seen, rose hues on a vibrant navy field. Lots of expensive-looking abstract art is on the walls, and glass-and-chrome end tables are set at each corner of the room, with copies of *Forbes* and *The Wall Street Journal* laid out in ranks. A sweet blonde who probably gets an extra couple of grand a year for being so good-looking is behind a fancy rosewood desk, taking names.

Sandy has hold of my lapel in the lightest way, instructing me in a murmur. The young lawyers who hustle by in their shirt-sleeves probably cannot even see his lips move. I am not to hold a discussion, Sandy says. He will ask the questions. My presence is intended as he puts it, merely as a stimulant. Above all, he says, I am to remain collected, whatever the climate of our reception.

'Do you know something?' I ask.

'One hears things,' Sandy says. 'Speculation is pointless when we will so soon know answers firsthand.' Sandy, in fact, hears many things. A good defense lawyer has an intricate network. Clients bring information. Reporters. Sometimes there are cops who are friends. Not to mention other defense lawyers. When I was prosecutor, the defense bar seemed to be a kind of tribe, always on their tom-toms whenever there was any piece of news that they could properly communicate. Sandy had told me that Della Guardia subpoenaed Horgan to the grand jury right after Nico took office and that Raymond tried to resist on grounds of executive privilege. Sandy knows this, he has said, from an excellent source. Given this skirmishing, I would expect continuing hostility between Raymond and Nico, but Sandy's reaction when he saw Raymond's name on the witness list implies other knowledge. Sandy, of course, would never betray the confidence of whoever it is who gave him a notion of Raymond's intentions.

Horgan's secretary comes out to retrieve us, and halfway to his office, Raymond himself is there. He is in his shirt-sleeves, without his coat.

'Sandy. Rusty.' He claps me once briefly on the shoulder as he shakes my hand. He has put on more weight, and his gut is straining against the lower buttons on his shirt. 'Have you fellas ever been up here?'

Raymond takes us on a tour. With the incentives of the tax code, the law firms and corporations have become the new Versailles. Raymond tells us about the artwork, names I know he has learned only from magazines. Stella. Johns. Rauschenberg. 'I especially like this piece,' he says. Squiggles and squares. In a conference room, there is a thirty-foot table milled from a single piece of green malachite.

Sandy asks about Raymond's practice. Mostly federal work so far, Raymond says, which he thinks is a good thing. He has a grand jury going great guns in Cleveland. His client sold parachutes to the Defense Department; they contain defective rope. 'A purely inadvertent oversight,' Raymond tells us, with a knavish smile. 'One hundred ten thousand pieces.'

Finally, we arrive at Raymond's office. They have given him a corner and he has the fancy views, west and south. The Wall of Respect has been reinstalled here with a few additions. A panoramic shot of the dais at Raymond's last inauguration is at the center now. With forty others, I am there, way off on the right.

I had not noticed a young man until Raymond introduces him. Peter something. An associate. Peter has a pad and pen. Peter is the prover. He will cover Raymond in the event there is later controversy about what he said.

'So what can I do you for?' Raymond asks, after he has called out for coffee.

'First,' says Sandy, 'Rusty and I both want to thank you for taking the time to meet. You are very gracious.'

Raymond waves this off. 'What can I say?' A non sequitur of sorts. I think he means to suggest he wants to help without saying that.

'I think it best, I am sure you understand,' says Stern, 'that Rusty not take part in our conversation. I hope you do not mind if he simply listens.' As he says this, Sandy glances toward Peter, who has raised his pad and is already relentlessly making notes.

'Sure, it's your ball game.' Raymond starts fussing on his desk, brushing at dust neither I – nor he – can see. 'I'm surprised you wanted him to come. But that's up to you guys.'

Sandy flexes his brow characteristically, one of those Latin gestures reflecting something too delicate or imprecise to say.

'So what do you want me to tell you?' Raymond again asks.

'We find your name on Della Guardia's witness list. That, of course, motivates our visit.'

'Sure,' says Raymond, and throws up his hands. 'You know how it is, Alejandro. The guy sends you a party invitation, you gotta go to the ball.' I have seen this bluff, hearty manner from Raymond a thousand times before. He gestures too much; his broad features are always tending toward a smile. His eyes seldom meet those of the person to whom he is speaking. This was how he negotiated with defense lawyers. I'm a great guy, but I just can't help. When his visitors left, Raymond would often call them names.

'So you will be appearing by subpoena?'

'You bet.'

'I see. We received no statement. Do I take it that you have not spoken to the prosecutors?'

'No, I've talked to them a little bit. You know, I talk to you, I talk to them. We had some troubles at first. Mike Duke had to work some things out. I've sat down with Tom Molto a few times now. Shit, more than a few times. But you know, it's one on one. I haven't signed a statement or anything like that.' A bad sign. Very bad. Panic and anger both are rising in me, but I try to stave them off. Raymond is getting star-witness treatment. No formal statements to minimize the inconsistencies that would endanger him on cross-examination. Multiple sessions with the prosecutor, because he is so important to the case.

'You mention troubles,' says Sandy. 'There is no question of immunity, I take it?'

'Shit no. Nothing like that. It's just that some of these guys around here, my new partners – This whole thing makes them nervous. It could be a little embarrassing for me, too.' He laughs. 'That's a hell of a way to start out. I'm here three days and I get a grand-jury subpoena. I bet Solly Weiss loved that,' he says, referring to the firm's managing partner.

Sandy is silent. He has his hat and briefcase positioned decorously in the center of his lap. He studies Horgan, without apology, searching him. The man is volunteering nothing. Stern becomes like this at moments, suddenly abandons all his comfortable civility and seems to sink beneath the surface of things.

'And what have you told them?' Sandy finally asks quietly. He is very still.

'My partners?'

'Certainly not. I was wondering what we might expect in terms of your testimony. You've been on this side of things before.' Sandy subsides into his more familiar tone, gentle and indirect. When he asked what Raymond told them, a second ago, it was like a flash of light suddenly reflected. His mettle was at once obvious and fully summoned.

'Well, you know, I don't want to get into a word-for-word.' He nods in the direction of the young man taking notes.

'Of course not,' Sandy says. 'Topics. Areas. Whatever you feel you can comfortably tell. It is very difficult from the outside even to guess sometimes what a witness might be called to discuss. You know this yourself, so well.'

Sandy is probing for something that I do not completely understand. We could get up now and leave if we were merely here to accomplish the previously announced purpose of our visit. We know where Raymond Horgan stands. He is not a friend.

'I'm going to testify about Rusty's conduct of the investigation. How he told me he'd be interested in handling it.

193

And a later conversation we had, about aspects of my personal life – '

'Just a second.' I can take no more. 'How *I* was interested in handling the investigation? Raymond, you asked me to take the case.'

'There was a conversation between us.'

From the corner of my eye, I note Stern raising a hand, but I fix on Horgan.

'Raymond, you *asked* me. You told me that you were busy with the campaign, it had to be in the best hands, you couldn't worry about somebody else lousing this up.'

'That's possible.'

'That's what happened.'

I look to Stern, seeking support. He is sitting back in his chair, staring at me. He is simply furious.

'I'm sorry,' I say quietly.

Raymond goes on, oblivious to my exchange with my lawyer.

'I don't remember that, Rusty. Maybe that's what happened – as you said, I was busy with the campaign. But the way I remember it, we had a conversation, a day, two days before the funeral, and at the end of that conversation we had agreed that you'd be handling the case, and the idea that you handle it, it's my feeling that that was more your idea than mine; I was receptive, I admit that, but I remember some surprise about the way things ended up.'

'Raymond – What are you trying to do to me, Raymond?' I look at Sandy, who has his eyes closed. 'Can't I just ask him that?'

But I have finally pushed things beyond the crest; Raymond is traveling full speed downhill on his own momentum. He leans as far as he can across his desk.

'What am I trying to do to you?' He repeats the question twice, growing flushed. 'What were *you* trying to do to *me*, Rusty? What the hell are your fingerprints doing all over that goddamn glass? What's all this bullshit of sitting in my office asking about who I'm fucking, and never then, when it would have been friendly, or two weeks before, when I assigned you to that investigation – which, as I remember, I bawled you out a couple times for not pushing – ' He turns abruptly to Sandy and points. 'That's something else I'm going to testify to,' he tells Sandy, then looks back at me. ' – Never, two weeks before, when it was the professional thing to have done, *never* at any time do you tell me you were dicking the same gal. I've spent a whole long time on that conversation, Rusty, asking myself what the hell you were doing there? What *were* you doing?'

This scene is more than Peter the associate can handle. He has stopped writing entirely and is just watching us. Stern points at Peter.

'Under the circumstances, I am advising my client to make no response. Clearly he would like to.'

'So that's what I'm going to testify to,' Raymond tells Sandy. He stands up and ticks the points off on his fingers. 'That he wanted the case. That I had to chew his ass repeatedly to move it. That he was more interested in finding out who else was fucking Carolyn than who had murdered her. And that when push finally came to shove, he sat in my office and gave us all a bunch of happy horseshit that he'd been nowhere near Carolyn's apartment that night. That's what I'll testify to. And I'll be goddamned pleased to do it.'

'Very well, Raymond,' says Sandy. He picks up his hat, a gray felt homburg, off the chair on which he laid it in the midst of his efforts to quiet me.

I stare directly at Horgan. He looks back.

'Nico Della Guardia was honest about the fact that he was out to screw me,' Horgan says.

Sandy steps between us. He hauls me to my feet, both hands on my arm.

'Enough,' he declares.

'Son of a bitch,' I say as we are moving briskly ahead of Peter, on our way out, 'Son of a bitch.'

'We know where we stand,' Stern says quietly. As we enter the reception area, he tells me in the barest sibilance to please hush. This enforced silence sits in my mouth like a bit. As the elevator sinks, I find myself with a bursting desperation to speak, and I grab Sandy's arm as we reach the ground floor.

'What is it with him?'

'He is a very angry man.' Stern walks determinedly through the marble lobby.

'I see that. Has Nico convinced him that I'm guilty?'

'Probably. Certainly he thinks you could have been a good deal more cautious, particularly on his behalf.'

'I wasn't a faithful servant?'

Sandy makes another of his Latin movements; hands, eyes, brow. He has other matters on his mind. As he walks, he cocks a grave eye in my direction.

'I had no idea that Horgan had an affair with Carolyn. Or that you had conversed with him on that subject.'

'I didn't remember the conversation.'

'No doubt.' says Stern in a tone which implies that he doubts me a good deal. 'Well, I think Della Guardia will be able to use that to his advantage. When was it that this relationship took place between Raymond and Carolyn?'

'Right after she stopped seeing me.'

Sandy stops. He makes no effort to mask his pain. He talks to himself an instant in his native tongue.

'Well, Nico is certainly coming closer to a motive.'

'But he's still some distance,' I say hopefully. He still cannot prove the principal relationship between Carolyn and me.

'Some,' Sandy tells me. There is a deliberate flatness in his expression. He is clearly quite put out with me, both for my performance upstairs and for keeping so significant a detail from him. We will have to speak at length, he says. Right now he has a court call. He puts his homburg on and ventures into the blazing heat without glancing back at me.

In the lobby I feel instantly bereft. So many emotions are surging that there is a kind of dizziness. Most of all, there is caustic shame for my own stupidity. After all these years, I still failed to recognize how these events would impact on Raymond Horgan, although now the trajectory of his emotions seems as predictable as a hyperbolic curve. Raymond Horgan is a public man. He has lived to make a reputation. He said he was not a pol, but he has a pol's affliction: he thrives on acclamation, he yearns for the good opinion of everyone. He does not care about my guilt or innocence. He is devastated by his own disgrace. His own chief deputy indicted for murder. The investigation, which he let me run, sabotaged right before his face. And he will have to sit upon the witness stand and broadcast his own indiscretions. There will be tavern jokes for years about being a deputy P A *under* Raymond Horgan. Between his conduct and mine, the office will sound more active than a Roman bath. Worst of all is the fact that the murder took Raymond from the life he really loved; it changed the course of the election; it sent him here to his glass-and-steel cage. What infuriates Raymond, inspires his rage, is not really that I committed this crime. It is that he believes he was intended to be another victim. He said as much when he finally let things loose. I screwed him. I killed Carolyn to bring him down. And I succeeded. Horgan thinks he has the whole thing figured out. And he has clearly planned his vengeance.

I finally leave the building. The heat is intense; the sun is blinding. I feel instantly unsteady on my feet. Compulsively, I try to calculate the one thousand subtle impacts on the trial of Raymond's testimony and his evident hostility to me, but that soon gives way. Ideas come and go erratically. I see my father's face. I cannot make things connect. After all these weeks, after all of this, I feel that I am finally going to go to pieces, and I find, stunningly, that as I turn about in the street, I am praying, a habit of my childhood, when I would try to cover my bets with a God in whom I knew I did not much believe.

And now, dear God, I think, dear God in whom I do not believe, I pray to you to stop this, for I am deathly frightened. Dear God, I smell my fear, with an odor as distinct as ozone on the air after a lightning flash. I feel fear so palpably it has a color, an oozing fiery red, and I feel it pitifully in my bones, which ache. My pain is so extreme that I can barely move down this hot avenue, and for a moment cannot, as my backbone bows with fear, as if a smelted rod, red-hot and livid, had been laid there. Dear God, dear God, I am in agony and fear, and whatever I may have done to make you bring this down upon me, release me, please, I pray, release me. Release me. Dear God in whom I do not believe, dear God, let me go free.

22

In the United States, the prosecution in a criminal case may not appeal the outcome. This is a constitutional principle, declared by the US Supreme Court. An American prosecutor, alone among all the advocates who stand before the bench – among the sophisticates and hacks, the collection lawyers in their rayon suits, the bankruptcy moguls, the divorce-court screamers, the gold-chained dope lawyers or the smooth likes of Sandy Stern, the big-firm 'litigators' who perform even routine courtroom tasks in pairs – the prosecutor alone is without right to seek review of a judge's trial rulings. Whatever the majesty of his office, the power of the policemen he commands, the bias in his favor jurors always bring to court, a prosecutor is often under a continuing duty to endure in silence various forms of judicial abuse.

Nowhere, while I was a PA, was that obligation more regularly or onerously borne than in the courtroom of Judge Larren Lyttle. He is sly and learned and indisposed by the experience of a lifetime to the state's point of view. The habits of twenty years as a defense lawyer, in which he regularly manhandled and belittled prosecutors and police, have never left him on the bench. And beyond that, he has a black man's authentic education in the countless ways that prosecutorial discretion can be used to arrogantly excuse unreasoning caprice. The random and complete injustices which he witnessed on the streets have become a kind of emotional encyclopedia for him, informing each decision that is made almost reflexively against the state. After two or three years, Raymond gave up coming to court to argue. The two of them would bellow at each other as they must have done in their old law office. Then

Larren would bang his gavel, more adamant than ever, and declare a recess so that he and Raymond could make up back in chambers and plan to have a drink.

Judge Lyttle is on the bench, receiving status reports on other cases, when Stern and I arrive. It is always as if there is a spotlight. He is the only person you see – handsome, mercurial, extraordinarily prepossessing. Judge Lyttle is a big human being, six foot four or five and broad across. His first fame came as a football and basketball hero at the U., where he went on scholarship. He has a full head of medium-length African hair, most of it gone gray, a big face, enormous hands, a princely style of oratory, with a large voice, full across all the male ranges. His intelligence, which is mighty, is also somehow transmitted by his presence. Some say Larren sees his future on the federal bench; others guess that his real goal is to succeed Albright Williamson as the congressman from the district north of the river, whenever it is that Williamson ceases defying age and his cardiologist's predictions. Whatever his inclinations, Larren is someone whose prospects and personal powers make him in these parts a man of capital importance.

We were summoned here yesterday morning by a phone call from the judge's docket clerk. With the filing of the defendant's pre-trial motions two days ago, His Honor desires to hold a status hearing on my case. I suspect that he is going to rule on some of our requests, and perhaps discuss a trial date.

Sandy and I wait in silence. Kemp has stayed behind. The three of us spent yesterday together and I told them everything I knew about each witness Nico has listed for the case. Stern's questions remained precise and limited. He still did not ask me if I screwed Carolyn that night, or was there for any other reason, or whether, notwithstanding my prior proclamations, I own any instrument that might conform to the crack atop her head.

I spend these moments, familiar downtime in a courtroom lawyer's life, looking about. The reporters are all here again, although the sketchers have stayed home. Judge Lyttle, politic in the ways a judge can be, treats reporters well. There is a table set aside for them against the western wall and he always gives the press room a call before issuing any decision of import. The courtroom where the course of the rest of my life will be determined is a jewel. The jury box is set off by a walnut rail and descending baubles, round spheres of beautifully grained wood. The witness stand is similarly constructed and abuts the judge's bench, which is well elevated and covered by a walnut canopy supported by two red marble pillars. The docket clerk, the bailiff, and the court reporter (whose job is to write down every word spoken in open court) are in a well before the bench. A few feet in front of them, two tables have been placed, finely hewn, again in darker walnut, with carefully turned legs. These tables for the lawyers on trial sit perpendicular to the bench. The prosecution, by tradition, will sit nearer the jury.

When all the other business is finished, our case is called. Some of the reporters creep up to the defense table to better hear the proceedings, and the assembly of lawyers – and me – convene before the bench. Stern, Molto, and Nico state their names. Sandy notes my presence. Tommy shoots me a little grin. I bet he's heard about our meeting with Raymond last week.

'Gentlemen,' Judge Lyttle begins, 'I asked you here because I thought we could do a little work to move this case along. I have some motions from the defendant and I'm prepared to rule on them, unless the prosecutors are particularly anxious to make a response.'

Tommy speaks in Nico's ear.

'Only to the motion to disqualify Mr Molto,' Nico says.

Naturally, I think. An entire office working for him, and he's still gun-shy about putting things on paper.

Larren says that he will leave the motion to disqualify to the end, although he has some thoughts about it.

'Now the first motion,' Larren says, with the stack of paper right before him, 'is a motion to set an immediate trial date. And I've thought about this, and as the prosecutors know, the *Rodriguez* case pled earlier this morning, so I will be free for twelve trial days beginning three weeks from today.' Larren looks to his calendar. '18 August. Mr Stern, can you be here?'

This is an extraordinary development. We had expected nothing sooner than the fall. Sandy will have to set everything else aside – but he barely hesitates.

'With pleasure, Your Honor.'

'And the prosecution?'

Nico at once begins to back and fill. He has a vacation planned. So does Mr Molto. There is still evidence to be developed. With that, Vesuvius erupts.

'No, no,' says Judge Lyttle, 'I will hear none of that. No, sir, Mr Delay Guardia.' He pronounces Nico's name that way, as if he is trying to incorporate the nickname. With Larren, you can never tell. 'These charges here – These charges are the most serious crime – What else could you do to Mr Sabich? A prosecutor his entire professional life, and you bring charges like this. We all know why Mr Stern wants a quick trial. There're no secrets here. We've all been tryin cases for a good part of our lives. Mr Stern has looked at the evidence you have provided by way of discovery, Mr Delay Guardia, and he doesn't think you have much of a case. He may not be right. I wouldn't know about that. But if you come into this courtroom chargin a man with a crime, you better be ready to prove it. Right now. Don't be tellin me about what's going to develop. You can't leave this hangin over Mr Sabich like that old sword of Damocles. No, sir,' Larren says again. 'We're gonna have a trial three weeks from today.'

My blood is ice. Without excusing myself, I take a seat at the head of the defense table. Stern glances back momentarily and seems to smile.

'Now, what else have we got?' says Larren. Just for an instant, as he looks about, there is a private smile. He can never quite hide his satisfaction with himself for trashing a prosecutor. He passes quickly on our motions for production. Every one is granted, as they should be. Tommy complains a little bit about the motion to produce the glass. He reminds the court that the prosecution has the burden of proving a chain of custody – that is, that the glass was never out of the state's hands – an impossibility if the glass is turned over to the defense.

'Well, what is it that the defense wants to do with this glass?'

I stand immediately. 'I want to take a look at it, Your Honor.'

Sandy gives me a corrosive glance. With his hand on my forearm, he puts me back down in my seat. I will have to learn: it is not my place to speak.

'Fine,' says Larren, 'Mr Sabich wants to look at the glass. That's all. He's got that right. The prosecution has got to show him the evidence. You know, I've looked over the discovery and I understand why Mr Sabich might want to look very carefully at that glass. So that motion will be allowed.' Larren points at me. It is the first real notice he has taken of my presence. 'And by the way now, Mr Sabich, you of course will be heard through counsel, but if it's your desire to speak yourself, you have that right. At any time. When we have our conferences in chambers or during the proceedings, you have every right to attend. I want you to know that. We all know Mr Sabich is a fine trial lawyer, one of the finest trial lawyers we have in these parts, and I'm sure he'll be curious about what we're doin from time to time.'

I look at Sandy, who nods, before I answer. I thank the court. I tell him I will listen. My lawyer will speak.

'Very well,' the judge says. But his eyes hold the light of a warmth that I have never seen from him in court. I am a defendant now, in his special custody. Like a chieftain or a Mafia don, he owes me some protection while I am in his domain. 'Next we have this motion to get into the apartment.'

Molto and Nico confer.

'No objection,' Nico says, 'so long as a police officer is present.'

To that, Sandy instantly objects. A few moments of typical courtroom skirmishing follow. Everybody knows what's going on. The prosecutors want to figure out what we are looking for. On the other hand, they have a valid point. Any disturbance of the contents of Carolyn's apartment will hinder their ability to make further use of the scene for evidentiary purposes.

'Well, you have pictures by now,' Larren says. 'Every time I have one of these cases, I wonder if the prosecutors haven't formed some kind of alliance with Kodak.' The reporters all laugh and Larren himself smiles. He is like that. He loves to entertain. He directs his gavel at Della Guardia. 'You can have a trooper by the door so you can be sure that no members of the defense remove anything, but I'm not gonna let you snoop on what they're lookin at. The prosecution's had four months to look all over that apartment,' Larren says, including in his count the month when I was head of the investigative team. 'I think the defense is entitled to a few minutes in peace. Mr Stern, you draft an appropriate order and I'll sign it. And let's be sure that you give notice in advance to Ms Polhemus's administrator or executor or whoever represents her estate, so they know what the court intends to allow.

'Now, let's talk about this motion to disqualify Mr Molto.' This is our request to prevent Tommy Molto from acting as one of the trial lawyers on the case, because Nico has said Molto may be a witness.

Nico starts right in. To disqualify one of the prosecutors with three weeks to trial would be an onerous burden. Impossible. The state could never be ready. I do not know if Nico is looking for more time, or trying to defeat the motion. He is probably not sure himself.

'Well, look now, Mr Della Guardia, I'm not the person who told you to put Mr Molto on your witness list,' Judge Lyttle says. 'I cannot imagine how you thought you were going to proceed with a prosecutor who might be a witness. A lawyer may not be an advocate and a witness in the same proceeding. We've been doin business in our courts the same way for about four hundred years now. And I do not intend to change it for this trial, no matter how important it is to any of the participants, no matter how many reporters show up from *Time* or *Newsweek* or any place else.' Judge Lyttle pauses and squints toward the reporters' gallery, as if he only now had noticed them there.

'But let me say this –' Larren stands up, and wanders behind the bench. Five feet off the ground to start with, he speaks from an enormous height. 'Now, I take it, Mr Delay Guardia, that the statement you are speaking of is the one where Mr Sabich responds to Mr Molto's accusation of murder by saying, "You're right."'

'"Yeah, you're right,"' says Nico.

Larren accepts the correction, bowing his large head.

'All right. Now, the state has not offered the statement yet. However, you've indicated your intentions and Mr Stern has made

203

his motion for that reason. But this is what occurs to me. I really am not sure that statement will come into evidence. Mr Stern hasn't made any objection yet. He would rather see Mr Molto disqualified first. But I imagine, Mr Delay Guardia, that when we get there Mr Stern is gonna say that this statement is not relevant.' This is one of Larren's favorite means of assisting the defense. He predicts objections he is likely to hear. Some of them – like this one – are clearly going to come. Others never would have occurred to defense counsel. In either event, when formally made, the objections foretold inevitably succeed.

'Your Honor,' says Nico, 'the man admitted the crime.'

'Oh, Mr Delay Guardia,' says Judge Lyttle. 'Really! You see, that is my point. You tell a man he's engaged in wrongdoing and he says, "Yeah, you're right." Everyone recognizes that's facetious. We all are familiar with that. Now, in my neighborhood, had Mr Sabich come from those parts, he would have said, "Yo' momma."'

There is broad laughter in the courtroom. Larren has scored again. He sits on the bench, laughing himself.

'But you know, in Mr Sabich's part of town, I would think people say, "Yeah, you're right," and what they mean is "You are wrong."' Pausing. 'To be polite.'

More laughter.

'Your Honor,' Nico says, 'isn't that a question for the jury?'

'On the contrary, Mr Delay Guardia, that is initially a question for the court. I have to be convinced this evidence is relevant. That it makes the proposition for which it is offered more probable. Now, I am not ruling yet, but, sir, unless you are a good deal more persuasive than you have been so far, I expect that you will find me ruling that this evidence is not relevant. And you might want to keep that in mind in addressing Mr Stern's motion, because if you're not going to be offering that evidence, or relying on it in cross-examination of the defendant, why then, I'd have to deny the defendant's motion.'

Larren smiles. Nico, of course, is screwed. The judge has as much as told him that the statement will not be admitted. Nico's choice is to lose Molto and make a futile effort to introduce the evidence, or to keep Tommy and abandon the proof. It is really no choice at all for him – better to take half a loaf. My statement to Molto has just disappeared from this case.

Molto approaches the podium. 'Judge –' he says, and gets no further. Larren interrupts. His face drains of all good humor.

'Now, Mr Molto, I will not listen to you address the admissibility of your own testimony. Maybe you can convince me that that time-honored rule prohibiting a lawyer from bein a witness in a case he tries shouldn't be applied here, but until you do, I will not hear further from you, sir.'

Larren closes business quickly. He says he will see us for trial on 18 August. With one more glance toward the reporters, he leaves the bench.

Molto is still standing there, his look of disgruntlement plain. Tommy's always had a bad habit for a trial lawyer of allowing his dissatisfaction to be evident. But Judge Lyttle and he have been going at each other now for many years. I may not have recalled Carolyn's service in the North Branch, but I could never have forgotten Larren and Molto. Their disputes were notorious. Exiled by Bolcarro to that judicial Siberia, Judge Lyttle applied his own rough justice. The cops were guilty of harassment, unless proven otherwise. Molto, beleaguered and bitterly unhappy, used to claim that the pimps and junkies and sneak thieves, some of whom made daily appearances in Larren's courtroom, would rise to applaud him when he assumed the bench for the morning call. The police despised Judge Lyttle. They invented racial epithets that showed the same imagination which put humankind upon the moon. Larren had been downtown for years by the time I finished the Night Saints investigation and Lionel Kenneally was still complaining whenever he heard Larren's name. There was one story Kenneally must have told me ten times about a battery case, brought by a cop who claimed that the defendant had resisted arrest. The cop, named Manos, said he and the defendant had gotten into a tussle shortly after the defendant called the cop a name.

What name? Larren asked him.

Here in court, said Manos, I'd rather not say, Judge.

Why, Officer, are you afraid you might offend those present? Larren gestured toward the forward benches, where the defendants on the morning call were seated, an assemblage of hookers, pickpockets, and junkie thieves. Speak freely, Judge Lyttle said.

He called me motherfucker, Your Honor.

From the benches there were whistles, catcalls, lots of joviality. Larren gaveled silence, but he was laughing, too.

Why, Officer, said Larren again, still smiling, didn't you know that is a term of endearment in our community?

The folks on the benches went wild: black-power salutes and a frenzy of stroking palms. Manos took all of this in silence. A minute later, when Molto rested, Larren directed a verdict for defense.

'And the great part,' Kenneally told me, 'is that Manos comes up to the bench then, stands there with his hat in his hand, and says to Lyttle, sweet as a school kid, "Thank you, motherfucker," before he walks away.'

I have heard this story from two other people. They agree on the final exchange. But both of them swear the last remark came from the bench.

23

Every week, usually on Wednesday night, the phone rings. Even before he starts I know who it is. I can hear him pulling on his goddamn cigarette. I am not supposed to talk to him. He is not supposed to talk to me. We both have our orders. He does not say his name.

How you doin? he asks.

Hanging in.

You guys okay?

Getting by.

This is a tough thing.

Tell me about it.

He laughs. No. I guess I don't gotta tell you. Well, you need anything? Anything I can do?

Not much. You're good to call.

Yeah, I am, but I figure you'll be runnin the joint again soon. I'm coverin my bets.

I know you are. What about you? How you doing?

Good. Survivin.

Schmidt still on your case? I ask, referring to his boss.

Hey, always. That's the guy. Screw him, I figure.

How tough are they making it on you?

These cupcakes? Come on.

But I know Lip is having a hard time. Mac, who has also called on a couple of occasions, told me they pulled him back into McGrath Hall, took him off the Special Command in the PA's office. Schmidt has got him chained to a desk, signing off on other dicks' reports. That is bound to drive him crazy. But Lip always was doing a high-wire act with the department. He had to keep dazzling the crowds to hold off his detractors. Plenty of people were waiting to see him fall. Now he has. Cops will always figure that Lipranzer knew and let me hide it. That's just the way they think.

I'll call next week, he always promises at the end of every conversation.

And he does, faithfully. Our talks do not seem to vary more than a line or two. About a month along, when it was becoming clear to everyone that this was serious, he offered money. I understand these kinda things can be expensive, he said. You know a bohunk's always got some dough salted away.

I told him Barbara had come through in the pinch. He made a remark about marrying a Jewish girl.

This week, when the phone rings, I have been waiting.

'How you doin?' he asks.

'Hanging in,' I say.

Barbara picks it up, just in time to hear that exchange.

'It's for me, Barb,' I say.

Unaware of our arrangement, she says simply, 'Hi, Lip,' and puts the phone back down.

'So what's goin on?'

'We're going to trial now,' I say. 'Three weeks. Less.'

'Yeah, I know. I seen the papers.' We both hang on that for a while. There is nothing Dan Lipranzer can do about his testimony. It is going to break my back, both of us know it, and there is no choice. He answered Molto's question the day after the election, before Lip could guess the score; and I tend to think that the answers would have been the same, even if Lip knew the consequences. What happened happened. That's the way he would explain it to himself.

'So you gettin ready?' he asks.

'We're working real hard. Stern's amazing. He really is. He's the best by a time and a half.'

'That's what they say.' When he pauses, I recognize the click of his lighter. 'Well, okay. Anything you need?'

'There is,' I say. If he hadn't asked, I wasn't going to say anything. That's the deal I made with myself.

'Shoot,' he tells me.

'I've got to find this guy Leon. Leon Wells. You know, the guy who's supposed to have paid off the PA in the North Branch? The defendant in the court file you dug up, the one with Carolyn and Molto? Stern hired some skip tracer and he came back with a complete zip. As far as he can tell, no such guy even exists. I don't know any other way to go. I can't have a heart-to-heart with Tommy Molto.'

This private investigator was named Ned Berman. Sandy said that he was good, but he seemed to have no idea what he was doing. I gave him copies of the pages of the court file. Three days later he was back saying he could not help. The North Branch, man, in those days, he said, it was a real zoo. I wish you luck. I really do. You couldn't tell out there who was doing what to who.

Lipranzer takes some time with this request, more than I expected. But I know the problem. If the department finds out he helped in the preparation of my defense, they will can him. Insubordination. Disloyalty. Fifteen years plus, and his pension, in the dumper.

'I wouldn't ask, you know I wouldn't. But I think it might really matter.'

'How?' he asks. 'You thinkin Tommy's kinky on this? Set you up to keep you from lookin?' I can tell that even though he is trying not make judgments, Lipranzer regards that notion as farfetched.

'I don't know what to say. You want to hear me say I think it's possible? I do. And whether he's sandbagging me or not, if we could get that kind of stuff out, it would look real bad for him. Something like that can really catch a jury's attention.'

He is silent again.

'After I testify,' he says. 'You know, those guys have got their eye on me. And I don't want anybody askin me any questions where I got to give the wrong answer under oath. A lot of people would like to see that. When I get off the stand, they'll ease up. I'll work on it then. Hard. Okay?'

It is not okay. It is likely to be too late. But I've asked for much too much already.

'That's great. You're a pal. I mean that.'

'I figure you'll be runnin the joint again soon,' he says. He says, 'I'm just coverin my bets.'

Tee ball, again. The summer league. In this circuit, mercifully, there are no standings, for the Stingers are only marginally improved. In the heavy air of the August evenings, the fly balls still seem to mystify our players. They fall with the unhindered downward velocity of rain. The girls respond better to tutoring. They throw and bat with increasing skill. but the boys for the most part seem unreachable. There is no telling them about the merit of a measured swing. Each eight-year-old male comes to the plate with dreams of violent magic in his bat. He envisions home runs and wicked liners. For the boys, there is no point in the repetitive instructions to keep the ball on the ground.

Nat, surprisingly, is something of an exception. This summer he is changing, beginning to acquire some worldly focus. He seems newly aware of his powers, and of the fact that people regard the manner in which you do things as a sign of character. When he takes his turn at bat and hits, I watch the way his eyes lift as he comes around first base before he sprints for second. It is not enough to say that he is merely imitating the players on TV, because what is significant is that he noticed in the first place. He is starting to care about style. Barbara says he seems more particular about his clothes. I would be more delighted by all of this were I not wary about the motives for this sudden maturation. He has not reached and developed so much as he has been plucked by the heels from his dreaminess. Nathaniel has turned his attention to the world, I suspect, because he knows that it has caused so much trouble for his father.

After the game, we head home alone. No one has been so heartless as to suggest we skip the picnic, but it is for the best. We attended once after the indictment, and the time passed so fitfully, with such sudden ponderous silences arising at the mention of the most ordinary topics – work to which I do not go; TV detective shows that turn on predicaments like mine – that I knew we could not return. These men are generous enough to accept my presence among themselves. The risk I pose is for the kids. We all must think about the months ahead, the impossibility there would be of explaining where I'd gone – and what I did. It is unfair to hobble these splendid evenings with the omen of evil. Instead, Nat and I depart with a friendly wave. I carry the bat, the glove. He goes along stomping out dandelions.

From Nathaniel, there are no words of complaint. I am pathetically touched by this, by my son's loyalty. God only knows what mayhem his friends are wreaking on him. No grownup can fully imagine the smirking wisecracks, the casual viciousness he bears. And yet he refused to desert me, the vessel from which this pain has poured. He does not dote. But he is with me. He pulls me to my feet from the sofa to work with him on the slider; he accompanies me at night when I venture out to get the paper and a gallon of milk. He walks beside me through the small woods between our subdivision and the Nearing village green. He shows no fear.

'Are you scared?' I ask suddenly tonight as we are walking.

'You mean scared you won't get off?' The trial looms so near, so large, that even my eight-year-old knows at once what I must mean.

'Yes.'

'Naw.'

'Why not?'

'I'm not, that's all. It's just a bunch of junk, right?' He squints up at me, from beneath the bill of his cockeyed baseball cap.

'In a manner of speaking.'

'They'll have this trial, and you'll tell what really happened, and that'll be the end of it. That's what Mom says.'

Oh, bursting, bursting heart: that's what his mom says. I put my arm around my son, more amazed than ever by his faith in her. I cannot imagine the lengthy therapeutic sessions between mother and child in which she has pitched him up to this level of support. It is a miracle which Barbara alone could have achieved. As a family, we are bound together by this symmetry: in the world, I love Nat most, and he adores his mother. Even at this scrappy age, full of the furious energy of a person of eight, he softens for her as no one else. She alone is allowed to hold him at length; and they enjoy a special sympathy, communion, a dependence that goes deeper even than the unsounded depths of mother and child. He is more like her than me, high-strung and full of her driving intelligence, those dark and private moods. She equals his devotion. He is never out of her imagination. I believe her when she says she could never wrest from herself the same emotion for another child.

Neither of them parts from the other comfortably. Last summer Barbara spent four days in Detroit, visiting a college friend, Yetta Graver, who she discovered is now a professor of mathematics. Barbara called twice a day. And Nat was like a running sore, crabby, miserable. The only way I could quiet him for bed was by imagining for him precisely what his mother and Yetta were doing at that moment.

They are in a quiet restaurant, I would tell him. Each of them is eating fish. It is boiled with very little butter. They each have had a glass of wine. At dessert they will break down and eat something they find too tempting.

Pie? asked Nat.

Pie, I said.

My son, the one I always dreamed of, fell asleep thinking of his mother eating sweets.

24

'Hi,' Marty Polhemus says.

'Hi,' I answer. As I came off the landing and caught my first glimpse of the figure and the long hair, I thought it was Kemp, who I'm supposed to meet here. Instead, I find this boy, who I have not even thought about for months. We stand alone in the hallway outside Carolyn's apartment looking at one another. Marty extends his hand and shakes mine firmly. He has no obvious reluctance, almost as if he is pleased to see me. 'I didn't expect to see you,' I finally say, casting about for some way to ask why he is here.

From his shirt pocket, he pulls a copy of Judge Lyttle's order allowing us to inspect the premises. 'I got this,' says Marty.

'Oh, I get it now,' I say out loud. 'That was only a formality.' The judge ordered us to notify the lawyer for the estate, a former PA named Jack Buckley. Jack apparently sent the notice on to the boy. 'The idea was just to let you object if you mind us going in and looking at some of Carolyn's things. You didn't have to be here.'

'That's okay.' This boy sort of shucks and bows as he talks. Back and forth. He shows no sign of leaving.

I try to make conversation, ask what he is up to. 'Last time we talked you were planning to flunk out and go back home.'

'I did,' he says, without ceremony. 'Actually, I got like suspended. I flunked physics. And I made a D in English. I was pretty sure I was going to flunk that, too. I went home six weeks ago. I just drove back here yesterday to get together all my junk.'

I apologize and explain that from his presence I assumed that things had worked out.

'Well, they did. Work out. I mean, so far as I'm concerned.'

'How'd your father take it?'

He shrugs.

'He wasn't real happy. About the D especially. That like hurt his feelings. But he said I had a tough year. I'll work for a while and go back.' Marty looks around at nothing in particular. 'So anyway, when I got that thing, I thought I'd like to come by and see what it was all about.'

The psychologists have a term, 'inappropriate.' That is this kid. Just sort of shooting the breeze outside the apartment where his mother was killed with the guy who everybody thinks did it. For a second, I wonder if he even knows what's going on. But the caption was right on the notice: PEOPLE VERSUS SABICH. And he could not have missed the buildup to the indictment in the papers. He has not been gone that long.

I do not get a chance to probe further, because Kemp comes along then. I can hear him on the stairs. He is arguing, and when he turns the corner off the landing I see with whom – Tom Glendenning, a big cop I never much liked. Glendenning is a white man's white man. Lots of ethnic and racial cracks. Not kidding around either. His whole sensibility revolves around the fact that he was born white and is now a cop. He treats everybody else like they're intruders. No doubt he'll be just as happy to view me that way. The more there are, the better Tom feels. Kemp is explaining that Glendenning may not enter while we view the apartment, and Glendenning is saying that's not what he understands from Molto. Finally, they agree that Glendenning will go downstairs and use the phone. While he's gone I introduce Kemp to Marty Polhemus.

'You're right,' Glendenning says when he comes back. 'That judge entered such an order.' The way he says 'that,' you know what he's thinking.

Kemp rolls his eyes. He is a good lawyer but still awfully Ivy League. He will not hesitate to let people know when he regards them as fools.

A large phosphorescent-orange notice with an adhesive backing has been applied to the door of Carolyn's apartment. It states that this is a crime scene, sealed by order of the Superior Court of Kindle County, and that entry is forbidden. The notice overlaps the threshold so that the door cannot be opened. The locks have been filled with plastic blocks. Glendenning cuts the notice with a razor, but it takes him some time to clear the locks. When he finishes, he produces Carolyn's key ring from his pocket. It has a large red-and-white evidence tag on it. There is a door handle lock, and a dead bolt. As I told Lipranzer a long time ago, Carolyn did not fool around.

With the keys in the lower lock, Glendenning turns and, without a word, frisks Kemp and me, then Marty. This will prevent us from planting anything. I show him a pad of paper I have in my hand. He asks for our wallets. Kemp starts to object, but I motion him to be quiet. Again, without a word, Glendenning does the same to Marty, who already has his wallet in his hand.

'Jeez,' says Marty. 'Look at all this stuff. What am I ever going to do with it?' He just wanders in ahead of Kemp and me. I pass a look with Jamie. Neither of us knows if we have the authority to keep him out, or if there is any reason to bother. Glendenning calls in after him.

'Hey there. Don't touch anything. Nothing. Just them can touch. All right?' Marty seems to nod. He drifts through the living room toward the windows, apparently to check the view.

The air in here is stale and heavy, used up and burned out by the summer heat. Something somewhere in here may be rotting; there is a faint smell. Although the temperature outside is moderate today, the apartment, with the windows sealed, never cooled after last week's intense heat. It must be close to 85 degrees.

I never believed in ghosts, but it is unsettling to be back. I feel a little curl of strange sensation working its way down from the bottom of my spine. The apartment seems oddly settled, especially since everything has been left largely as it was found. The table and mauve seating piece are still overturned. On the light oak floor, just off the kitchen, an outline of Carolyn's body has been chalked. But everything else seems to have acquired some added density. Beside the sofa, on another glass table, a little inlaid box remains which I had purchased for Carolyn. She had admired it at

Morton's the day I walked over there with her during the McGaffen trial. One of the red dragons on her Chinese screen assesses me with its fiery eye. God, I think. God, did I ever get myself in trouble.

Kemp motions to me. He is going to start looking about. He hands me a pair of plastic gloves, loose ones like Baggies with fingers. There's no real need for this, but Stern insisted. Better not to be fighting about fingerprints Tommy Molto claims they discovered long before.

I stop a minute by the bar. It's on the wall directly by the kitchen. I thought I could see what I'm looking for from the police photographs of the scene, but I want to be certain. I stand three feet from the glassware and count the tumblers lined up on a towel. It is on one of the glasses of this set that my prints have been identified. There are twelve of them here. I count them twice to be sure.

Jamie comes beside me. He whispers, 'Where in the hell do we look?'

He wants to see whether there are accessories on hand used by Carolyn for birth control.

'There's a john over that way,' I say quietly. 'Medicine cabinet and vanity.'

I tell him I will check the bedroom. I look first inside her closet. Her smell is on everything; I recognize the clothes I saw her wear. These sights stir mild sensation, buffeting against something that wants this all suppressed. I don't know if it is an impulse to be clinical or the sense – which I always previously seemed to check at the door here – of what is properly forbidden. I move on to her drawers.

Her bedside table, a chubby-looking piece with clubbed Queen Anne feet, holds the telephone. This is as likely a spot as any, but when I open the single drawer I see nothing but her panty hose. I push them around and find a phone directory, a skinny volume covered in light brown calf's leather. The coppers always miss something. I can't resist. I check under *S*. Nothing. Then I think of *R*. Yes. At least I made the book. My work and home numbers are listed. I graze a minute. Horgan is here. Molto is not listed by name, but there is somebody called *TM*, which is probably him. I realize I should see about her doctors. *D* is it. I write the names down and put the paper in my pocket. Outside I hear a stirring. For some reason my first thought is that it is Glendenning, who has decided to ignore the dark-skinned judge and snoop. I flip the pages on the book to protect what I have found, but when the figure passes by the door, it is only Marty wandering. He looks in and waves. The page I turned is *L*. 'Larren,' it says right at the top. There are three numbers listed. Well, I think. That must have been a cozy group out in the North Branch. Everybody's here. Then I think again. Not quite. I check *N* and *D*, even *G*. Nico never made it. I tuck the book back in under the panty hose.

Marty is lurking at the bedroom door.

'Pretty strange, huh?'

That it is. I nod sadly. He tells me that he is going to wait outside. I try to let him know that he is free to leave, but the kid is dense and doesn't get the hint.

When I find Kemp, he is going through the living room.

'There's nothing here,' he tells me. 'No foam, no cream. I don't even find a case for a diaphragm. Am I missing something? Do women hide that stuff?'

'Not that I know of. Barbara keeps hers in the top drawer of the dresser. I wouldn't have any ideas about anyone else.'

'Well, if the chemist says contraceptive cream is present, and it's not seized from the apartment,' Kemp says, 'you tell me where it's at.'

'I guess I took it,' I say, 'when I grabbed the diaphragm.'

With both Kemp and Stern, I have fallen into this habit, speculating in the first person on what Nico will say I did. Jamie, especially, finds it amusing.

'Why would you do that?'

I consider for a moment. 'Maybe it would hide the fact that I took the diaphragm.'

'That doesn't make sense. It's supposed to be rape. What difference does it make what the hell she did when she *wanted* to have sex?'

'I guess I wasn't thinking clearly. If I had been, I wouldn't have left the glass on the bar.'

Kemp smiles. He likes the byplay, fast words.

'This helps,' he says. 'There's no way around it. I want to get hold of Berman,' he says, referring to the PI. 'He should search himself, so he can testify about it. He'll be available in about an hour. Wait until Glendenning hears he has to wait. He'll blow a gut.'

The four of us meet outside the apartment and watch Glendenning lock the door. He pats each one of us down again. Glendenning, as Kemp predicted, refuses to wait for Berman. Kemp tells him that he has to, the court order gives us access for the day.

'I don't take orders from any rock 'n' roll defense lawyer,' says Glendenning. Even when I was on his side, I thought this guy was all charm.

'Well, let's go see the judge, then,' Kemp says. Jamie got Glendenning's number quick. The copper looks to the ceiling like this is the most ridiculous thing he's ever heard, but by now he's trapped. He and Kemp pound down the stairway, exchanging words. I am left with Marty Polhemus.

'Nice guy, huh?' I ask Marty.

He asks me, in all seriousness, 'Which one?'

'I was talking about the policeman.'

'He seemed all right. He said that what's-his-name, Mr Kemp, used to be in the Galactics.' When I confirm that, the boy predictably says 'Wow.' Then he goes silent. He still seems to be waiting for something.

'I talked to them, you know. The cops.'

'Did you?' I am thinking about the glassware by the bar.

'They asked me about you, you know? About when you came out to see me.'

'Well, that's their job.'

'Yeah, they wanted to know if you like said anything about your relationship with her, I mean with Carolyn. You know?'

I have to exert control to avoid a reflex to pivot. I had forgotten. I had forgotten that I told this goddamned kid. That is Nico's

218

evidence, that is how he's going to prove up the affair. A thick bilious feeling cuts deep in my throat.

'They asked me a couple of times, you know. I said – I mean, I thought we had a real talk, you know?'

'Sure,' I say.

'And I told them that you didn't say anything about that.'

I look at the boy.

'Okay?' he asks.

I am, of course, supposed to remind him to tell the truth.

'Sure,' I say again.

'I don't think you're the guy who killed her.'

'I appreciate that.'

'It's like karma,' he says. 'It isn't right.'

I smile. I lift my hand to direct him to the landing, and just like that it hits me. It's like running into a wall, the recognition and the panic. I am so frightened that my legs begin to give out, actually buckle, and I reach for the railing. You fool, I think, you fool. He's wired. He is wearing a tape recorder. Nico and Molto wired him up. That is what he's doing here, that's why he does not seem right. He isn't. He follows us into the apartment and watches everything we do, then gets me out here to suborn him. And I've just convicted myself. I'm gone. I feel that I am going to faint. I falter again, but this time I turn backward.

Marty extends his hand. 'What is it?'

When I look at him I know I'm crazy. Absurd. He is dressed for the season, a tight T-shirt and shorts. Not even a belt. Nobody can hide equipment under that. I watched Glendenning frisk him. And it's not there in his eyes either. All I see is this spaced-out kid, kindly, timid, terribly lost.

I have suddenly sweated through my shirt. I am wrung out now and weak. My pulse is beating far up in my arms.

'I'm okay,' I tell him, but Marty takes my elbow anyway as we start down the stairs. 'It's the place,' I say. 'It does bad things to me.'

25

Three a.m. When I awake my heart is racing and cool traces of sweat are abrading my neck, so that in the idiocy of sleep I am trying to loosen my collar. I grope; then lie back. My breath is short, and my heartbeat thunders intermittently in the ear against the pillow. My dream is still clear to me: my mother's face in agony; that worn cadaverous image as she neared the end, and worse, her look of lost, unspeaking terror.

When my mother became sick, and quickly died, she was in the most peaceful period of her adult life. She and my father were no longer living together, although they still worked side by side each day in the bakery. He had moved in with a widow, Mrs Bova, whose urgent bearing when she came into the shop I can remember even from the years before her husband died. For my mother, whose life with my father had been a dominion of fear, this arrangement became a kind of liberation. Her interest in the world outside her suddenly increased. She became one of the first of the regular callers on those listener-participation talk shows. Tell us what you think about interracial dating, legalizing marijuana, who killed Kennedy. She stacked the dining-room table with old newspapers and magazines, pads and index cards on which she made notations to herself, preparing for tomorrow's programs. My mother, who was phobic about venturing beyond our apartment building or the shop, who had to begin her preparations early in the morning if she was going to depart her home sometime that afternoon, who from the time I was eight sent me to the market so that she could avoid leaving the house – my mother became a local personality of sorts for her outspoken views about various worldly controversies.

I could not reconcile this development with the accommodations I had made long before with myself to accept her wildly verging eccentricities, or the narrow margins of her former life.

She had been twenty-eight, four years my father's senior, when they were married, the sixth daughter of a Jewish union organizer and a lass from Cork. My father wed, I'm sure, for her savings, which allowed him to open up the shop. Nor was there ever any sign that my mother had married for love. She was an old maid and, I would guess, far too peculiar to gather other suitors. Her behavior, as I witnessed it, was apt to be excessive and ungovernable, with manic tours from pinnacles of rosy hilarity to hours of brooding looks. Sometimes she became frantic. She was forever running to ransack her crowded dresser drawers, rummaging in her sewing box as she made high-pitched excited noises. Because she seldom left home, her sisters made it a habit to look after her. This was a brave endeavor. When my aunts visited, my father would assail them in loud conversation with himself as busybodies, and he was not above actual threats of violence if they came when he was drunk. The two who ventured most often, my Aunts Flo and Sarah, were both bold, determined women, their father's daughters, and they were apt to control my father with stern looks and fearless demeanor, not much different than if they were confronting some barking cur. They were undeterred in their unannounced mission to protect the meek – Rosie (my mother) and, especially, me. For me these sisters were a hovering presence throughout my childhood. They brought me candies; they took me for haircuts and bought my clothes. They supervised my upbringing in such routine fashion that I was in my twenties before I recognized their intentions – or their kindness. And somehow, without ever realizing it had happened, I grew to know there were two worlds, my mother's and the other one dwelled in by her sisters, the one to which I eventually recognized I, as well, belonged. It was a fixed star of my youth to think that my mother was not, as I put it to myself, regular; to know that my adoration of her was a purely private matter, unintelligible to others and beyond my power to explain.

Do I really care what she would think now? I suppose. What

child would not? I am almost glad she did not live to witness this. In her last few months she was with us. We were still living in the city in a one-bedroom apartment, but Barbara refused to see my mother anywhere else. She slept on a daybed in the living room from which she seldom rose. Barbara, most of the time, sat on a hard wooden chair drawn close. Near the end, my mother spoke constantly to Barbara. Her head was laid on her pillow, her face sadly reduced by disease, her eyes narrowly focused, their light growing weak. Barbara held her hand. They murmured. I could not make out the words – but the sound was constant, like a running tap. Barbara Bernstein, daughter of a sleek suburban matron, and my mother, of roaming mind and indelibly sweet disposition, voyaged to one another, crossed the straits of lone-liness, while I, as ever, was too full of private grief to make my own approach. I watched them from the door: for Barbara, the mother who made no demands; for Rosie, a child who would not disregard her. When I took Barbara's place, my mother held my hand. I had the decency to tell her often that I loved her; she smiled weakly, but seldom spoke. Near the end, it was Barbara who gave her the shots of Demerol. A few of the syringes are still downstairs in a box of odd keepsakes of my mother that Barbara maintains: antique bobbins and index cards; the gold-tipped Parker pen she used to make notes for her radio appearances.

I walk through the dark to find my slippers, slide my robe from the closet. In the living room, I sit, feet up, huddled in a rocking chair. Lately I have been thinking of taking up cigarettes again. I feel no cravings, but it would give me something to do in these abject hours in the dead of night when I am now so often awake.

A game I play with myself is called What Is the Worst Part? So many things seem trivial. I do not care much now about the way the women gape at me when I walk around in the village center. I do not worry about my reputation, or the fact that for the rest of my life, even if charges are dropped tomorrow, many people will cringe reflexively whenever they hear my name. I do not worry about how hard it will be for me to find work as an attorney if I am acquitted. But the steady emotional erosion, the sleeplessness, the manic anxiety I cannot pretend about or minimize. What is worst are these midnight wakings and the instants before I can gather myself, when I am sure that the terror is never going to end. It is like groping for the switch plate in the dark, but I am never certain – and here the terror is the worst – I am never sure that I will find it. As the search becomes more and more prolonged, the little bit of sense that holds forth in me erodes, gives way, bubbles off like a tablet dropped into water, and the wild blackness of some limitless and everlasting panic begins to swallow me.

That is what is worst; that and my worries about Nathaniel. On Sunday, we will put him on a train for Camp Okawaka near Skageon, where he is scheduled to remain for the three weeks the trial is projected to last. Recalling this, I quietly tread the stairs and stand in the dark hall outside his door. I listen until I can catch the rhythm of his breath, and then force my own breathing down to that same measure. As I watch Nat sleep, the weirdness of science overcomes me: I think of atoms and molecules, skin and veins, muscle and bones. I try to comprehend my son for an instant as a compilation of parts. But that fails. We cannot ever enlarge the realm of our final understanding. I know Nathaniel as the hot mass of my feelings for him; I behold him as something no smaller or more finite or reducible than my passions. He will not piece or parse. He is my boy, gentle and beautiful in sleep, and I am grateful, grateful so that my heart is sore and breaking, that in this rough life I have felt such tenderness.

If I am convicted, they will take me away from him. Even Larren Lyttle will send me to prison for many years, and the thought of missing the remainder of his young life shatters me, breaks me into pieces. Oddly, I feel little conscious fear of prison itself. I dread the exile and the separation. The thought of confinement can make me ill at ease. But the actual physical horrors I am sure to suffer are seldom in my mind, even when I pierce myself with the thought of the extreme consequences I may face.

And yet I know. I have spent days at Rudyard, the state pen, where every murderer is sent. I have been there usually to interview a witness, but the sights are chilling. The bars are heavy iron slats, painted flat black, two inches deep, one-half inch wide, and behind them are all these bastards who now – now it strikes you – are so much the same. The black guys chattering their manic raging stuff. The white guys in their rolled-up stocking caps. The Latinos who look out with pointy-eyed rage. They are collectively every man you have avoided in a hallway or a bus station, every kid you picked out in high school as destined to be a bum. They are the ones who always wore their deficits like scars, headed here almost as certainly as a skyward-shot arrow plunging back to earth.

About this group it is no longer possible to harbor any kind of sentiment. I have heard every horror story. And I know that these grisly anecdotes are some of the unseen ink that blackens my dreams. For me this will not be far from torture. I know about the nighttime shivs, about the showers where blow jobs are given in the open. I know about Marcus Wheatley, one of the guys I tried to get to talk in Night Saints, who hosed somebody on a dope deal down there, and was laid on his back in the weight room, told to put up his hands, and then given a barbell with 250 pounds on each end, which asphyxiated him, even while it acted half like a guillotine. I know about the demographics of that neighborhood, 16 percent murderers, and more than half the inmates there for some form of violent crime. I know about the gray food. The four men in a cell. The odor of excrement that is overpowering on certain tiers. I know that every month there are areas where the gang control becomes so complete that the guards refuse to walk through for days. I know about the guards themselves and the eight of them who were convicted in the federal court for a New Year's party they threw in which they used shotguns to line up twelve black prisoners whom they took turns beating with flagstones and bricks.

I know about what happens to men like me there, because I know what happened to some I helped to send. I know about Marcy Lupino, who, whenever my thoughts loiter here, is the person most likely to come to mind. Marcello was a regular type, your basic hustling American, a CPA who early in his career did a little work setting odds for some of the boys from his old neighborhood. Eventually Marcy's accounting practice prospered and he determined that he no longer required outside employment, at which time John Conte, one of the Boys, informed him that his was not the kind of job that he was free to quit. And that's the way it went. Marcy Lupino, respected CPA, PTA president, and member of the board of directors of two banks, a guy who wouldn't monkey with the books of his biggest client, left his office every afternoon at 3:30 p.m. sharp to set the spread on ball games, to tote the odds for tomorrow's ponies. All well and good, until one day when a federal snitch gave away a wire room. The IRS came through the door and found Marcy Lupino among half a dozen other people and three million dollars in betting slips. The feds wanted him to talk in the worst way. But Marcy was very good at arithmetic. Two years on a gambling beef, mail fraud, wire fraud, racketeering charges, whatever the feds could put to him, was not worth ten minutes of what John Conte and the Boys would do. They would cut out his testicles and feed them to him, make him chew. And this, Marcy Lupino knew, was not a figure of speech.

So Mike Townsend from the Organized Crime Strike Force called me. He wanted to provide Marcy with incentives. We charged Marcy stateside, and when he was convicted he went to Rudyard instead of the federal overnight camp he had been counting on, a place with a salad bar and tennis courts, a place where he would teach bookkeeping to inmates working on college degrees and copulate with Mrs Lupino every ninety days as part of the furlough program. Instead, we sent him off in manacles, chained to a man who had put out his infant daughter's eyes with his keys.

Six months later Townsend called and we took a trip north to see if Lupino had responded. We found him in a field with a hoe. He was scraping at the ground. We reintroduced ourselves, hardly a necessity. Marcy Lupino took his hoe, propped it under his arm, and leaned on it as he wept. He cried like I have never seen a man cry; he shook from head to toe, his face turned purple, and the water poured from his eyes, truly, as from a faucet. A little fat bald-headed forty-eight-year-old man, crying as hard as he could. But he would not talk. He said one thing to us: 'I got no teet'.' Nothing else.

As we were walking back, the guard explained.

Big buck nigger, Drover, wanted Lupino as his babe. He's the kind, man, nobody says no, not even the Italians in this joint. He gets himself into Lupino's cell one night, takes out his dingus, and tells Lupino to suck. Lupino won't, so Drover takes Lupino's face and bangs it on the bunk rail until there is not a whole tooth left in Lupino's head; some aching roots, some pieces, but not one tooth.

Warden's got a rule, the guard says. You get bandages for your wounds, we'll sew you up, but no special treatment unless you talk. Fuckin Lupino ain't getting his false teeth until he tells who did the tap dance on him. And fuckin Lupino, he ain't tellin, he knows what's good for him, nobody here is that dumb. No, the guard says, he ain't tellin. And ol' Drover, he is laughin, he says he done a real good job, and that his big Johnson goes in there now, smooth as silk; he says he been in many pussies that don't feel that good. The guard, a fine humanitarian, leaned on his shotgun and laughed. Crime, he reported to Townsend and me, sure don't pay.

Run, I think now as I sit in the dark contemplating Marcy Lupino. Run. The thought always comes that suddenly: run. As a prosecutor, I could never understand why they stayed around to let it fall, to face trial, sentencing, prison. But they remained for the most part, as I have. There is $1,600 in my checking account and I have no other money in the world. If I looted Barbara's trust, I would have enough to go, but then I would probably lose the only real motive I have for freedom – the chance to see Nat. And even if I could spend summers with him in Rio or Uruguay or wherever it is that they do not extradite for murder, the powers of even a desperate fancy are too meager to imagine how I would survive without a language I know or a skill those cultures would recognize. I could simply disappear to the center of Cleveland or Detroit, become somebody different, and never see my son again. But the fact is that none of these are visions of what I recognize as life.

Even in these lightless hours, I want the same things I wanted when I got off the bus at night in the village green in Nearing. We are so simple sometimes, and fortified so strangely. I sit here in the dark with my heels drawn against me, and as I shiver, I imagine the odor of the smoke of cigarettes.

26

'People versus Rožat K. Sabich!' calls Ernestine, Judge Lyttle's docket clerk, into the crowded courtroom. She is a stern-looking black woman, six feet tall. 'For trial!' she cries.

Not much is like the first day of a murder trial. Sunup on the morning of battle; Christians against lions back in Rome. Blood is on the air. Spectators have crammed themselves into every linear inch available along the public benches. There are four full rows of press, five sketch artists at the head. The judge's staff – his secretary and law clerks, who are not ordinarily present – are in folding chairs against the rear wall of the courtroom, next to his chambers door. Bailiffs, armed for this solemn occasion, are positioned at the forward corners of the bench beside the marble pillars. The atmosphere is busy and intense, full of a racing murmur. No one here is bored.

Judge Lyttle enters and the room comes to its feet. Ernestine makes her announcements. 'Oyez, oyez. The Superior Court for the County of Kindle is now in session, the Honorable Larren L. Lyttle, Judge Presiding. Draw near and give your attention and you shall be heard. God save the United States and this Honorable Court.' Ernestine bangs her gavel. When everyone is seated, she calls my case for trial.

The lawyers and I move to the podium. Stern and Kemp; Molto and Nico; Glendenning has appeared and will be the case investigator, sitting with the prosecutors. I stand behind the lawyers. Judge Lyttle looms above, his hair newly cut and smoothly groomed. It is 18 August, a few days short of two months since I was indicted.

'Are we ready to call for a jury?' Larren asks.

'Judge,' says Kemp, 'we have a few matters that we can address while you are bringing up the prospective jurors.' Kemp's role on this case will be Law Man. Stern has put him in charge of research and Jamie will address the judge with regard to points of law, outside the jury's presence. When they are in the box, he will not say a word.

From the courtroom phone, Ernestine calls the clerk's reception room and asks for a venire, citizens summoned for jury duty who will be questioned by the judge and lawyers to determine if they should serve in this case.

'Judge,' Kemp says again, 'we have received all the production you ordered from the prosecution. With one exception. We have still not been given an opportunity to see that glass.'

Stern has instructed Jamie to raise this for reasons besides our curiosity about the glass. He wants Judge Lyttle to know that the prosecutors are conforming to the judge's dim expectations. It works. Larren is upset.

'What about this, Mr Delay Guardia?' Nico clearly does not know. He looks for Molto.

'Judge,' says Tommy, 'we'll take care of it after court.'

'All right,' says Larren. 'That will be done today.'

'Also,' Kemp says, 'you have not ruled on our motion to disqualify Mr Molto.'

'That is correct. I have been waiting for the prosecutor's response. Mr Delay Guardia?'

Tommy and Nico exchange glances and nod to one another. They will proceed according to their prior agreement, whatever that is.

'Your Honor, the state will not call Mr Molto. So we suggest that the motion is moot.'

Stern steps forward and asks to be heard.

'Do I understand then, Your Honor, that Mr Molto will not be called under any circumstances – that his testimony is forsworn throughout the case and at all stages?'

'That's right,' Larren agrees. 'I'd like us all to be clear at the start, Mr Delay Guardia. I don't want to be hearin later about you didn't expect this or you didn't expect that. Mr Molto is not testifying at this trial. Correct?'

'Correct,' Nico says.

'Very well. I will deny the defendant's motion on the representation of the prosecutors that Mr Molto will not be called as a witness at this trial.'

Ernestine whispers to him. The prospective jurors are in the corridor.

So in they come, seventy-five people, twelve of whom will soon be in charge of deciding what happens to my life. Nothing special, just folks. You could skip the summonses and the questionnaires and grab the first seventy-five people who walked by on the street. Ernestine calls sixteen to sit in the jury box, and directs the remainder to the first four rows on the prosecution side, from which the bailiffs have dismissed the spectators amid great grumbling, sending them to form a waiting line out in the hall.

Larren starts by telling the venire what the case is about. He has probably seen a thousand juries chosen during his career. His rapport is instantaneous: this big, good-looking black man, kind of funny, kind of smart. The white people take to him too, thinking, probably, they all should be like this. Nowhere in a trial is Larren's advantage to the defense likely to be greater than at this juncture. He is skilled in addressing juries, canny in divining hidden motivations, and committed to the foundation of his soul to the fundamental notions. The defendant is presumed innocent. Innocent. As you sit here you have gotta be thinking Mr Sabich didn't do it.

'I'm sorry, sir. In the first row, what is your name?'

'Mahalovich.'

'Mr Mahalovich. Did Mr Sabich commit the crime that he is charged with?'

Mahalovich, a stout middle-aged man who has his paper folded in his lap, shrugs.

'I wouldn't know, Judge.'

'Mr Mahalovich, you are excused. Ladies and gentlemen, let me tell you again what you are to presume. Mr Sabich is innocent. I am the judge. I am tellin you that. Presume he is innocent. When

229

you sit there, I want you to look over and say to yourself, There sits an innocent man.'

He goes through similar exercises, expounding upon the state's burden to prove guilt beyond a reasonable doubt and the defendant's right to remain silent. Talking to a thin, grey-haired lady in a shirtwaist dress, who is seated in the chair beside the one Mahalovich once occupied:

'Now don't you think, ma'am, that an innocent person oughta get up there and tell you it's not so?'

The lady is torn. She saw what happened to Mahalovich. But you don't lie to a judge. She touches her dress at the collar before she speaks.

'I would think so,' she says.

'Of course you would. And you have to presume that Mr Sabich thinks the same thing, since we're presumin that he's innocent. But he doesn't have to do that. Because the Constitution of the United States says he doesn't have to. And what that means is that if you sit as jurors on this case, you have promised to put that thought out of your mind. Because Mr Sabich and his lawyer, Mr Stern, may decide to rely on that constitutional right. The folks who wrote the Constitution said, God bless you, sir, God bless you, Mr Sabich, you don't have to explain. The state's got to prove you guilty. You don't have to say a thing if you don't want. And Mr Sabich can't really receive that blessing if any of you have it in your mind that he should explain anyway.'

As a prosecutor, I used to find this part of Larren's routine unbearable, and Nico and Molto both look pale and upset. No matter how many times you tell yourself that the judge is right, you can't believe that anybody ever thought it was going to be explained so emphatically. Nico looks particularly drawn. He listens with an alert, humorless expression. He has lost weight and there is a new darkening in the sallow skin beneath his eyes. To get a case of this stature prepared in three weeks is a terrible burden, and he has an office to run as well. Moreover, it must have occurred to him often how much he has put on the line. He has taken klieg lights and run them across the sky telling the near world to watch Nico Della Guardia. If he loses, he will never have the same credibility in office. His silent campaign to be earmarked as Bolcarro's successor will be finished not long after its start. His career, much more than mine, hangs in the balance. I have lately come to realize that my career, after this indictment and the hoopla of this trial, is probably over in any event.

Next, Larren takes up the subject of publicity. He questions jurors about what they have read. For those who are being coy he points out the article announcing the start of the trial on the front page of today's *Trib*. Jurors always lie about this. People who want to get out of jury service usually find a way. The ones who come to the courthouse are, for the most part, eager to serve and less willing to confess to obvious disqualifications. But Larren slowly wins the truth from them. Nearly everybody here has heard something about this case, and over about twenty minutes Judge Lyttle tells them that is worthless information. 'Nobody knows anything about this case,' he says, 'because there has not been a word of evidence heard.' He excuses six people who admit that they will not be able to put the publicity out of their minds. It is unsettling to consider what the others, subjected to Nico's media splash, must think about the case. It's hard to believe that anyone can really fully put aside those preconceptions.

Late in the morning, questioning about the jurors' back-grounds begins – this process is called *voir dire*, truth-telling, and it continues throughout the afternoon and into the second morning. Larren asks everything he can think of and the lawyers add more. Judge Lyttle will not allow questioning directed to the issues of the case, but the attorneys are permitted to roam freely into personal details, limited largely only by their own reluctance to give offense. What TV shows do you watch, what newspapers do you read? Do you belong to any organizations? Do your children work outside the home? In your house, are you or your spouse in charge of the monthly bookkeeping? This is the subtle psychological game of figuring out who is pre-disposed to favor your side. Consultants now earn hundreds of thousands of dollars making such predictions for lawyers, but an attorney like Stern knows most of this by instinct and experience.

To pick a jury effectively you must know the case you want to try. Stern has not said anything to me, but it is becoming clearer that he has a strong notion not to offer evidence for the defense. He thinks he can whittle away at Nico's proof. Perhaps my actions in the past, when I have been beyond control in spite of his instructions, have convinced him I would be a poor witness in my own behalf. No doubt the decision to testify or not will be mine in the end. But I suspect that Stern is simply trying to move things to the point that I am convinced we can win without my testimony, before he forces my hand. In any event, he has spent little time talking to me about the defense case. Mac and a few of the judges have agreed to appear as character witnesses. Stern also has asked me about neighbors who would be willing to offer that kind of testimony. Clearly, though, he wants to try a reasonable-doubt case. At the end, if all goes as he hopes, no one will know what happened. The state will have failed to meet its burden of proof and I should be acquitted. With that goal, we need jurors bright enough to appreciate the legal standard and strong enough to forthrightly apply it – people who will not convict merely because they are suspicious. For that reason Sandy has told me that he thinks younger jurors will be better overall than old. In addition, they may be more in tune with some of the nuances of male and female relations that so strongly flavor the case. He wants, in other words, people who might believe that co-workers adjourn to a woman's apartment for reasons other than sexual intercourse. On the other hand, he has said, older people will have more immediate respect for my past attainments, my position, and my reputation.

Whatever the plans, you usually go in the end on gut impressions. Certain jurors just seem to be people you think you like, folks you can talk to. On the second morning, as we begin making our choices, Stern and Kemp and I have few disagreements. We huddle together at the counsel table, directing our decisions to prospective jurors taken up in groups of four. Barbara is invited by Sandy to come up from the nearest spectator bench to join in our consultation. She places her hand lightly on my shoulder, but offers no comment. Standing close to me as we confer, dressed in a dark blue silk suit and, again, a matching hat, she conveys an impression of somber dignity, of grieving well restrained. Overall, the effect is a little like the Kennedy widows. She is playing her small part well. Last night, after the *voir dire* started, Sandy explained to Barbara that he would be calling on her in this fashion. At home, she expressed appreciation for Sandy's courtesy and I explained to her that courtesy was not his prime intent. Stern again wants all the jurors to see at the outset that my wife is still on my side and that we, in this modern age, defer to the opinions of women.

The defense gets to excuse ten jurors without explanation – so-called peremptories. The prosecution gets six. Nico's plan seems to be pretty much the inverse of ours, although with fewer challenges he does not have the same opportunity to shape the panel. In general, he seems to be looking for his voters, older ethnic types, generally Roman Catholics. For that reason, without having planned to do it earlier, we strike all the Italians.

I am more comfortable with the group that we end up with than was often the case when I was a prosecutor. There is a preponderance of younger people, many of them single. A female drugstore manager in her late twenties. A young woman who is an accountant with a brokerage house. A twenty-six-year-old man is an assembly-line foreman, and another fellow about his age runs restaurant services at a local hotel and fiddles part-time with computers. There is a young black woman who does auditing at a local insurance company. Among the twelve, we have a divorced female schoolteacher, a secretary for a local rail line, a man who retired last year from running a high school music program, and an auto mechanic; also a Burger King management trainee, a retired nurse's aide, and a cosmetics saleswoman from Morton's. Nine whites, three blacks. Seven women, five men. Larren also seats four alternates, who will hear the evidence but not take part in deliberations unless one of the twelve regulars falls ill or is otherwise excused.

With the jury chosen, early in the second afternoon we are ready to start my trial.

*

At ten minutes to two we arrive again at the courthouse for opening statements. The atmosphere is now the same as yesterday morning. The lull of jury selection is past and the blood urge is on the air. The adrenalized excitement of beginning becomes a kind of painful irritant that I feel seeping into my bones. Kemp calls me into the hallway outside the courtroom, and we walk some distance to get away from the gaggle of unhappy onlookers for whom the bailiffs have not been able to find seats. Out here you can never be certain who is listening. The best journalists would not report something they overheard, but you can never tell who is talking to the prosecutors.

'I want to say something,' Jamie tells me. He has chopped a good two inches off the curled edges of his pageboy, and he is turned out in a distinguished blue pinstriped suit purchased from J. Press in New Haven. He is handsome enough to have chosen Hollywood instead of law. From comments, I have come to realize that he made enough money playing his guitar to be quite comfortable without working. Instead, he is in the office, reading cases, writing memos, conferring with Stern and me until eleven and twelve o'clock at night.

'I like you,' Jamie says.

'I like you, too,' I answer.

'And I really hope you beat this thing. I've never told a client this before. But I think you will.'

There are no more than a year or two's worth of clients in Jamie's life and so the comment is not worth that much as a prediction, but I am touched by his good feeling. I put a hand on his shoulder and I thank him. He did not tell me, of course, that I am innocent. He knows better than to be convinced of that; the evidence is against me. Probably if you shook him awake in the middle of the night and put the question, he would tell you he does not know.

Stern appears now. He is almost jaunty. His flesh is invigorated by the high excitement; the broadcloth of his shirt is so white and free of creases that it appears almost holy as it meets his full cheeks. He is about to give the opening statement in the most noted case of his career. Suddenly I am full of envy. I have not thought in all the months about how much fun it would be to try this case, an understandable omission. But those old inclinations suddenly surge forth amid this supercharged air. The big Night Saints case, a twenty-three-defendant conspiracy which I tried with Raymond, had a fraction of this attention, but it was still like taking hold of a live wire, a drumming excitement that did not stop, even in sleep, for seven weeks. Like motorcycling or mountain climbing: you know that you have been here. I am sad suddenly, briefly despairing over my lost trade.

'So?' Sandy asks me.

'I told him I thought that he would win,' says Kemp.

Stern speaks Spanish; his eyebrows shoot up toward the hairless crest of his scalp.

'Never out loud,' he says. 'Never.' Then he takes my hand and faces me with his deepest look. 'Rusty, we will do our best.'

'I know,' I say.

Coming back into the courtroom, Barbara, who has gone back and forth from the U. over lunch, emerges from the crowd to hug me. It is half an embrace, one arm firmly around my waist. She kisses my cheek, then wipes away the lipstick with her hand. She talked to Nat.

'He wants you to know he loves you,' she says. 'I do too.' She says this in a cute way, so that the tone, in spite of her good intentions, is somewhat equivocal. None the less, she has done her best. It is the right time and the right place for maximum performance.

The jury files in from the waiting room, where they will eventually deliberate. It is located right behind the jury box. The divorced schoolteacher actually smiles at me as she takes her seat.

Larren explains the function of opening statements: a prediction of the evidence. A forecast. 'It is not an argument,' he says. 'The lawyers will not set forth the inferences which they think arise from the proof. They will simply tell you in an unvarnished fashion what the actual evidence will be.' Larren says this no doubt as a warning to Delay. In a circumstantial case, a prosecutor needs some way at the outset to make a jury see how it all fits together. But Nico will have to do this carefully. However Della Guardia feels about Larren, the jury is in love with the judge already. His charm is like a floral scent he emits into the air. Nico will gain nothing from being upbraided.

Larren says, 'Mr Delay Guardia,' and Nico stands. Trim, erect, bristling with anticipation. A person at the very top.

'May it please the court,' he says, the traditional beginning.

Right from the start, he is surprisingly bad. I know immediately what has happened. The time constraints and the burden of running the office have impinged severely on his preparation. He has never gone over this before. Some of it is being improvised, perhaps in response to Larren's warning right before he began. Nico cannot shake his drawn, nervous look, and he cannot find a rhythm. He keeps hesitating in spots.

Even with Nico's inadequate preparation, much of this is difficult for me to hear. Nico may lack his usual style and organization, but he is still hitting the high spots. The counterpoint of the physical evidence against what I said and did not say to Horgan and Lipranzer is, as I always feared, particularly effective. On the other hand, Delay misses points of emphasis. He tells the jury too little about things he should be the one to disclose. A smart prosecutor usually seeks to defuse defense evidence by mentioning it first, demonstrating from his own mouth that his case can stand the defense's strongest blows. But Nico does not adequately detail my background – he fails to say that I was second-in-command of the office – and, in describing my relationship with Carolyn, he omits any mention of the McGaffen trial. When Stern gets up, in his own quiet way he will make these abbreviations appear to be concealment.

In the area of my relations with Carolyn, Nico makes the only deviation from what we had predicted. Nico's problem is deeper than I, or even Stern, had understood. Delay does not simply lack proof of my relationship with Carolyn. he has not even correctly guessed what occurred.

'The evidence,' he tells the jury, 'will show that Mr Sabich and Ms Polhemus had a personal relationship that had gone on for

236

many months, at least seven or eight months before the murder. Mr Sabich was in Ms Polhemus's apartment. She called him on the phone. He called her. It was, as I say, a personal relationship.' He pauses. 'An intimate relationship.

'But all was not well in this relationship. Mr Sabich was, apparently, very unhappy. Mr Sabich was, it seems, intensely jealous.'

Larren on the bench has swung about and now is glaring. Nico is doing what the judge warned him about, arguing rather than simply describing his witnesses and exhibits. In his agitation, the judge glances now and then in Sandy's direction, a signal for Sandy to object, but Stern is quiet. Interruptions are discourteous, and Sandy is himself in court. More important, Nico is at the point in his oration where he is saying things that Stern knows he may not prove.

'Mr Sabich was jealous. He was jealous because Ms Polhemus was seeing not only him. Ms Polhemus had formed a new relationship, a relationship that apparently infuriated Mr Sabich.' Another weighty caesura. 'A relationship with the prosecuting attorney, Raymond Horgan.'

This detail has never before found public life. Nico undoubtedly cabined it to protect his new alliance with Raymond; but he cannot help himself, he is still Nico, and he actually turns to the press rows as he lets this news into the world. There is an audible stirring in the courtroom, and Larren, with the mention of his former partner, finally loses his cool.

'Mr Delay Guardia!' he thunders, 'you were warned, sir. Your remarks are not to be in the nature of closing argument. You will confine yourself to a *sterile* recitation of the facts or your opening will be over. Do I make myself clear?'

Nico faces the bench. He actually looks surprised. His prominent Adam's apple bobs as he swallows.

'Certainly,' he says.

Jealousy, I write on my notepad, and pass it to Kemp. Given the choice between no motive and a motive he cannot quite prove, Nico has chosen the latter. It may even be the smarter gamble. But at the end, he will be working hard to stretch the facts.

Stern moves to the podium as soon as Nico is through. The

judge offers a recess, but Sandy smiles gently and says he is prepared to go on right now, if the court please. Sandy is unwilling to let Nico's remarks accumulate force on reflection.

He steps around the podium and rests one elbow on it. He wears a brown suit, tailor-made, that conforms subtly to his full shape. His heavy face is still with portent.

'How are we to answer this,' he asks, 'Rusty Sabich and I? What can we say when Mr Della Guardia tells you about two fingerprints but not another? What can we say when the evidence will show you gaps and suppositions, gossip and cruel innuendo? What can we say when a distinguished public servant is put on trial on the basis of circumstantial evidence which, as you will be able to determine, does not approach that precious standard of reasonable doubt?

'Reasonable doubt.' He turns, he steps, he comes two feet closer to the jury. 'The prosecution must prove guilt beyond a reasonable doubt.' He harks back to everything they heard over the last two days from Judge Lyttle. At the outset, Stern has locked arms before the jurors with that mighty and learned jurist, a particularly effective device in light of Larren's first putdown of Delay. Sandy uses the term 'circumstantial evidence' repeatedly. He mentions the words 'rumors' and 'gossip.' Then he talks about me.

'And who is Rusty Sabich? Not simply, as Mr Della Guardia told you, a top deputy in the prosecuting attorney's office. *The* top deputy. Among a handful of the finest trial lawyers in this county, this state. The evidence will show you that. A top graduate of the University Law School. A member of the *Law Review*. Clerk to the Chief Justice of the State Supreme Court. He gave his career, his life to public service. To stopping and preventing and punishing criminal behavior, not' – Stern glances contemptuously towards the prosecutors – 'to committing it. Listen, ladies and gentlemen, to the names of some of the persons whom the evidence will show you Rusty Sabich brought to justice. Listen, because these are persons whose wrongdoing was so well known that even you who are not regularly in this courthouse will recognize these names, and, I am sure, will once again be grateful for Rusty Sabich's work.' He spends five minutes talking about the Night Saints and

238

other cases, longer than he should, but Della Guardia is hard put to object after Sandy endured his opening without complaint.

'He is the son of an immigrant, a Yugoslavian freedom fighter who was persecuted by the Nazis. His father came here in 1946 to a land of freedom, where there would be no more atrocities. What would Ivan Sabich think today?'

I would squirm were I not under the sternest orders to show nothing. I sit with my hands folded and look ahead. At all moments, I am to appear resolute. Lamentably, Stern did not give me a preview of this portion. Even if I testify, I will not testify to this – not that the prosecutors would be likely to disprove it.

Stern's manner is somehow commanding. The accent lends an intrigue to his speech, and his considered formality gives him substance. He makes no predictions of what the defense will show. He steers clear of promising my testimony. Instead, he focuses on deficiencies. No evidence, not a scintilla of direct evidence that Rusty Sabich handled any murder weapon. No sign that Rusty Sabich took part in any violence.

'And what is the cornerstone of this circumstantial case? Mr Della Guardia told you many things about the relationship of Mr Sabich and Ms Polhemus. He did not tell you, as the evidence will show, that they were co-workers, that they worked as trial lawyers, not as lovers, on a case of tremendous importance. He did not mention that. He left that for me to tell you. All right, then, I have, and the evidence will show that to you, too. You should mind closely what the evidence shows you, and does not show you, about the relationship of Rusty Sabich and Carolyn Polhemus. Mind that closely in this circumstantial case where Mr Della Guardia seeks to prove guilt beyond a reasonable doubt. I tell you flatly, flatly, that the evidence will not show you what Mr Della Guardia has said it would. It will not. You see this case will not involve facts, but rather supposition upon supposition, guess upon guess –'

'Mr Stern,' says Larren mildly. 'You seem to be falling into the same trap as Mr Della Guardia.'

Sandy turns; he actually bows in an abbreviated way.

'I am so sorry, Your Honor,' he says. 'He seems to have inspired me.'

A laugh, a small one, from everyone. The judge. A number of members of the jury. A small laugh at Delay's expense.

Sandy turns back to the jury, and remarks as if he were speaking to himself: 'I must keep myself from getting carried away by this case.' Then he plants his last seed. No commitments, just a few words.

'Well, one cannot help asking why. As you listen to the evidence, ask why. Not why Carolyn Polhemus was murdered. That regrettably is something no one will be learning from this proof. But why Rusty Sabich sits here falsely accused. Why offer a circumstantial case, a case that is supposed to show guilt beyond a reasonable doubt and does not?'

Sandy stops. He tilts his head. Perhaps he knows the answer; perhaps he does not. He speaks softly.

'Why?' is the last thing that he says.

27

They cannot find the glass.

Nico admits this as soon as Stern and Kemp and I arrive on the third morning of trial. The first witnesses will be called today.

'How in the world?' asks Stern.

'I apologize,' says Nico. 'Tommy tells me he forgot about it at first. He really did. Now they're looking high and low. It'll turn up. But I have a problem.' Della Guardia and Stern stroll away, conferring. Molto watches them with obvious concern. He seems reluctant to leave his place at the prosecution table, like a whipped dog. Really, Tommy does not look well. It is too early in the trial to be as exhausted as he appears. He has a yellow cast to his skin, and his suit, the same as yesterday's, does not seem to have had any time to rest. I would not be surprised if Molto never made it home last night.

'How can they lose a piece of evidence like that?' Kemp asks me.

'Happens all the time,' I answer. The Police Evidence Center, over in McGrath Hall, has more unclaimed items than a pawnshop. Tags get knocked off; numbers are reversed. I started many cases with evidence misplaced. Unfortunately, Nico is right: the glass will turn up.

Stern and Della Guardia have agreed to advise the judge of this development, before he takes the bench. We will all go back to chambers. This will save Nico from a public whipping. Stern's concession on points like this, minor courtesies, is the kind of thing that has made him popular around the PA's office. Other lawyers would demand to be on the record so that Nico could take a hiding before the press.

We all wait a moment in the judge's outer office, while his secretary, Corrine, keeps an eye on the phone light to see when the judge completes the call he is presently taking. Corrine is stately and large-chested, and the courthouse wags regularly speculated on the nature of her relationship with Larren, until last fall, when she married a probation officer named Perkins. Larren has always been a ladies' man of some renown. He divorced about ten years ago, and over time I've heard a lot of tales about him drinking Jack Daniel's in the pretty-people night spots down on Bayou Boulevard, that pickup strip which certain sages refer to as the Street of Dreams.

'He says come right in,' Corrine tells us, putting down the phone after a brief conversation with the judge to announce our group. Kemp and Nico and Molto precede us. Stern wants a moment with me to confer.

When we enter, Nico has already begun telling the judge the problem. He and Kemp are in armchairs before the judge's desk. Molto sits a distance away on the sofa. The chambers, the judge's inner sanctum, have a distinguished bearing. One wall is solid with the gold-toned spines of the state law reports, and Larren also has his own Wall of Respect. There is a large picture of the judge and Raymond, among a number of photos of the judge with politicians, mostly black.

'Your Honor,' Nico is saying, 'I learned the first time last night from Tommy –'

'Well, I thought Tommy indicated yesterday that you had the glass and he simply had overlooked this matter. Tommy, I'll tell you something right now.' The judge is on his feet behind his desk, looking rather regal in a purple-toned shirt with white collar and cuffs. He has been roaming in his books and papers as he listens, but now he turns about and points a stout finger at Molto. 'If I have the same kind of bullshit from you in this case I've had in the past, I'll throw you in the lockup. I really will. Don't be tellin me one thing and meanin something else. And I want to say this right in front of the prosecuting attorney. Nico, you know we've always gotten along. But there's a history here.' The judge tips his large head in Molto's direction.

'Judge, I understand. I really do. That's why I was concerned as soon as I learned of the problem. I really do believe that it's an oversight.'

Larren glances balefully at Della Guardia from the corner of his eye. Nico does not even flinch. He is doing a pretty good job. He has both hands in his lap and is making his best effort to appear the suppliant. This is not an attitude that comes to him naturally, and his readiness to humble himself before the judge is actually quite winning. There must have been hell to pay last night between Molto and him. That's why Tommy looks so bad.

Larren, however, is not about to let the subject go. As usual he has caught all the implications quickly. For better than a month the prosecutors have been promising to produce a glass they knew they could not find.

'Isn't this somethin?' the judge asks. He looks, for support, to Stern. 'You know, Nico, I don't issue these orders just for the hell of it. You do with your evidence as you like, but really – Who had this glass last?'

'There's some disagreement, Judge, but we believe it was the police.'

'Naturally,' says Larren. He looks off toward the distance in disgust. 'Well, you see what we have here. You have defied an order of the court. The defense has not had an opportunity to prepare. And you have given an opening statement, Nico, in which you must have referred to this evidence half a dozen times. Well, that's your problem now. When you find the glass, assuming you find it, then we'll determine whether or not it comes into evidence. Let's go try this case.'

Nico's difficulties, however, are more complex than one angry judge. The state case has been prepared with the witnesses expected in an established sequence, referred to as an order of proof. The first person to testify is supposed to describe the crime scene, and accordingly, he will mention the glass.

'Not in my courtroom,' says Larren. 'No, sir. We're not gonna be talkin anymore about evidence that nobody can find.'

Stern finally speaks up. He announces that we have no objection to Delay proceeding as he had planned.

'Your Honor, if the prosecution fails to find the glass, we will object to any further evidence regarding it.' He means, of course, the fingerprints. 'But for the time being, there is no purpose to delay, if Your Honor will permit it.'

Larren shrugs. It's Sandy's lawsuit. This is the subject Sandy and I discussed in the judge's outer office. If we object, we can make Nico take witnesses out of the order he had planned, but Sandy thinks the advantage is greater if Nico's first witness has to explain that a piece of evidence is missing. Better that they look like Keystone Kops was how Stern put it. The disorganization will make a poor impression on the jury. Besides, there is little damage to me in the bare fact that a glass was found. And as I pointed out to Kemp, the police-evidence custodians will eventually locate the glass; they always do.

'I would think you should give Mr Stern an order of proof so that he has notice of when we're coming to this area again.'

Molto speaks up. 'We have one, Judge. We'll give it to them right now.' Tommy fiddles in the sloppy heap of papers on his lap, and eventually passes a sheet to Kemp.

'And let's put this on the record,' Larren says. Nico's punishment. He must explain this screw-up in public after all.

While the lawyers are before the bench, repeating our chambers conference in the presence of the court reporter, I examine the order of proof. I am eager to know when Lipranzer will be testifying. The sooner he does, the sooner the search for Leon can resume. I have tried to get Sandy's PI to look further, but he claims there is nothing to do. The list, however, provides no good news. Lip is scheduled toward the latter part of the case. Leon and I will have to wait.

Even in my disappointment, I recognize that Tommy and Nico have constructed their case with care. They will begin with the murder scene and the collection of the physical evidence, and will then start a slowly accelerating demonstration of why I am the murderer. First will come their proof, equivocal as that is, of my relationship with Carolyn; then my questionable handling of the investigation; near the end they will offer the various bits of evidence that put me at the murder scene: the fingerprints, the fibers, the phone records, the Nearing maid, the blood test results. Painless Kumagai will testify last and, I suppose, offer an expert opinion on how it was done.

Up on the bench Larren is still chewing Nico out, for the record.

'And the prosecutors will immediately advise the defense when the evidence is located. Is that correct?'

Nico promises.

With that matter settled, the jury is brought in, and Nico announces the name of the prosecution's first witness, Detective Harold Greer. He enters from the corridor and stands before Larren to be sworn.

As soon as Greer is up there, it is obvious to all of us why Nico wanted to maintain the predetermined order of proof. Juries for obvious reasons tend to remember the first witness, and Greer is impressive, a huge, well-spoken black man, calm and orderly in his presentation of himself. With or without the glass, he is the image of competence. The department is full of officers like Greer, men and women with the IQs of college professors who became cops because it was, within their horizons, the best thing available.

Molto is doing the questioning. He looks rumpled but his direct examination is well prepared.

'And where was the body?'

Greer was the third officer on the scene. Carolyn was discovered about 9:30 a.m. She missed an eight o'clock meeting and a nine o'clock court call. Her secretary called the super directly. All he did, he told me months ago, was push the door open and look around. He could see then he needed the cops. The beat guys called for Greer.

Greer describes what he observed and the way the evidence techs did their work under his direction. Greer identifies a sealed plastic packet that contains the fibers that were lifted from Carolyn's body, and a larger packet that contains her skirt, from which more of the Zorak V fibers were obtained. Molto and he

245

smooth over the glass. Greer describes finding it on the bar, watching the evidence techs seal the Baggie.

'And where is the glass at present?'

'We've had a little trouble locating it. It should turn up in the police evidence room.'

Next Molto raises the specter of the removed diaphragm. Greer says that in a thorough search of the apartment he found no contraceptive device. Then, with all the little bits of evidence which the police discovered inventoried before the jury, Molto moves to his climax.

'Based on your experience in nine years as a homicide detective, and the appearance of the scene, did you have any opinion as to what had taken place?' Molto asks.

Stern makes his first objection before the jury.

'Your Honor,' Stern scolds, 'this is speculative. This cannot be regarded as an expert opinion. Mr Molto is asking about a hunch.'

Larren strokes his cheeks with his big hand, but shakes his head. 'Overruled.'

Molto repeats the question.

'Based on the position of the body,' Greer responds, 'the way it was tied, the signs of disturbance, the open window over the fire escape, on first looking at the scene I was of the opinion that Ms Polhemus had been murdered in the course of, or as the result of, a sexual assault.'

'A rape?' asks Molto, a leading question, not usually permitted on direct examination but harmless under the circumstances.

'Yes,' says Greer.

'And were police photographers at the scene?'

'They were.'

'What, if anything, did they do?'

'I asked them to take a number of photos of the scene. And they did that.'

'In your presence?'

From the evidence cart the prosecutors wheeled into court this morning, Molto takes the collection of photos I looked at four months ago in my office. He shows each to Sandy before he presents them to Greer. Molto has set his examination up cleverly. Usually a judge will limit the prosecution's use of photos in a murder case. It is grisly and prejudicial. But by emphasizing the appearances, which the prosecution of course will argue were staged, Tommy has deprived us of the usual grounds for objections. We sit, attempting to appear implacable, while Greer describes each of the gruesome photos and identifies them as having accurately reflected the scene. When Molto offers them, Sandy approaches the bench and asks the judge to look them over himself.

'We can do with just two of the body,' Larren says. He removes another two, but he allows Molto to pass the ones admitted among the jurors at the end of Greer's examination. I do not dare to look up often, but I can sense from the stillness in the box that the blood and Carolyn's contorted corpse have had the effect the prosecutors hoped. The schoolteacher will not be smiling at me again for quite a while.

'Cross-examination,' says the judge.

'Just a few matters,' says Sandy. He smiles a bit at Greer. We will not be challenging this witness. 'You mentioned a glass, Detective. Where is that?' Stern starts to look among the exhibits Greer identified.

'It's not here.'

'I am sorry. I thought you testified about it.'

'I did.'

'Oh.' Sandy appears flustered. 'But you do not have it?'

'No, sir.'

'When was the last time you saw it?'

'At the scene.'

'You have not seen it since?'

'No, sir.'

'Have you tried to find it?'

Greer smiles, probably the first time since he took the stand. 'Yes, sir.'

'I see from your expression you have put some effort into this?'

'Yes, sir.'

'And the glass still cannot be found?'

'No, sir.'

'And who would have handled it last?'

'I don't know. Mr Molto over there has got the evidence receipts.'

'Oh.' Sandy turns in Tommy's direction. Molto appears faintly amused. It is Sandy's playacting that he finds humorous, but the jury of course does not realize that is the source of this slight grin. To them Tommy must appear somewhat arrogant. 'Mr Molto has them?'

'Yes, sir.'

'Ordinarily he would have the evidence, too?'

'Yes, sir. The prosecutor gets the evidence and the original tags.'

'So Mr Molto has the tag but not the glass?'

'That's right.'

Sandy turns again to Molto. While looking at him, Stern says, 'Thank you, Detective.' He appears to ruminate before he again faces the witness.

Stern spends a few minutes on the details of the collection of various pieces of evidence. When he reaches the diaphragm he pauses with some apparent emphasis.

'A contraceptive device was not the only item you failed to find, is that right, Detective?'

Greer's face narrows. He did not find the Hope Diamond or Aunt Tillie's missing lace hankie. The question can't be answered.

'Well, Detective, you and the officers under your command made a very thorough search of the apartment, did you not?'

'We certainly did.'

'And yet, sir, you failed to find not merely a diaphragm but also any cream or jelly or other substance that could be expected to be utilized with it – is that not correct?'

Greer hesitates. He had not thought of this before.

'That's correct,' he says at last.

Nico turns immediately to Tommy. They are seated fifteen feet in front of me, facing the jury. I've never had the chance before to watch my opponents. From the prosecutor's table you focus on the jurors. Nico is whispering. It seems to be something like,

Where the hell is the stuff? A couple of the jury members respond alertly to this part of the examination.

Stern is about to sit down when I ask him to bring the photos over. Sandy casts me a black look. This is proof that Stern would just as soon be forgotten. I motion to him again, however, and he hands me the stack. I finally find the picture of the bar and make my point to Stern. He bows briefly to me before returning to the witness.

'You identified this photograph, Detective Greer, State Exhibit 6-G?'

'Yes, sir.'

'It reflects the bar where you found this glass?'

'It does.'

'Tell me, sir – this would be easier if we had the glass, but is your recollection of it good?'

'I think so. It's like the ones in the picture.'

'Just so. The glass you seized was one of this set of barware laid out here on this towel?' Sandy has turned the photograph around so both Greer and the jurors can see the portion of the picture Stern means to indicate.

'Right.'

'Count the glasses, would you?'

Greer lays his finger on the photo and does it slowly.

'Twelve,' Stern repeats. 'So the missing glass would make thirteen?'

Greer knows this is peculiar. He waggles his head. 'I guess so.'

'An odd set?'

Molto objects, but Greer answers, 'Very,' before Larren can rule.

'Really,' Sandy says to me when we break for lunch, 'I appreciate your thoughts, Rusty, but you must share them with us before the last moment. This detail may be significant.'

I look at Stern as we are heading out of court.

'I just noticed,' I tell him.

The prosecutors have a dismal afternoon. I never tried a case as a deputy PA that did not have a low spot, a trough, a place where my evidence was weak. I used to talk about walking through the Valley of Death. For Nico, as we've long known, the valley is trying to prove what went on between Carolyn and me. His hope, quite clearly, is to get just enough evidence before the jury that they can make a comfortable guess. The overall plan Molto and he seemingly made was to start strong with Greer, stagger through this portion, and then dash for home, with the physical evidence providing a note of rising credibility. A reasonable strategy. But all the lawyers come to court after lunch knowing that these hours will belong to the defense.

The state's next witness is Eugenia Martinez, my former secretary. She clearly sees this as her moment. She comes to the stand in a broad slouch hat and dangling earrings. Nico presents her testimony, which is succinct. Eugenia testifies that she has been employed in the PA's office fifteen years. For two of those fifteen years, ending last April, she worked for me. One day last September or October, in answering the phone, Eugenia picked up the wrong line. She heard just a few words of conversation, but she recognized the voices as those of Ms Polhemus and me. I was talking about meeting Ms Polhemus at her home.

'And how did they sound to you?' asks Nico.

'Object to "sound,"' says Stern. 'It calls for a characterization.'

'Sustained.'

Nico faces Larren. 'Judge, she can testify to what she heard.'

'What she heard, but no opinions.' From the bench, Larren addresses Eugenia. 'Ms Martinez, you cannot tell us what you thought when you heard the conversation. Just the words and the intonation.'

'What was the intonation?' Nico asks, back close to where he wanted to be.

Eugenia, however, is not ready for the question.

'Nice-like,' she finally answers.

Stern objects, but the response is too innocuous to merit exclusion. Larren flips a hand and says that the answer may stand.

Nico is having a difficult time with something important.

Again, I am struck by how difficult it has been for him to prepare.

'Did they sound intimate?' he asks.

'Objection!' Stern shoots to his feet. The question is leading and unfairly suggestive.

Larren again takes off on Nico before the jury. The question was clearly improper, Larren says. It is stricken and the jurors are ordered to disregard it. But there is method to Nico's breach. He was trying to find some way to signal Eugenia.

He asks, 'Could you further describe the tone of the remarks you heard?'

Stern objects with force. The question has been previously asked and answered.

Larren peers down. 'Mr Delay Guardia, I suggest that you move on.'

Suddenly help comes to Nico from an unexpected source.

'He say "my angel,"' Eugenia volunteers.

Nico faces her, stunned.

'That's what he say. Okay? He say he be comin at eight o'clock and call her "my angel."'

For the first time since the trial began my composure fails before the jury. I let out a sound. My look, I'm certain, is inflamed. Kemp lays a hand on mine.

'My angel!' I whisper. 'For Chrissake.'

Over his shoulder, Stern looks at me severely.

Suddenly ahead of where he expected to be, Nico sits down.

'Cross-examination.'

Sandy advances on Eugenia. He speaks as soon as he reaches his feet, not waiting to arrive at the podium. He has maintained the same scolding expression which only seconds ago he turned on me.

'For whom do you work now in the prosecuting attorney's office, Ms Martinez?'

'Work?'

'Whose typing do you do? Whose phones do you answer?'

'Mr Molto.'

'This gentleman? The prosecutor at the table?' Eugenia says yes. 'When Mr Sabich was forced to take leave because of this investigation, Mr Molto advanced to Mr Sabich's position, is that right?'

'Yes, sir.'

'And that position is one of considerable authority and influence in the PA's office, is that right?'

'Number-two man,' answers Eugenia.

'And Mr Molto was in charge of the investigation that brought him Mr Sabich's job?'

'Objection!'

'Your Honor,' Sandy says to the judge, 'I am entitled to develop bias. The woman is testifying before her employer. Her perception of his motives is important.'

Larren smiles. Stern is developing more than that, but his excuse will pass. The objection is overruled.

The court reporter rereads the question and Eugenia answers yes. Sandy, in his opening touched only lightly on the election and the change of administration. This is his first attempt to develop rivalry for power as a theme. It will answer, in part, his question to the jury in his opening statement about why the prosecutors might move ahead on an insufficient case. It had never struck me that he might do that by picking on Molto rather than Della Guardia.

'Now, in the course of investigating Mr Sabich, did Mr Molto ask you to speak to a police officer about what you remembered of Mr Sabich's relationship with Ms Polhemus?'

'Sir?'

'Didn't you speak in May to Officer Glendenning?' Tom is in and out of court, but right now he is here and Sandy points at him, seated in uniform at the prosecutor's table.

'Yes, sir.'

'And you knew that the investigation was a very important one, particularly to your boss, Mr Molto, did you not?'

'Seemed like.'

'And yet, madam, when you were asked about Mr Sabich's relationship with Ms Polhemus, you never told Officer Glendenning that you heard Mr Sabich call Ms Polhemus "my angel," did you?' Sandy says it with a special cold emphasis. He appears furious with the perjury. He has Glendenning's report in his hand.

Eugenia suddenly recognizes that she is trapped. She gets a slow, unwilling look and sags a little. She probably had no idea that the defense would know what she said before.

'No, sir,' she says.

'You didn't tell Officer Glendenning that you recalled Mr Sabich using any term of endearment, did you, madam?'

'No, sir.' She is brooding; I have seen this look a hundred times. Her eyes close; her shoulders draw around her. This is when Eugenia is at her meanest. 'I never said anythin like that.'

'Not to Mr Glendenning?'

'No time.'

Sandy, before I do, recognizes where Eugenia is going. She has thought of a way out. He walks a few steps toward her.

'Didn't you testify five minutes ago, madam, that Mr Sabich called Ms Polhemus "my angel"?'

Eugenia draws herself up in the witness stand, fierce and proud.

'No way,' she says loudly. Three or four of the jurors look away. One of them, the man who is learning about hamburgers, laughs out loud, just one little hiccup.

Sandy studies Eugenia. 'I see,' he finally says. 'Well, tell me, Ms Martinez, when you answer Mr Molto's phone these days do you listen in on *his* conversations?'

Her thick eyes go sidelong with contempt. 'Nope,' she says.

'You would not listen a moment longer than you had to in order to recognize that someone is on the line, is that not correct?'

This, of course, is Eugenia's problem. She probably heard a good deal more pass on the telephone between Carolyn and me than she has disclosed. But even with the PA and his chief deputy prosecuting the case, she cannot admit to eavesdropping. The winds of fortune change too quickly, and Eugenia, a bureaucratic animal, knows that such an admission would eventually be the long-awaited dynamite to dislodge her from her sinecure in civil service concrete.

'What you heard, you heard in an instant?'

'That's all.'

'No more?'

'No, sir.'

'And you tell us it was "nice-like"? Were those not your words?'

'What I say, yes, sir.'

Stern comes and stands beside Eugenia. She weighs about two hundred pounds. She is broad-featured and surly, and even dressed in her finest, as she is today, she still does not look very good. Her dress is much too loud and is stretched tight over her bulk.

'You base this answer,' he asks, 'on your experience in such things?'

Sandy is poker-faced, but a couple of the jurors get it. They look down as they smile. Eugenia certainly gets it. Killers' eyes do not grow colder.

Stern does not ask for an answer.

'And this conversation about meeting at Ms Polhemus's apartment took place last September, you say?'

'Yes, sir.'

'Do you remember that Mr Sabich and Ms Polhemus tried a case together as co-prosecutors last September?'

Eugenia stops. 'Uh-uh,' she says.

'You do not remember the McGaffen case? A child, a little boy, had been hideously tortured by his mother? His head put in a vise? His anus burned with cigarettes? You do not remember Mr Sabich securing the conviction of this –' Stern makes it look as if he is searching for a word, before he ends with 'woman?'

'Oh, that one,' she says. 'I recall.'

'The McGaffen case, I take it, was not recalled in your discussions with Mr Molto?'

'Objection.'

Larren ponders.

'I will withdraw it,' says Stern. He's made his point to the jury. Prosecutor Molto seems to be taking it in the shorts so far today. He has the tag for the missing glass. He has inspired Eugenia's perjury.

'Ms Martinez, do you remember how warm it was in Kindle County last year around Labor Day?'

Her brows close. She has taken enough of a beating that she is trying to cooperate.

'Past 100 two days.'

'Correct,' Stern says, improperly. 'Is the PA's office air-conditioned?'

Eugenia snorts. 'Only if you believe what they say.'

Laughter throughout the courtroom. The judge, the jury, the spectators. Even Stern finally smiles.

'I take it you try to leave as soon as the day ends when the heat is like that?'

'You got that right.'

'But the prosecutors, when they are in the midst of a trial, do not leave at the end of the day, do they?'

She looks at Sandy suspiciously.

'Isn't it commonplace, in your experience, for the deputy PAs to prepare for the next day of trial in the evenings?' Stern asks.

'Oh yes.'

'Now, madam, would you not prefer to work in air conditioning rather than the PA's office on a very warm evening?'

'Objection,' Nico says. It's largely pointless.

'I'll let it stand.'

'Sure would.'

'You don't know of your own knowledge that Ms Polhemus's apartment was air-conditioned, I take it?'

'No, sir.'

'But you do know that the riverfront is much closer to the PA's office than Mr Sabich's home in Nearing?'

'Yes, sir.'

Whatever the jury makes of Eugenia, it is probably favorable compared to their opinions of Mrs Krapotnik, who is called next. Her few minutes on the witness stand achieve the level of pure burlesque. Mrs Krapotnik is a widow. She does not say what Mr Krapotnik died from, but it is hard to believe that Mrs Krapotnik was not partly the cause. She is heavy-bosomed and garishly made up. Her hair is reddish, teased out so that it stands like a shrub, and her jewelry is thick. A difficult human being. She refuses to answer questions and narrates, free-flow. Mrs Krapotnik explains as she is going along that the late Mr Krapotnik was an entre-preneur of sorts. He bought their loft building on the riverfront when, as Mrs K. puts it, 'the neighborhood was still a mess, with trucks and junk, whatever.' She nods to the jury when she says this, confident that they know what she means. Mr Krapotnik directed the refurbishment of the property himself.

'He was a visionary. Do you know what I'm saying? He saw things. That place – you know what was in there? Tires, I'm not kidding, Mr Dioguardi. Tires. Really, you could not believe the smell. I am not squeamish and it is embarrassing to say it, but one time he took me in there, I swear to God I thought I would retch.'

'Madam,' Nico says, not for the first time.

'He was a plumber. Who thought he knew real estate? Yes, Mr Dioguardi?' She squints. 'Is that your name? Dioguardi?'

'Della Guardia,' says Nico, and casts his face despairingly toward Molto, seeking help.

By and by Mrs Krapotnik reaches Carolyn. She was their tenant originally when she moved in almost a decade ago. During the conversion craze, the building went condo and Carolyn bought. Listening to Mrs Krapotnik, I write Kemp a note. 'Where does a probation officer going to law school at night get the money to rent on the waterfront?' Kemp nods. He has thought of the same thing. For almost a decade, Carolyn lived on the second floor and Mrs Krapotnik the first. Carolyn sent flowers, not really the right thing, when Mr Krapotnik died.

Nico is eager to get Mrs Krapotnik out of there. The lady is beyond control. He does not bother asking about the night Carolyn was murdered. Any identification Mrs Krapotnik made at this point would be sorely impeached by her prior failures.

Instead, Nico simply asks, 'Do you see in the courtroom, Mrs Krapotnik, anyone you have seen in the vicinity of Ms Polhemus's apartment?'

'Well, I know I seen that one,' she says. She throws both hands and her bangle bracelets in the direction of the judge.

Larren covers his face with both hands. Nico pinches the bridge of his nose. The laughter in the spectator sections is suppressed, but seems after an instant to grow. Mrs Krapotnik, recognizing that she has blown it, looks about desperately. She points at Tommy Molto, seated at the prosecutor's table.

'Him too,' she says.

Molto makes matters worse by turning to see if there is anyone behind him.

By now the jurors are laughing.

Nico retreats to the evidence cart and brings Mrs Krapotnik the photo spread from which she has previously identified a snap of me. She looks at the spread, glances up in my direction, and shrugs. Who knows?

'Do you recall previously identifying photograph number 4?' Nico asks.

This time she says it out loud: 'Who knows?' When Nico closes his eyes in frustration, she adds, 'Oh, all right. I said it was him.'

Nico heads for his seat.

'Cross-examination.'

'One question,' says Stern. 'Mrs Krapotnik, I take it your building is air-conditioned?'

'Air condition?' She turns to the judge. 'What's his business if we got air condition?'

Larren stands to his full height and places his hands on the far side of the bench, so he is canted over Mrs Krapotnik, five or six feet above her head.

'Mrs Krapotnik,' he says quietly, 'That question can be answered yes or no. If you say anything else I will hold you in contempt.'

'Yes,' says Mrs Krapotnik.

'Nothing further,' says Stern. 'Your Honor, the record will reflect that there was no identification of Mr Sabich?'

'The record will reflect,' says Judge Lyttle, shaking his head, 'that Mr Sabich was one of the few persons in the courtroom Mrs Krapotnik missed.'

Larren leaves the bench, with the laughter still ringing.

Afterward the reporters crowd around Stern. They want a comment from him on the first day's testimony, but he will make none.

Kemp is packing back into Sandy's large trial case the docu-

257

ments – duplicates of statements and exhibits – that we withdrew during the day and which now litter the table. I am helping, but Stern takes my elbow and steers me toward the corridor.

'No gloating,' he says. 'We have a long night's work. Tomorrow they will be calling Raymond Horgan.'

How familiar it all seems. I come home at night with the same laborer's weariness that has always followed a day in court. My bones feel hollowed out by the high-voltage impulse of the day; my muscles have a neuralgic tenderness from the adrenalized super-heating. My pores, it seems, do not close down rapidly, and the low-tone body sweat of high excitement continues through the evening. I return home with my shirt encasing me like a package wrapper.

Sitting in court, I actually forget at certain moments who is on trial. The performance aspect is of course not present, but the premium on close attention is large. And once we get back to the office, I can be a lawyer again, attacking the books, making notes and memos. I was never short on intensity. When the bus pulls into Nearing shortly before 1 a.m. and I walk down the lighted and silent streets of this gentle town, the feelings are all known and, because they are known, safe. I am in a harbor. My anxiety is stanched; I am at peace. As I have for years, I stop by the door, in a rocking chair, and remove my shoes, so that when I go upstairs I will not disturb Barbara, who by now must be asleep. The house is dark. I absorb the silence and, finally alone, reflect on the events of the day. And in this moment, stimulated perhaps by all the talk of her, or simply by the momentary feeling that I have at last receded to the better past, or even by an unconscious recollection of other stealthy re-entries to my home, I am startled as Carolyn rises before me, rises as she rose for me that month or so when I thought I had found Nirvana, naked to the waist, her breasts high and spectacularly round, the nipples red, erect, and thick, her hair full of static from our bedroom romping, her sensuous mouth parted to offer some clever, salacious, stimulating remark. And again I am made almost without the power of movement by my own desire, so fierce, so hungry, so wanton. I do not care that it is mad, or hopeless: I whisper her name in the dark. Full of shame and longing, I am like a piece of crystal trembling near the breaking pitch. 'Carolyn.' Hopeless. Mad. And I cannot believe my own conviction, which is not really an idea but instead that deep embedded thing, that rope of emotion which is a wish that I could do it all again. Again. Again.

And then the ghost recedes. She folds into the air. I sit still, spine stiffened in my chair. I am breathing quickly. It will be hours now, I know, before I can sleep. I grope in the hall cabinet for something to drink. I should make my mind work over the meaning of this nighttime visitation. But I cannot. I have the sensation, as determined as the longing of only moments before, that it is all past. I sit in the rocking chair in my living room. For some strange reason, I feel better with my briefcase, and I place it in my lap.

But its protection is incomplete. The wake of this intrusion leaves the currents of my emotions roily and disturbed. In the dark I sit, and I can feel the force of the large personages of my life circling about me like the multiple moons of some far planet, each one exerting its own deep tidal impulses upon me. Barbara. Nat. Both my parents. Oh, this cataclysm of love and attachment. And shame. I feel the rocking sway of all of it, and a moving sickness of regret. Desperately, desperately I promise everyone – all of them; myself; the God in whom I do not believe – that if I survive this I will do better. Better than I have. An urgent compact, as sincere and grave as any deathbed wish.

I drink my drink. I sit here in the dark and wait for peace.

28

The first thing I notice as Raymond Horgan comes into the courtroom ·s that he has on the same suit he wore to bury Carolyn, a subtle blue serge. The added weight does not detract from his public bearing. You would describe him now as burly, and still, in the rolling way he walks, a person of stature. He and Larren exchange the same sage grin while Raymond is sworn. Seated, Horgan looks outward to assess the crowd in a composed professional manner. He nods to Stern first, then his glance crosses mine and he acknowledges me. I do not move. I do not allow an eyelash to flutter. At this moment I wish with all my heart that I may be acquitted, not for the general sake of freedom, but so that I can see the look on Raymond Horgan the first time he has to face me on the street.

Here in the courtroom, awaiting Raymond's entry, there was more of that epic atmosphere, the extra amperage of a special moment – four hundred people on edge, an urgent undertone in the courtroom murmur. Today, I notice, the press gallery is larger by a row and a half, and the journalistic first-string is on hand – the ancnor people and columnists. I have been surprised during the trial by the extent to which the reporters have been willing to honor Stern's injunctions to keep wide berth of me. Now that they have their file footage of me entering the courthouse, which they can show with each night's story on TV, Barbara and I are able to come and go in relative peace. Now and then someone – usually a journalist whom I have known for years – will stop me with a question in the hallway I refer all these matters to Stern. Last week I also encountered a freelance journalist from New York who says he is considering writing a book about the case. He believes it will make good reading. I declined his invitation to buy me dinner.

I would be oblivious to the press were it not for the morning papers. I have stopped watching the accounts on TV. The summaries seem so inept that they make me furious, even when the errors favor me. But I cannot avoid the headlines, which I see on the paper-dispensing machines as we drive into the city. The two dailies seem to have sworn a feud to see which can take the lead in trashy tabloid coverage of the case. Nico's revelation in opening of Raymond's amours with Carolyn produced tasteless headlines for two days. PA SEX the *Herald* blared, with all kinds of kickers and subheads. It is impossible that the jury does not view these headlines, too. They pledged during *voir dire* not to read the papers, but that is a promise few trial lawyers trust.

In the jury box, at the moment, there is a considerable stirring. The jurors seem far more excited to see Raymond than was the case, for example, when they first glimpsed Nico during the *voir dire*. Then I noticed only a few of the prospective jury members leaning over to one another and nodding in Delay's direction. Horgan brings a greater aura to the courtroom. He has been well known for most of everybody's adult life. He is a celebrity; Della Guardia is a replacement. Perhaps the suggestion of fleshy intrigue Nico floated in opening also contributes to the high interest. It is clear, however, that as Stern weeks ago predicted, we have reached a critical juncture in this trial. Each juror has revolved his chair to face the witness stand. As Molto comes to the podium to begin the direct examination, the large courtroom is quiet.

'State your name, please.'

'Raymond Patrick Horgan,' he answers. 'The third.' With that he grins very briefly up at Larren. A private joke. I never knew that Raymond was a third. Amazing, sometimes, what comes out under oath.

Molto again has readied himself with care for the examination. Raymond clearly knows what is coming, as he should, and he and Tommy develop a nice rhythm at once. Horgan's hands are folded. In his blue suit and finest public manner, he looks serene. All his beguiling charm is present; his candor. His gruff baritone is reduced one marking on the volume register in an effort at understatement.

Tommy is taking his time. They are going to get everything they can from Horgan, recover quickly from yesterday's debacle in the war of impressions. They cover Raymond's background. Born right here. High school on the East End at St Viator's. Two years' college, then his dad died. He became a cop. Seven years on the force, was already a sergeant when he graduated from night law school. I am afraid for a moment that Molto is going to bring out the fact that Raymond practiced law with Larren, but that is elided. Horgan simply says it was a three-man partnership, doing primarily criminal work. After sixteen years in practice, politics.

'Some elections I won,' says Raymond, 'some I lost.' With that he turns to smile fondly at Nico at the prosecutor's table. Delay rears his half-bald head from taking notes and beams back. My God, how they look at each other! The fastest friends. The jurors seem delighted by this alliance, forged on well-known past adversity. The smiling schoolteacher watches the unspoken exchange between the two with apparent delight. I feel my soul sinking. This will be a very hard day.

'And do you know the defendant, Rožat Sabich?'

'I know Rusty,' Raymond says.

'Do you see him here in court?'

'I do.'

'Would you point to him and describe what he is wearing.'

'Next to Mr Stern. Second at the defense table, in a blue chalk-stripe suit.'

This is a formality to establish that the Sabich spoken of is me. Yesterday with Eugenia, Sandy rose and agreed – 'stipulated' is the term – to the identification so that we did not have to go through this exercise in finger-pointing. But now Stern quietly says to me, 'Stand.' I do. I rise slowly and face Raymond Horgan. I do not smile or grimace, but I am sure my abject fury is plain. Certainly Raymond's affability fades somewhat, even while his hand is in the air.

'That's him,' says Raymond quietly.

Molto breezes through the history of my association with

Raymond. Sandy will bring it out in detail anyway. Then he asks Raymond about Carolyn. Here Horgan becomes instantly somber. He lets his eyes fall to the rail of the witness box and says, 'Yes, I knew her, too.'

'What was the nature of your relationship?'

'I met her first as a probation officer. For eight years she was employed as a deputy prosecuting attorney in our office, and for a very brief time at the end of last year we had a personal relationship as well.'

Nice, succinct. They move to the murder. Molto never mentions the election, but it emerges in Raymond's answers by reference.

'And is there any practice in the PA's office in supervising police investigations?'

'Certainly in a major case – and this was a very major case in my mind – there was a practice to assign a deputy PA to guide and assist the police.'

'Who made the assignment in this case?'

'Well, to short-circuit things a little bit, I would say that Mr Sabich and I decided that he should have that role in this case.'

Tommy for the first time pauses. Raymond, it seems, may have backed down a little as a result of his meeting with Stern and me. Molto did not expect that. He asks again:

'How did Mr Sabich get that assignment?'

'I don't really remember whether I suggested it or he did. Like everybody else, I was confused and upset at that time. He got the case. But he was glad to have it. I remember that. He was not reluctant at all, and promised to pursue it vigorously.'

'Did he?'

'Not to my way of thinking.' This is objectionable as a conclusion but Stern does not want to interrupt. One of his thick fingers has been laid from his chin to his nose and he watches intently, not even bothering to take notes. At many times his concentration in court is trance-like. He shows very little, just absorbs. I have the same sense that I did when we were in Horgan's office that Sandy's calculations are not about facts or strategy but character. He is trying to figure Horgan out.

Raymond registers his complaints with my handling of the case,

263

including having to urge me to speed up the fingerprint and fiber reports. The impression comes through clearly that I was dogging it. Then he describes the conversation in his office that night we both first realized he was going to lose.

'He asked me if I had been intimate with Carolyn.'

'And what did you tell him?'

'The truth,' says Raymond, quite simply. No big deal. 'We'd been on for three months, then off.'

'And when you told him this, did Mr Sabich express surprise in any way?'

'None at all.'

I get it. They're going to reason backward. I asked, but I knew anyway. What is their theory? That I was outraged when I found out? Or that I gave in to the weight of accumulated grievances? Neither one makes complete sense, when you suppose, as Nico has, that my relationship with Carolyn was ongoing. Not having the right facts always hurts. I can feel many of the jurors watching me now, trying to read in me the truth of the prosecutors' surmise.

'And at any time in this conversation or at any time earlier, did Mr Sabich inform you that he himself had a personal relationship with Ms Polhemus?'

Sandy is instantly back to life, on his feet.

'Objection. Your Honor, there is simply no proof of record of any personal relationship between Mr Sabich and Ms Polhemus.' A good tactic, if for no other reason than to break the rhythm now and draw the jury back to yesterday. But this obstacle we are throwing up still presents a painful straddle for me. We cannot continue to make an issue of this failure of proof if I am going to get on the witness stand and tell the jury that everything Stern contested for two weeks is true, that Carolyn and I indeed had a warm romance. This is one of the many delicate means that Stern is employing seemingly to discourage my testimony.

'We-e-e-ll,' drawls Larren. He turns around in his chair. 'I would say *almost* no proof.' A nice comment for the defense. 'I'm gonna let the question stand, but I want to give the jury a limiting instruction.' He faces them. 'Ladies and gentlemen, Mr Molto is asking a question based on an assumption. It's up to you to decide, based on the evidence you hear in court, whether that assumption is true. Just because he says this doesn't make it so. Mr Stern says there is not sufficient evidence to warrant that assumption, and at the end of the case that will be one of the things for you to determine. Proceed, Mr Molto.'

Molto repeats the question.

'Certainly not,' says Raymond. The Gaelic humor has now left his face.

'Is that something you would have wanted to know?'

'Objection.'

'Rephrase it, Mr Molto. Is it something that the witness would have expected Mr Sabich to tell him, based on the witness's understanding of his office's practices?' It is rare for Larren to be so helpful to the prosecutors. I can see that Raymond is having the impact I long feared.

When the question is put as the judge suggested, Raymond buries me.

'I certainly did expect that. I never would have allowed him to handle that investigation. It raises more questions that it answers. The public should know that things are being done for professional, not personal, reasons,' he adds, a gratuitous shot. Stern, in front of me, frowns.

Molto then takes Raymond to the end. The meeting in his office. Horgan faithfully recounts my outbursts in spite of Mac's and his warnings.

'Describe Mr Sabich's appearance as he left the meeting.'

'He looked quite excited, I would say. Very upset. He seemed to have completely lost his composure.'

Molto looks at Nico, then says he has nothing further on direct.

Larren takes a recess before cross. In the john, as I come out of a stall, I find Della Guardia two sinks down. His hair is too thin now to comb; instead, he tries to tickle it into place with his fingertips. His eyes flick a little bit when he notices me in the mirror.

'Not a bad witness, huh?' he asks. His intent is hard to divine. I don't know if this is a casual aside or gloating. I keep getting the feeling that Nico is out of place emotionally. He is not oriented in this case – like offering me his hand on the day of the arraignment. He has never been the kind of person to make a frontal approach to unpleasantness, especially once someone has reached him. I remember when he divorced Diana; even though she had been running around, he took her back into the apartment for a few weeks when she was thrown out by the other guy. Nico reads something in my hesitation. 'I mean, you have to admit, he is not a bad witness.'

I dry my hands. I realize now what it is. Nico still wants me to like him. God, human beings are strange. And maybe Nico even has his redeeming side. Horgan at this moment would be cold as a saber's edge. It seems pointless at this little minute to resist him. I smile a bit. I use his nickname.

'Better than Mrs Krapotnik, Delay.'

'Now, Mr Horgan, you mentioned that you had a personal relationship with Ms Polhemus? Is that correct?'

'It is.'

'And you also told us that you believe Mr Sabich should have informed you that he had had such a relationship as well?'

'At a later time,' says Raymond carefully. He wants to rule out jealousy on his part. 'I felt when the investigation began he had a professional obligation to tell me.'

'Have you any personal knowledge, Mr Horgan, that there was ever such a relationship between Mr Sabich and Ms Polhemus?'

'That's the point,' says Horgan. 'He never told me.'

Sandy does not take getting stuck cheerfully. He looks at length toward Horgan. He wants the jury to notice that Raymond Horgan is taking shots.

'Please answer the question I asked you. Do you remember it?'

'I do.'

'But you chose not to answer it?'

Raymond's mouth moves without words. 'I apologize, Mr Stern. I have no personal knowledge of such a relationship.'

'Thank you.' Sandy strolls. 'But assuming there was something to reveal, you believe an honest official would make such disclosures to someone in a responsible position?'

'I do.'

'I see,' says Stern. He takes a moment to face Raymond. Sandy is short and soft, but in the courtroom he emits tremendous power. He is clearly equal to Raymond Horgan, who, too, is looking very firm. He sits there with his reddened Irish bulk, his hands folded, waiting for Sandy to take him on. Assuming that he comes out of this intact, Raymond's combination of prominence and skill is likely to make him the leading defense attorney in this city. His nearest rival will be the man who is examining him now. In the years ahead there are no doubt going to be a number of multiple-defendant cases in which they will sit together as co-counsel. In a very real sense, preservation of his relationship with Raymond is of far more practical importance for Stern than anything that happens to me. The rule of life in the defense bar ordinarily is to go along and get along. The state is the only professional enemy these guys want to have.

Recognizing all of that, I have put my hostility aside and told Sandy that he has my blessings to treat Raymond gently. As Stern has pointed out before, Raymond's credibility, born of years in the public light, will make him hard to successfully assail, in any event. But it is clear from Stern's demeanor that he will be neither courtly nor accommodating to Raymond. Perhaps Stern believes the direct was too damaging to simply absorb. But I am surprised that Sandy has begun any attack this abruptly. There are some favorable things Raymond will have to concede – compliments on my performance in the office in the past, for example. The traditional wisdom is that you take what a witness will give before you slap him.

'And you applied these standards for disclosure to yourself as well?'

'I tried.'

'Certainly you would give all appropriate information to someone on your staff doing a job for you?'

'Again, Mr Stern, I'd try.'

'And certainly the case concerning Ms Polhemus's death was a very important case in your office?'

267

'Given its political significance, I would call it critical.' Raymond looks in my direction as he says this. His eyes are hard as ball bearings.

'But even though you yourself saw this as a critical case, you did not give Mr Sabich all the information at your disposal about the matter, or about Ms Polhemus, did you?'

'I tried.'

'Did you? Was it not very important to know everything Ms Polhemus was working on, so that any person who might have a motive to do her harm could be identified?'

Raymond suddenly sees where this is going. He sits back in his chair. But he still tries to fight.

'That wasn't the only thing that was important.'

Bad mistake. Lawyers really are lousy witnesses. Raymond is going to deny that Carolyn's docket was an important source of leads. Sandy embarrasses him badly in the next few moments. People in law enforcement often fear reprisals from those they prosecute? Such reprisals all too frequently occur? Law enforcement would be impossible if prosecutors and police could be assaulted, maimed, murdered by those they investigate? Certainly when Ms Polhemus was killed it was a thought, indeed it was speculated in the press, was it not, that a former defendant might have been her attacker? Raymond sees he's lost after a few questions, and answers simply yes.

'So all of Ms Polhemus's cases were important? It was important to know whom she was investigating, what she was looking into?'

'Yes.'

'And in spite of knowing that, Mr Horgan, you personally removed a file from Ms Polhemus's drawer after the investigation of her murder began, didn't you?'

'Yes.'

'A very sensitive matter, was it not?'

Larren has observed the cross, lying back in his chair. For the most part he has appeared faintly amused by this contest between two well-known professionals. Now he interrupts.

'What's the relevance of this, Counsel?'

Sandy for a moment is wordstruck.

'Your Honor, I think that the relevance of this is clear.'

'Not to me.'

'The witness has testified on direct examination that Mr Sabich did not bring to his attention information that Mr Horgan regarded as pertinent. The defendant is entitled to explore Mr Horgan's standards in this regard.'

'Mr Horgan was the prosecuting attorney, Mr Stern. You're mixing apples and oranges,' says the judge.

Relief comes from an unexpected source. Della Guardia is on his feet.

'We have no objection to this line of questioning, Judge.'

Larren lets his glance linger in Nico's direction. Molto immediately grabs Delay's forearm. I assume that Nico wants the discussion about professional standards to continue in the belief that it will further educate the jury about the extent of my deviation. But he is well out of place here. For one thing, Horgan is not his witness. And I take it from the heated way that Molto speaks to him as Delay resumes his seat that Nico does not recognize the drift of Sandy's questioning. I wonder if he even knows about the B file or has just forgotten. I make a note which I will give to Stern at the break: Who did Horgan tell *re* B file? Molto? Nico? neither?

With new daylight, Sandy quickly proceeds.

'As I said, this was a very sensitive matter, was it not?'

'Yes.'

'It involved allegations –'

Larren again injects himself, more faithful than a Labrador.

'We don't need the details of the internal workings of the prosecuting attorney's office or of its investigations, many of which, I remind you, Mr Stern, are protected by rules of grand-jury secrecy. This was a sensitive case. Let us move on.'

'Of course, Your Honor, I had no interest in disclosing any secrets.'

'Of course not,' says Larren. He smiles with apparent disbelief and turns toward his water carafe, which, it so happens, is in the direction of the jury. 'Proceed.'

'And, in fact, this case was so sensitive, Mr Horgan, that you assigned it to Ms Polhemus without informing any other person in your office that you had done so. Yes?'

'Yes.'

Sandy quickly lists everyone in the office who was not told: Mac. The Special Investigations Chief, Mike Dolan. Three or four more names. He ends with me. Raymond acknowledges each.

'And you gave the file to Mr Sabich only when he personally informed you that a file appeared to be missing from Ms Polhemus's office, is that not true?'

'True.'

Sandy takes a little tour around the courtroom to let all of this sink in. Raymond has been tarnished. The jury is paying close attention.

'Now, Ms Polhemus was an ambitious woman, was she not?'

'I suppose it depends on what you mean by ambitious.'

'She enjoyed being in the public eye, she wanted to progress in your office, did she not?'

'All true.'

'She wanted to handle this case?'

'As I recall.'

'Now, Mr Horgan, you assigned this case to Ms Polhemus, this highly sensitive matter to her, this case that only you and she knew about, this case she was eager to handle while you two were personally involved, correct?'

Raymond begins to roll again in his seat. He knows that Stern will spare him nothing now. He has hunkered down a little, so that to my eye it looks as if he is trying to duck.

'I really don't recall exactly when I made that assignment.'

'Let me remind you, then.' Sandy gets the file jacket, shows Raymond the docketing date, reminds him of his direct testimony about when he and Carolyn were dating. 'So,' he concludes, 'you assigned this very sensitive case to Ms Polhemus while you were personally involved with her?'

'That appears to be when it happened.'

Stern stands still and looks at Horgan.

'The answer to the question,' says Raymond, 'is yes.'

'Your failure to inform anyone of this assignment contradicted established procedure in your office, did it not?'

'I was the prosecuting attorney. I decided when there would be exceptions to the rules.' He has picked up Larren's hint.

'And you made an exception for Ms Polhemus?'

'Yes.'

'With whom you were – Strike that. Ordinarily such a case would have been assigned to a lawyer with more experience in such matters. would it not?'

'That's a consideration ordinarily.'

'But that wasn't a consideration here?'

'No.'

'And this remained your secret with Ms Polhemus, did it not, even after your relationship with her ended?'

'True,' says Raymond. He smiles for the first time in a while. 'There was no change in my conduct.'

'Because you were embarrassed?'

'It didn't occur to me.'

'And when Mr Sabich was trying to assemble all the information in the office about Ms Polhemus's cases, it did not occur to you that you had gone to her office and put the file in your drawer?'

'I suppose it didn't'

'You were not attempting to conceal anything, were you, Mr Horgan?'

'I was not.'

'There was an election campaign taking place, was there not?'

'Yes.'

'A tough campaign?'

'Brutal.'

'A campaign in which, as it turned out, you were losing?'

'Yes.'

'A campaign in which your opponent, Mr Della Guardia, had been a deputy in your very office and had many friends there?'

'That's true.'

'And you were not concerned, Mr Horgan, in the midst of this brutal campaign about word leaking out, through one of Mr Della

Guardia's friends, that you had given choice assignments to an assistant with whom you were sleeping?'

'Maybe it crossed my mind. Who knows, Mr Stern? It was not an ideal situation.'

'Far from it,' says Stern. 'I ask you again, sir, were you not trying to hide the fact that you had had an affair with a member of your staff?'

'It wasn't something I ordinarily talked about, if that's what you mean.'

'No indeed. It could be viewed as unprofessional.'

'It could be, but it wasn't. We were both adults.'

'I see. You had confidence in your judgment, notwithstanding this affair?'

'Very much so.'

Stern has gradually approached Horgan. Now he takes the last few steps and reaches out to touch the rail of the witness stand, so that he stands only a few feet from Raymond.

'And yet, sir, you come to this courtroom where the life of a man who served you faithfully for a dozen years now hangs in the balance, and you tell us that you would have none of the same confidence in him?'

Horgan's look locks with Stern's. From where I am, I cannot quite see Raymond's expression. He finally faces about and when he does he has his tongue tucked into his cheek. He is looking now in Della Guardia's direction, somewhat sheepishly. I am not sure if he is seeking help or casting apologies.

'I wish he had said something, that's all. It would have looked better for him. It would have looked better for me.'

One of the jurors says, 'Hmm.' I hear the sound, but do not see whom it came from. Others are looking toward the floor. It is hard to figure why this seems to have such impact. Nothing has changed the fingerprints, or the fibers, or the records from my phone. But it has been a splendid moment for the defense. Molto and Nico have brought Raymond Horgan to this courtroom as the model of propriety, the arbiter of standards. Now it turns out that things have been overblown. Just as he did in representing Colleen McGaffen, Sandy Stern has found the message to this

272

jury that he wishes to send but never speak aloud. So what? he is saying. Suppose it is true that Sabich and the decedent had been intimate. Suppose that he chose, wisely or not, to keep that to himself. It is still no different from what Horgan did. If I was too embarrassed to confess aspects of my past conduct, everyone should understand. The knot between what I did not say and what I did has been untied; the juncture has been severed between murder and deceit.

Sandy walks away. He lets Horgan sit. Raymond sighs a couple of times and removes his handkerchief. As Stern paces by our table, he places his hand on my shoulder and I cover it with mine. A spontaneous gesture, but it seems to go down well with one or two jurors who notice.

'Let us turn to another subject, Mr Horgan. How did you meet Mr Sabich?'

Sandy is still strolling, headed back now toward the witness, and below the table I motion to him, no. I forgot to tell him not to ask that question.

'Perhaps we should not loiter with ancient history,' says Sandy casually. 'I shall withdraw that question, if the court please. As a matter of fact, Your Honor, if this would be a convenient point, perhaps we could all do with some lunch.'

'Very well,' says Larren. He seems particularly sober after Raymond's performance. Before he leaves the bench, Judge Lyttle glances back at Horgan, who has still not moved.

29

'So what did you think of this morning? Hmm?' asks Stern. He reaches for the relish tray. 'You must try the corn willie, Rusty. Such a simple dish, but really very well prepared.'

Stern has worked through lunch each day preceding, but you can tell that it is not his chosen routine. A civilized life includes a meal at noontime, he would say, and today, Horgan or not, he takes me to his dining club for lunch. It is on the forty-sixth floor of Morgan Towers, one of the tallest buildings in town. From here you can see the river bend and sway, the serried ranks of the city skyline, which these days looks mostly like so many shoe boxes end on end. If you had a telescope you could probably make out my home in Nearing.

I would have expected to become closer to Sandy. I am fond of him, and my respect for his professional abilities, never slight, has grown progressively. But I would not say that we have become friends. Perhaps it is because I am a client, charged with murder no less. But Stern's view of human capacity is itself large enough that I doubt any one act, no matter how heinous, would disqualify someone from his affections. The problem, if there is a problem, is the man and his inner restraints. He draws his lines in his professional life and I doubt anyone passes. He has been married thirty years. I have met Clara once or twice. Their three children are now spread all around the country; the youngest, a daughter, will finish at Columbia Law School next year. But as I think about it, I do not know many other people who claim to be close to Stern. He is a pleasant companion on any social occasion, and he is a polished raconteur. I remember that a friend of Barbara's father told me years ago that Stern tells marvelous stories in Yiddish, a skill I, of course, cannot confirm. But there are sharp limits on Sandy Stern's sense of intimacy. I know very little of what he really thinks, particularly about me.

'I have two comments about this morning,' I say, as I help myself to corn. 'I thought it went very well, and I enjoyed it a great deal. The cross has been brilliant.'

'Oh well,' says Stern. Sandy, despite his fine manners, is a considerable egotist, like every other noted trial lawyer. He shakes his head, but then takes a moment to savor my praise. A number of the reporters and courtroom observers whispered their compliments as we were on the way over here. Stern, only halfway through the cross, still wears the light air of triumph. 'He did it to himself, really. I do not think I recognized before the start of this case how vain a person Raymond is. Even so, I do not know how far it takes us.'

'You embarrassed him very badly.'

'Apparently. He is bound to remind me of it someday. But this is not our problem now.'

'I was surprised Larren was so protective of Raymond. If I had to guess, I would have bet that he'd have bent over backward to appear neutral.'

'Larren has never been afraid of being regarded as a man with his own affinities.' Sandy sits back as a waiter sets down his plate. 'Well,' says Stern, 'I only hope we do as well at the next critical juncture. I am not as optimistic.'

I do not understand what he is talking about.

'There are two pivotal cross-examinations in this trial, Rusty,' he says. 'We are only in the midst of the first.'

'What's the other – Lipranzer?'

'No.' Stern frowns a bit, unhappy, apparently, merely with the prospect of Lip's testimony. 'Detective Lipranzer for us will be primarily a holding action. In that case, we will be hoping, merely, to ease the sting. No, I was thinking of Dr Kumagai.'

'Kumagai?'

'Oh yes.' Sandy nods to himself. 'You see, of course, that the physical evidence is the center of the prosecutors' case. But in order to fully utilize that evidence, Nico must call a scientific expert. Della Guardia cannot stand before the jury at the end of the case and offer only conjecture on how this act took place. His theories must be buttressed by a scientist's opinions. So he will call Kumagai.' Sandy samples his lunch with obvious appreciation. 'Forgive me for being didactic. I am unaccustomed to counseling trial lawyers. At any rate, Kumagai's testimony becomes critical. If he performs well, he will solidify the prosecution case. But his testimony also offers an opportunity for us. It is really the only chance we will have to blunt the edge somewhat of the physical evidence – the fingerprints, the fibers, all of these items that are normally unassailable. If we make Kumagai look dubious, the physical evidence, all of it, suffers as well.'

'And how do you do that?'

'Ah,' says Stern, somewhat wistfully, 'you ask all the difficult questions. We must turn our attention to that shortly.' He taps his bread knife and casts his eyes toward the skyline, not really focused on it. 'Kumagai is not a pleasant individual. A jury will not warm to him. Something will suggest itself. In the meantime,' Stern says, looking back to me abruptly, 'what was this blunder I almost made? Something awful would have been disclosed when I asked how you and Horgan met?'

'I didn't think you wanted the jury to hear about how the Yugoslavian freedom fighter went to federal prison.'

'Your father? Oh dear. Rusty, I must apologize to you for that improvisation the other day. It came to me as I was there. You understand these things, I am sure.'

I tell Sandy that I understand.

'Your father went to jail? How did that happen? Horgan represented him?'

'Steve Mulcahy. Raymond just covered a couple of the court calls. That was how we met. He was very nice to me. I was quite upset.'

'Mulcahy was the other partner?' In those days it was Mulcahy, Lyttle & Horgan. 'He has been dead many years. We are talking about some time ago, I take it.'

276

'I was still in law school. Mulcahy was my professor. When my father got the first summons, I went to him. I was terribly embarrassed. I thought character and fitness might keep me out.'

'Of the bar? My Lord! What was the crime?'

'Taxes,' I say. I take the first bite of my lunch. 'My father didn't file for twenty-five years.'

'Twenty-five years! Oh my. How is your fish?'

'Good. Would you care for a little?'

'If you don't mind. Thank you. You are much too kind. They really do this very well here.'

Sandy chats on. He is serene and comfortable amid the silver-plate table settings and the waiters in pastel cutaway coats. His retreat. In forty-five minutes he will resume cross-examining one of the most prominent lawyers in the city. But like all virtuosos he has a well-deserved faith in his instincts. He has worked hard. The rest is inspiration.

When the meal is near its end, I show Sandy the notes I made this morning. 'Oh yes,' he tells me. 'Very good.' Some matters he is determined not even to respond to. 'You are falsely accused and he says you seem to lack composure? Really, this is too silly to repeat.'

At another table, he sees a friend, an older red-haired man. Sandy departs for a second to greet him. I review the pad I have brought along from the courthouse, but most of it has been covered in our discussion. Instead, I look out toward the city and, as usual, think about my father with despair. I had been wildly angry with him throughout that episode, both because of my own discomfiture and because I felt he had no right to seek attention after ignoring my mother's illness, then in its initial stages. But as I watched my father in Mulcahy's outer office, a worm of pain began to eat at my heart. In his distraction, my father, usually rigid about his personal hygiene, had failed to shave. His beard grew quickly and his cheeks were whitish with the stubble. He held the felt brim of his hat in his fingers and turned it in his hands. He had a tie on, which he seldom wore; the knot was a kind of crumbled mess pulled off to the side, and his shirt was soiled around the collar. He did not seem to fill his chair, or even his clothing. He looked at his feet on the floor. He appeared much older than he was. And terribly afraid.

I do not believe I had ever seen my father visibly frightened before that. His almost invariable mien was of a rough-tempered, sullen indifference. I did not wonder what produced the change. My father seldom spoke to me about his history. Virtually everything I knew came from his relatives. The shooting of his parents; my father's flight; the camps of one side or the other where my father passed the last years of his youth. They ate a horse, my cousin Ilya told me once when I was nine or ten. The story inspired nightmares for most of a week. An old nag had died. It keeled over in the night and froze. It lay in the snow for three days, and then some guard allowed it to be dragged beyond the barbed-wire fence of the compound. The inmates attacked it; they pulled off the hide with their bare hands and grabbed at the flesh. Some meant only to take something to cook, but others in their panic began to eat it there. My father had seen that. He came to America. He had survived. And now in a lawyer's office, almost three decades later, he could foresee a repetition. I was twenty-five years old, and I understood more of my father's life then, and how his deprivations, in that odd heredity of material effects, had become my own – I recognized more of that in a moment than in all the time before. And I was overcome by grief.

Mulcahy pled my father guilty. The assistant US attorney promised not to recommend more than a year in jail, and old Judge Hartley, a soft touch, gave him only ninety days. I saw him just once while he was in. I had no stomach for it, and my mother by then was nearing the end.

When I asked how he was, he looked around, as if he were only now seeing the place for the first time. He was chewing on a toothpick.

I been in worse, he told me. He had regained all his old harshness, and I found it more upsetting than his fear. Iron-headed, ignorant, he embraced his deepest misfortunes with a kind of pride. The things for which not only he, but I, eventually, had come to suffer he claimed as badges of achievement. He had played in the Olympics of confinement. He could survive a local jail. He had no gratitude to me; no apologies for my shame, or for his stupidity. No knowledge of his real prison. It was late in his life; he died not quite three years later. But the truth is that for everything that went before, it was not until that moment that I finally gave him up.

The afternoon's cross begins where I thought the morning's might, in those areas where Horgan is our witness. Stern starts with the calls in March from my phone to Carolyn's. Horgan promptly recollects the recidivist rapist indictment she was trying to draw together that month, and he acknowledges that one of the chief deputy's primary functions is to assist in the drafting of charges, especially in complex cases. Raymond does not resist Stern's suggestion that Carolyn's trial schedule and my crowded daytime calendar could easily have led to those consultations taking place by phone at night, or, at least, to calls aimed at scheduling meetings about the proposed indictment.

From the calls, Stern moves on to the conversation in Raymond's office the Wednesday after the election. By offering my statement that I was at home the night Carolyn was murdered, the prosecution has, in essence, put in evidence of my defense and Stern elaborates upon it.

Sandy emphasizes that my statement was voluntary. Ms MacDougall encouraged Mr Sabich not to speak? You, Mr Horgan, asked him not to speak? You, sir, in the strongest terms? You told him to keep his mouth shut? Yet he spoke, and he was clearly quite provoked, was he not? Nothing calculated in his manner? His remarks appeared spontaneous? Stern develops at length a prosecutor's learning about the hazards to an investigation subject of talking. The implication, carefully teased out, is that any person of my background who'd had time to contemplate the prospect of confrontation would have known better than to speak up, especially in this fashion. A man who had been at the scene, Stern is suggesting, who had done what the prosecutors say I did, and who was in charge of the investigation, would know better than to choose a lie so easily exposed. Only a person who truly had not been there and who was ignorant of the real circumstances could be provoked by fresh insult to burst out with this truthful response, which chance has bizarrely undermined. Watching Stern do the cross, I foresee his closing argument, and perceive clearly the reasons for keeping me off the stand. Rusty Sabich made his spontaneous explanation the day he was first confronted. What else is there really that he can add now, so long after the fact?

With my version before the jury, Stern goes about building my credibility. He takes Raymond on an extensive tour of my achievements as a deputy PA. He begins, in fact, with *Law Review* and goes through the succeeding years. When Molto finally objects that this is unnecessary, Sandy explains that Horgan has questioned my judgment in the direction of the Polhemus investigation. It is appropriate that the jury know the full extent of my professional background, so that they are able to recognize that what has been portrayed as unwillingness or insubordination may merely be a disagreement between two veteran prosecuting attorneys. The logic of this position is largely unassailable and Larren directs Molto to resume his seat. The canonization of St Rožat goes on.

'And so, nearly two years ago now,' Sandy eventually asks, 'when Mr Sennett, then your chief deputy, moved to San Diego, you turned to Mr Sabich to fill that spot?'

'I did.'

'And is it fair to say that the chief deputy is the person in the office in whose judgment you place the greatest confidence?'

'You could say that. I regarded him as the best lawyer for the job.'

'All right. You had 120 other deputies?'

'About that.'

'Including Mr Della Guardia and Mr Molto?'

'Yes.'

'And you chose Mr Sabich?'

'I did.'

Nico looks up, irked, but neither he nor Molto objects. Sandy works like a jeweler, tapping, tapping at his themes of past resentments. Two of the jurors seem to nod.

'And you did not think Mr Sabich would commit a crime, you had absolute and complete confidence in his judgment and integrity, based on working closely with him for more than a decade?'

The question is compound, and argumentative, but also obvious. 'Let it stand,' says Larren when Molto objects. Raymond weighs the answer.

'That's fair,' he finally says. This small concession seems to have had a substantial effect in the jury box. I see now why Stern attacked Raymond at the outset. He had a point to make. Not with the jury – but with Raymond Horgan. Matters are not as clear to Raymond as they were when he walked into the courtroom.

'Just so. And it was not necessary for him to check with you on all matters to be sure that he was proceeding in exactly the manner you wished?' Stern asks. I take it that he is trying to minimize the significance of my delay in pursuing the fingerprint report.

'I always gave the people who worked for me some leeway.'

'Well, is it not true, Mr Horgan, that in conducting the investigation of Ms Polhemus's murder, Mr Sabich knew that you had trusted his judgment on many occasions in the past, including on many substantial matters?'

'I don't know what he knew, but I had obviously approved of his judgment in the past on a lot of things.'

'For example,' says Sandy, without any indication of what is coming, 'you gave Mr Sabich the authority to decide where and when to fire Mr Della Guardia.'

Nico, understandably, erupts. Larren is disturbed. He calls immediately for a conference with the lawyers outside the jury's presence. Some judges hold these meetings, known as sidebars, in the courtroom at the side of the bench away from the jury. Larren's practice – designed to keep the jury from overhearing the lawyers' arguments – is to leave the courtroom entirely and stand in the small anteroom outside his chambers.

Della Guardia, Molto, Kemp, Stern, the court reporter, and I all follow the judge out the back door to the courtroom behind his bench. It is clear even before everyone has assembled that the judge is put out with Stern. He regards the last question as a cheap shot.

'Now what are we going to do here?' he demands of Sandy. 'Relive ancient history day by day? We are not gonna turn this lawsuit into a contest over personalities.'

Molto and Nico are both talking. Any past antagonism between the prosecutor and the defendant is irrelevant, they say. Judge Lyttle is clearly inclined to agree.

'Your Honor,' says Stern, 'we do not accuse Mr Della Guardia personally of bad faith. But we believe this is a circumstance indicating how and why he might be misled.' Without saying it, Stern is focusing again on Molto. He has been careful to pick on him, and not Nico, from the start. Della Guardia is a popular person in this town right now, and known to the jurors. Molto is a cipher. Perhaps Sandy also means to take advantage somehow of the unequivocal promise made at the start that Molto would not testify.

'Why Mr Della Guardia might be misled, Mr Stern, is irrelevant. What the prosecutor thinks of his case is no matter to this jury. Lord knows, you don't want to start gettin into that.'

'Your Honor,' says Stern solemnly, 'it is the theory of the defense that Mr Sabich has been framed in this case.'

From this huddled group, I take a step backward myself. I am stunned. Stern had so thoroughly rejected this tactic weeks ago that I had given it no further thought. And things seemed to be going so well without it. Was Horgan's direct that devastating? I no longer understood my own lawyer's theory of defense. Just a moment ago, I thought he was working up one of his delicate unspoken messages to the jury: Molto wanted Sabich's job. He pressed too hard to make a case in order to obtain it, and Della Guardia failed to recognize this because he, even unconsciously, was nursing a grudge of his own. That was vintage Sandy Stern, an artful assessment of human frailty, quietly communicated, designed to diminish the prosecutors' credibility and to demonstrate how this grotesque error – accusing me – came to be made. This is the kind of believable undercurrent juries eagerly receive. But this is a blunderbuss technique, one which, I had come to agree with Stern, was not worth the risk. Certainly I was not prepared for this change of direction without consultation. And on the record. These corridor conferences are available to the public. The reporters at the break will crowd around the court reporter and beg her to read her notes. I can see the headline: SABICH FRAMED, LAWYER SAYS. Lord knows what the jurors will think, if any of them fail to miss the unavoidable. Improvising, Sandy has raised the stakes.

In the meantime, Nico walks up and down the corridor snorting. 'I don't believe it,' he says two or three times.

Larren looks to Molto for a response.

'Ridiculous,' Molto says.

'Your denial is noted for the record. I mean your response on the point of evidence. If Mr Stern is truly going to endeavor to prove that the case against Mr Sabich has been manufactured, then I suppose this history of antagonism is relevant for those purposes.'

That of course is one reason why Stern may have gone down the road now, to get normally inadmissible proof before the jury.

'I must say,' the judge says, 'Mr Stern, that you are playing with fire. I don't know where this is gonna lead us. But I'll tell you two things. You had better be prepared for the prosecution's response. Because the prosecutor will be entitled to quite a bit of latitude in answering. And secondly, proof of this charge better be forthcoming or I'll strike all the cross-examination on this theme and I'll do that in the jury's presence.' Larren from his considerable height looks down at Stern directly. At this juncture, most defense lawyers, caught running out of bounds, back off and withdraw the question.

Stern says simply, 'I understand. Your Honor, I think, will see exactly how this will develop. We will offer evidence addressed to the issue.'

'Very well.'

We return to the courtroom.

'What the hell is he doing?' I ask Kemp as we sit down again at the defense table. Jamie shakes his head. Sandy has not conferred with him either about this.

Stern quickly leaves the subject of Nico's firing and moves on to smaller matters. He makes a few more minor points at random and then comes back to the counsel table to confer.

'Almost done,' he whispers to Kemp and me. 'I have one further area. Anything more?'

I ask what he was doing out in the hallway and he places his hand on my shoulder. He says he will discuss it later. Kemp tells Sandy he has nothing else and Stern once more addresses the witness.

'Just a few more questions, Mr Horgan. You have been most patient. We spoke earlier about a file you assigned Ms Polhemus, a very sensitive case. Do you recall that part of the examination?'

'I believe I'll remember it for quite some time,' says Raymond. He smiles, though.

'Did you know, Mr Horgan, that Mr Molto was involved in the case described there?'

Nico is on his feet first, bellowing in outrage. Larren for the first time before the jury shows anger with Stern.

'Sir, I have warned you about this area of inquiry.'

'Your Honor, it is relevant to the defense position I set forth earlier at sidebar.' He means the frame-up theory. Stern is being elliptical in order to keep the content of the hallway conference from the jury, who were not supposed to hear that conversation. 'I must tell the court that we have every intention of continuing to investigate this file with the jury, and to offer evidence about it when it is our turn. Indeed, this is the proof I alluded to.' Stern is saying that we are going to put in proof about the B file to support the charge that the case is manufactured. Again, I am astounded by his position. The judge sits back; he rests his hands atop his head and puffs out his cheeks to blow off steam.

'For the time being, we have heard enough,' he says.

'Two questions more,' says Sandy with magisterial authority, and turns back to Horgan without waiting for the judge to tell him he may not.

'Did Mr Molto ever ask you about that file?'

'As I recall, yes. After I resigned as PA he went over everything Rusty – Mr Sabich – had done on the Polhemus case.'

'And Mr Molto had that file then?'

'He did.'

'And do you know what investigation, if any, he conducted of the allegations contained there?'

'I do not.'

'I'll answer that,' says Nico suddenly. He is standing. He has quite clearly lost his temper. His color is up and his eyes are wide. 'He took no action. He wasn't going to chase Rusty Sabich's red herrings.' This speech before the jury would ordinarily be grossly improper. But it is precisely the kind of riposte that Larren's warning in the hallway seemed to invite, and Della Guardia has taken full advantage of the opportunity. No doubt he and Tommy discussed this on the way back in from the corridor and decided that Nico would attempt to make a spirited defense of Molto in the jury's presence. Stern ventures no objection. Instead, he slowly turns to face Molto.

'Mr Della Guardia,' he says, 'perhaps we will all learn something about red herrings.' He pauses. 'And scapegoats.'

Those are the last words from Stern on Raymond's cross.

Larren recesses for the week. On Fridays he hears motions in other cases. I wait for some explanation from Stern of his new tactics, but he goes on picking up papers from the defense table. Raymond stops by to shake Sandy's hand on his way from the courtroom. He wanders wide of me.

Finally Stern comes to see me. He wipes his face with his handkerchief. He appears relaxed. Leaving aside the last bit, the cross-examination of Horgan went exceptionally well.

I am too concerned, however, to congratulate him.

'What is this?' I ask. 'I thought you told me we weren't going down the road to accusation.'

'Clearly, Rusty, I changed my mind.'

'Why?'

Stern gives me his Latin smile: the world is full of mystery.

'Instinct,' he replies.

'And what evidence are we going to offer?'

'Now you remind me,' he says. He is quite a bit shorter than I am and he cannot comfortably swing his arm around my shoulder. Instead, he uses another confidential gesture and touches my lapel. 'For the time being, I will have to leave that concern to you,' he says, and turns away.

30

Tonight I say that I am bushed and leave Stern and Kemp early, but there is an appointment that I want to keep. I called after court, and good to his word, Lionel Kenneally is here, in a neighborhood tavern called Six Brothers. The cabbie gives me a peculiar look when he drops me. It is not that there are no white people around here. There are a few stoical families holding on against the Ricans and the blacks, but they do not wear chalk-striped suits and carry briefcases. Instead, their shingle-sided bungalows are tucked in among the warehouses and factories which cover most of every block. There is a sausage plant across the street, and the air is heavy with the scent of spices and garlic. The tavern is like so many others out this way: just a joint with Formica tables, a vinyl floor, lights over the mirrors. Above the bar, there is a neon Hamm's sign which casts weird shadows from the reflective spangles of the continuous waterfall.

Kenneally does not even wait for me. Instead, he starts to move when I enter and I follow him back to a smaller room with four tables where he says he won't be bothered.

'So what the fuck is this about?' He is smiling but his tone is not altogether friendly. I've got the frigging watch commander out with an indictee, an enemy of the state, an accused homicidal felon. It is no place for a ranking police officer to be seen.

'I appreciate your coming, Lionel.'

He waves that off. He wants me to get down to business. A woman pokes her head in. I decline to drink at first, then think better of it and order a Scotch-rocks. Lionel already has a whiskey in his hand.

'I need to ask you some questions I should have asked when I came out to see you in the district in April.'

'About?'

'About what the hell was going on out in the North Branch eight or nine years ago.'

'Meaning?' His look is close: he does not want to get led astray.

'Meaning, was somebody taking money?'

Kenneally bolts his drink. He's thinking.

'You know you're hot fucking stuff, don't you?' he asks.

'I see the papers.'

He looks at me. 'You going down on this thing?'

I tell him the truth.

'I don't think so. Stern is a magician. He's got three of the jurors thinking about inviting him for dinner, you can tell from the looks on their faces. He cut a good piece out of Horgan today.'

'They say downtown that Nico doesn't have the horses. They say he went too soon, Molto forced his hand. They say if he had any brains he would've got you in a room with a tape recorder and somebody you trust instead of lettin Mac make him tell you what he had.' I recognize now that what I thought might be a glaze of alcohol is anger. Lionel Kenneally is pissed. He's heard enough about the case to figure that he did something he doesn't do frequently: made an error in judgment. 'Myself, I figure you might be goin down anyway. Sure as fuck, you didn't tell me you were in there handlin her glassware when you was out here before.'

'You want me to tell you I didn't kill her?'

'Fuckin-A right I do.'

'I didn't kill her.'

Kenneally stares, a fierce, immobile look. I know my delivery was too measured to provide him with any assurance.

'You are one fuckin strange son of a bitch,' he says.

The barmaid, wearing one of those old ruffled tops to show the beginning of her cleavage, comes in with my drink. She also puts another tumbler of whiskey in front of Lionel K.

'You know,' I tell Kenneally as I sip, 'that is something I never understood about myself. I mean, my old lady was as weird as those women downtown carrying around shopping bags, and my old man had spent most of World War II eating dead horses and stuff such as that, which does some work on your cerebrum, believe me. Everything in my whole life was weird. And until this happened, I really thought I was Joe College. That's who I wanted to be and that's what I thought I was. Really, I thought I was fucking Beaver Cleaver, or whoever the boy next door is these days. I really did. And about the only thing I've gotten out of this experience to date is hearing you tell me I am one strange son of a bitch and listening to that little harp string that sounds in my chest when somebody, even if he's half-crocked, has said something that is really right. So I thank you.' I tap his glass with mine.

I am not sure that Lionel particularly enjoyed this routine. He watches me for a minute.

'What'd you come here for, Rusty?'

'I already told you. Just answer that one question.'

Kenneally sighs. 'Ain't you a fuckin pip. One question, all right? And what's said here stays here. It's me and you. I ain't listenin to any fuckin sob stories about your constitutional rights or that shit. Nobody's fuckin callin me to testify against the PA. That happens, world's gonna think you confessed right here tonight.'

'I have the ground rules.'

'Your short answer is, I don't exactly know. Maybe I heard some things, all right? But that wasn't my show. Things out this way were a little loose. You know what I'm sayin? Remember, we're talkin before Felske stepped in shit.' Felske was a bail bondsman who used to take care of certain cops for referring him business. When the bail law was reformed, permitting personal-recognizance bonds and obviating the need for outside sureties, Felske and his coppers maintained their income by selling the coppers' assistance on occasion. Sometimes the cops would talk a witness into not showing up. Sometimes the cops would forget things when they testified. Felske, however, made such a proposition one day to a man with an electronic lapel pin. The copper involved, named Grubb, flipped for the FBI and took down

Felske and three other officers. That was five years ago. 'Back then, this was a wide-open place.'

'Was Tommy Molto one of the people you heard things about?'

'I thought you said one question.'

'It had subparts.'

Kenneally doesn't smile. He looks down in his drink.

'In this job, you learn you better not say never.' Kenneally laughs. 'Lookit you. Right?' He laughs again. He is still angry with himself. All of this is against his better judgment. 'But Molto,' he says. 'Never. He's from the fuckin seminary. He'd bring his rosary to court. No chance this guy would take.'

'Was Carolyn involved with whatever was going on?'

He shakes his head. He is not saying no. He is refusing to answer.

'Look. I don't owe you, Rusty. Okay? I thought you done your job like a professional guy. You come out here before people in the suburbs even knew from gangs, and you worked hard. I give you credit. What else you done, you done. But you come into the projects with me in the middle of the night. You got your fuckin hands dirty. But don't push, all right. There guys I owe. You ain't one.'

Cop loyalty. He won't even drop a dime on a dead lady. Kenneally drinks his drink and looks out the door.

'Did Carolyn have anything going with Molto? You know, a personal thing?'

'Jesus. What's your hang-up with Molto? Guy's strange like everybody else.'

'Let's just say he's my best alternative.'

'What the fuck does that mean?'

I wave the question off.

'Well, I don't see that guy even catchin a whiff of Polhemus. You seen him. Buddy Hackett, right? They were friends, that's all. Buddies. Sometimes she'd smooth shit out for him.' Kenneally takes another drink. 'It wasn't him she was bangin.'

'Who?'

'No chance,' he says. 'You got enough.'

'Lionel.' I really don't want to beg. He will not look at me. 'This isn't gossip, for Chrissake. This is my goddamned life.'

'The nigger.'

'What?'

'She was sleepin with the nigger.'

I don't get it at first. Then I do.

'Larren?'

'You been out at the North Branch. You remember how it was. It was like everybody used to work in one room. Three doors, and all of em let you into one office. PO. PA. Nick Costello was signin in the coppers who come out to testify. He had a desk there. Judge's chambers used to open up there, too. He'd get off the bench noontime, she'd go sashaying in. They weren't makin no secret of it.

'Fuck,' says Kenneally, 'I halfway told you last time you was out here. Don't you remember? I told you how she fucked her way to the top. I couldn't figure Horgan hiring her. That's who got her in. Your old buddy there, Judge Motherfucker. He and Horgan got some kinda tie-in.'

'They were law partners,' I say. 'Years ago.'

'Figures,' says Lionel. He shakes his head in disgust.

'And you won't tell me whether Carolyn was dirty?'

He raises a finger. 'I'm gonna leave,' he says. He's quiet for a while. 'Sometimes she'd smooth things out, like I say. Molto and the judge, they didn't get along so well. Maybe you heard them stories.'

'A number.'

'You know, she was everybody's pal back then. The PO. Sometimes she'd get the judge to lay off. Sometimes she'd get Molto to take two steps back. She was kinda the referee. Maybe you're right. Maybe Molto was really carryin a big fuckin torch for her. Maybe that's why he had sand in his ointment whenever he had to go before the judge. Who knows? Go figure people,' he says.

I can tell that I've had everything now that I'm going to get. This last little bit was strictly for charity.

I pick up my briefcase and leave money for the drinks.

'You're a good sod, Kenneally.'

'I'm a fuckin fool, is what I am. Halfa downtown's gonna be talkin about this tomorrow. Whatta I tell em we said?'

'I don't give a shit. Say what you want. Tell them the truth. Molto knows what I'm looking for by now. Maybe that's why I'm in this soup to begin with.'

'You don't believe that.'

'I don't know,' I tell him. 'Something's not right.'

31

We spend the weekend at work, both days. My assignment is to prepare for the end of the state's case, when the defense, as a matter of routine, makes a motion for a directed verdict of acquittal – a request that the judge terminate the trial, declaring that there is not enough evidence for a reasonable jury to convict. This is usually futile. In ruling on the motion, the judge is required to evaluate the evidence in the light most favorable to the state, meaning, for example, that for the purposes of this decision Judge Lyttle will have to accept Eugenia's testimony, right down to her angels. However, a directed-verdict ruling is unreviewable; the state may not appeal. As a result some judges – Larren quite notoriously – use this as a device for imposing the result they favor. Thus, while our prospects are dim, Stern wants to make as strong a presentation as possible. My assignment is to find cases which in some fashion condemn the absence of proof of motive in a circumstantial case. I pass hours in the library.

Sunday morning we meet to talk strategy. Sandy still does not want to speak in detail about the defense case. He makes no mention of my testimony or that of other witnesses. Instead, we analyze the remainder of the state's proof. Lipranzer is supposed to testify Monday. The state's case will now begin to gather speed. Their physical evidence will be coming in: the fibers, the phone records, the fingerprints (assuming they can find the glass); the maid who thinks she saw me on the bus; and Kumagai.

Stern again emphasizes the point he made to me the other day at lunch: our need to raise doubt in some way about Kumagai. If we cannot, the prosecutors will reach the end of their case having built up tremendous momentum; that, in turn, may force Sandy to change his strategy for our presentation. This is one reason Stern is unwilling to arrive at any final opinions about what we should do. Together Kemp and Stern and I puzzle out ways to attack Kumagai. Stern has examined Painless a number of times and he shares the common opinion that Kumagai is an unpleasant hack. The jury will not be eager to believe him. There are old stories about Painless which I share; finally, I mention that his police department personnel file, where complaints about Kumagai's past performance might be jacketed, would be a good source for us to examine.

'Excellent,' says Stern. 'How wonderful to have a prosecutor on our side.' He directs Jamie to draft at once a trial subpoena for the file, and another for records of the Pathology Lab, so we can see what else Painless was up to in April. We have not issued most of our subpoenas, inasmuch as many of the deputy sheriffs who serve them tend to alert the prosecutors, giving the PAs an opportunity to combat the evidence gathered or, even worse, to utilize it themselves if it is helpful to the state. But now that the prosecution case is almost complete, we should proceed. Jamie forages through his old notes to be sure we do not miss any of the items we have said we wanted to acquire. He drafts subpoenas for each of Carolyn's doctors, identified from her little phone book, which I found in her apartment.

'And you wanted to subpoena the phone company,' Kemp says to me, 'so we can look at their backup data at the MUDs from your house.'

'Don't bother with that,' I say quickly. I do not look up, but I can feel the weight of Kemp's startled glance upon me. Stern, however, goes on, without dropping a beat.

'Perhaps if it is not productive to raise questions,' says Sandy, 'we should consider stipulations.' A stipulation is a statement agreed to by the prosecution and defense which recites what a witness would say, so that he need not be called. As Stern thinks aloud about that possibility, he becomes more convinced it is the right way to proceed. We will agree to the testimony not only of the phone company representatives but also the Hair and Fiber experts and the forensic chemist. By doing that, we will shorten the time in which this damaging evidence is actually before the jury. Della Guardia may not accept the proposal, but he is likely to. For the prosecutor, there is always a blessing in not having to come forward with your proof.

With these decisions made, Kemp and I return to the library, a central conference room in Stern's suite where the statute books and law reports are shelved floor to ceiling in dark oak cases on each of the four walls. I work at one table, Kemp at another. I become aware after a few minutes that Jamie is watching me, but I still do not look up.

'I don't get it,' he finally says out loud, giving me no choice. 'You said there was something wrong with those phone records.'

'Jamie, cut me a break. I've thought about it since.'

'You said we should look into whether or not they'd been doctored.'

The intensity in his eyes is not really anger. There is something vulnerable. As he seldom does, Quentin Kemp, in his cowboy boots and tweed sportcoat, looks undefended and young. He thinks of himself as much too hip to be capable of being misled.

'Jamie, it's something I said. Okay? Under the circumstances. You understand.'

But I can see that he does not understand at all. It bothers me, and the look in his eye, his knowing that now he can't believe me. I fold my pad and put on my coat. Sandy is still in his office when I tell him I am leaving for the night. He is studying the reams of scientific evidence that Nico produced in response to our motions. Spectrographs. Print charts. The full report of Carolyn's autopsy. He is dressed in casual clothes, a handsome sweater and slacks, and he seems relaxed under the green glass shade of an auditor's lamp, smoking his precious cigar.

Lipranzer is on the stand on Monday morning. Nico takes care to keep him away from me. The prosecution team walks down the corridor with Lip, just as Ernestine is calling court to session. Lipranzer is wearing a suit, something he hates to do, but he still looks more like a convict than a policeman. It is an awful double-knit thing with a kind of carpetbag pattern. His duckass hairdo is particularly slick. I end up holding the door as Lip enters the courtroom, and in spite of the presence of Nico in front of him and Glendenning behind, Lipranzer gives me both a wave and a wink. I am fortified just to see him again.

Nico handles Lip well. It is his best examination of the trial so far. He is matter-of-fact and gets what he has to quickly. He knows that Lip is not friendly. He will tell the truth, but – so different from Horgan – is awaiting any opportunity to bite Nico's heels. Delay is careful not to give him the chance. If he is professional, he knows he can count on Lip to act the same way. They are both suppressed and brief.

'Did Mr Sabich ever tell you that he had a personal relationship with Carolyn Polhemus?'

'Objection.'

'On the same basis as with Mr Horgan, Mr Stern?' the judge asks.

'Indeed.'

'The objection will be overruled. Ladies and gentlemen, I'm sure you remember what I told you last week about questions based on assumptions. Because Mr Della Guardia is sayın it, doesn't make it so. You may proceed.'

I have wondered how Lip will answer the question. But he says simply, No. Nico did not ask whether I suggested that such a relationship might exist, or whether it was clearly understood by both of us, a question Della Guardia in fact cannot properly put. He asked if I told him, and Lipranzer has responded correctly. Hedged in by the formalities of the rules of evidence, our truth-finding system cuts off the corners on half of what is commonly known.

In a clipped, almost British way, Nico elicits the fact that I told Lip not to collect the MUD records from my home. And he also brings out from Lipranzer the occasions on which he had to remind me to request computer analysis of the finger-prints found on the glass and elsewhere in Carolyn's apartment. It all emerges between the two of them with a strange undercurrent. I am sure the jury knows something is not right here. And Nico is smart enough at the end to let them know what it is. When he has got what he needs from Lipranzer, he sets up the cross, by showing bias. He asks about the cases that Lip and I have worked together.

'Would it be fair to say that by now the two of you have formed a kind of prosecutorial or investigative team?'

'Yes, sir.'

'And as a result of working as a team, have you formed a personal friendship?'

'Definitely.'

'A close friendship?'

Lip's eyes skate toward me for a moment.

'I suppose so.'

'You trust him?'

'I do.'

'And he knows that?'

Stern objects: Lip can't answer about what I know, and the prosecutor is leading. The witness has already characterized the relationship. Larren sustains the objection on all grounds.

'Well, let me put the question like this: Were you assigned to the case initially?'

'No, sir.'

'Who was assigned?'

'Harold Greer, a detective from the 18th District, where the crime occurred.'

'Is he a competent investigator?'

'In my book?'

Nico is careful here, in order both to avoid objections and to keep Lip from zinging him.

'Has Mr Sabich ever expressed to you any reservations about Harold Greer's abilities?'

'No, sir. Everybody I know thinks of Harold Greer as a top-grade cop.'

'Thank you.' Nico smiles, savoring the bonus. 'And who, to your knowledge, decided to make this a Special Command matter and bring you in on this case, Detective Lipranzer?'

'Mr Sabich requested my assignment, if that's what you're askin. He had Mr Horgan's say-so.'

'To your knowledge, Detective Lipranzer, does the defendant have a closer personal relationship with anyone on the police force?'

Lip shrugs. 'Not that he's mentioned.'

Nico struts a little.

'So it's fair to say, Detective, is it not, that you are the person on the city police force least likely to suspect Mr Sabich of murder?'

The question is objectionable. Stern starts to move, then ceases, with his hands poised on the arms of his chair. This time I am keeping pace with him. He has seen Lip hesitate and knows that Nico, by improvising, has made his first error. He has given Lipranzer an opening and is going to take a blow.

'I would never believe that,' Lip says simply. He leans on 'never.' Just right. That will sit well with the jury. He's not going out of his way to nose Nico. But he's taken the opportunity to make his feelings known.

Sandy rises to cross. We talked last night about not crossing Lip at all. Stern did not want to emphasize Nico's favorable points. But apparently the direct went even better for the state than Stern anticipated. Nico's direct has opened the door to a kind of catalogue of the successes Lip and I have scored together as a way of explaining why I would choose him for this case. Stern runs through them one by one.

'And as a matter of fact,' says Stern, when he is at the end of that, 'even in the midst of this murder investigation you and Mr Sabich were inquiring about yet another matter, weren't you?'

Lip is puzzled.

'Wasn't there a file, which had been stored in Mr Horgan's drawer –'

Sandy does not get any further before Nico is on his feet yelling. Larren picks up his gavel and points it at Stern.

'Mr Stern. I have told you on too many occasions that I do not wanna be hearin any more about that file during the prosecutor's case. You went much too far while Mr Horgan was testifying and I'm not gonna abide any reoccurrence.'

'Your Honor, this evidence is critical to our defense. We intend to continue exploring the matter of this file when it is our turn to present evidence.'

'Well, if this is critical to your defense, then we can talk about calling Detective Lipranzer back at that time. But I advise you, sir, to move on to another area of inquiry, because I have not heard near enough to let you go chasin that hare all over the courtroom at this time. Am I clear?' Judge Lyttle peers over the bench with an impressive concentration of his features.

Stern does his little cut-rate bow, inclining his head and shoulders. I find myself disconcerted by Sandy's lapse of judgment. He has taken a beating in the presence of the jury, a setback which was entirely predictable, and I still do not understand what he is trying to accomplish. He's already cast his shadow over Molto with that file. Why does he harp on it? The jury is bound to be disappointed, particularly when he keeps promising to produce evidence that we do not have in hand. We cannot offer the letter I found in the B file, because it is hearsay. I do not understand Stern's bluff, and he is cavalier whenever I steer him toward the subject. He treats it as if it is just another courtroom effect.

Stern, in the meantime, has come back to the defense table.

'Now, Detective Lipranzer, Mr Della Guardia asked you some questions about the telephone records.' Sandy holds up the documents. 'As I understand your testimony, it was you who raised the matter of his home number with Mr Sabich, is that right?'

'Yes, sir.'

'He did not bring it up?'

'No.'

'He did not ask you in advance not to obtain the records from his home? Am I right?'

'Absolutely correct.'

'In point of fact, he informed you at the start that you might find calls from Ms Polhemus to one of his phones?'

'In his office, right.'

'He didn't ask you or tell you not to seek any records for that reason, did he?'

'No, sir.'

There is a ringing emphasis to all of Lip's answers. Stern is putting on a demonstration now, showing what a cross-examiner can do with a friendly witness. But it is all too clear. There is no resistance. Lip is more or less allowing Stern to testify. He quickly endorses Stern's proposal that it was Lipranzer's own idea not to obtain my home records. He considered them irrelevant; I simply acquiesced in the suggestion, saying, as people often do, that a subpoena was best avoided since it might upset my wife. Sandy returns to counsel table for a document. He numbers it, and hands it to Lip for identification. It is the original subpoena *duces tecum* to the phone company.

'Now, what prosecutor issued that subpoena?'

'Rusty. Mr Sabich.'

'His name appears as the authorizing signatory on the face, does it not?'

'Yes.'

'And by its terms does that subpoena require production of these very records?'

'According to what it says?'

'That's my question.'

'The answer is yes. The subpoena would cover these records.'

'Does it contain any exemption for Mr Sabich's home?'

'No.'

'And any time you or anyone else wanted to examine the records of Mr Sabich's home, this subpoena would require the production of those records?'

'Yes.'

'As a matter of fact – please do not answer if this is beyond your knowledge – when Mr Molto and Mr Della Guardia decided that they wanted those records, they relied on the authority of this subpoena to obtain them, did they not?'

'I think that's right.'

'And so Mr Sabich stands on trial here on the basis of evidence that he himself subpoenaed, correct?'

The courtroom ruffles. Nico objects. 'The question is argumentative.'

Larren shakes his head benignly.

'Mr Della Guardia, you're tryin to show here that Mr Sabich hindered the gathering of evidence, as a way to prove guilty knowledge. And the prosecution is entitled to do that, but the defense is entitled to show that the evidence that is being presented was actually gathered through his efforts. I don't know how else they meet your proof. Overruled.'

'I repeat,' says Stern, standing before Lipranzer, 'Mr Sabich is being tried here with evidence he himself subpoenaed.'

'Right,' says Lip. Eager as a recruit, he adds, 'Just like the fingerprints.'

'Just so,' says Sandy. He proceeds to the fingerprints. It was Sabich who personally visited McGrath Hall, met with Lou Balistrieri, demanded that the prints be processed. True, Sabich was busy, running the entire PA's office while Horgan campaigned, but again it was his own efforts that produced the evidence now being used in an attempt to convict him.

'Did he obstruct you?' Sandy asks at the end.

Lip sits straight up in his chair. 'No.'

'Did he impede you?'

'Not in my book.'

'Indeed, Detective, I believe you told Mr Della Guardia that even if you had known of this evidence, your respect and affection for Rusty Sabich after many years' association is such that you would never have suspected, let alone believed, that he had committed this murder. Is that right?'

The way Lip hesitates, I fear for a moment that Stern has gone too far. But then I see that Lip is merely making his own ungainly effort at dramatic effect.

'Never,' he repeats, and Stern sits down. As he does, he smiles furtively at me, a gesture meant largely for the jury. Nonetheless, for the first time I have the feeling that the jurors are not satisfied by Stern's performance. It is unconvincing. This tour de force still does not explain why I did not volunteer to Lip the information about the calls from my phone, especially the one on the night of the murder. Stern's cross does not offer any reason why I could not work with Harold Greer, whose appearance is surely far more impressive to the jury than Lipranzer's. It does not show what alternatives I had to going to Lou Balistrieri when Lipranzer – not to mention Horgan – was nagging me to do that. And this last exchange, while touching in its awkwardness, is simply baloney. No one could fail to be discomfited by the discovery of the phone records and prints. The doubtful nature of the cross is emphasized by Lip's obedient response to Stern's guidance. It is all too clear: Lipranzer is a friend, willing to be misled. The jury will not fail to perceive this. It is as I always feared. The rule of equal and opposite reactions applies in the courtroom as well. Due in large part to his visible reluctance, Dan Lipranzer has been the most damaging witness against me to date.

The afternoon continues the downward movement. The stipulations are prepared and read. Coming on the heels of Lipranzer's testimony, the revelation of the actual content of the telephone records is crushing. Nico reads the stip himself. He has finally caught the measure of this jury. They are a bright bunch and want the facts delivered without varnish. Nico assumes a flat, understated tone and looks up just a little when he finishes reading so that he can watch the evidence drive home. The jurors are attentive to him and I feel the weight of their calculations. I discover that, as a defendant, you experience the lows in the courtroom far more acutely than as an advocate. My afternoon settles into a feeling of weakness, suppression with a coefficient of palpable nausea.

The stipulation about the carpet fibers is lengthy, but it has a similar impact. By agreeing to forgo the testimony, Nico, in theory, lost the drama of a live presentation. But the technical witnesses tend to be dry and overly involved. The written summaries are direct enough to have some bite. There is no chance this way that Stern can engage in any of his masterful misdirection or minimization. The facts, as they are, emerge with painful salience. The one favorable aspect – that none of my clothing matched any of the fibers found – is too easily explained. The clothes I wore that night were discarded – with the murder weapon. Or simply did not shed. These conclusions, inevitable and arithmetically direct, seem to thicken the air of the courtroom. I can sense them taking place in every quarter. And with them a kind of hush or calm inhabits the place, a dawning resolution. It is more than the mid-afternoon lull. Instead, it seems that all of the observers, including the jurors, have perceived a change in direction, a swing of momentum more in line with original expectations. It has taken the prosecutors longer than it should have, but they are assuming control of the trial, proving their case.

As usual, it is Molto, heedless and overeager, who begins to drag me back from the abyss. When the last stipulation is read, he asks for a corridor conference.

'What is it?' asks Larren when we are all assembled.

'Judge,' he says, 'we are ready to proceed with the fingerprint expert. There is just one small difficulty.'

Kemp eyes me with wicked glee. The difficulty, so called, is obvious to both of us: They have not found the glass. Jamie's smile is welcome. It is the first sign of any renewed warmth between us in better than a day, and it comes at the right moment, for the members of the defence have each been wordless and grim all afternoon. During the 3:30 recess, I encountered Stern in the john and we did not say a thing aloud. He gave me one of his Judeo-Latin shrugs. His eyes were listless. We knew this was coming, he seemed to say. Our time on the high wire has ended.

Now, in the small anteroom to his chambers, Judge Lyttle fulminates. Molto still cannot do anything right in Larren's eyes.

'Are you telling me that you have completed your search and this object absolutely cannot be found?'

'Judge –' he starts to say.

'Because that's one set of facts. And I'll have to rule on that basis. But if you're tellin me that you think the thing is gonna turn up but it's convenient right now for you to go ahead without it, then that's quite another. We aren't gonna be talkin about proceeding now and discovering the evidence later. Am I understood?'

Nico catches Tommy's arm. He tells the judge they would like to take one more night.

'That's fine, then,' Larren says. 'Do I take it that you're moving for an adjournment for the day?'

Nico crisply says, 'Yes.' It is clear that the day's success has fortified him. He can tolerate adversity without distress. His old confidence seems to possess him again.

'Your Honor,' says Stern. 'I hope the court has not decided to let the prosecution proceed with the fingerprint evidence in the absence of the glass. Certainly, if Your Honor please, we would ask to be heard on that question.'

'I quite understand,' says Larren. 'You may want to do some research on this issue, Mr Stern. And I'll be happy to hear you. And I can tell you right now, I'm not eager to let anybody get up on the witness stand in my courtroom and give his opinions about what he says was once observed on some physical object that nobody can even find anymore.' He casts a rough-tempered glance toward Molto. 'So you look in the books tonight and I'll listen to you. And, Mr Della Guardia, if I were you, I'd roll up my shirt-sleeves and get over to that evidence room myself.'

'Yes, Your Honor,' says Nico dutifully.

Stern gives me a meaningful look from beneath his extended brow as we head into the courtroom. He seems to be inquiring. It is almost as if he thinks that I can account for the glass's absence. Perhaps it is merely a sense of promise that gives Sandy this expression. If Larren were to keep the prosecutors from presenting the fingerprint evidence, the case against me would certainly fail. Stern is not sure whether or not he should be hopeful. Nor am I.

'Would he really think about keeping out that proof?' I ask Stern as we stand behind counsel table. We are waiting for the jury to return to the courtroom, so that the judge can tell them they are being dismissed for the day.

'It strikes me as a serious question of evidence. Is it not? We must study tonight.' More time for Kemp and me in the library. I nod, accepting Stern's unspoken instruction.

About 9:30 that night, Kemp comes back to Stern's small library to tell me that I have a call. He remains behind to inspect the series of cases I have copied from the reports of the state supreme and appellate courts, while I go to the receptionist's desk, where Jamie has picked up the phone. A line is blinking, on hold. I assume it is Barbara. She usually calls about now, hoping to review the day's evidence for a few moments; and every evening I go through an arabesque of diffidence and contained response.

The truth is that I have done my best to avoid Barbara since the days immediately before the trial. I have suggested she go to sleep each night before I return; I have eaten dinner with Stern and Kemp, enjoining her even from leaving me a meal. I cannot stand to have her abstracted curiosity turned on this evidence like some high-powered light. I do not want those late-night scenes where we chew over the events of my trial as we did those malefactors I accused. It would make me unbearably ill at ease to hear Barbara engage in close analysis of the tactical decisions undertaken in this trial for my life. Most of all, I do not wish to get drawn into discussions of my discomfort. With the evidence being trotted out each day before us, I know the conclusions she might reach, and in my present state I could not abide that confrontation – to allay suspicions or confirm them.

But when I pick up the phone, it is not Barbara's voice I hear.

'How'd I do?' Lip says. 'I thought they were goin to give you a medal or somethin with all these terrific things you and I done.'

'You were great,' I tell him. There is no point in the truth.

'Fuckin Delay, I'll tell you,' he says. 'Schmidt come to see me this mornin before I got on. He says a little birdie wanted to make sure that I got the message that if I fucked around on the stand, I'd be walkin beats in the North End by myself in the middle of the night. Nice subtle stuff with this guy.'

I make a sound, general agreement. I have sent a few such messages myself from time to time – to coppers who have a peculiar friendship with defense counsel; who know the defendant from the 'hood. It's part of the job.

'I thought maybe we could get together tonight,' Lip says. 'Talk about that thing I said I'd help you with.' He means finding Leon. 'How about I drive you home? You be there a while?'

'Another two hours probably.'

'That's good for me. They got me working 4:00 to midnight. I'll take my coffee early. Corner Grand and Kindle at 11:30? I'll be drivin the unmarked Aries.'

We work it like a spy movie. I am in the lobby until the car hoves into sight and Lip is barely at the curb five seconds before he is moving. Now that he is off the witness stand, the pressure on him has lessened, but there are many people who would tell him that the better part of wisdom right now lies in staying away from me. He pulls around the corner so quickly that the rear end gives way a little bit on the pavement, which is slick from a light rain.

I compliment him again on his testimony. 'It was good,' I say, 'because you played it straight.'

'I'm tryin,' he says, and reaches for his radio, which is putting out a tremendous ruckus. 'This is great,' says Lip, of the radio. 'We're workin on a dope bust with the G-men to make up for that fiasco in April and these guys can't get on the air together often enough to make sure nobody gets turfed. They better hope their subject don't have a scanner, because he couldn't miss this posse comin.'

I ask about what is going down.

'It's cute,' says Lip. 'They got a nice-lookin little female agent in a mink coat that got seized last time the Strike Force went in on Muds Corvino's bolita game. She's makin out to be some dope-crazed suburbanite and she's gonna buy ten keys of coke from somebody in Nearing.'

'Probably one of my neighbors,' I say. 'There's a guy down the block named Cliff Nudelman whose nose is redder than Rudolph's.'

We are quiet, listening to the radio traffic. Cops and robbers. I feel a vague melancholy when I admit to myself that I miss it. There is lots of static because of the rain. Thunder and lightning must not be far off. I am reluctant to mention Leon first, but I finally ask how Lip is doing.

'I haven't started,' he says. 'I will. First thing. Only I haven't got a fuckin idea where I oughta look. That's what I wanted to hear. You got some suggestions?'

'I don't know, Lip. It shouldn't be that hard to find a faggot named Leon. Go interview waiters. Or interior decorators.'

'Probably moved to San Francisco, you know. Or died of AIDS or some crap.' I refuse to respond to Lip's suggestion that his efforts will be futile. We are quiet a moment; the radio barks. 'Can I ask a question?' he says after a while. 'Is this really so important?'

'To me?'

'Yeah.'

'Damn right.'

'Can I ask why? I mean, you really think this jamoche's gonna give you somethin?'

I tell him what I told him before. 'I *want* to find something, Lip. That's the most honest way I can put it.'

'On Molto?'

'On Molto. Right. That's the way I've got it figured. As much as I can figure at all.' We are down near the bus terminal, a bleak place at any hour, but especially at midnight with rain. I look out toward it, a sad hulk in the dark. Lip's dwindling faith in me hangs in here with a misty sadness of its own. More even than the risks, that is what bothers him. From his own perspective he's figured it out. I want to use this thing with Molto as a diversion – as Nico put it, a red herring. Lip's reluctance is obvious to both of us, and it is a dismal sign of where I am that I must lever him with our friendship to make him do what I know he would resist for almost anyone else. 'Let's run a sheet at least. Berman, Sandy's PI, says he couldn't even get a rap sheet out of the department.'

'I told you, man, they closed down tight on this thing. They're gonna be in Kenneally's shit in a big way for givin you the time of day.'

I take a moment.

'How did you hear about that?'

'Watch commander don't get anywhere that people don't notice.' The rain beads on the window. The air is close. I understand the spy stuff on the street corner now. 'What'd he tell you?' Lip asks.

'Not much. He told me that Carolyn and Larren used to be an item a long time ago. What do you think of that?'

'I think she got around,' says Lipranzer, 'same thing I always thought.'

'He said that Larren clouted her into the PA's office through Raymond.'

'That fits,' says Lip.

'That's what I thought.'

'He tell you anythin else?'

'More ancient history. You know: the North Branch used to be a dirty old place, but he thinks Molto was clean.'

'And you believe him? About Molto?'

'I don't want to.'

'I wouldn't take that guy's advice on clean or dirty, I'll tell you that. God only knows where he's comin from.'

'What is it with you and Lionel?'

'Not my kinda cop,' says Lipranzer simply. We have crossed the Nearing bridge by now and have entered the sudden dark of the suburban neighborhoods, out of the garishness of the highway's yellow sulfur lights. 'I worked out his way when I started, you know.'

'I didn't know that.'

'Yeah,' he says. 'I seen him in action. Not my kinda cop.'

I decide I won't ask.

Lip looks out the windshield. The shadows of the wipers move across his face.

'We're talkin twelve, fourteen years ago now,' he says at last. 'Things were different. I'm the first to admit that. Okay? Everybody's on the pad back then. All right? Everybody.' Lip looks straight at me and I know what he means. I find it unsettling. 'The pimps, the barkeeps, they just put up the dough. You didn't even talk about it. It was there. So I'm not castin stones, okay?'

'But one night, I'm comin out of a place – two, three in the mornin – squad comes runnin down the street full speed and stops dead. First I think it's me he wants. So I come a little closer. But he don't even see me. It's Kenneally. You know, he's a sergeant by then, so he's ridin alone, beat supervisor. And he's lookin across the street. Right in a doorway. There's a hooker, okay? Black gal. You know, she's got the skirt on up to her chin, and leopard top or some such shit. Anyway, I hear him whistle. You know? Like for a dog or horse. Big loud number like that. And he pulls the black-and-white into the alley. Gets out and looks down the street toward this pro, and he's pointing like this.' Lip shoots an index finger down toward his groin. 'Big smile. And this lady, she waits and she waits. And he keeps pointin and smilin. He says somethin I don't quite hear. Don't say no. Somethin like that. Anyway, she goes slow down the street like, Oh, man, don't tell me, draggin her purse like she's got maybe an anvil inside. And Kenneally's got his big smile. Sits down right there in the squad. All I see is his legs stickin out the door, his shorts down around his ankles, and this lady on her knees while she's workin. Fucker didn't even take off his hat.'

Lip swings into my driveway. He takes the car out of gear and lights a cigarette. 'He ain't my kinda cop,' he says again.

32

The trial's first pitched battle over an issue of law occurs the next day and occupies the entire morning. Nico describes a six-hour item-by-item search of the police evidence room. They cannot find the glass. Both sides have prepared written memoranda addressed to whether testimony about the fingerprints on the glass may none the less be received. Kemp wrote our brief sometime after midnight. Molto must have started later than that, since Nico said they were in the warrens of the evidence room past one o'clock. Each man wears the hazy red-eyed look of a lawyer on trial. Larren retires to his chambers to read both briefs, then returns to hear oral argument. At the start, it is supposed to be only Nico and Stern addressing the court, but each turns so often to his second that before long all four lawyers are talking, with the judge interrupting, posing hypothetical questions and, on occasion, thinking out loud. Stern makes his points with greater vehemence than at any time during the trial. Perhaps he senses an opportunity for triumph; perhaps desperation is gathering after yesterday's sobering events. He keeps emphasizing the fundamental unfairness of forcing the defendant to confront scientific testimony whose basis we have had no chance to assess. Nico, then Molto, repeatedly state that the so-called chain of custody has gone un-contested. Whether the glass can be found or not, the testimony of Greer, Lipranzer, and Dickerman, the lab supervisor, will establish, taken together, that the prints were identified from lifts obtained from the glass the day after the murder.

The back-and-forth between the lawyers is endless, and I find my spirits in a sickening spiral, escalating, then instantly descending from elation to bitter lament. It is clear that the judge is undecided. This is one of those issues, of which there are so many during a trial, where a judge is within legal boundaries no matter what he does. The authorities support a ruling for either side. The way Larren gives it to Nico and Tommy about the carelessness of the police makes me certain, at moments, that the evidence is going to be excluded. But the prosecutors are frank about the devastation that this would bring to their case, and without saying it aloud, they hint at the impropriety of disposing of a celebrated prosecution as the result of police negligence. In the end, this thought appears persuasive and Larren rules against the defense.

'I'm gonna admit this testimony,' the judge says, shortly after the court clock has reached noon. Then he explains the basis of his ruling for the record, so that the court of appeals can assess his judgment, if it ever comes to that.

'I must say that I'm pretty reluctant to do so, but I am influenced by its obvious importance to the case. Naturally, that same fact, given the overall tone of some of the things that have occurred here' – the judge looks toward Molto – 'leads me to understand the defense's skepticism. They are right that they have not had the opportunity to examine an object of physical evidence. On the other hand, the object itself is not gonna be presented. The absence of this exhibit is attributed to the police evidence room. I want to note for the record that the police evidence room custodians have been guilty for years of this kind of slipshod record keeping and handling of exhibits. This is probably the most dramatic, but certainly not the only example that we all know about. And I must say that it is that knowledge, derived outside the record, that influences me to allow the testimony. The fact of the matter is that the best-intentioned prosecutors – and I by no means am ruling on the intentions of Mr Della Guardia or of Mr Molto, who seems to have had the glass last –' Again Larren stares darkly at Tommy. Did Greer really say that? I wonder. '– but the best-intentioned prosecutors cannot seem to control what happens to exhibits once they leave their hands. It could be that there is bad faith here. I will be lookin out for further evidence of that, and if there is that kind of bad faith, then this prosecution is gonna end. Period. But overall, that thought strikes me as so unpalatable that I'm gonna assume it isn't true. So I will admit this proof, over objection, and with my own reservations noted. I am, however, gonna give the jury a strongly worded limiting instruction, which I want to take some time to craft over the lunch hour. We will resume at two o'clock.'

The judge leaves the bench, asking the lawyers to remain for a few moments so he can have their thoughts on the instruction he wants to draft. Sandy is philosophical. It is clear now that he believed we were going to win. I explain what has occurred to Barbara, who appears particularly upset by Larren's ruling. 'It isn't fair,' she tells me. 'You haven't even had a chance to look at it.'

'I understand,' I say. 'It's one of those calls a judge gets to make.' I'm not trying to be heroic. All along I have tested Larren against my own internal barometer. On this one, I would have ruled the same way.

I go to the john. When I come out, Nico again is at the sink, washing his hands as he feints left and right to see the position of his hairs under the light.

'Well, Rusty,' he says. 'Are we going to be hearing from you next week?'

Under the state discovery laws, the defense is under no obligation to inform the prosecution of its witnesses. Whether or not the defendant will testify is often the most closely guarded secret of the defense camp. The prosecution should rest tomorrow. Assuming the judge takes a day for arguments on the directed-verdict motion, our case will begin next Monday. If the prosecutors receive no indication of our intentions, they will not know whether to spend the weekend preparing for cross-examination or closing arguments. Most of the time, you end up strung out in both directions.

'I'm sure Stern will tell you, Delay, whenever we make up our minds.'

'I have a sawbuck that says you're coming.' Nico is playing games, testing my nerve. He is a lot harder than he was during our encounter here last week. This is the crafty Delay of old.

'Maybe you'll win,' I tell him. 'You got the cross?'

'Had to,' he says. 'I couldn't cross Barbara. She's too nice a lady.'

Again Nico is probing. He wants to know if Barbara will testify to support my alibi. Perhaps he's trying to see if I flinch at the thought of Molto working over my wife.

'You're just a softie, Delay.' I look at myself in the mirror. I've had enough of this conversation. Nico, upbeat with the pleasant current of events the last two days, will not let it go.

'Don't let me down, Rusty. I really want to hear it. You know, sometimes I wonder. I think, How could the guy I knew do a thing like that? I admit it. I wonder sometimes.'

'Nico, if I told you what really happened, you wouldn't want to believe it.'

'Now, what does that mean?'

I turn away and he takes my elbow.

'Really, what does that mean?' he asks. 'This isn't that crap about Tommy framing you, is it? I mean, that's for the papers, Rusty. This is Delay.' He touches his shirt. 'You can't believe that. That's a bunch of crap. I mean, off the record, all that shit. Me and you. Right here. Old buddies. Nobody repeats anything. You're telling me you believe that crap?'

'Where's the glass?'

'Oh, screw that. The cops lose everything. We both know that.'

'He seemed to have primed the pump with Eugenia.'

'What? You really think he told her to say "my angel"? Come on. He heated her up too much. I admit that. And that was stupid. I told him that. I *told* him that. He's compulsive. You know. He was very fond of Carolyn. Very close to her. He considered her one of his closest friends. Big sister kind of thing almost. Looked up to her. He's very committed to this case.'

'Did you ever look at that file, Nico?'

'The one from Raymond's drawer?'

'Do some homework. On your own. You may get some surprises. About big sister and little brother.'

Nico smiles and shakes his head to show he isn't buying it. But I can tell that I've gotten under his skin now. I enjoy the advantage.

I've had Nico's number for years. I dry my hands on one of the paper towels, with my mouth pursed to show that I will say no more.

'So that's it, huh? That's the big secret. Tommy done it. That's what I'm waiting to hear?'

'Go ahead, Delay,' I say quietly, while my back is to him. 'I'll give you a preview. One question. Right here. Me and you, as you say. Off the record. Just the old buds. Nobody repeats anything to anyone else.' I revolve and look at him directly.

'Did you do it?' he asks.

I knew he would. Sooner or later somebody had to put it right to me. I finish drying my hands, and I summon up everything in me that belongs to the truth, every badge of sincerity I own in my manner.

'No, Nico,' I say very quietly, and look him dead in the eye, 'I did not kill Carolyn.'

I can see that I reach him: some kind of enlargement in the pupils; his eyes become darker instantly. Some tone seems to change in his face.

'Very good,' he says at last. 'You'll be very good.' Then he finally smiles. 'So this has been kind of a bitch, huh? Falsely accused and all of that?'

'Go fuck yourself, Delay.'

'I knew I'd hear that, too.'

Both of us come out of the john laughing. When I look up, I see that I have attracted the attention of Stern and Kemp, who are standing a short distance down the corridor conferring with Berman, the private investigator. He is very tall, with a large belly and a loud tie. Stern's look is nettled. Perhaps he is upset to see me with Nico, but it seems that he has been interrupted. He waves his hand, dismissing the other two, and returns to the courtroom. Kemp walks off with Berman a few steps, then comes back to me. We watch Delay follow Sandy inside.

'I won't be here this afternoon,' Jamie says. 'Something came up.'

'Something good?'

'Very good, if it pans out.'

'Is this a secret?'

Jamie looks back at the courtroom door.

'Sandy said not to discuss it right now. Don't raise false hopes. He wants to be cautious. You understand.'

'Not really,' I say.

Berman, some distance away, tells Jamie they have to go. Kemp touches my sleeve.

'If it works out, you'll be delighted. Trust me.'

My look, I'm sure, is abject, confused and thwarted by my own attorneys. But I know I cannot object. I myself have taught Jamie Kemp to be frugal with his confidence. I educated him in professional skepticism, in believing that the best judgment waits.

'Something came up with one of the subpoenas,' he says. Berman calls again: They told the guy they'd be there at one. Jamie backs away. 'Trust me,' he says once more before he jogs off down the hall.

'Ladies and gentlemen,' Larren reads to the jury. 'You are about to hear the testimony of a fingerprint expert, Maurice Dickerman, concerning evidence he claims to have identified on a certain glass. In considering this evidence you must – I say *must* – bear in mind that the defense has had no chance to examine that glass. The testimony is proper, but it is up to you to determine what weight to give it. The defense hasn't had any opportunity to see what scientific explanation there may be for the prosecution's evidence. They have had no opportunity to see whether there was some form of chicanery – I'm not sayin there was, but I'm tellin you that the defense hasn't had the chance to get a scientist of their own to say yea or nay about that. They haven't had a chance to see if there's some mistake. An innocent mistake, but still a mistake. They haven't even had the chance to see if some other scientist would look at the glass and say those were another person's fingerprints.

'And I am instructing you as a matter of law, ladies and gentlemen, that when this case is over and you are deliberating on it, that you are entitled to consider not just this testimony but the failure of the prosecution to make the glass available to the defense. And it is permissible – I'm not tellin you what to do – but it is permissible for that one fact alone to raise a reasonable doubt in your mind which would require Mr Sabich's acquittal.

'All right. Proceed.'

Molto, at the podium, takes a moment to stare up at the judge. By now both men have abandoned pretense. There is an outright hatred between them, and it is visible and intense. In the meantime, the force of Larren's limiting instruction settles over the courtroom. The defense, in this instant, has staged a nine-run rally. The fingerprint evidence has been impeached from the mouth of the judge. Acquittal, he says, is a permissible conclusion. The suggestion that an error has been made, that there has been a mistake, is like a cut to the bone in a criminal trial.

Morrie Dickerman comes to the witness stand. The pure professional. An angular New Yorker with large, dark-framed glasses, Morrie finds fingerprints fascinating. He used to like me because I would sit there and listen to him. Morrie is as good as Painless Kumagai is bad – the kind of grab bag of abilities you encounter in public service. He sits there with his photographs and slides and shows the jury how it is done. He explains how prints are made, a residue of oils left by certain persons, at certain times. Some people don't ever leave prints. Most people will leave prints at some times and not at others. It depends on how much they sweat. But when they leave a print, it is unique. No one fingerprint is like any other. Morrie lays all of this out in his openhanded way, then nails my butt to the barn door in the last five minutes of his testimony with his pictures of the bar, the glass, the lifts, and enlargements from my county employee's file card. All the matching points of comparison have been identified with red arrows. Morrie, as usual, has prepared well.

Stern spends some time on his feet, studying the photographic blowup of one of my fingerprints from the glass before he begins. He turns the picture toward Morrie.

'What time on April first was that fingerprint made, Mr Dickerman?'

'I would have no idea.'

315

'But you're certain it was made on the first of April?'

'No way to tell that, either.'

'I'm sorry?' Stern draws his mouth downward in mock surprise. 'Well, certainly you can tell us that it was made around April first?'

'No.'

'Well, how long can fingerprints last?'

'Years,' says Dickerman.

'I'm sorry?'

'It can be years before the oils break down.'

'What is the oldest fingerprint you have taken in all the time you have worked for the police department?'

'In a kidnapping case, I took a fingerprint off the steering wheel of an abandoned car that had to be three and a half years old.'

'Three and one half years?' Stern makes a sound. He is a marvel. The man who laid waste to Raymond Horgan now feigns gentle-spirited befuddlement, deference to the expert. He acts as if he is slowly figuring all of this out as he goes. 'Then Mr Sabich could have handled this glass six months earlier when he was at Ms Polhemus's apartment in connection with the McGaffen trial?'

'I can't tell you when Mr Sabich handled it. I can tell you it has two of his fingerprints. That's all.'

'Suppose Mr Sabich had touched it for some reason – merely had an unnoticed drink of water, or only the interior of the glass had been rinsed after he used it – is it possible that his prints would remain?'

'Yes. And by the way, it is theoretically possible that the entire glass could have been immersed. Usually soap and water will remove the oils, but there are cases in the literature where finger-prints have been identified even after the object was rinsed in soap and water.'

'No,' says Sandy Stern in wonder.

'I've never seen that,' says Dickerman.

'Well, at least we know that no one else handled the glass, because there were no other fingerprints on it.'

'No.'

Stern goes still. 'I'm sorry?'

'There's another latent.'

'No,' says Stern again. He is laying it on self-consciously. There is an odd theatricality to Sandy. Early in the trial the jury had not seen him enough to know that he was acting. Now in our second week, he is more broad in some gestures, as if to acknowledge the deliberateness of his behavior. I know and you know, he is saying to them. An act of confidence. So they understand that he is not really trying to put anything past them. 'You mean there is another fingerprint on the glass?'

'That's what I mean.'

'Could it be, sir, that Mr Sabich touched the glass months before, and someone else handled the glass on April first?'

'It could be,' says Dickerman evenly. 'It could be anything.'

'Well, we know Mr Sabich was there that night because his prints are on many other objects in the apartment, are they not?'

'No, sir.'

'Well, there must be some things. For example, the window latches were opened. Were there identifiable prints there?'

'Identifiable, sir. But not identified.'

'These were the fingerprints of someone, but not Mr Sabich?'

'Or Ms Polhemus. We excluded her.'

'A third person left those prints?'

'Yes, sir.'

'Just as with the glass?'

'True.'

Stern goes through the entire list of locations within the apartment from which lifts were taken without discovery of my prints. The coffee table that was upset. The fireplace tools printed with the thought that one might be the murder weapon. The surface of the bar. The cocktail tables. The window. The door. Five or six other places.

'And Mr Sabich's prints appeared in not one of those places?'

'No, sir.'

'Only on this glass that can no longer be found?'

'Yes, sir.'

'One place?'

'That's all.'

'He would have left prints throughout the apartment had he been there, would he not?'

'He might have. He might not have. Glass is an unusually receptive surface.'

Stern, of course, knew the answer.

'But the table,' asks Stern, 'the windows?'

Dickerman shrugs. He is not here to explain. He is here to identify fingerprints. Stern makes the most of Dickerman's inability and for the first time since we started, looks directly to the jury, as if for consolation.

'Sir,' says Stern, 'how many other identifiable prints were there of a third person, not Mr Sabich, not Ms Polhemus?'

'Five, I think. One on the latch. One on the window. A couple on the liquor bottles. One on a cocktail table.'

'And are any of those made by the same person?'

'I wouldn't know.'

Stern, who has still not left the side of the defense table, bends forward a bit to indicate that he does not understand.

'I'm sorry?' he says once more.

'No way to tell. I can tell you whoever it is has not been printed by the county, because we did a computer run. They don't have a criminal record. They haven't worked for the county. But they could be five different people or the same person. It could be the cleaning lady or a neighbor or some boyfriend. I can't tell you.'

'I don't understand,' says Stern, who understands very well.

'People have ten fingers, Mr Stern. I don't know that unknown A isn't the index finger, and B is the third finger. Plus left hand and right hand. There's no way to tell without knowns to work from.'

'Well, certainly, Mr Dickerman –' Stern stops. 'Which prosecutor supervised your activities after Mr Sabich?'

'Molto,' says Dickerman. You get the feeling at once that Morrie does not care for Tom very much.

'Well, certainly he asked you to compare these five unidentified prints to see if two of them might be from the same finger?'

Very good, I think to myself. Excellent. This is the kind of detail that I always overlooked as a prosecutor. I thought about the defendant, and the defendant of course thought about everybody else.

But when Dickerman answers, 'No, sir, he did not,' one of the jurors, the part-time computer jock, turns away shaking his head. He looks straight at me, like, Can you believe this? I am astounded that we have come back so far from yesterday. The juror turns to the person beside him, the young woman who runs the drugstore, and they exchange remarks.

'It can be done overnight,' says Dickerman.

'Well, I'm sure,' says Stern, 'that Mr Molto may remember now.' Stern is about to sit down. 'Do you know, Mr Dickerman, why Mr Molto did not ask you to make that comparison of the other prints?' A good trial lawyer never asks why, unless he knows the answer. Stern does, as I do. Neglect. Too much to do and not enough time to do it. The problem of focus. Any answer will suffice to raise doubts about Molto.

'I assume he didn't care,' says Dickerman. He is trying to downplay the significance of the omission, but his answer has an ominous air, as if Molto would not be concerned about the truth.

Stern, who has never moved from the defense table, stands there one second more.

'Just so,' he says. 'Just so.'

Molto approaches the podium and Ms Maybell Beatrice, who works as a domestic in Nearing, is called. I am relieved to see Tommy up there again. For all of Nico's sloppiness, he now seems to have found his place in the courtroom. Tommy is far less adaptable. In the PA's office there was always a kind of cultural divide, a barrier over which my friendship with Nico was ultimately stranded. Raymond picked an elite corps, young lawyers with law-school credentials he liked and, after an apprenticeship, set them to work on Special Investigations. We prosecuted the guilty and rich for bribery and fraud; we ran long-term grand-jury investigations; we learned to try cases against the likes of Stern, lawyers who argued law to the judges and nuance to the jurors.

Molto – and Della Guardia – never rose above the advanced prosecution of street crimes. Tommy's particular mix of pride and passion has been nurtured too long in the homicide courtrooms and branch courts. Those are places where no holds are barred, where defense lawyers use every cheap strategy and device, and prosecutors learn to imitate them. Tommy has become the kind of prosecutor that the PA's office too often breeds: a lawyer who can no longer make out the boundaries between persuasion and deception, who regards the trial of a lawsuit as a series of gimmicks and tricks. I thought at the start that it would be his molten-hot personality that would be a detraction for the state. Instead, the burden he attaches to the prosecution is his inability to escape from his experience. He is brighter than Nico, with a gimlet-eyed cleverness, and he is always prepared, but by now every person in the courtroom suspects that his zeal has no limit. He will do anything to win. Whatever the old rivalry or jealousy surrounding Carolyn, I take it that this trait as well must be a partial source of the antipathy between the judge and him.

And it is the same thing that keeps my curiosity high about Leon and the B file, and whatever shadows lurk in Molto's past. I found Nico's comment about Molto's close relations with Carolyn intriguing. Who knows exactly how she beguiled him? More and more, like everyone else here, I find myself persuaded that there is something sinister in Molto's character. It is too easy for Molto to justify all of his behavior; there is no obvious catch point below which he won't sink. What started out as another of Stern's courtroom illusions seems to have acquired a life of its own. I have wondered, as I have tried to guess at the revelation that Kemp is off chasing, if Molto is not the target. Certainly as Stern has gone on with the old defense lawyer's artifice of placing the prosecutor on trial, Molto has responded poorly. He makes what is perhaps his biggest blunder yet in his direct examination of this Nearing maid.

Ms Beatrice says that she saw a white man on the eight o'clock bus one Tuesday night in April. She does not know what Tuesday night it was, but it was Tuesday, because she works late on Tuesdays, and it was April, because she remembered it as last month when she first spoke to the police, who were doing random interviews in the bus station in May.

'Now, ma'am,' Molto says, 'I ask you to look around the courtroom to see if there is anyone you recognize.'

She points at me.

Molto sits down.

Stern begins cross. Ms Beatrice greets him without apprehension. She is an elderly woman, quite stout, with a lively and kindly face. Her gray hair is drawn back in a bun, and she wears round wire-rimmed glasses.

'Ms Beatrice,' says Stern amiably. 'I take it that you are the kind of person who gets to the bus station a bit early.' Stern knows this, of course, because of the time shown in her police interview.

'Yes, sir. Ms Youngner run me up each night at quarter to so's I can buy me a paper and a Baby Ruth and get me a seat.'

'And the bus on which you go into the city is the same bus that comes out of the city, is that right?'

'Yes, sir.'

'It terminates – that is, it ends its run in Nearing and goes back in?'

'It turn round in Nearing, that's right.'

'And you are there each night when the bus arrives at a quarter to?'

'Quarter to six. Most every night, yes, sir. 'Cept Tuesday, as I explain.'

'And the people coming home from downtown get off the bus and walk past you, is that right, and you have occasion to see their faces?'

'Oh, yes, sir. They looks tired and weary, many a them.'

'Now, ma'am – well, I shouldn't ask you this –' Stern looks again at the report of the police interview. 'You are not saying you recognize Mr Sabich as the man you saw on the bus that Tuesday night are you?' There is nothing to lose with the question. Molto's direct has left the impression that is, in fact, the case. But Ms Beatrice makes a face. She shakes her head most emphatically.

'No, sir. They is somethin here I like to explain.'

'Please do.'

'I knowed I seen this gentleman.' She nods to me. 'I tol' Mr Molto that many a time. I seen this man when I go to get on the bus. Now I recollect, they was a man on that bus one Tuesday night, cause I works late that night on account of Ms Youngner don't get home till near 7:30 on Tuesdays. And I recollect he was a white man, cause we don't get many white gentlemens that ride on the bus going into town that time a night. Now I just can't remember whether 'twould be this man or another man. I know he look real familiar to me, this man do; but I can't say that's cause I seen him in the station or cause I seen him on the bus that night.'

'You have some doubt that it was Mr Sabich you saw that night.'

'That's right. Can't say 'twas him. Coulda been him. I just can't say.'

'Have you spoken with Mr Molto about your testimony?'

'Many a time.'

'And have you told him all of what you've just told us?'

'Oh, yes, sir.'

Sandy turns in Molto's direction with a look of silent and lofty reproof.

After court, Stern tells me to go home. He takes hold of Barbara and draws her toward me.

'Take your pretty wife to dinner. She certainly deserves some reward for her fine support.'

I tell Stern that I was hoping we would begin talking about the defense, but Sandy shakes his head.

'Rusty, you must forgive me,' he says. As chairman of the Bar Association's Committee on Criminal Procedure, he is responsible for a formal dinner to be given tomorrow night in honor of the retirement of Judge Magnuson, who has sat as a felony judge for three decades. 'And I must spend an hour or two with Kemp,' he adds offhandedly.

'Would you like to tell me where he has been?'

Stern screws up his face.

'Rusty, please. Indulge me.' He again takes Barbara's arm and mine. 'We have some information. I will tell you that. It bears on my examination tomorrow of Dr Kumagai. But it is not worth repeating now. It may be a complete misunderstanding. I do not wish to raise false hopes. You are better off in the dark, rather than having your expectations dashed. Please. Accept my advice on that. You have been working long hours. Take an evening off. Over the weekend, we can discuss a defense, if it comes to that.'

'"If it comes to that"'? I ask. His meaning is elusive. Is he proposing we rest – offer no evidence? Or is this new information so explosive that the trial will come to a halt?

'Please,' Sandy says again. He begins leading us out of the courtroom. Barbara now intervenes. She takes my hand.

So we have dinner at Rechtner's, an old-fashioned German place near the courthouse which I have always liked. Barbara seems especially cheerful after the pleasant developments today. She, too, was apparently affected by the dour events of yesterday. She suggests a bottle of wine and, once it is open, questions me about the trial. She enjoys the opportunity to finally have me at close quarters. Clearly, my unavailability has frustrated her. She asks serial questions with her large dark eyes still and intent. She is very concerned about the Hair and Fiber stipulation of yesterday. Why did we choose that, rather than testimony? She requires a full account of everything the lab report revealed. Then she inquires at length about Kumagai and what his testimony is expected to show. My responses, as they have been throughout, are laconic. I answer briefly, telling her to eat her meal, while I try to contain my discomfort. As ever, there is an aspect to Barbara's interest that I find frightening. Is her wonder truly as abstracted as it seems? Is it the procedures and puzzles that attract her, more even than their impact on me? I try to shift the conversation, asking what we hear of Nathaniel, but Barbara realizes she is being put off.

'You know,' she says, 'you're getting like you were before.'

'What does that mean?' A terrible evasion.

'You're like that again – distant.'

I am where I am and she complains. Even with the wine, a jolt of galvanic anger rockets through me. My face, I imagine, is like my father's, with that monumental look of something dark and untamed. I wait until it has passed.

'This is not an easy experience, Barbara. I am trying to get through it. Day by day.'

'I want to help you, Rusty,' she says. 'However I can.'

I do not answer. Perhaps I should be angry, but as always happens, in the wake of rage I am left in the lightless caverns of the deepest sadness of my life.

I reach across the table and take both her hands between mine.

'I have not given up,' I say. 'I want you to know that. It is very hard now. I am just trying to get to the end. But I am not giving up on anything. I want as much left as possible, if I get the chance to start again. All right?'

She looks at me with a directness she seldom has, but she finally nods.

As we are driving home, I ask again about Nat, and Barbara tells me, as she has not before, that she has had a number of calls from the director of his camp. Nathaniel is waking twice a night with screaming nightmares. The director, who originally put this off under the rubric of adjustment, has now decided that the problem is acute. The boy is more than homesick. There is a special anxiety about my fate which has been exaggerated by being away. The director has recommended sending him home.

'How does Nat sound on the phone?'

Barbara has called him twice, during luncheon recesses, the only time he can be reached. I have been with Stern and Kemp on both occasions.

'He sounds fine. He's trying to be brave. But it's one of those things. I think the director is right. He'll be better off home.'

I readily agree. I am touched and, with whatever perversity, heartened by the depth of my son's concern. But the fact that Barbara has kept this to herself plays on old strings. I find myself once more on the brink of anger, but I tell myself that I am unreasoning, irrational. The idea, I know, is not to increase my burdens. Yet she has a flawless and undetectable way of keeping things to herself.

As we unlock the door, the phone is ringing. I imagine that it is Kemp or Stern, finally ready to share the big news, whatever it is. Instead, it is Lipranzer, who still does not give his name.

'I think we got somethin,' he says. 'On that matter.' Leon.

'Can you talk now?'

'Not really. I just want to be sure you're free tomorrow night. Late. After I'm off.'

'After midnight?'

'Right. Thought maybe we could go for a drive. See a guy?'

'You found him?' My heart picks up. Amazing. Lipranzer found Leon.

'Seems like. I'll know tomorrow for sure. You're gonna love this one, too.' In the phone, I hear someone speaking nearby. 'Look, I gotta go. I just wanted to let you know. Tomorrow night,' he says. He laughs, a rare sound from Dan Lipranzer, especially in these times. 'You're gonna love it,' he says.

33

'Doc-tor Kumagai,' says Sandy Stern in a tone which from its first syllable bristles with derision. It is five past two, the beginning of the afternoon session, and these are the first words of a cross-examination which both Kemp and Stern have promised me privately will be the most eventful of the trial.

Tatsuo Kumagai – Ted to his friends – the state's final witness, faces Stern, limp with indifference. His hands are folded. His brown face is placid. To this audience, he presents himself as a man without need of expression. He is an expert, an unaffected observer of facts. He is dressed in a blue pincord suit, and his abundant black hair is folded in a small pompadour. His direct examination this morning was the first occasion on which I've seen Painless testify and he was somewhat better than I expected. The medical terminology, and his unique speech patterns, caused the court reporter to interrupt a number of times to ask for answers to be repeated or spelled. But he has an undeniable presence. His native arrogance is translated by the witness chair into a developed confidence becoming an expert physician. His qualifications are impressive. He has studied on three continents. He has given papers all over the world. He has testified as a forensic pathologist in homicide cases throughout the United States.

These credentials emerged as part of the lengthy process of qualifying Painless as an expert. Unlike a so-called occurrence witness, who is confined to telling what he saw or heard or did, Painless is charged with considering all of the forensic evidence and rendering an opinion on what occurred. Prior to his appearance, various stipulations were read. The forensic chemist's

326

analysis. The results of blood tests. On the stand, Painless used these facts and his own examination of the body to provide a comprehensive account. On the night of 1 April, Ms Polhemus had had sexual relations, almost certainly consensual in nature. This opinion was based on the presence of a 2 percent concentration of the chemical nonoxynol-9 and various jelly bases, indicating the use of a diaphragm. The man with whom Ms Polhemus had intercourse was, as I am, a type-A secreter. Soon after she had had sex – the relative time indicated by the depth within the vagina of the primary seminal deposit – Ms Polhemus was bludgeoned from behind. Her attacker was right-handed, as I am. This can be determined from the angle of the blow to the right side of her head. His height cannot be approximated without knowing her posture at the time of the attack or the length of the murder weapon. The best indication from the cranial wound is that she had reached her feet, if only briefly, when she was struck. The diaphragm was apparently removed at this time, and Ms Polhemus, already dead, was bound. Without Stern's objection, Painless testified that the presence of the spermicidal compound, coupled with the unlocking of the doors and windows, led him to believe that a rape had been simulated in order to conceal the murderer's identity, and that the murderer was someone familiar with the methods of detection of crime and Ms Polhemus's routine responsibilities in the P A's office.

When Nico had led Painless through this summary, he asked if his opinion of how the crime occurred had ever been communicated to me.

'Yes, sir, I met Mr Sabich about 10 or 11 April this year and we discuss this case.'

'Tell us what was said.'

'Well, Mr Sabich try to convince me that Ms Polhemus must have die accidentally as part of some kind of deviant sexual activity, in which she had voluntarily been bound.'

'And how did you respond?'

'I say that was ridiculous, and I explain what the evidence show really occur.'

'And after you informed Mr Sabich of your theory of what occurred, did you have any further discussion?'

'Yes. He became quite upset. Angry. He stood up. He threaten me. He say that I better be careful or he gonna prosecute for tamperin with an investigation. There's some more, but basically, that's it.'

Both Stern and Kemp on either side of me watched Painless do his stuff with a calm approaching the beatific. Neither one bothered to take notes. I do not yet know what is coming, although that is my choice.

Kumagai made a mistake, Kemp told me when I arrived at their offices this morning. A big one.

How big? I asked.

Enormous, said Kemp. Huge.

I nodded. To myself I thought that if it were somebody other than Painless, I would be more surprised.

Do you want to know what it is? Kemp asked me.

Strangely I found Stern's assessment was right. It was better not to know details. Simply hearing that there was some outsized error was enough to steer me directly to the peripheries of my deepest rage. I had no desire to enter that region of disorder.

Surprise me, I told Kemp. I'll hear it in court.

Now I wait. Painless sits there, unfluttered, impassive. At lunch, Kemp told me he believed that Kumagai's career could be over tonight.

'Doc-tor Kumagai,' Stern begins, 'you have testified here as an expert, is that right?'

'Yes, sir.'

'You have told us about your papers and your degrees, have you not?'

'I answer questions about that, yes.'

'You said you have testified on many prior occasions.'

'Hundreds,' says Painless. Each answer has a kind of screw-you brittleness. He means to be a smart guy and tough, the better of any cross-examiner.

'Doctor, has your competence ever been called into question, to your knowledge?'

Painless adjusts himself on the stand. The assault has begun.

'No, sir,' he says.

'Doctor, is it not true that many deputy prosecuting attorneys over the years have complained about your competence as a forensic pathologist?'

'Not to me.'

'No, not to you. But to the chief of police, resulting in at least one memorandum being placed in your personnel file?'

'I don't know about that.'

Sandy shows the document first to Nico, then to Kumagai on the stand.

'No, I never seen that,' he says at once.

'Do you not have to be notified under police regulations of any addition to your personnel file?'

'Could be, but you ask what I remember. I don't remember that.'

'Thank you, Doctor.' Sandy removes the documents from Kumagai's hands. As Stern is strolling back to our table, he asks, 'Do you have any nicknames?'

Kumagai stills. Perhaps he is wishing that he had acknowledged the letter.

'Friend call me Ted.'

'Aside from that?'

'Don't use nicknames.'

'No, sir, not that you use. But by which you are known?'

'I don't understand question.'

'Has anybody ever referred to you as Painless?'

'To me?'

'To anyone, to your knowledge?'

Again Painless takes a moment to shift around in his seat.

'Could be,' he says finally.

'You do not enjoy that nickname, do you?'

'Don't think about it.'

'You acquired that nickname some years ago from the former chief deputy prosecuting attorney Mr Sennett, in an unflattering context, did you not?'

'If you say.'

'Mr Sennett told you to your face, did he not, that you had bungled an autopsy and that the only person who found working with you painless was the corpse, because it was dead?'

The laughter thunders in the courtroom. Even Larren is chuckling up on the bench. I shift in my seat. Whatever Stern has better be good, because for the first time he has abandoned his innate decorousness. His cross so far verges on the cruel.

'I don't remember that,' says Painless coldly when the room has come back to order again. Over the years he has grown adroit in his knowledge of the rules of evidence. Every cop and PA in Kindle County knows that story. Stan Sennett would be happy to tell it from the stand. But the judge is not likely to allow such a diversion, called collateral impeachment. Painless has drawn his shoulders around him. He looks out at Stern, waiting for more. He has apparently taken some pleasure in what he regards as his own small triumph.

'Now, Mr Della Guardia and Mr Molto are two persons from the PA's office with whom you have worked with less – let us say disagreement, is that right?'

'Sure. They my good friends.' On this point, Painless has apparently been well schooled. He will acknowledge his contacts with Tommy and Delay, in order to minimize their importance.

'Did you discuss this investigation with either one of them while it was in progress?'

'I talk to Mr Molto sometime.'

'How often did you speak to him?'

'We stay in touch. We talk now and then.'

'Did you talk to him more than five times in the first few weeks of April?'

'Sure,' he says, 'if you say.' Painless is taking no chances. He knows that subpoenas are out. He can't be sure whose MUDs we have obtained.

'And you talked in detail about this investigation?'

'Mr Molto's a friend. He ask what I'm doin, I tell him. We talk about public information. Nothin from the gran jury.' Painless resumes his satisfied smile. These answers, of course, have been the subject of prior discussion with the prosecutors.

'Did you tell Mr Molto the results of the forensic chemist's analysis prior to conveying them to Mr Sabich? I am talking specifically about the specimen which showed the spermicidal jelly.'

'I understand,' says Painless curtly. He looks directly over at Tommy. Molto has his hand over part of his face, and with Kumagai's glance, he straightens up and takes it away.

'I think so,' says Kumagai.

He has not quite finished his response when Larren interrupts.

'Just a second,' says the judge. 'Just *one* second. The record will reflect that Prosecuting Attorney Molto has just made a gesture which I recognize to be a signal to the witness in connection with his last answer. There will be further proceedings with regard to Mr Molto at a later time. Proceed, Mr Stern.'

Tommy is crimson as he struggles to his feet.

'Your Honor, I am terribly sorry. I don't know what you are talking about.'

Neither do I, and I was watching Molto. But Larren is inflamed.

'This jury is not blind, Mr Molto. And neither am I. Proceed,' he says to Stern, but his anger is too great to store away and he immediately wheels his chair around in Molto's direction and gestures with the gavel. 'I warned you. I told you before. I am very upset with your conduct during this trial, Mr Molto. There will be proceedings.'

'Judge,' says Tommy despairingly.

'Resume your seat, sir. Mr Stern, proceed.'

Stern comes over to the table. I explain what I saw. He, too, observed nothing. But Stern does not let the incident pass. In a mincing tone he asks, 'It is fair to say, Dr Kumagai, that you and Mr Molto have always had good communication, is it not?'

The question evokes a few snickers, especially from the reporters' section. Kumagai blinks with disdain and fails to answer.

'Dr Kumagai,' asks Stern, 'It is your ambition, is it not, sir, to become coroner of Kindle County?'

'I like to be coroner,' says Painless with disarmingly little hesitation. 'Dr Russell doing a good job now. Couple years he retire, maybe I put in for the job.'

'And the PA's recommendation would help you obtain that position, would it not?'

'Who knows?' Painless smiles. 'Can't hurt.'

Grudgingly, I must admire Delay. Kumagai is his witness and he has obviously counseled him to play it straight about whatever was going on during the election campaign. Nico quite clearly wants to have some prosecutorial candor to troop before the jury to make up for some of Molto's gaffes. And his judgment strikes me as correct. If it were not for the incident with the judge a moment ago, it would all sit pretty well.

'By April, had you and Mr Molto ever discussed the possibility of you becoming coroner, Dr Kumagai?'

'I say. Mr Molto and me friends. I talk about what I wanna do, he talk about what he wanna do. Talk all the time. April. May. June.'

'And in April you also spoke about this investigation a number of times before you received the forensic chemist's report?'

'I'd say so.'

'Now, that report, sir, concerned the semen specimen which you had taken from Ms Polhemus during the autopsy, is that right?'

'Right.'

'And it is that specimen which has been identified as being of Mr Sabich's blood type and as containing chemicals consistent with the use by Ms Polhemus of a birth-control device – a diaphragm. Am I correct?'

'You are correct.'

'And the presence in that specimen of this birth-control chemical, the spermicide, is critical to your opinion, is it not?'

'All facts important, Mr Stern.'

'But that fact is particularly important, because you, sir, want us to believe that this tragic incident merely had the appearance of a rape, do you not?'

'Don't want you to believe nothin. I give you my opinion.'

'But it is your opinion – to get down to brass tacks, as they say – that Mr Sabich tried to make this look like a rape, correct?'

'If you say so.'

'Well, is that not what you are trying to suggest? You and Mr

Molto, and Mr Della Guardia? Let us be plain with these people.' Sandy points to the jury. 'Your opinion is that this was a staged rape. And that the way it was done suggests some knowledge of investigative techniques and of Ms Polhemus's regular duties in the PA's office, correct?'

'That's what I say on direct.'

'And all of that points to Mr Sabich, does it not?'

'If you say so,' Painless says eventually, with a smile. You can see his reluctance to believe that Stern is inept enough to implicate his own client. But Sandy keeps forcing the issue, saying more than Kumagai would risk on his own, and Painless takes his characteristic pleasure in someone else's misfortune.

'And all of those deductions depend in the end on the presence of spermicidal jelly in the specimen you sent to the forensic chemist, do they not?'

'More or less.'

'Much more than less, is it not?'

'I would say.'

'So this specimen, and the presence of the spermicide, is critical to your expert opinion?' says Stern, arriving at the point where he was a moment ago. This time Painless concedes. He shrugs his shoulders and says all right.

'Now, does your expert opinion, Dr Kumagai, take any account of the fact that no spermicidal jelly was found in Ms Polhemus's apartment? Are you familiar with that testimony that was given here by Detective Greer?'

'My opinion of scientific evidence. I don't read the transcript.'

'But are you familiar with that testimony?'

'I heard about it.'

'And are you not concerned, as an expert, that your opinion depends on the presence of a substance not found in the victim's belongings?'

'Am I concerned?'

'That is my question.'

'Not concerned. I got an opinion on scientific evidence.'

Stern gives Painless the long look.

'Spermicide came from somewhere, Mr Stern. I don't know

where lady hides this stuff. It's in the specimen. Test says what it says.'

'Just so,' says Sandy Stern.

'You stipulated,' says Kumagai.

'That the spermicide was in the specimen you sent. Yes, sir, we did agree to that.' Sandy walks around the courtroom. I still cannot guess what it is that Kumagai missed. Until Painless mentioned the stipulation I was ready to bet that the spermicide was misidentified.

'Now, sir,' says Stern, 'your initial impressions at the time of the autopsy took no account of the presence of a spermicide, did they?'

'Can't remember now.'

'Well, think back, please. Was it not your original theory that the person who had last had intercourse with Ms Polhemus was sterile?'

'Don't recall.'

'Really? You told Detective Lipranzer that Ms Polhemus's attacker seemed to have a condition in which he produced dead spermatozoa, did you not? Detective Lipranzer has already testified once before the jury, I am sure it would be no problem for him to return. Please reflect, Dr Kumagai, is that not what you said?'

'Maybe. Very preliminary.'

'All right, it was your very preliminary opinion. But it was your opinion then?'

'I guess.'

'Now, do you recall the physical findings that led you to that opinion?'

'No, sir.'

'As a matter of fact, Doctor, I am sure it is difficult for you to recall, unaided, any autopsy within days of when it took place, is that right?'

'Sometime.'

'How many autopsies do you do in a week, Dr Kumagai?'

'One, two. Sometime ten. Depends.'

'Do you remember how many you performed in the thirty days surrounding Carolyn Polhemus's death?'

'No, sir.'

'Would you be surprised to know that it was eighteen?'

'Sound right.'

'And with that number, it is obvious, is it not, that the specifics of any one examination may slip your mind?'

'True.'

'But when you spoke to Lipranzer the details were fresher. Were they not?'

'Probably.'

'And you told him then that you believed the attacker was sterile?'

'I say, I somewhat remember that.'

'Well, let us review for a moment the findings you presently recall that might have led to that preliminary opinion.'

Sandy runs through it quickly. The rigor mortis, blood coagulation, and digestive enzymes established the time of death. The primary deposit of male fluids in the rear of the vagina, away from the vulva, indicated that Carolyn had spent little time on her feet after sex, meaning that intercourse had occurred near the time of her attack. And there was an absence in the fallopian tubes of any live spermatozoa, which one would expect to find ten to twelve hours after intercourse, assuming no contraception had been used.

'And to explain those phenomena, particularly the dead spermatozoa, you theorized that the attacker was sterile. It did not occur to you at first, Doctor, that a spermicide had been used, did it?'

'Apparently not.'

'As you look back, you must think you were a fool to have missed something so obvious as the use of a contraceptive spermicide?'

'Make mistakes,' allows Painless with a flip of his hand.

'You do?' asks Stern. He eyes the state's expert. 'How often?'

Kumagai does not answer that. He recognizes his miscue.

'Mr Stern, I find no birth-control device. No diaphragm. Apparently, I assume no birth control used.'

'But certainly, Dr Kumagai, an expert of your stature could not have been so easily misled?'

335

Kumagai smiles. He knows he is being taunted.

'Any single fact important,' he says. 'Kind of thing that murderer knows.'

'But you yourself were not trying to mislead Detective Lipranzer when you gave him your initial impression, were you?'

'Oh no.' Painless shakes his head vigorously. He has been prepared for that suggestion.

'You must have been convinced, Doctor, at that time, that birth control had not been used – so convinced that you considered the use of a spermicide to be out of the question?'

'Look, Mr Stern. I got an opinion. Chemist has results. Opinion changes. Lipranzer know opinion's preliminary.'

'Let us consider some alternatives. For example, Dr Kumagai, you would be convinced that birth control would not be used by a woman who knew she could not bear children, correct?'

'Sure,' he says. 'But Ms Polhemus got a child.'

'So the evidence has shown,' remarks Stern. 'But let us not consider the particulars of Ms Polhemus. Just bear my example in mind. If a woman knew she could not conceive, it would be unreasonable for her to use a spermicide, would it not?'

'Sure. Unreasonable.' Painless agrees, but his answers are growing slower. His eyes seem thick. He has no idea where Stern is headed.

'Absurd?'

'I'd say.'

'Can you, as a forensic expert, conceive of any reason that such a woman might use a diaphragm or a spermicide?'

'We not talkin about a lady in menopause?'

'We are speaking of a woman who knows without question that she cannot conceive.'

'No reason. No medical reason. I think of nothin.'

Sandy looks up at Larren. 'Your Honor, may the court reporter mark the last five questions and answers so that she can read them back later, if need be?'

Kumagai conducts a slow survey of the courtroom. He looks at the judge, the reporter, finally the prosecutors' table. He is actually frowning now. The trap, whatever it is, has been set. Everyone knows it. The reporter attaches a clip to the narrow sheaf of stenographic notes.

'Is it not your expert opinion, Dr Kumagai,' asks my lawyer, Alejandro Stern, 'that Carolyn Polhemus was a woman who knew she could not conceive?'

Kumagai looks out at Stern. He bends over the microphone before the witness chair.

'No,' Painless says.

'Please do not rush yourself, Doctor. You did eighteen autopsies in those weeks. Would you not rather consider your original notes?'

'I know the lady use birth control. You stipulate,' he says again.

'And I, sir, say once more that we stipulated to the chemist's identification of the specimen that *you* sent.'

Stern returns to our table. Kemp is already holding aloft the document Sandy wants. Stern drops a copy with the prosecution and delivers the original to Kumagai.

'Do you recognize the notes of your autopsy of Ms Polhemus, Dr Kumagai?'

Painless flips a few pages.

'My signature,' he says.

'Would you please read aloud the short passage marked by the paper clip?' Sandy turns to Nico. 'Page 2, Counsel.'

Kumagai has to change glasses.

'"The fallopian tubes are ligated and separated. The fimbriated ends appear normal."' Kumagai looks down at the sheet he has read from. He pages again to the end. He is frowning, deeply now. Finally he shakes his head.

'Not right,' he says.

'Your own autopsy notes? You dictate them as you are conducting the procedure, do you not? Surely, Doctor, you are not suggesting you made a contemporaneous error?'

'Not right,' he says again.

Stern comes back to the defense table for another piece of paper. I have gotten it by now. I look up to him as he takes the next document from Kemp. I whisper:

'Are you telling me that Carolyn Polhemus had her tubes tied?'

337

It is Kemp who nods.

The next few seconds are blank. Weirdly, unaccountably, I feel alone, locked in my own teetering sensations. An essential connection has been interrupted. For a moment it is like *déjà vu*. I cannot make out reasons. What takes place in the courtroom seems remote. I am aware, in a dislocated way, that Painless Kumagai is being devastated. He denies two or three more times that it is possible that Ms Polhemus had had her fallopian tubes surgically separated to prevent conception. Stern asks if other facts might affect his opinion and pushes into Kumagai's hands the records of the West End gynecologist who performed the tubal ligation six and a half years ago, after Carolyn aborted a pregnancy. It was this doctor, no doubt, whom Kemp went to meet yesterday afternoon.

'I ask you again, sir, would these records alter your expert opinion?'

Kumagai does not answer.

'Sir, is it now your expert opinion that Carolyn Polhemus knew she could not conceive?'

'Apparently.' Kumagai looks up from the papers. In my confusion, I find that I actually feel sorry for him. He is slow now, hollow. It is to Molto and Nico he speaks, not Stern or the jury. 'I forgot,' he tells them.

'Sir, is it not absurd to believe that Carolyn Polhemus used a spermicide on the night of April first?'

Kumagai does not answer.

'Is it not unreasonable to believe that?'

Kumagai does not respond.

'There is no reason known to you that would explain why she might do that, is there, sir?'

Kumagai looks up. There is no way to tell if he is thinking or simply being ravaged by shame. He has taken hold of the beveled rail of the witness stand. He still does not answer.

'Shall I have the court reporter read back your answers to the questions I asked a few moments ago?'

Kumagai shakes his head.

'Is it not clear, Dr Kumagai, that Carolyn Polhemus did not use a spermicide on April first? Would that not be your expert opinion? Does it not seem to you, sir, as an expert and a scientist, the most obvious reason that no trace of a spermicide could be found in her apartment?'

Kumagai seems to sigh. 'I cannot answer your questions, sir,' he says with some dignity.

'Well, answer this question, Dr Kumagai: Is it not clear, given these facts, that the specimen you sent to the chemist was not taken from the body of Carolyn Polhemus?'

Kumagai now sits back. He pushes his glasses back up on his nose.

'I have a regular procedure.'

'Are you telling this jury, sir, that you have a clear recollection of taking that specimen, marking it, sending it on?'

'No.'

'I repeat: Is it not likely that the specimen containing the spermicide, the specimen identified as containing fluids of Mr Sabich's blood type, was not taken from the body of Carolyn Polhemus?'

Painless shakes his head again. But this is not denial. He does not know what occurred.

'Sir, is it not likely?'

'It is possible,' he finally says.

From the jury box, clear across the courtroom, I can hear one of the men say, 'For Chrissake.'

'And that specimen, Dr Kumagai, was sent, was it not, while you were having these regular conversations with Mr Molto, am I right?'

With this, Kumagai finally rediscovers his spark. He draws himself up in the chair.

'Do you accuse me, Mr Stern?'

It is some time before Stern speaks.

'We have had enough unsupported accusations for one case,' he says. Then, before resuming his chair, Stern nods in the direction of the witness, as if to dismiss him. 'Doc-tor Kumagai,' he adds.

*

After court, Jamie Kemp and I sit in Stern's conference room describing Kumagai's cross-examination for a small audience composed of Sandy's secretary, the private investigator Berman, and two law students who work in the office as clerks. Kemp has brought out a bottle of champagne, and one of the young people has turned on a radio. A fine actor, Kemp does a burlesque in which he plays the parts of both Stern and Kumagai. He repeats Stern's most damaging questions in an insistent tone, and then falls in a chair, where he beats his feet and makes the sounds of a person being choked. We are roaring when Stern comes through the door. He has on a tuxedo, or, more properly, part of it: only the striped trousers and the boiled shirt; a red bow tie, not yet knotted, is through his collar. Inspecting the scene he is livid; a fierce anger grips all his features. You can tell that he is struggling to keep himself in check.

'This is inappropriate,' he says. He is speaking to Kemp. 'Entirely inappropriate. We are on trial. This is not the time to congratulate ourselves. We may not bring a trace of smugness to that courtroom. Juries sense such things intuitively. And they resent it. Now, if you would please clean this up, I wish to speak with my client. Rusty,' he says, 'when you have a moment.'

He wheels and I follow Stern to his office with its soft, almost feminine interior. I suspect that Clara had a hand in the decoration. Everything is done in the same creamy tone. Full-length drapes cover the windows, and furnishings upholstered in Haitian cotton crowd the office, so that it feels as if you are being pushed into a seat. Stern has a heavy crystal ashtray at each corner of his desk.

'It's my fault more than Jamie's,' I say when I enter.

'Thank you, but you are not charged with making judgments at this time. He is. That was entirely inappropriate.'

'It was a great triumph. He's worked hard. We were enjoying it. He was trying to put your client at ease.'

'You need not defend Kemp to me. He is a first-rate attorney and I value his work. Perhaps I am to blame. As a case is headed toward conclusion I always become tense.'

'You should savor today, Sandy. No lawyer gets many crosses like that, especially of the state's expert.'

'That is so,' says Stern, and he indulges a brief whimsical smile. 'What a colossal blunder.' He makes a sound, a groan of sorts, and shakes his head. 'But that is past now. You have been very insistent and so I wanted to take one moment with you to discuss the case for the defense. I wish there were more time, but I have committed myself months ago to this dinner for Judge Magnuson. Della Guardia will be there, so we will all be evenly disadvantaged.' He smiles in appreciation of his own understated humor. 'At any rate, your defense: Decisions on these matters are always the client's. If you wish, I will give you my advice. If not, feel free to dictate. I am at your disposal.' As I anticipated all along, Sandy has waited until we are clearly ahead on points before allowing me to make my decisions. I know what he would suggest.

'You think we'll even get the chance to offer a defense?'

'You mean, do I think Judge Lyttle will direct a verdict for us tomorrow?'

'In your view, is that possible?'

'I would be surprised.' He takes up his cigar from the ashtray. 'Realistically, my answer is no.'

'What's left that ties me to the crime?'

'Rusty, there is no need for me to lecture you. But you must remember that the inferences at this stage must be taken in the light most favorable to the prosecution. Even Kumagai's direct testimony, preposterous as it now seems, must be credited for purposes of the motion. And the answer to your question is that the evidence, in any light, ties you to the scene. Your fingerprints are there. Carpeting which could be yours is there. The phone records show you were in contact. And all of this was concealed.

'On a more practical level, no judge is eager to usurp the jury's role as decision maker in a case of this stature. He invites criticism, and perhaps more importantly, he leaves a sense abroad that the case was never fairly resolved. I regard the prosecution evidence, as it stands, as paper-thin. It is likely that the judge sees it the same way. But he would no doubt prefer to have the jury discharge you. If, unaccountably, they fail in that responsibility, he can grant a motion for acquittal post trial, notwithstanding the verdict. I would consider that far more likely in this case.'

He makes sense, but I was hoping he would say something else.

'So that brings us to the question of a defense,' Stern says. 'Certainly if we proceed we must offer certain documents. We want to establish that Barbara was at the U., as you claimed. So we will present the computer log to demonstrate she signed on shortly after eight o'clock. We want to show that the rent-a-car and taxi companies have no records to support the notion that you traveled to the city on the night of April first. The gynecologist's records we spoke of today must, of course, be offered. Other odds and ends. I take all of that as given. Whether we bring on testimony is the question.'

'Who would you consider calling?'

'Character witnesses. Certainly Barbara.'

'I don't want her to testify,' I say at once.

'She is an attractive woman, Rusty, and there are five men on the jury. She can support your alibi, quite effectively. No doubt she is willing.'

'If I testify, and she's sitting in the first row smiling at me, the jury will know that she supports my alibi. There's no need for her to get chewed up.'

Stern makes a sound. I have disrupted his plans.

'You don't want me to get up there, do you, Sandy?'

He does not answer at first. Instead, he brushes a trace of cigar ash from the pleats on his shirt.

'Are you reluctant because of my relationship with Carolyn?' I ask. 'I won t deny it, you know.'

'I know that, Rusty. And I do not find that encouraging. I think it would give a large boost to the state, which they desperately need. Frankly, we run some risk that the same facts might also emerge on Barbara's cross-examination. The confidential communications privilege would probably prohibit inquiry into your admissions to your wife about your affair, but one can never be certain. Overall, it is probably not worth the chance.' Stern seems casual in admitting that I was right after all – it really does not make much sense to talk about calling Barbara. 'But disclosure of these matters is not my principal concern about your testimony,'

Sandy says, getting to his feet. He feigns stretching, but I know by now that he wants to come sit beside me on the couch, the place where he delivers all the bad news. He adjusts a picture of Clara and the children on the white birch credenza behind his desk; then, most naturally, settles next to me.

'Rusty, I prefer to see the defendant take the stand. No matter how often and how insistently jurors are told that they must not hold a defendant's silence against him, it is an impossible instruction to follow. A jury wants to hear a denial, particularly when the defendant is a person accustomed to presenting himself in public. But in this case I am against it. We both know this, Rusty: Two groups of persons make good witnesses. Those who are essentially truthful. And skilled liars. You are an essentially truthful person and would ordinarily make a fine witness in your own behalf. Certainly, you have years of training in how to communicate with a jury. I have no doubt that if you were to testify to everything you knew you would do so convincingly and that you would be acquitted. Deservingly, I might add.'

He looks at me briefly, a quick but penetrating expression. I am not positive whether that is a vote of confidence in my innocence or another comment on the poor quality of the state's case, but I sense the former and I find myself pleasantly surprised. With Stern, of course, it is possible that he has offered that now only to sweeten this pill.

'However,' he says, 'I am convinced after observing you for several months now that you will not testify to everything you know. Some matters remain your secret. Certainly at this juncture I do not wish to pry. I mean that sincerely. With some clients persuasion is called for. With others you would just as well not know. In a few cases, it is best to leave things undisturbed. That is my sense here. I am confident that the choice you have made is a deliberate one, and well considered. But be that as it may, when one comes to the witness stand determined to tell less than the truth, he is like a three-legged animal in the wild. You are not a skillful liar. And if Nico blunders into this area of sensitivity, whatever it is, things will go very badly for you.'

A pause, a silence just a bit longer than need be, passes between us.

'We must assess the case as it is,' Stern says. 'We have not had a bad day yet for the defense. Well, perhaps one. But there is not a piece of evidence that stands untarnished. And this afternoon we have dealt a blow from which the state is not likely to recover. It is my best professional judgment that you should not testify. Whatever your chances – and I admit that I think after today they are quite good – whatever your chances, they are best this way.

'Having said all of that, let me remind you that it is your decision. I am your attorney. And I will present your testimony, if you choose to give it, with confidence and conviction – no matter what you choose to say. And certainly no choices need be made tonight. But I wanted to let you begin your period of final reflection with my own views in mind.'

He is gone a few moments later, his tie knotted and his perfect jacket removed from its hanger behind the door. I remain in his office, made somber by his remarks. This is the closest Stern and I have come to a heart-to-heart. His candor, after so many months of suppression, is disturbing, no matter how kindly or elegantly phrased.

I wander down the hallway with the thought in mind to have another glass of champagne. Kemp's light is still on. He is at work in his small office. Over one of the filing cabinets, merely pasted to the wall, is a poster. Dropped out against a vibrant red background is a young man in a spangled jacket. He is playing a guitar, and the photo has caught him in motion so that his hair stands on end like a dandelion gone to seed. The word GALACTICS crosses from corner to corner in white caps. I am sure that few people who walk in recognize the Jamie Kemp of a decade ago.

'I got you in some hot water with the boss,' I say. 'I apologize.'

'Shit, that's my own fault.' He points to a chair. 'He's the most disciplined human being I know.'

'And one hell of a lawyer.'

'Isn't he? Have you ever seen anything like what went on today?'

'Never,' I tell him. 'Never in twelve years. How long have you guys had that stuff?'

'Sandy noticed the line in the autopsy Sunday night. We got the records from the gynecologist yesterday. You want to hear something? Stern thinks it was just a mistake. He feels Kumagai does everything half-ass. When he got the chemist's results, he went on from there and forgot about the autopsy. I don't buy that.'

'No? What do you think?'

'I think you were set up.'

'Well,' I say, after an instant, 'I've thought that a lot longer than you.'

'I believed it,' says Kemp. 'Most of the time.' I am sure he is thinking about the phone records again, but he does not mention them. 'Do you know who did it?'

I take a moment with that.

'Why wouldn't I tell my lawyers?'

'What do you think about Molto?'

'Maybe,' I say. 'Probably.'

'What does he get out of it? Keeps you from looking into that file? What do you call it? The B file?'

'The B file,' I repeat.

'Except he can't believe you're not going to mention it, if he puts it to you.'

'Yeah, but look at the position I'm in. Would you rather be accused by the chief deputy P A, or some wild man you're trying to nail for murder? Besides, he wouldn't know how far along we were. He'd just want to keep anybody from going forward.'

'That's pretty amazing, don't you think? Bizarre?'

'That's probably one reason I don't quite believe it.'

'What are the others?'

I shake my head. 'I'll have a better idea tonight.'

'What's tonight?'

I shake my head again. For Lipranzer's sake I cannot take any chances. This will be between only him and me.

'Is this do-it-yourself night?'

'That it is,' I say.

'You better be careful. Don't start doing Della Guardia any favors.'

'Don't worry,' I say. 'I know what I'm doing.' I stand up and consider my last statement, one of the most farfetched I have recently made. I bid Kemp good night and go back down the hallway to look for the champagne.

34

Like Santa Claus or the demons that come out in the woods, Lipranzer arrives at my home after midnight. He seems lively and unusually good-humored as Barbara greets him at the door in her nightclothes. Awaiting Lip, I have felt not the slightest inclination to sleep. Instead, the events of the day have combined in such a fashion that for the first time in months I have a sensation which I recognize as something more than hope aborning. It is like the closed eyelids' trembling reception of new daylight. Somewhere inside, there is faith reignited that I am going to be free. In that mellow luminescence, I have passed the most pleasant time in weeks with my wife. Barbara and I have been drinking coffee together for hours, talking about the demise of Painless Kumagai and Nathaniel's scheduled return on Friday, the prospect of a renewed life a balm upon us.

'Downtown they're sayin some wild things,' Lipranzer tells both of us. 'Right before I pulled out of the Hall, I talked to a guy who had just heard from Glendenning. They say Delay's talkin about dismissin the case and Tommy is kickin and screamin and trying to think up a new thing. Could that be right?'

'It could be,' I say. At the mention of Nico dismissing, Barbara has taken hold of my arm.

'What the hell happened in that courtroom today?' Lip asks.

I start to tell him the story of Kumagai's cross-examination, but he has already heard it.

'I know that,' he says, 'I mean, how is it possible? I told you that little jerk said the guy was shootin blanks. I don't care how many times he denied it. One thing, Ted Kumagai is history.

There ain't a soul in the Hall not saying he'll be suspended by next week.'

As Kemp predicted. By now, I find my feelings of sympathy pinched.

Barbara sees us out the door. 'Be careful,' she says. Lipranzer and I sit a moment in the driveway in the unmarked Aries. I perked another pot of coffee – this one with caffeine – when Lip arrived, and Barbara has given him a second cup for the road. He is sipping on it as we sit there.

'So where are we going?' I ask.

'I want you to guess,' he says. It is, of course, a little late to go visiting. But I learned this approach from the coppers a long time ago. If you've got to find someone, the best time to be looking is in the dead of night, when almost everybody's at home. 'Gimme your shot on Leon,' Lip says. 'You know, tell me about him.'

'I have no idea. He's got some kind of job that he wants to keep. That was clear from the letter. So he has to make a good buck. But he lives on the edge. I don't know. Maybe he owns a restaurant or a bar, with some straight partners. He could be anything semi-respectable. He runs a theater company, how's that? Am I close?'

'You'd never get close. Is he white?'

'Probably. Pretty well off, whatever he is.'

'Wrong,' says Lipranzer.

'No shit?'

Lipranzer is laughing.

'All right,' I say, 'twenty questions is over. What's the scoop?'

'Feature this,' says Lipranzer. 'He's a Night Saint.'

'Come on.'

'Sheet as long as my arm. Gang crimes has got all kinds of intelligence on him. This guy's like a lieutenant now. Whatever they call them, a deacon. Runs things on two floors in the projects. He's been up there for years. Apparently, he figured that all his hard-ass pals wouldn't think much of him if they found out he's runnin out to the Public Forest to suck white boys' cocks. That's his thing. Mojoleski's got a snitch, gay as a jaybird, teaches high school, who gave him all kinds of information on this jamoche. Seems like he and Leon went sneakin around together for years.

This guy was Leon's teacher. Eddie somethin. Nine out of ten, that's the fella who's been writin letters.'

'Son of a bitch. So where are we going? Grace Street?'

'Grace Street,' says Lipranzer.

The words are still enough to settle a shiver near my heart and my spine. Lionel Kenneally and I spent a few evenings in there. Early mornings, actually. Three a.m., four. The safest time for a white man.

'I give him a call,' says Lipranzer. 'He's an affluent type. Got a phone and everything. In his own name, by the way. That P.I. Berman did a hell of a job. Anyway, I called about an hour ago. Said I was givin away newspaper subscriptions. He wasn't interested, but he said yeah, when I asked if I was talkin to Leon Wells.'

A Night Saint, I think as we drive toward the city. 'A Night Saint,' I murmur out loud.

I became familiar with the Grace Street projects during my fourth year as a deputy P A. By then, I had joined Raymond Horgan's fair-haired coterie, and he selected me to lead a large-scale police/grand-jury investigation of the Night Saints. This assault on the city's largest street gang was announced by Raymond just in time to become the centerpiece of his first re-election campaign. For Raymond, it was an ideal issue. Negro gangsters were not popular with anybody in Kindle County, and success would permanently dispel his bleeding-heart image. The Saints investigation was my initial trip to the spotlight, the first time I worked with reporters at my side. It took almost four years of my life. By the time Raymond ran for re-election again, we had convicted 147 identified gang members. The press heralded Raymond Horgan's unprecedented triumph, and never mentioned that more that 700 Saints remained on the street, doing all the old things.

The Saints' genesis would make some sociologist a reasonably good dissertation. Originally they were the Outlaws of the Night, a small, not particularly well-disciplined street gang in the North End. Their leader was Melvin White. Melvin was a fine-looking

American, with one sightless eye, milky and wandering, and, for balance perhaps, a dangling turquoise earring, three inches long, in the opposite ear. His hair tended toward the straight and was worn in Gorgon fashion, resembling, if anything, an unkempt Rastafarian tangle. Melvin was a thief. He stole hubcaps, guns, mail, the change from vending machines, and all manner of motorized vehicles. One night Melvin and three of his pals killed an Arab gas-station owner who drew on them while they were emptying his register. They pled to involuntary manslaughter, and Melvin, who up until then had only visited state youth camp, went to Rudyard, where he and his three buddies got to meet men to admire. Melvin emerged four years later in a caftan and phylacteries and announced that he was now Chief Harukan, leader of the Order of Nighttime Saints and Demons. Twenty other bloods dressed just like him settled in the same part of town, and within the next twelve months they all began, as they put it, involving themselves in the community. Melvin gathered his followers to him in a deserted apartment building he called his ashram. He preached from a loudspeaker on weekends and evenings. And during the day he taught those inclined how to steal.

Initially, it was mail. The Saints had people in the post office. Many, in fact. They stole not only checks and the tickets to events but account information, so that they could pass forgeries at any bank. Harukan had what for lack of anything else has to be called the vision to recognize the principles of capitalist enterprise, and his profits were reinvested, usually in decimated real estate in the North End purchased at county scavenger sales. Eventually entire blocks were Saint-owned. The Saints drove up and down in their big cars. They blasted their horns and played their radios. They hustled the daughters of the neighborhood and made hoodlums, willingly or not, of the sons. Harukan, in the meantime, emerged as a political figure. The Saints gave away food on the weekends.

As they became better established, Melvin led the Saints into smack. Entire buildings became processing centers. Guys with chemistry degrees would cut the heroin with quinine and lactose while two dudes with M-16s watched them. In a second area six women, each one stark naked to prevent any body-cavity smuggling, made up dime bags, closing them off with seal-a-meals. Out on the streets in Saintland, high-grade heroin was sold from stands. There were drive-up windows in garages to which white kids from the suburbs could come down to score, and on weekends the traffic was so bad that some mogul in caftan and shades would be down there with a whistle telling people where to go. Once or twice the newspapers tried to write about what was going on, but the coppers didn't like it. There were policemen on the take, something the department has traditionally preferred to ignore, and the cops who weren't taking were just scared. The Saints killed. They shot, they garroted, they stabbed. They murdered, of course, in dope squabbles; but they also killed because of minor differences of opinion, because someone insulted the upholstery in somebody's 'mobile, or because of an innocent brushing of shoulders on the street. They ran six square blocks of this city, their own little Hey Dude fascist arena, a quarter of their terrain occupied by the Grace Street projects.

I have heard it said on many occasions that these projects were drawn from the same architectural plans as the student dormitories at Stanford. Suffice it to say, there is no resemblance now. The small balconies at the rear of each apartment have been curtained off with chicken wire to end the rain of suicides, infants, drunks, and persons pushed, who, over the first five years, became a sauce upon the pavement below. Most of the sliding glass doors to the balconies have been replaced with plywood sheets; and from the balconies themselves a wide variety of objects hang, including laundry, garbage cans, gang banners, old tires, car parts, or, in winter, anything that profits by being kept out of the heat. No sociologist can portray how far the life in these three concrete towers is from the existence most of us know. It is not Sunday school, was Lionel Kenneally's favorite phrase. And he was right; it was not. But it was more than cheap irony or even rabid racism could comprehend. This was a war zone, akin to what was described by the guys I knew who came back from Nam. It was a land where there was no future – a place where there was little real sense of cause and effect. Blood and fury. Hot and cold. Those were terms that had some meaning. But you could not ask anybody to do anything that involved some purchase on what might happen next year, even next week. At times when I listened to my witnesses describe the daily events of project life, in the disconnected way most of them had of doing that, I would wonder if they were hallucinating. Morgan Hobberly, my star, a reformed Saint who, truly, got religion, told me that one morning he rolled out of bed to the sound of gunfire outside his door. When he investigated, he found himself caught between two bloods trying to zap each other with carbines. I asked Morgan what he did. 'Back to sleep, babe. Not my thing. Pulled my pill over my head.'

In truth, my four years of investigation succeeded only because of Morgan Hobberly. The whole heroic incursion into gang life, which Stern has trumpeted before my jury on a dozen occasions, came down to one piece of luck: finding Morgan. An organization like Harukan's did not have the kind of membership who could not be bought. Dozens of them were informants for the police or the federal agencies. But Melvin was smart enough to have a few of them out there doing counter-intelligence work. We were never sure what was right, since we got, through our sources, two or three different stories at any one time.

But Morgan Hobberly was the real thing. He was on the inside. Not particularly because he wanted to be, but because the Saints enjoyed having him around. Everybody knows a Morgan Hobberly. He was born cool, given to grace the way some people are born to music, or horses, or high jumping. His clothes just hung on him right. His movements were lithe. He was not so much beautiful as composed, not so much handsome as present. Aloof was not the right word as much as magical. There was a vibration he stirred in me that somehow reminded me of my feelings for Nat. And because some moral voice that Morgan took for divine told him one morning that Harukan's ways were evil, Morgan secretly went to work for the state. We put a body recorder on him and he sat in the meetings of chieftains. He gave us the numbers of phones that we connected to pen registers and, eventually, tapped. In the seventy days that Morgan Hobberly helped us, we gathered virtually all the evidence for trials that lasted another two years.

He did not make it, of course. The good, they say, never do. It was Kenneally who told me they'd found Morgan. They had a call from the Public Forest district command, he said, and it didn't sound encouraging. When I arrived, there was already that funny scatter of cops and paramedics and reporters familiar to a murder scene. Nobody wants to talk to anybody else; nobody wants to be near the body. People were all over, shot out in different places like spores. I couldn't figure where he was. Lionel was there already, with his hands dug deep in his windbreaker. He gave me that low look of his, the varlet's eye. We fucked up bad, he was saying; and then his eyes drifted back enough for me to guess the general direction.

He had died of drowning. So Coroner Russell later determined – I would not let Kumagai near the body. He had died of drowning, the coroner found, in the waste pool of a public outhouse. That was where he was. Upside down, with his head, and his two broken shoulders, pushed through the wooden seat. Rigor mortis had set in, so that his legs were spread at a kind of scarecrow angle, and his plain twill workpants and raveled nylon socks and worn oxfords created an atmosphere of unbearably humble address. His skin – the band of flesh visible where the pants and socks didn't meet – was purple, a royal shade. I stood in that tiny wooden shack, where a fly or two still buzzed even though it was now November, where the air was rank even without the summer heat, and contemplated Morgan Hobberly's strange humor and the ether on which I always thought that he could float. I believed less then in angels and ghosts, because I had thought surely that this was one man who, as he made his way through the world, could not be touched.

Lipranzer is looking cold – not unemotional or distant, but actually cold, although the nighttime temperature in August is still verging on the seventies. His shoulders are hunched close and his windbreaker is zipped tight. I know him well enough to recognize this is a sign of discomfort, if not fright. On this turf, I am probably more experienced.

'How you doin, Charlie Chan?' I ask him as we head up the concrete staircase.

'Me no likee this one, boss,' he says. 'Uh-uh. No fuckee way.'

In the projects, a staircase is a building's main thoroughfare. The elevators are seldom operable, and when they are, nobody will get on them anyhow, since there is no mercy for him who finds himself between floors with a carload of Saints. Instead, all commerce is transacted in this stairwell. Dope is sold here; wine is drunk here; love is made. It is near 3 a.m. and still this vertical Ganges is not completely deserted. Near floor 4 two young men are drinking something in a bag and trying to romance a young woman whose head is lolled back against the cinder blocks. 'How you doin, brother?' they say to a black man who happens to be climbing up ahead of us. To Lip and me, they say nothing, but their looks are insolent and cold, and Lip, without missing a step, flips out his tin as we are going past. He does not want to be mistaken for an ordinary white man.

At the top of the stairway, the eighth floor, Lip holds a finger to his lips and quietly pulls the steel fire door back. I follow him into the corridor, a typical project hallway; brightly lit to discourage intruders, trash along the sides in isolated pieces, an uncut smell of human use. About halfway down the wall, the sheetrock has been smashed out in a shape which for all the world resembles someone's head. In a hallway like this, one of Lionel Kenneally's guys shot Melvin White, the night after we returned the first round of indictments. I was outside to supervise the arrests, but it was about twenty minutes after we all heard the gunfire before the coppers would let me go in. By then the ambulance had arrived, and I went up with the paramedics. Along with the surgeons, they eventually saved Melvin's life, making way for his return to Rudyard. When I saw him, however, Harukan's chances did not seem good. They had laid him out in the middle of the hallway next to his automatic rifle. He was making a sound too labored, too desperate to be called groaning, and his stomach and his arms, which lay upon it, were painted with blood. Between his hands, a little twisted purple piece of tissue protruded. And above him stood Stapleton Hobberly, Morgan's brother, who had begun snitching for us after Morgan was killed. Stapleton had his penis in his hands. He was urinating in Melvin White's face while a number of coppers lounged against the walls and watched.

And what the fuck am I supposed to say if this guy dies of drowning? one of the paramedics asked me.

Now Lip is rapping on the door.

'Open up, Leon! Wake up! It's the po-lice. Come on, man. We just wanna talk.'

We wait. The building, in a way that is almost beyond the threshold of detection, seems more silent now. Lip raps again with the flat of his palm. There is no kicking this door in. They are all reinforced steel.

Lipranzer shakes his head. And at that moment the door suddenly, silently, swings open. It is very slow. Inside, the room is totally black, no sign of light. Somehow an extraordinary adrenal rush has begun. If I were to pick out the details that key this response, I could only identify the little metal click, but even before that there is an instantaneous perception of alarm. Danger is palpable in the air, as if the threat of harm were an odor, a stirring like wind. When I hear the sound of the gun being readied, I realize that we are perfect targets, standing backlit in the bright hallway. Yet clear as the thought is, I have no impulse to move. Lipranzer, though, is going. Somewhere along he has said, 'Motherfucker,' and as he is on the way down, he slides in my direction and cuts my legs out from under me. I land, painfully, on an elbow and roll away. We both end up lying on our bellies on the floor, staring at one another from either side of the door. Lipranzer has his pistol gripped with both hands.

Lip closes his eyes and yells at top volume.

'Leon, I am the po-lice! This man is the po-lice! And if your piece is not out here in ten seconds, I am callin this in, they are blasting your ass away before you can say shit. Now I'm gonna start countin!' Lip gets to his knees and presses his back to the wall. He motions with his chin for me to do the same thing. 'One!' he yells.

'Man,' we hear, 'if you are the po-lice, how am I gone know it. Huh? How am I gone know it?'

Out of his windbreaker, Lip draws his creds – the star and his picture i.d. He inches toward the doorway, then allows only his hand to cross its plane as he pitches them in.

'Two!' Lip yells. He is backing away. He points up at the lit exit sign. We are going to run for it soon. 'Three!'

'Man, I'm puttin on the lights now. Okay? Okay? But I'm keepin my piece.'

'Four!'

'Okay, okay, okay.' The gun scutters over the tiles and lands against the molding of the hallway with a thump. A heavy black item. Until it stopped, I thought it was a rat. Light from the apartment angles out of the threshold.

'Out here, Leon,' Lip yells. 'Down on your knees.'

'Oh, man.'

'Down!'

'Shee-it.' He comes knee-walking right out the doorway, his arms extended before him. He is quick and comical now. The cops, man. Always *so* serious.

Lip pats him down. Then he nods. And the three of us get to our feet. Lip snatches his creds back. Leon has on a black sleeveless T-shirt and a red headband. On the bottom, he is wearing only his Jockey shorts. Apparently we roused him. A smooth-skinned, powerfully built man.

'I'm Detective Lipranzer. Special Command. I'd like to come in and talk.'

'And who's he, man?'

'He's my goddamned friend.' Lip, who still has his gun in his hand, pushes Leon. 'Now get back inside.' Leon goes first, Lip covers the doorway; with his gun held by his face, he flashes from post to post, staring inside. Then he goes in to search. After a moment he emerges and motions me in. He holsters his pistol again, at his back, under the coat.

'Man, would we have been a headline,' I say to him, my first words since this started. 'If he was shooting, you might have saved my life.'

Lip makes a face, meant to disparage me. 'If he was shooting, you were dead by the time I knocked you down.'

Inside, Leon is waiting for us. His apartment is a galley kitchen and a couple of rooms. There is no sound of anyone else, but he is seated on a mattress on the floor of the living room. He has put on his pants. A plastic alarm clock and an ashtray are by the bed at his feet.

'We want to ask you a couple of questions,' Lip says. 'If you're straight, we're out of your face in five minutes.'

'Hey, man. You come in here three clock in the mornin. Come on, man. Gimme a break. Call Charley Davis, man, he's my 'torney, man. Talk to him, Jack, cause I'm tired and I'm goin to sleep.' He leans back against the wall and closes his eyes.

'You don't need an attorney, Leon.'

Leon, still with his eyes closed, laughs. He has heard that one before.

'You got immunity,' Lipranzer tells him. 'This guy's a PA. Aren't you?'

Leon opens his eyes in time to see me nod.

'See, now you have immunity.'

'7-7-2,' says Leon, '5-8-6-8. That's his number, man. Charley Davis.'

'Leon,' says Lip, 'about eight, nine years ago you dropped fifteen hundred bucks on a deputy PA to make some problems you had go away. Do you know what I'm talking about?'

'No chance, man. Okay? I mean, you come bustin into my home, three clock in the mornin, man, askin me shit like that. Am I a fool, man? Huh? Am I a fuckin fool? I'm gone be talkin to some fuckin white-ass po-liceman about shit like that? Come on, man. Go home. Let me sleep.' He closes his eyes again.

Lip makes a sound. For some reason I get the idea that he is going back to his gun, and I have an impulse to stop him, but instead he walks slowly over to Leon. He crouches, right at the head of his bed. Leon has watched him approach, but he closes his eyes once Lipranzer has reached his level. Lip takes his index finger and jabs Leon a couple of times in the forearm. Then Lip points at me.

'See that guy? That guy's Rusty Sabich.'

Leon opens his eyes. Captain Saint Killer. Right in his living room.

'Bullshit,' says Leon.

'Show him your card,' says Lipranzer.

I am hardly prepared for this, and I have to empty the pockets of my sportcoat. In the process I discover that my coat is gray across its entire front with the hallway's soil. I have brought along the documents Lip obtained months ago from Leon's court file, my appointment diary, my wallet. In there I find one dog-eared card. I give it to Lipranzer, who hands it to Leon.

'Rusty Sabich,' says Lipranzer again.

'So?' asks Leon.

'Leon,' says Lip, 'how many of your blood brothers do you think have been on his pad, huh? Twenty-five? Thirty-five? How many Saints do you think he's paid to snitch? You go back to sleep, Leon, and Rusty Sabich is gonna get on the phone tomorrow morning. He's gonna tell every one of them how you go out to the Forest to suck off white boys. He's gonna give them who and when and where. He's gonna tell them how they can find out all about this stone faggot deacon they got, name of Leon Wells. Okay? You think this is bullshit? This is not bullshit, my man. This is the guy who let Stapleton Hobberly take a piss in Harukan's face. Have you heard that story, huh? Now, all we want is five minutes of your time. You tell us the absolute truth and we're gonna leave you alone. We gotta know a couple of things. That's all.'

Leon has not moved much, but his eyes are wide open as he listens to Lipranzer. There is no more play in his expression.

'Yeah, man, and next week, you need somethin else and you be bustin in the door at three clock in the mornin pullin this shit again.'

'We'll tell you right now if we're ever gonna need anythin else. Just as soon as you answer our questions.' What we'll need is for Leon to come down to court testify, if he nails Molto. But Lip knows the ropes; you don't tell them that for a while. 'Now don't bullshit me, Leon. Here's my first question: Did you or did you not pay fifteen hundred to make that case go away?'

Leon makes a sound. He sits up straight.

'That fuckin Eddie,' he says. 'You already know, man. Right? So why you be botherin me?'

'Leon,' says Lip quietly. 'You heard my question.'

'Yeah, man. I paid fifteen hundred.'

My heartbeat has become very solid now. Thump thump. I expect to see my pocket jumping when I look down at my shirt.

I speak for the first time.

'Did the woman have anything to do with it? Carolyn? The probation officer?'

Leon laughs. 'Yeah, man. You might say that.'

'What?'

'Come on, man,' he says. 'Don't shit me. That bitch set the whole thing up, man. You know that. She tell me I don't have to be mopin round, she know how to take care of everythin. Real smooth. Real smooth. Man, I bet she did it a hundred times. Tell me where to go. How to bring the bread, man. Very cold lady. You hear me?'

'I do.' I crouch down now like Lipranzer. 'And was she there when you made the drop?'

'Right there. Sittin right there. Very cool. You know, man; "How you do. Sit right there." Then the dude start talkin.'

'He was behind you?'

'You got it. She be tellin me when I come in. Don't turn round, just do what the man say.'

'And he told you to put it in the desk?'

'No, man. The desk where I was. He say just leave it in the top drawer.'

'That's what I mean. It was the P A's desk, right?'

'Yeah. That desk.'

'And you paid him, right?' asks Lipranzer. 'The P A?'

Leon looks at him with irritation.

'No, man, I ain't gone be payin no little toad P A. Am I a fool? He gone take my bread, man, and be saying, Oh no, can't do it, just got the word from downtown. I heard enough of that shit.'

Lipranzer looks over to me. He has not gotten it yet. But I have. Just now. Finally, God, am I dense. Dense.

'So who was it?' asks Lip.

Leon mugs. He does not like to tell a policeman anything he does not already know. I say it for him.

'The judge, Lip. Leon paid the judge. Right?'

Leon nods. 'Black dude. Was him, too, man. Behind me? I could tell the voice when I heard him in court.' Leon snaps his fingers, trying to get the name. But there is not any need for him to bother. It's right on the order of dismissal. I take it out of my pocket to check. There's no missing that signature. I've seen it dozens of times in the last two months. It's as distinctive as everything else Larren does.

'So what is it?' Lip asks. It is nearly five now and we are sitting in Wally's, an all-night joint by the river. They used to be famous for doughnut holes, before the national chains got hold of that idea, too. 'Larren's porkin her and takin the money to keep her in style?'

Lip is still wired. On the way here, he stopped at some hole in the wall, a blind pig he knew about, and came out with a half pint of peach brandy, of all things. He drank it down like a Coke. He still had not shaken off our initial encounter at the doorway.

God, he said to me. Sometimes I hate bein a cop.

Now I shake my head at his questions. I don't know. The only thing I have figured out for certain in the last hour is that this is what Kenneally didn't want to tell me when I saw him last week. That Larren was taking. That's what pissed off the coppers back then. The judge was doing it, too.

'What about Molto?' asks Lip. 'You figure he was in?'

'I figure he was out. I don't see Larren Lyttle in any triangles. Nico said Molto always looked up to Carolyn. She probably asked him to dismiss cases and he just obliged. I'm sure he had the hots for her like everyone else.' All very Catholic and suppressed, of course. That would make sense, too. That's the fuel that's kept Molto's engine running at high speed. Unresolved passion.

We talk it over like this for most of an hour. Eventually it gets late enough to have breakfast and we both order eggs. The sun is coming up now, over the river, that spectacular profusion of rose-colored light.

I suddenly think of something and laugh. I laugh too hard, with an embarrassing lack of control. A bout of juvenile hilarity. My thought is ridiculous, not really funny at all. But it has been a long and very odd day.

'What?' Lip asks.

'All these years I've known you, and it never really dawned on me.'

'What's that?'

I start laughing again. It's a moment before I can speak.

'I never realized you carry a gun.'

35

Barbara rolls over as I approach the side of the bed in my pajamas.

'Are you getting up now?' She squints toward the clock. It is 6:30. 'It's early, isn't it?'

'I'm going to bed,' I tell her.

She starts and rolls to her elbow, but I wave that it is not worth talking about. I do not think I will sleep, but I do. I dream of my father in jail.

Barbara waits until the last minute to wake me, and we have to race. The traffic on the bridge is thick, and court is already in session when we arrive. Kemp and the two prosecutors are before the judge. Nico is talking. He looks dour and drawn, and his manner in addressing the judge can only be described as agitated.

I sit down next to Stern. Barbara had called to tell him we would be late, but she diplomatically omitted any mention of why. I spend the first moments of my whispered conference with Sandy assuring him that we are both in good health. Then he explains what is happening:

'The prosecution has entered their hour of desperation. I will tell you about it when the judge breaks. They want Molto to testify.'

I thought that was what Nico was talking about. When he is done exhorting the judge, Larren looks down and says simply, 'No.'

'Your Honor –'

'Mr Delay Guardia, we went over this carefully the first day of the trial. You may not call Mr Molto.'

'Judge, we had no idea –'

'Mr Delay Guardia, if I were inclined to allow Mr Molto to testify, then I oughta declare a mistrial right now, because if this case ever got to the court of appeals – *ever*, I say hypothetically – but if it ever got there, they would turn it around and send it right back. Mr Stern asked the first day of trial about Mr Molto's testimony and you said No how and No way, and that's how it stands.'

'Judge, you said that we would be entitled to some leeway if the defense proceeded with this frame-up theory. You said that.'

'And I allowed you to stand before the jury and make one entirely improper statement in their presence. Do you recall what occurred while Mr Horgan was on the witness stand? But I should have had more faith in Mr Stern's professional acumen than to suppose he would venture down that road without reason. I didn't know then, Mr Della Guardia, that the state's chief piece of evidence was going to disappear after last being seen with Mr Molto. I didn't know that Mr Molto and the chief pathologist were going to manufacture evidence, or testimony – and I tell you, sir, that is a reasonable interpretation of the events of yesterday. I'm still considering the question of what happens with Mr Molto. But one thing that isn't gonna happen is that he gets up on the witness stand and makes matters worse. Now, what's the other thing you wanted to bring up?'

Nico is silent, his head bowed for a second. When he straightens up, he takes an instant to adjust his jacket.

'Judge, we're going to call a new witness.'

'Who is that?'

'Dr Miles Robinson, Mr Sabich's psychiatrist. He was on our witness list. We omitted him from the order of proof, but I informed Mr Stern about the change last night.'

Beside Stern, I have tensed. He has his hand on my arm to prevent a more precipitous reaction.

'What the hell is this?' I whisper.

'I was going to discuss this with you this morning,' says Stern quietly. 'I've spoken with the doctor. I will give you my estimate of what the prosecutors are up to in a moment.'

'And what's the problem?' asks Larren. 'Mr Stern objects to calling the witness without notice?'

Stern stands. 'No, Your Honor. I object to the witness's testimony, but not on that basis.'

'State your objection, Mr Stern.'

'Your Honor. We object on two grounds. Whatever the enlightened view may be of psychotherapy, many persons continue to regard it as a stigma. This testimony therefore risks serious prejudice to Mr Sabich. More important, I expect that Mr Molto – who as I understand it will be questioning Dr Robinson – will elicit material that would violate the physician-patient privilege.'

'I see,' Larren says again. 'Are you moving to suppress?'

Stern looks down at me. Something is on his mind. He leans in my direction, then seems to think better of it.

'Your Honor – my remarks are likely to give offense, for which I apologize. But I believe they are appropriate and necessary to articulating my client's interests. Judge Lyttle, I question the prosecutors' motives in offering this proof. I perceive no factual basis for overcoming the testimonial privilege that prevents a physician, certainly a psychotherapist, from testifying about his treatment-oriented conversations with a patient. I believe that this testimony is offered knowing that the defense must move to suppress it, and that the court must allow that motion. When that occurs, the prosecutors will have someone else to blame when this case reaches the end for which we all now know it is destined.'

Nico becomes fiery. He pounds on the podium, incensed by Stern's suggestion that he and Molto are out to trick-bag the judge.

'I deny that,' he says. 'I deny that! I think that is an outrage!' He does another of his stomping routines, revolving away, and ends up at the prosecutors' table, staring fiercely at Stern as he drinks a cup of water.

Larren is quiet for a long time. When he speaks he makes no comment on what Stern has suggested.

'Mr Della Guardia, on what basis will you seek to overcome the privilege?'

Nico and Molto confer. 'Your Honor, we expect the evidence to

363

show that Mr Sabich saw Dr Robinson on only a few occasions. As a result we believe that Mr Sabich's statements were not for the purpose of seeking treatment and are outside the privilege.'

I have heard all I can handle. Aloud, if under my breath, I remark, 'What bullshit.'

Perhaps the judge hears me. Certainly he looks in my direction.

'Listen here,' says Larren, 'this case hasn't gone very well for the state. Any jackass would know that, and nobody here is a jackass. But if you think, Mr Delay Guardia, that I'm gonna let you elicit privileged testimony so that you can try to pull a rabbit out of a hat, you better have another think or two. I can't and I won't allow that. Now, sir, I'm not gonna suppress this testimony. I don't have any comments on Mr Stern's observations. I don't know whether he's right. I will only say that it is appropriate to adjudicate a claim of privilege on a question-by-question basis. If you wanna put this witness on in the jury's presence, be my guest. But I'll tell you right now that you're on the edge as it is. The conduct of one of the prosecutors has been deplorable. And if he starts attempting to elicit privileged material in the jury's presence, then you're at your peril. Have you conferred with Dr Robinson so that you know the permissible areas of inquiry?'

'Dr Robinson has refused to meet with us.'

'Well, good for him,' says Larren. 'You do what you want, Mr Delay Guardia. But you better have a lot you can get from this witness. Because I can only imagine what this jury is thinkin by now.'

Nico asks for a moment to confer. He and Molto walk together to a corner of the courtroom. Tommy is vehement. He has a high color, and he swings his hands emphatically. I am not surprised when Nico announces that they intend to proceed.

So the jury is brought back to the box and Miles Robinson comes to the witness stand. He is in his mid-sixties, trim, with white hair cropped very close. He is soft-spoken and exceedingly dignified. In another era, he would have been called an octaroon. He is fairer than I am, but he is black. I met him briefly many years ago when he was called as a witness in an insanity case. The nation's leading expert on memory loss. He is a full professor at the medical school at the U., co-chair of the Psychiatry Department. When I had my troubles, he seemed pretty clearly to be the best shrink I could think of.

'Do you know Rusty Sabich?' Molto asks, as soon as Robinson has stated his name, his office address, and his profession.

Dr Robinson turns to the judge.

'Do I have to answer that, Your Honor?'

Larren leans over. He speaks kindly.

'Dr Robinson, Mr Stern over there' – he points – 'represents Mr Sabich. Anything he does not think you ought to be obliged to answer, he will object to. Otherwise, you should answer the questions posed. Don't worry now. He's highly qualified.'

'We've spoken,' says Robinson.

'Very good, then,' says the judge. 'Reread the question, please,' Larren tells the court reporter.

'Yes,' says Robinson when that has been done.

'How do you know him?'

'He was my patient.'

'How many times did you see him?'

'I checked my records last night. Five times.'

'From when to when?'

'February to April of this year. April third was the last time.'

'April third?' asks Molto. He faces the jury, who refuse to look at him. He means, however, to call attention to the fact that my last session was two days after the murder.

'Yes, sir.'

'Did Mr Sabich ever discuss Carolyn Polhemus with you?'

The doctor-patient privilege protects conversations, not acts. Up until now Molto has not asked Robinson to repeat anything I have said. With this question, however, Stern quietly comes to his feet.

'Objection,' he says.

'Sustained,' says the judge distinctly. He has folded his arms over his chest, and he glares down at Molto. It is clear that he shares Sandy's perception of the motives here. And he has conceived of his own politic compromise. He will let Robinson take the stand, and then sustain objections to any questions of consequence.

'Your Honor, may I have the basis of that ruling?' asks Molto. He looks up to the bench defiantly. Lord, how these men hate each other. By now it would require an archaeological dig to get through the sedimentary layers of resentments built up over the years. Some of it has to have been Carolyn. Molto is too primitive not to have been jealous. Did he know, back in their days in the North Branch, about the other dimension to Larren's relations with her? I puzzled on that most of the night. Who knew what about whom back then? And what does Larren think Molto knows now? Tangled webs. Whatever else, it is clear that the dispute between these men by now has nothing to do with me.

'Mr Molto, you know the basis of the ruling. It was discussed before the jury entered. You have established a physician-patient relationship. Any communications are privileged. And if you question another of my rulings in the jury's presence, sir, your examination will end. Proceed.'

'Dr Robinson, isn't it true that Mr Sabich stopped seeing you?'

'Yes, sir.'

'Your treatment of him ceased?'

'Yes, sir.'

'Judge, I submit that these conversations are not privileged.'

'You are in contempt, Mr Molto. Proceed with your examination.'

Molto looks over to Nico. Then he lets it all out. He considers his armaments and reaches for the nuclear bomb.

'Did Rusty Sabich ever tell you that he had killed Carolyn Polhemus?' There is the abrupt sound of people gasping throughout the courtroom. But I realize now why Nico was pounding on the podium. This is the question they brought Robinson here to answer. Nothing marginal like whether I used to sleep with her. They are taking one last blind shot. The judge, however, is enraged.

'That is all,' he screams. 'That is all! I have had it with you, Mr

Molto. Had it! If the other questions are privileged, how isn't that one?'

I whisper to Stern. He says to me, 'No,' and I say to him, 'Yes,' and I actually take his elbow and push him to his feet. There is a rare tone of uncertainty as he speaks.

'Your Honor, we would not object to the question, as phrased, being answered.'

Larren and Molto are both slow to respond, the judge because of his wrath and Molto in sheer confusion. They both finally comprehend at the same time.

Molto says, 'I move to withdraw the question.'

But the judge knows what is occurring.

'No, sir. You will not make an inquiry so prejudicial in the presence of the jury and then seek to withdraw it. So the record is clear, Mr Stern, are you waiving the privilege?'

Stern clears his throat.

'Your Honor, the question does seek to elicit privileged communications, but in my view the question, as framed, can be answered without invading the privilege.'

'I see,' says Larren. 'Well, I suppose that's right. If it goes one way. You ready to take your chances?'

Stern's eyes trail off toward me for an instant, but he responds clearly, 'Yes, Your Honor.'

'Well, let's listen to the answer, then. We'll know where we stand. Ms Court Reporter, would you please read back Mr Molto's last question.'

She stands, with the stenographic tape in her hand. She reads in a flat voice:

'Question by Mr Molto: "Did Rusty Sabich ever tell you that he had killed Carolyn Polhemus?"'

Larren holds up a hand so that the court reporter can resume her seat and prepare to take down the response. Then the judge nods to the witness.

'The answer to the question,' says Robinson in his measured way, 'is no. Mr Sabich never told me anything like that.'

The courtroom ruffles in a fashion that it has not to date, with an air of release. The jurors nod. The schoolteacher smiles at me.

Molto will never give up.

'Did you ever speak in any way about the subject of murdering Ms Polhemus?'

'Objection to that question and to all further questions concerning communication between Mr Sabich and the doctor.'

'The objection is sustained. The objection is taken as a limiting motion and is granted. Any further inquiry being prohibited or irrelevant to these proceedings, I intend to terminate this examination. Dr Robinson, you are excused.'

'Your Honor!' shouts Molto. But Nico instantly has him by the arm. He leads Tommy away from the podium, as they exchange words. Nico nods to humor him, but he seems to have a firmness, a resolve that does not partake of Tommy's outrage.

The judge looks only at Nico.

'Do I take it, Mr Delay Guardia, that the state rests?'

Nico answers. 'Yes, Judge. On behalf of the people of Kindle County, the state rests.'

Larren will dismiss the jury now for the weekend and hear the motion for a directed verdict. He turns to them:

'Ladies and gentlemen, I would ordinarily ask you to leave the courtroom at this point in time. But I am not going to do that. Your service in this case is now over –'

I do not understand these words at first, but when I feel Jamie Kemp's arms around me, then Stern's, I know what has occurred. My trial is over. The judge has gone on speaking. He tells the jurors that they may stay if they please. I am weeping. I put my head down on the table for a moment. I am sobbing, but I lift my head to listen, as Larren Lyttle sets me free.

He is addressing the jury:

'I have reflected on this case at length over the last twenty-four hours. At this time, normally a defense lawyer makes a motion for a judgment of acquittal. And most often a judge decides to let the case proceed. Usually there is enough evidence so that a reasonable jury might find a defendant guilty. I think it's fair to say that there ought to be. No man ought to be brought to trial without sufficient evidence that some fair people might conclude beyond a reasonable doubt that he is guilty. I think justice requires that. And I think that in this case justice has not been done. I understand the prosecutors have suspicions. Before yesterday, I might even have said that there were reasonable grounds for suspicion. Now I'm not so sure of that. But I cannot let you deliberate on evidence like this, which is so clearly inadequate. It would be unfair to you and – most importantly – to Mr Sabich. No person should be held on trial on evidence such as this. I have no doubt that your verdict would be a ringing not guilty. But Mr Sabich should not have to live with this specter a moment longer. There is no proof of motive here, no concrete evidence that there was ever an intimate relationship. There is no effective proof, so far as I am concerned, after yesterday, to give any reasonable person grounds to believe that Mr Sabich even had carnal relations with Ms Polhemus on the night of her death. And, as we have just seen, there is not a shred of direct proof that he murdered Ms Polhemus. Perhaps he was there that night. The state might be entitled to that inference. If the prosecutors had ever found that glass, I might be more confident. But under all the circumstances, I cannot let the case proceed.'

'Your Honor.' Nico is on his feet.

'Mr Della Guardia, I understand you are despairing at this time, but I am speaking and I would like you to hear me out.'

'Your Honor –'

'I have a few words to say about Mr Molto.'

'Judge, I want to move to dismiss.'

Larren starts, actually draws back. In the courtroom, there is a larger stir and then the serial sound of people moving. I know without looking back that the reporters are fleeing for their phones. The TV guys will have to get their camera vans down here. Nobody was planning for the shit to hit the fan at this point. Larren bangs his gavel and demands order. Then he opens his large hand to indicate that Nico may proceed.

'Judge, I just wanted to say a couple of things. First, it seems like a lot of people have started to think that this case is some kind of frame-up or sham. I deny that. I want to deny that. On behalf of all members of the prosecution. I think we were right to bring this case –'

'You had a motion, Mr Delay Guardia?'

'Yes, Judge. I hoped when I came to court this morning that you would let the case go to the jury. Some judges would, I think. I think that's the right thing. But some judges probably wouldn't. And since you've apparently made up your mind –'

'I certainly have.'

'For Mr Sabich's sake, I don't think there should be any question about whether this was a proper legal decision on your part or not. I disagree with you. We do disagree. But I don't think it's fair to pretend that I think you're outside the law. And I certainly don't want anyone thinking I'm looking for excuses.' Nico turns, if only barely, to look over his shoulder in the direction of Stern. 'So for those reasons, I would like to accept your judgment and move to dismiss this case.'

'That motion is allowed.'

Larren stands.

'Mr Sabich, you are discharged. I cannot tell you how sorry I am that any of this has taken place. Not even the pleasure of seeing you free can make up for this disgrace to the cause of justice. I wish you Godspeed.'

He bangs his gavel. 'Case dismissed,' he says, and leaves.

36

Turmoil. My wife. My lawyers. Reporters. Onlookers, I do not know. They all wish to touch me. Barbara is the first. The feeling of her arms around me so firmly, her breasts girdled against me, her pelvis squeezed against mine is astonishingly stimulating. Perhaps this is the first sign of the regeneration of my life.

'I am so glad.' She kisses me. 'I am so glad for you, Rusty.'

She turns from me and hugs Stern.

Today, I elect to make my once-only exit through the heating plant. I do not wish to face the press's disordered melee. I gather Barbara, Stern, and Kemp toward the end of the lobby and then we drop out of sight. But of course there is no escaping. Another gaggle is waiting when we reach Stern's building. We make our way upstairs with little comment. From somewhere a luncheon has appeared in the conference room, but there is no opportunity to eat. The phones ring. And the secretaries soon report that the reception room is a mob scene, with reporters spilling out into the halls. The hungry monster must be fed. I cannot deny Stern this moment. He deserves it, and the consequences of this kind of success in a celebrated case, in terms of both economics and professional stature, will enlarge Stern's career for years to come. He is now a lawyer of national standing.

And so, after half a corned-beef sandwich, we all descend to the lobby of the building to again confront the jostling, shouting crowd of reporters, the microphones, the recorders, the brilliant lights that rise up around me like a dozen new suns. Stern speaks first, then me. 'I don't think that anybody, under these circumstances, can say anything adequate, especially in a short period of time. I am very relieved that this is over. I will never fully understand how it happened in the first place. I am grateful that I was represented by the best lawyer on the face of the earth.' I dodge the questions about Della Guardia. I am still not settled in my own mind. There is already a large part of me that is content with the idea that he was merely doing his job. No one asks about Larren, and I do not mention his name. In spite of my gratitude, I doubt that after last night I could bring myself to praise him.

Back upstairs, there is now champagne, the same vintage as Kemp popped the night before. Was Stern preparing for victory, or does he always keep a case on ice? There are still many visitors in the offices. I stand among them with Kemp and Stern and drink toasts to Sandy. Clara is here, Sandy's wife. Mac arrives. She weeps as she embraces me in her chair.

'I never had any doubt,' she says.

Barbara finds me to say that she is going to leave. She has some hope that Nat's return can be advanced one day. Perhaps the camp director can arrange a seat on the DC-3 that flies back and forth from Skageon. This will require many phone calls. I see her out through the lobby. She embraces me again. 'I am so relieved,' she says, 'so, so glad it turned out this way.' But something between us is impenetrably sad. I cannot, right now, fully imagine Barbara's inner states, but I think that even in this moment of rapturous gratefulness and relief she recognizes that something suspended still remains. In the aftermath of all of this, to go beyond our old troubles will require a treacherous journey across nearly unspannable chasms to grace and forgiveness.

In Stern's offices people keep arriving. A number of cops are here, lawyers around town who have come to congratulate Sandy and me. I feel ill at ease among the many outsiders, so few of whom I know. And my initial euphoria is long past, given way to a suppressed melancholy. At first I believe I am exhausted, and full of pity for myself. But eventually I recognize that my disturbance seems to arise, like black oil percolating from the earth, from something more particular, an idea that seems to demand time for contemplation, and quietly as I can, I leave. I do not say that I am going. I slip out with the excuse that I am finding the head. Then I drift out of the building. It is late afternoon. The shadows are longer and off the river a breeze is up that is rich and full of summer.

The night editions of the papers are on the stands. The *Tribune* head is half a page: JUDGE FREES SABICH. And the kicker: Calls Prosecution 'A Disgrace.' I pay my quarter. 'Decrying a "disgrace to the cause of justice" Kindle County Superior Court Judge Larren Lyttle today dismissed murder charges against Rožat K Sabich, former Chief Deputy in the Kindle County prosecuting Attorney's Office, ending Sabich's eight-day-old trial. Judge Lyttle sharply criticized the case presented by Kindle County Prosecuting Attorney Nico Della Guardia and stated at one point that he believed some of the evidence against Sabich, a former political rival of Della Guardia's, was manufactured by the prosecution.' Both papers play it the same way. Nico takes it in the chops. A made-up case against a past political opponent. Ugly stuff. It will run coast to coast. My friend Nico will be doing the hurt dance for a long time to come. The press, blind as ever to half tones or grays, makes no mention of Nico's final gesture of decency in dismissing the case.

I go down to the river. The city is strangely quiet tonight. A new place with outdoor tables on the riverbank is open and I have two beers and a sandwich. I hold the sports page up before me, a way to avoid responding to the lingering gazes of occasional passers-by, but for the most part I am engaged in a kind of numb reflection. I call Barbara near six, but there is no answer. I hope she is on the way to the airport. I want to get home to see Nat. But before that there is one stop I have to make.

The front door is open when I return to Stern's office, but the suite is almost deserted. I hear only one voice, which I know just by its word-blank rumble to be Stern's. I follow the sound to Sandy's rich office. From what I hear in the hallway, I take it that he is discussing another lawsuit. The lawyer's life, I think, as I catch sight of him there. This morning Sandy Stern won the best-known case of his career; tonight he is working. There is a brief open before him while he talks on the phone. Copies of the afternoon editions of both papers have been tossed aside onto the sofa.

'Ah yes,' he says, 'Rusty has just come in now. Yes. No later than ten tomorrow morning. I promise.' He replaces the receiver. 'A client,' he says. 'So, I see you returned.'

'I'm sorry I ran out.'

Sandy raises a hand. No explanation is needed.

'But I wanted to see you,' I tell him.

'That happens,' says Stern. 'I have clients, after trials such as this, very intense experiences, who are coming back for days, weeks really. It is very difficult to believe it is over.'

'That's sort of what I'd like to talk about,' I say. 'May I?' I take one of Sandy's cigars, which he has often offered. He joins me and selects one as I hold his humidor. We smoke, lawyer and client. 'I wanted to thank you.'

Sandy raises his hand the same way he did before. I tell him how much I admired his defense of me, how seldom I was inclined to second-guess. You are, I say, the very best. This praise appears to run over Sandy with the soothing effect of a bath of warm milk. With this last compliment he does little more than laugh and tip his cigar, one of his courtly gestures, helpless before the truth.

'I also have been thinking about things, and I'd like to know what happened in that courtroom today.'

'Today?' asks Sandy. 'Today you were acquitted of serious charges.'

'No, no,' I say, 'I want to know what really happened. Yesterday you explained to me why Larren would have to let the case go to the jury. And today he acquitted me, without so much as a motion from the defense.'

'Rusty, I made an estimate of what the judge might think. What lawyer do you know who possesses the ability to always correctly predict judicial inclinations? Judge Lyttle decided not to expose you to the risk of an unsupported jury verdict, which might have increased the pressure on him to turn away from what he thought was right. We should both be grateful to him for his perspicacity and his fortitude.'

'Last night your estimate was that the state's case was good enough to go to the jury.'

'Rusty, I am by nature pessimistic. Certainly you cannot take me to task for my discipline. If I had predicted victory and the result were otherwise, I could understand your concern. This I do not.'

'Don't you?'

'We both know that the prosecution's case was not strong to start and that it weakened as it progressed. Some rulings were favorable. Some witnesses balked. Some cross-examinations succeeded. One piece of evidence was unaccounted for. Another was clearly mischaracterized. The state case failed. We have each seen that happen before on many occasions. And matters went from bad to worse for them today. Consider Dr Robinson's testimony this morning. That was very telling.'

'You really think so? I didn't tell him I killed Carolyn. So what? I'm a lawyer. A prosecutor. I know better than to confess to anyone.'

'But to visit a psychiatrist two days after the murder, to have the advantage of this most intimate of professional relationships and to make no culpable statement of any kind – Rusty, this was significant proof, elicited by the prosecution, no less. Perhaps if I had known of it, I would have not made the prediction which I did last night.' Sandy frowns somewhat; his eyes are slightly averted. 'At a moment like this, Rusty, of such sudden change, I have seen persons react strangely. You should not allow your thoughts about events themselves to cloud your appraisal of matters.'

Very diplomatic. Don't let the fact that you killed her influence your judgment as a lawyer. This mild betrayal of me, subtle though it is, is so much out of character that I am now certain I am right.

'I've been in these courtrooms a dozen years now, Sandy. Something is wrong.'

Stern smiles. He puts down his cigar. He clasps his hands.

'There is nothing wrong here. You are acquitted. The system so operates. Go home to your wife. Is Nathaniel back yet? That should be a marvelous reunion for all of you.'

I refuse to be distracted. 'Sandy, what accounts for what happened today?'

'The evidence. Your lawyer. The lawyers on the other side. Your own good character, which was well known to the judge. Rusty, what else is it that you think I can tell you?'

'I think you know what I know,' I tell him.

'Which, Rusty, is what?'

'About the B file. About Larren and Carolyn. About the fact that she used to carry money to him.'

Shock – acute surprise – is not in Sandy Stern's emotional range. His faith in his own worldliness is such that he would never allow anything to so affect him. But his expression now gathers intensity. His mouth draws. And he turns his cigar toward him and considers the ash before he looks back to me.

'Rusty, with all respect, you have been through a great deal. I am your friend. But I am also your lawyer. Lawyer. I keep your secrets. But I do not tell you mine.'

'I can handle the facts, Sandy. I assure you I can. I've dealt with a lot the last few months. And as you told me last night, I'm very good at keeping a secret. I just have this bizarre commitment to learning the truth. I'd like my sense of irony complete.'

I wait and Stern at last gets to his feet.

'I see the problem. You worry about the judge's integrity.'

'With cause, wouldn't you say?'

'No, I would not agree.' Stern perches on the sofa arm, a white nubby fabric. He takes a moment to loosen his tie. 'Rusty, what I say to you I know. How I know is not a concern for you. I have had many clients. Persons worry. They seek a lawyer's advice at times. That is all. And we speak now tonight and these things are never spoken of again by either of us. For my part, I tell you now, I have never said any of these things. Understood?'

'Very well.'

'You doubt Larren's character. You must forgive me, Rusty, a moment of philosophy, but not all human misbehavior is the result of gross defects of character. Circumstances matter, too. Temptation, if you will allow an old-fashioned word. I have known Larren throughout my career and I tell you that he was not himself.

His divorce left him in a state of disorder. He was drinking much too heavily. I understood he was gambling. He had fallen into this relationship with a beautiful and self-seeking woman. And his professional life was shattered. He had given up his practice when it was at its zenith, both in terms of his prominence and its financial rewards. I am sure he meant by this change to make up for the reversals in his personal life, and instead he found himself confined as an act of political vengeance in a judicial dumping zone, adjudicating matters of picayune importance which had no relation to what had attracted him to the bench at the outset. Larren is a powerful mind, able, and he heard for years about nothing but traffic tickets, tavern brawls, sexual interludes in the Forest – matters at the periphery of public justice. All of these cases end the same way, with the defendant discharged. It is only a question of labels: Case dismissed. Pre-trial supervision. Post-trial probation. The defendant in any event returns home. And Larren was in an environment whose thoroughgoing corruption was always one of this city's most distressing secrets. The bondsmen. The policemen. The probation officers. The lawyers. The North Branch was a beehive of illicit dealing. Do you think, Rusty, that Larren Lyttle was the first judge in the North Branch courthouse to fall by the wayside?'

'You can't be apologizing for him,' I say, and Stern's look becomes fomented – severe.

'Not for a moment,' he says strongly. 'Not for a moment. I do not for a moment condone what we speak of. It is a disgrace. Our public institutions crumble from such conduct. If such matters had been the object of proper accusation and proof, and were I the judge before whom they were tried, the prison sentences would be lengthy. Probably lifelong. Whatever my affinities or affections.

'But what happened happened in the past. Long in the past. Judge Lyttle, I tell you, would rather die – I mean this sincerely – die rather than corrupt his office in the Superior Court. This judgment is heartfelt and not merely a lawyer's sanctimony about a judge.'

'My experience as a prosecutor, Sandy, was that people aren't usually just a little corrupt. It's a progressive disease.'

'This is an episode in the past, Rusty.'

'You're confident it's over?'

'Very.'

'Is that another story, too? How it ended?'

'Rusty, you must understand that I do not have a historian's knowledge. I heard personalized accounts from certain individuals.'

'How did it end, Sandy?'

He looks down at me from the vantage of the sofa arm. His hands are on his knees. His face is without humor. Confidences are the core of Sandy Stern's professional life. To him these are intimate and sacred matters.

'My understanding,' he says finally, 'is that Raymond Horgan became knowledgeable of what was occurring and demanded that it cease. Some police in the 32nd District began to assemble evidence. Other persons with knowledge of that had deep fears that any probing of corruption in the North Branch would ultimately prove the undoing of many persons besides Judge Lyttle. It was frankly from one or two of these concerned persons that I heard this account. At any rate, they determined that the PA should properly be advised of an ensuing investigation.' Stern looks off for a moment. 'Perhaps,' he says, with the most remote of smiles, 'that was their lawyer's advice. Privately, I'm sure, it was calculated that Horgan would naturally inform his old friend of the perils to which he was exposed and counsel him at all costs to stop. I believe that is what occurred. I emphasize that I do not know whether or not I am correct. As you no doubt perceive, I am most uncomfortable with this kind of conversation, and I have never made any effort to confirm this information.'

I should have figured that Horgan was in the middle of this somehow. I take a minute. What is this feeling? Something between disappointment and derision.

'You know,' I say, 'there was a time when I thought Raymond Horgan and Larren Lyttle were heroes.'

'With justification. They did many heroic things, Rusty. Many.'

'And what about Molto? Did you ever hear anything about him?'

Stern shakes his head no.

'He was unsuspecting, as far as I know. It is difficult to believe that was really the case. Perhaps he was exposed to others' suspicions and refused to believe them. It is my understanding that he himself was somewhat in Carolyn's thrall. A lapdog. A devotee. I am sure she was able to manipulate him. In Latin America, one sees – or saw, when I was a young man – I have no idea of what transpires now – but when I was young I frequently met women of Carolyn's type, women who used their sensuality with what we might call an aggressive twist. In this day and age, there is something more troubling about a woman with such an old-fashioned and oblique approach to the avenues of power. It seems more sinister. But she was very skillful.'

'She was a lot of things,' I say. Ah, Carolyn, I suddenly think, with unbearable sadness. What was it that I wanted with you, Carolyn? Something in the moment makes me think that Stern has not quite got her right. Perhaps it is the past ordeal and its extraordinary end today; maybe it's amnesty week in Kindle County – no one may be blamed; perhaps it is only more of the same debased obsession – yet for whatever reason, even after all of it – *all* of it – as I sit here amid the cigar smoke and soft furniture, I still feel for her, and feel most of all now sympathy. It is possible that I misjudged Carolyn entirely. Perhaps she suffered from some birth defect, like a newborn come into the world with certain organs missing. Perhaps the feeling parts were absent in her, or subject to some congenital atrophy. But I do not believe that. She was, I think, like so many of the hurt and maimed who have passed before me: the synapses and receptors were in working order on her heart and feelings – but they were overloaded by the need to give solace to herself. Her pain. Her pain! She was like a spider caught in her own web. In the end, in her own monumental way, she must have been in torment. Surely that was no accident. I can only guess about the causes; what forge of cruelty produced her, I do not know. But there was some form of abuse, some long-practiced meanness from which she clearly meant to escape. She sought to re-create herself. She took on every lustrous role. A moll. A star. A person of causes. A conquistadora of wayward passion. A clever, hard-nosed prosecutrix, determined to master and punish those lesser types who could not contain ugly and violent impulse. But no disguise could change her. The heredity of abuse is so often more abuse. Whatever cruelty made her, she took in and, with self-delusion, wild excuses, but always, I would think, some straining residuum of pain, turned it back out into the world.

'And so,' asks Stern. 'Are you better satisfied?'

'About Larren?'

'What else?' He has apparently misinterpreted my moment of reflection.

'I'm hardly satisfied, Sandy. He had no business presiding over this case. He should have excused himself the minute it was assigned to him.'

'Perhaps that is so, Rusty, but let me remind you that Judge Lyttle had no idea when this case began that that file – the B file, as you call it – was going to be an element of your defense.'

'You did.'

'Me?' Stern waves at some of the smoke and passes a remark in Spanish that I do not understand. 'Am I, too, the target of complaint? Certainly you do not think that I planned to focus on that file at the threshold? And even then, Rusty, was I to make a motion for Judge Lyttle to excuse himself? How would you have framed it? The defendant asks the court to recuse itself because the alleged victim was once Your Honor's lover and partner in crime? Some matters are not for courtroom pleading. Really, Rusty. I do not mean to appear the cynic. And I share your concern for professional standards. But I suggest again that you are reacting to the shock of events. This punctiliousness, under the circumstances, is a bit surprising.'

'I don't mean to be a prig. If I am, I apologize. But I'm not concerned about form or technicalities. I have the feeling things were bent well out of shape.'

Stern draws back, removing his cigar. It is a long, slow motion meant to show surprise. But it is no longer opening night. I have seen all of Sandy Stern's best moves a number of times and I don't buy this one.

'Sandy, I've been thinking hard about things in the last few hours. Larren Lyttle's career was over if the circumstances of the

B file were fully explored. And you used every opportunity to tell him that you intended to do just that.'

'Really, Rusty. You must know things that I do not. I saw nothing to indicate that Judge Lyttle fully understood the import of that file. You must remember that its contents were never described in testimony. The file itself was never even in the courtroom.'

'Sandy, would you be offended if I told you that I still don't think you're sharing everything with me?'

'Ah,' says Stern. 'We have been too long together on this case. You begin, Rusty, to sound something like Clara.' He smiles, but I again refuse to be dissuaded.

'Sandy, it took a long time for this to sink in. I admit that. For a while I thought that it was just a bizarre coincidence. You know, I thought it was just lucky that your harping on that file took advantage of Larren's vulnerability. But, I realize now, that's not possible. You *meant* to catch the judge's attention. There was no other reason for you to keep referring to that file. The last time you did it – when Lip was on the stand? – we were way past the point where you needed to raise doubts about Tommy. By then, you knew all about Kumagai. You knew you were going to blow Molto away with that. But you went out of your way again to tell the judge we were going to offer proof about the file the first chance we got. You must have told him that, one way or the other, half a dozen times. You wanted Larren to believe that we were hell-bent on turning that file inside out in public. That's why you mentioned that whole business of a frame-up while Horgan was on cross. You wanted to create a record in which Larren would think he had no proper way to keep you from going ahead. And yet when you sat down with me to talk about a defense, you didn't mention word one about the file. We had nothing to offer.'

Stern is silent. 'You are a fine investigator, Rusty,' he says at last.

'And you're very flattering. Actually, I've had the feeling lately that I was fairly dull. There are still a lot of things I haven't figured out. Like what you mentioned a second ago. How *did* you know that Larren would realize that the B file concerned a case

381

where he'd been dirty? What else is there to the story?'

Stern and I stare at each other for a moment. His look is deeper and more complex than ever. If he is disconcerted, it is well concealed.

'There is no more to tell, Rusty,' he says at last. 'I made certain assumptions, particularly when I saw the judge's reactions with Horgan on the witness stand. They are very close, of course, and as I say, it is my understanding that Raymond would have been quite sensitive to the implications of that file. It seemed likely to me that he and Larren must have communicated about it sometime in the past. But I have no special knowledge. Just a lawyer's intuition.'

Horgan. That was what I missed. Raymond had to have told Larren about that file long ago. Stern is correct. For a moment I spin out the further calculations that follow. But that is not for now. I want to clear the books first with Stern.

'So let me see if I get it,' I tell him. 'You wouldn't dream of directly threatening the judge with exposure. That could be counterproductive, even disastrous. And it's simply not Stern's style. You had to find your own perfect and subtle way of doing things. You wanted Larren to worry about the file, but to believe that he alone perceived his problem. And so, at all moments you made it appear that the defense was in pursuit of Tommy Molto. You acted as if you thought he was the bad guy the file would expose. And the judge bought it. He did his best to steer us in the wrong direction. He did everything he could to make Tommy's zeal look sinister. Larren derided Molto's character. He held him in contempt. Accused him of manufacturing evidence, of signaling witnesses. But that was a double edge. The worse Tommy looked, the stronger your argument for going into the B file became, because it began to seem like this really was a frame-up, engineered by Molto to keep Sabich from discovering Tommy's twisted past. And so it was more and more important for Larren to end the trial. He could never take the chance of letting you go into that file, as you kept saying you wanted to do. Larren didn't know what would come out, but the worst thing, of course, was the truth. He could bet the ranch that whatever Tommy knew about the bad old past in the North Branch, he wouldn't keep it to himself. Molto might hold back to protect Carolyn and her memory – but not to save Larren's ass, at the cost of his own. And so, without so much as a motion from us, Judge Lyttle declares a TKO and sends me home. And, Sandy, there was one man in the courtroom who knew that was what had to happen. You figured it was coming all along.'

Stern's eyes are large and clear and somberly brown.

'Do you judge me so harshly, Rusty?'

'No. I share the Stern outlook. No one is above temptation.'

Sandy smiles at that, somewhat sadly.

'Just so,' he tells me.

'But tolerance doesn't require an absence of standards. I know I sound like a world-class ingrate, but I have to tell you I don't approve.'

'I did not act for my own benefit, Rusty.' He looks at me in that familiar way, lowering his chin so he can observe me from beneath his drawn brow. 'It was a situation in which I – in which we – found ourselves. I did not create it. My own recollection of some of the matters you refer to was refreshed as we proceeded. I dwelt on Molto initially because he was so much easier a target than Della Guardia. It was necessary to develop this theme of past rivalries, somehow. When certain other matters came to mind, it was convenient to continue in the fashion that you have described. But I did not mean to coerce the judge. It was for that reason that I made Molto our straw culprit, so that Judge Lyttle would not feel impelled to do something rash. Was I aware that this might create certain subterranean pressures on Larren as well?' Stern gestures – he nearly smiles. Again there is that mysterious Latin look, used this time as the most reluctant, if philosophical, form of acquiescence. 'As you put it, I assessed a point of vulnerability. But I think overall, in your analysis, you credit me with an intricacy of mind that no human being – certainly not I – possesses. I made certain judgments, instantaneously. This was not a charted course. It remained a matter of intuition and estimation throughout.'

'I'll always wonder, you know. About the outcome.'

'That would be inappropriate, Rusty. I understand your concern now. But I would hesitate before I accepted your view of the judge's ultimate ruling. His handling of this case was, I believe, evenhanded on the whole. Certainly, if he was seeking a convenient way to terminate the proceedings, he could have prohibited the prosecution from offering their fingerprint testimony, in the absence of the glass. Even Della Guardia, disappointed as he was, conceded that Larren's decision today was within the realm of the judge's legitimate discretion. Do you think Nico would have made that handsome gesture of dismissing the case if he believed Larren's assessment was unfounded? Judge Lyttle entered a proper decision, and had he not, I am confident you would have been acquitted. Isn't that what the jurors told the press?'

That is indeed what the papers reported. Three jurors told the media on the courthouse steps that they would not have voted to convict. But Sandy and I both know that the seat-of-the-pants impression of three laymen who have learned that the judge on the case called it a loser are worth very little – and are hardly determinative of what nine other people would have done, in any event.

Stern continues.

'As I say, I made judgments. If, in retrospect, either one of us regards them as questionable, then that should be a burden on my conscience, not yours. Your role is to accept your good fortune on its face, without further reflection. This is the legal significance of an acquittal. This matter is now entirely disposed of. I urge you to move forward. You will overcome this shadow on your career. You are a gifted lawyer, Rusty. I always regarded you as one of the finest of Horgan's prosecutors, probably the best. I was quite disappointed that Raymond did not have the sense to step aside last year and attempt to make the appropriate political arrangements so that you could have succeeded him.'

With that I smile. Now I know that the worst is really over. I have not heard that old saw in many months.

'I believe you are going to be all right, Rusty. I sense that.' For my part, I sense that Stern is about to say something regrettable; even, perhaps, that I have profited from this experience. I spare him the chance. I pick up my briefcase, which had been left here. Stern sees me to the door. We stand at the threshold, shaking hands, promising to speak, knowing that, whatever else, in the future we will have very little to say to one another.

FALL

37

Only the poets can truly write of liberty, that sweet, exhilarant thing. In my life, I have not known an ecstasy as dulcet or complete as the occasional instants of shivering delight when I again realize this peril is behind me. Over. Done. Whatever the collateral consequences, whatever the smirking, the unvoiced accusations, the contumely or scorn with which others might treat me, to my face or, more certainly, behind my back – whatever they say, the terror is over; the sleepless early-morning hours I spent trying to catapult myself ahead in time, envisioning a life of mindless toil during the day, and nights working like half the other inmates on my endless train of *habeas corpus* petitions and, finally, the wary fearful hours of half-sleep on some prison bunk, awaiting whatever perverse terror the night would bring – that horror is past me. And with a sense of earned relief. Every sin of my life seems truly expiated. My society has judged; no punishment is due. Every sticky cliché is right: an enormous weight has been lifted; I feel as if I could fly, like a million bucks, ten feet tall. I feel free.

And then, of course, the shadow moves, and I think what I have been through, with enormous anger and bitterness and a swooping descent into depression. As a prosecutor I lost cases, more, naturally, than I would have liked, and had my chance to observe the acquitted defendant in the instant of victory. Most wept; the guiltier they were, the harder they cried. I always thought it was relief, and guilt. But it is, I tell you, this disbelief that this ordeal, this – think of the word – trial has been endured for no apparent point but your disgrace, and your uncompensable damage.

The return to life is slow: an island on which a soft wind moves.

The first two days the phone does not stop. How people who did not speak to me for the last four months can imagine that I could accept their glib congratulations astounds me. But they call. And I am calculating enough to know they may be needed again; I accept their good wishes with some aplomb. But I spend most of my time alone. I am overwhelmed by the desire to be out in the waning summer and the stirring fall. One day I hold Nat out of school and we go fishing from a canoe. The day passes and we say almost nothing; but I am content to be with my boy and I feel he knows it. Other days I walk in the forest for hours. Very slowly, I begin to see things and therefore notice what I did not see before. My life for four months has been an oblivion, a hopeless storm of feeling so wild that there was nothing outside it. Every face that presented itself to my imagination did so with cyclonic impact in my interior reaches, which now, gradually, are growing still, and which, I finally realize, will in time again require movement.

For the present, I remain at home. My neighbors say that I should write a book, but I am not ready yet for any enterprise. It becomes clear quickly that Barbara finds my presence disconcerting. Her irritation with me, held so long in check, now returns in a peculiar fashion. She clearly feels unable to speak her mind. There are no overt complaints, no instants of shrill sarcasm. As a result she seems even more confined within herself than ever. I find her staring at me with an intense look, troubled, angry, I think. 'What?' I ask. Her chin dimples in disapproval. She sighs. She turns away.

'Are you ever going back to work?' she asks me one day. 'I can't get anything done with you around here.'

'I'm not bothering you.'

'You're a distraction.'

'By sitting in the living room? By working in the garden?' I admit that I am trying to provoke her.

She lifts her eyes to heaven; she walks away. Now she never rises to the bait. This battle, such as it is, must be fought in silence.

It is true that I have made no effort to secure employment. The checks continue to arrive every two weeks from the PA's office. Della Guardia, of course, has no justifiable cause to fire me. And it would turn the office on its head were I to return to work. Nico is under siege from the press. The national reports have increased the sense of local embarrassment. What might ordinarily have passed as mere incompetence in the administration of county affairs has been magnified into a major scandal through the lens of coast-to-coast attention. Nico Della Guardia has made us in Kindle County look to the world like benighted backwoods buffoons. The editorial writers and even the few local politicians of the opposing political party demand that Nico appoint a special prosecutor to investigate Tommy Molto. The local Bar Association has opened an inquiry to determine whether Tommy should be disbarred. The common belief is that Nico, in his ambition to vault himself into the mayor's office, pressed too hard and that in response Molto manufactured evidence, in league with Painless Kumagai. Nico's dismissal of the case is widely read as a confession. Only on occasion are other motivations suggested. I saw a Sunday piece by Stew Dubinsky which mentioned the B file and the aroma that surrounded the North Branch courthouse during those years. But nothing ever followed. Whatever the general understanding, I am not inclined to correct it. I will not exculpate Nico or Tommy or Painless. I still have no wish to tell what I know: that it was my seed taken from Carolyn; that those surely were my prints found on that glass in the apartment; that the carpet fibers detected were from my home; that all the calls the records showed were made from my phone. I will never be ready to brook the costs of these admissions. And there is a rough justice in this. Let Tommy Molto enjoy the experience of attempting to disprove what circumstance seemingly makes obvious. I accept the checks.

It is Mac's last act as chief administrative deputy in the P A's office, before taking the bench, to negotiate a date at which my stipend may end. Nico has suggested six more months. I demand an additional year as reparations. Nine months is ultimately agreed. In our final conversation on this subject, Mac honors our friendship mightily by asking me to speak at her induction. This is my first public outing. Ed Mumphrey, who presides in the ceremonial courtroom, introduces me as 'a man who knows a great deal about justice,' and the three or four hundred persons who have assembled to watch Mac become a judge rise to their feet to applaud me. I am now a local hero. Kindle County's Dreyfus. People regret some of the pleasure that they felt watching me be flogged. Yet it is not possible for me to forget how out of place I feel in society. The trial is still like a shell around me. I cannot reach out.

Because I am one of the three speakers at the ceremony, Nico is not present. But Horgan could not appropriately stay away. I attempt to avoid him, but later, amid the jostling by the hors d'oeuvres tables at the hotel reception, I feel a hand upon my arm.

Raymond has that blarney smile. He does not take the risk of offering his hand.

'How've you been?' he asks in a hearty way.

'I'm fine.'

'We should have lunch.'

'Raymond, I'll never do another thing in my life that you tell me I should.' I turn, but he follows me.

'I put that badly. I would really appreciate it, Rusty, if you would have lunch with me. Please.'

Old affections. Old connections. So hard to break; for what else do we have? I give him a date and walk away.

I meet Raymond at his law firm, and he suggests that if I don't mind, we will not go out. Both of us would be better off without some clever item in the I-On-The-Town column about how Raymond H. and acquitted Chiefdep buried the hatchet in Satinay's prime rib. Instead, Raymond has arranged a catered lunch. We eat shrimp rémoulade alone in an enormous conference room on that stone table that seems to be composed of a single quarried piece, a thirty-foot slab, polished and posted here as an auction block for the captains of industry. Raymond asks the obligatory questions about Barbara and Nat, and he talks about the law firm. He asks about me.

'I won't be the same,' I say.

'I imagine.'

390

'I doubt you can.'

'Are you waiting for me to say I'm sorry?'

'You don't have to be sorry. It doesn't do a damn thing for me, anyway.'

'So you don't want me to tell you I'm sorry?'

'I'm done giving you advice, Raymond, on how to behave.'

'Because I am.'

'You should be.'

Raymond does not miss a bite. He was prepared for some rancor.

'You know why I'm sorry? Because Nico and Tommy made me believe it. It never dawned on me that they had fucked around with the evidence. I figured they'd do as they were taught. They're gonna recall him, you know. Della Guardia? They're gonna try. There are petitions circulating right now.'

I nod. I have read as much. Nico announced last week that there were no grounds for the appointment of a special prosecutor. He expressed his confidence in Molto. And the papers and the TV editorialists pilloried him again. A state legislator made a speech on the floor of the House. This week's word is Cover-up.

'You know what Nico's problem is, don't you? Bolcarro. Bolcarro won't give him the time of day anymore. Augie's gonna sit on his hands on this recall, too. Nico will have to make it on his own. Bolcarro feels like he gave Nico a boost, and the next thing he knows, Della Guardia's a candidate for mayor. Sound familiar?'

I say, 'Mmm-hmm.' I want to sound bored. I want to sound petulant. I came here to make my anger plain. I have promised myself that I will not be concerned about how low I sink. If I feel like calling names, I will do it. Throwing punches. Tossing food. There will be no point below which I will not descend.

'Look,' he says suddenly, 'put yourself in my shoes. This was a hard thing for everybody.'

'Raymond,' I say, 'what in the fuck did you do to me? I ate your shit for twelve years.'

'I know.'

'You were out to ax me.'

'I told you, Nico made me believe it. Once you believe it, I'm sort of a victim in the whole thing.'

'Go fuck yourself,' I say. 'And when you're done fucking yourself, go fuck yourself again.' I wipe the corners of my mouth with the linen napkin. But I make no move to leave. This is just the beginning. Raymond watches me, bitterness and consternation moving through his ruddy face. Finally he clears his throat and tries to change the subject.

'What are you going to do, Rusty, with your career?'

'I have no idea.'

'I want you to know I'll help however I can. If you like, I'll see what's available here. If there's anything else in town that interests you, just say so. Whatever I'm able to do, I will.'

'The only job outside the P A's office that ever sounded good to me was something you mentioned – being a judge. Think you can do that? Do you think you can give me back the life I had?' I look at him levelly, intent on letting him know that this tear cannot be repaired. My tone is sardonic. No judicial candidate can carry the baggage of a murder indictment. But Raymond does not flinch.

'All right,' he says. 'Do you want me to explore that? See if I can find you a seat?'

'You're full of it, Raymond. You don't have that kind of clout anymore.'

'You may be wrong about that, my friend. Augie Bolcarro thinks I'm his best buddy now. Just as soon as he got me out of the way, he decided I could be useful. He calls me up with questions twice a week. I'm not kidding, either. He refers to me as an elder statesman. Isn't that something? If you'd like, I'll speak with him. I'll have Larren speak with him.'

'Don't do that,' I tell him quickly. 'I don't want your help. And I don't want Larren's, either.'

'What's wrong with Larren? I would figure you'd worship that guy.'

'He's your friend, for one thing.'

Horgan laughs. 'Boy, you came up here with one idea in mind, didn't you? You just want to piss all over me.' Raymond pushes the plate aside. 'You want to give me twelve years' backtalk in five minutes? Fine, go ahead and do it. But listen to me. I didn't set you up. You want to take a dump on somebody? Tommy deserves it. So does Nico, as far as I'm concerned. Join the crowd. If you want, I'm sure you can contact the Bar Association. They'll move you to head of the line and let you take a public crap all over both of them.'

'They already called. I told them I had nothing to say.'

'So why me, huh? I know you didn't like seeing me on the witness stand, but did I lie up there? I didn't say a goddamn thing that didn't happen. And you know that, brother.'

'You lied to *me*, Raymond.'

'When?' For the first time, he's surprised.

'When you gave me the B file. When you told me how Carolyn asked for it. When you told me that it was a bullshit allegation.'

'Oh,' says Horgan slowly. He takes a moment to adjust. But he does not falter. Raymond Horgan, as I always knew, is tough. 'Okay. Now I get it. Some little birdie has been whispering in your ear, huh? Who was it? Lionel Kenneally? He was always your asshole buddy. You know, there are a few things you might like to hear about him, too. Nobody's a hero, Rusty. You got your nose bent out of shape about that? Fine. I'm not a hero. Some other people weren't heroes. That has nothing to do with you being charged with murder.' He points at me, still unflummoxed.

'And how about my getting a fair trial, Raymond? Did you think about that? Did you know whether or not Larren was going to tool me because he wanted to keep that thing under wraps?'

'He's not that kind of guy.'

'He's not what kind of guy? We're talking about somebody who sold his robe. Come off it. The only thing he cared about – or you, for that matter – was making sure nobody found out. Let me ask you something, Raymond. How was it that my case got drawn to Larren? Who gave Ed Mumphrey the call?'

'Nobody gave Mumphrey any calls.'

'Just dumb luck, huh?'

'So far as I know.'

'Did you ever ask?'

'Larren and I didn't talk about your case. Ever. Not once that I

393

remember. I was a witness, and as strange as it may sound to you, we both behaved properly. Look,' he says. 'I know what you think. I know how it sounds. But, Rusty, you're talking about bullshit. It's something that happened to the guy nine years ago, when he had his head stuck completely up his ass.'

'How did it happen, Raymond?' I ask, my curiosity for a moment greater than my anger.

'Rusty, I don't know what the fuck went on. I talked to him about it exactly once. And the conversation didn't last any longer than it had to. He was drunk on his ass half the time in those days. You know, she was the PO. Guys on bond would give her their sob story. She started putting in a word with the judge. And he'd go along. I'm sure he thought it'd make her happier to lift her skirt. One day, one of these guys she's helped out gives her a C-note for her troubles. She brings it to Larren to figure out what to do. He thinks it's funny. She does, too. They go out and blow it on dinner. One thing leads to another. They had a high old time, I guess. He always thought it was like a fraternity prank. They both did.'

'And you hired her, knowing this?'

'Rusty, that's *how* I hired her. Larren was giving me all this hearts-and-flowers crap about how broke she was from paying off her law school tuition and making 11K a year as a PO. I said, Fine, I'd double her salary, but knock this shit off. I thought I'd leave her out there as a deputy. Nobody ever liked those assignments. And with two other deputies to watch her, what could she do? And instead, it turns out that she did a helluva job. A hell of a job. She wasn't long on scruples, but the lady had a lot of brains. And I finally got Larren transferred downtown. And he performed with real distinction. I'll go to my grave believing that. No one will ever be able to knock Larren's integrity on his handling of a felony case. A year later they were both so respectable they didn't even talk to one another. If she exchanged ten words with Larren in the last five, six years, I'd be amazed. And, you know, as the time passed, it got to the point that I could see what he saw in her. You know what came of that.'

This, of course, is the answer to what puzzled me last spring.

Why did Carolyn make her move first for me rather than Raymond, when she perceived the prospective vacuum at the head of the office? It was not my manliness, my dark good looks. I was fresher, nowhere near as wise. She probably figured Raymond would know better. He should have; maybe he even did. Maybe that's why she didn't end up with what she wanted, why Raymond gave no sign of having been pained. He saw her coming. He knew what to look for.

'Well, isn't that nice,' I say. 'Everything worked out. Until you get a certain piece of anonymous correspondence. And so you gave her that file to trunk.'

'No, sir. No way. I gave it to her. I didn't know what it was. I told her to look at it. And to bear in mind that she could never tell who might come looking over her shoulder. That's all I said. What do you want from me, Rusty? I'm seeing the gal by then. Am I supposed to pretend? If I was such a bum, I'd have done just what you said. Headed for the shredder with the thing.'

I shake my head. We both know he is much too careful for that. No way to tell who may come looking for the letter. That's the kind of job that a Medici like Raymond knows he should hand off. And with instructions that will never bounce back on him. Very artful. Investigate. See what's going on. And what goes unspoken is that if it has to do with Larren and you, clean the mess up very carefully. Carolyn certainly tried. I don't have to wonder anymore who had Leon's arrest file from the 32nd District.

'And when she got cooled, you ran and collected the file?'

'When she got "cooled," as you put it, I got a call from His Honor. You know, I had told him about the letter when the thing came in. So he's on the phone the day they find the body. Pure Larren, too. He's always been a sanctimonious asshole. He says to me, It might be politically sensitive, why don't I collect that file?' Raymond laughs. Alone. I do not relax my severe expression. 'Listen, Rusty, when you asked me, I gave you the thing.'

'You had no choice. And you tried to mislead me anyway.'

'Look,' he says, 'he's my friend.'

And the key to Raymond's black support. If Raymond had ever

395

prosecuted Larren Lyttle, or let somebody else do it, he could have just as well resigned as run for re-election. But I don't mention that. Disgust has finally displaced some of my anger.

I stand up to leave.

'Rusty,' he says to me, 'I meant what I said. I want to help you. You give me the high sign and I'll do whatever you want. You want me to kiss Augie Bolcarro's ass in Wentham Square at noon so he'll make you a judge, I'll do it. You want to work for the big bucks, I'll try to arrange that, too. I know I owe you.'

What he means is that he wants to keep me happy, now more than ever. But his genuflection is still soothing in a way. You cannot continue pounding a man who's on his knees. I say nothing, but I nod.

On the way to the door, Raymond again points out all the modern art along the walls. He apparently has forgotten that he gave the same dime lecture to Stern and me. As we're parting by the elevator, he reaches for me and tries to take me into an embrace.

'It was a terrible thing,' he says.

I break away. I actually shove him slightly. But there are people around and Horgan pretends not to have noticed. The elevator arrives. Horgan snaps his fingers. Something has come to mind.

'You know,' he says quietly, 'there was one thing I promised myself I was gonna ask you today.'

'What's that, Raymond?' I ask as I step inside.

'Who killed her? I mean, who do you think?'

I say nothing. I remain impassive. Then, as the elevator doors begin to close, I nod to Raymond Horgan in a gentlemanly way.

38

One day in October I am working in the yard and I feel an odd stirring. I am fixing the fence – removing the posts, sinking new ones in cement, nailing on the beeftail. For a moment I consider the tool with which I am working. A Whatchamacallit. It is an inheritance of sorts from my father-in-law. After his death, Barbara's mother brought all his yard and home equipment over here. The Whatchamacallit is a piece of black iron, a kind of cross between a hammer's claw and a crowbar. You can use it for anything. On the night of 1 April, it was used to kill Carolyn Polhemus.

Right after the trial I noticed that there was still a crust of blood and one blond hair clinging to the edge of one of the two teeth. I stared at the Whatchamacallit for a long time, then I took it to the basement and washed it in the laundry tub. Barbara came downstairs as I was doing it. She stopped dead on the stairway when she saw me, but I tried to appear jovial. I reached for the hot water and began to whistle.

I have picked it up a dozen times since then. I want to observe no fetishes, no taboos. And after a moment for reflection, I decide it is not the Whatchamacallit singing to me like a ghost. Instead, as I consider the grass, the roses and their thorns, the vegetable bed that I helped Barbara put in this spring, there is the sense of something in this house, this land that is irretrievably used up and old. I am finally ready for some considered changes. I find Barbara in the dining room, where she is grading papers. They are stacked across the table like my mother's magazines and notecards from her era as a radio personality. I sit down on the other side.

'We should think about moving back into the city,' I tell her.

I expect, of course, that this concession will bring from Barbara the radiance of victory. She has advocated this move for many years. Instead, Barbara puts down her pen and holds her forehead. She says, 'Oh, God.'

I wait. I know something awful is going to happen. I am not scared.

'I didn't want to talk about this yet, Rusty.'

'What?'

'The future,' she says, and adds, 'I didn't think that it would be fair to you. So soon.'

'All right,' I say. 'You've nodded in the direction of good taste. Why don't you tell me what's on your mind?'

'Rusty, don't be like that.'

'I'm like that. I'd like to hear.'

She folds her hands.

'I've taken a job for the January term at Wayne State.'

Wayne State is not in Kindle County. Wayne State is not within four hundred miles of here. Wayne State, as I recall, is in a city I have visited once, which is called Detroit.

'Detroit, right?'

'Right,' she says.

'You're leaving me?'

'I wouldn't put it like that. I'm taking a job. Rusty, I hate to do this to you now. But I feel I have to. They had hired me for the September term. I was going to tell you in April, but then all that craziness began –' She shivers her head with her eyes closed. 'Anyway, they were nice enough to give me an extension. I've changed my mind half a dozen times. But I've decided it's for the best.'

'Where's Nat going to be?'

'With me, of course,' she answers, her look suddenly fierce and aquiline. On this point, she means to say, there must not be even a thought that she might yield. It occurs to me, as a sort of reflex, that I could probably go to court and try to prevent that. But just now I have had enough of litigation. In its odd way, the thought inspires a smile, rueful and brief, a reaction which brings a vaguely hopeful look to Barbara.

'What do you mean you're not leaving me, you're taking a job?' I ask. 'Am I invited to Detroit?'

'Would you come?'

'I might. This isn't a bad time for me to start over. There are a few unpleasant things following me around here.'

Barbara immediately tries to correct me. She has thought all of this through, perhaps to salve her conscience, probably because there are always these geometries in her head.

'You're a hero,' Barbara says. 'They wrote about you in *The New York Times* and *The Washington Post*. I've been expecting you to tell me any day that you're going to run for office.'

I laugh out loud, but this is a sad remark. More than anything Barbara has said, it proves how far we have already drifted. We have again ceased communication. I have not told her enough for her to understand my own thoroughgoing revulsion with what has gone on in the interest of politics.

'Would it offend you if I moved somewhere closer than here so that I can see my son? Granting that we're not about to live in the same house.'

She looks at me.

'No,' she says.

I consider the wall for a moment. My God, I think. What happens in a life. And then I think once more of how this all began and pine, as I have so often lately. Oh, Carolyn, I think. What did I want with you? What did I do? But it is not as if I am entirely without an account.

I am nearly forty now. I can no longer pretend that the world is unknown to me, or that I like most of what I've seen. I am my father's son. That is my inheritance – the grimness of outlook bred of knowing that there is more cruelty in life than simple wits can comprehend. I do not claim that my own sufferings have been legion. But I have seen so much. I saw my father's hobbled soul, maimed by one of history's great crimes; I saw the torment and the need, the random and passionate anger that brings such varied and horrible misbehavior to our own streets. As a prosecutor I meant to combat it, to declare myself a sworn enemy of the crippled spirit that commits each trespass with force and arms.

But of course, it overcame me. Who can observe that panorama of negative capacity and maintain any sense of optimism? It would be easier if the world were not so full of casual misfortune. Golan Scharf, a neighbor, has a son born blind. Mac and her husband, in a moment of revelry, turn a corner and plunge into the river. And even if luck, and luck alone, spares us the worst, life none the less wears so many of us down. Young men of talent dull it and drink it all away. Young women of spirit bear children, broaden in the hips, and shrink in hope as middle years close in upon them. Every life, like every snowflake, seemed to me then unique in the shape of its miseries, and in the rarity and mildness of its pleasures. The lights go out, grow dim. And a soul can stand only so much darkness. I reached for Carolyn. With all deliberation and intent. I cannot pretend it was an accident, or serendipity. It was what I wanted. It was what I wanted to do. I reached for Carolyn.

And so now, still gazing at the wall, I begin to speak, saying aloud things that I had promised myself would never be spoken.

'I've thought a lot about the reasons,' I say. 'Not that anyone can fully comprehend them. Whatever you call that insane mix of rage and lunacy that leads one human being to kill another – it's not the kind of thing that's easy to understand in any ultimate way. I doubt anybody – not the person who does it or anyone else – can really grasp the whole thing. But I've tried. I really have tried. I mean, one thing I should say to start, Barbara, is that I apologize to you. I think a lot of people would find that laughable. That I would say that. But I do.

'And one more thing you've got to know. You have to believe it: she was never more important to me than you are. Never. I guess, to be unflinchingly honest, there must have been something there that I didn't believe I could find anywhere else. That was *my* failing. I admit it. But as you've told me yourself, I was absolutely obsessed with her. It would take hours to explain why. She had that power; I had that weakness. But I know goddamn well that I wouldn't have gotten over her for years, and probably never, as long as she was walking around. I mean, there is no such thing as justification here, or excuse. I'm not trying to pretend there is.

But at least we should both acknowledge the circumstances.

'I always figured it wasn't going to do anybody much good to talk about it. And I assumed that was what you'd figured. What happened happened. But naturally I've spent a lot of time thinking about exactly how it occurred. I could hardly help that. I guess every prosecutor learns that we live closer than we want to believe to real evildoing. Fantasy is a lot more dangerous than people like to say. You get this idea, this careful elaborate plan, it becomes actually stimulating to think about it, it titillates and thrills you, you dwell on it, and you take the first step toward carrying it out, and that is thrilling and titillating, too, and you go on. And in the end, once you edge up to it that way, telling yourself all along that no real damage has been done, it takes just one extraordinary moment, when you revel in the excitement, in the feeling of flying free, for the whole thing actually to occur.'

I finally look back. Barbara is on her feet now, standing behind her chair. Her look is quick and alarmed, as well it might be. No doubt she never wanted to hear this. But I go on.

'As I said, I really never thought I'd have to talk about this, but I raise it now, because I think once and for all it ought to be said aloud. There's no threat here. There's not even the shadow of a threat, okay? God knows what somebody in your position might think Barbara, but there is not a threat. I just want the cards on the table. I don't want there to be wondering about what either of us knows or thinks. I don't want that to be a factor in whatever it is we're going to do. Because all in all, even though you're probably amazed to hear me say all of this, and then say this, too, I expected, I guess the word is wanted, is *want*, to go on. There are a lot of reasons. Nat, first of all. Of course. And I also want to minimize the damage to our lives. But more than that, I do not want that mad act to have had no decent consequence. And basically, in trying to explain to myself how and why this woman was murdered – for what little rational impulses have to do with it, and for what little they are worth as explanations – I suppose I always thought that in part it was for us. For us. For the good of us. God knows a lot of it was simply for my benefit, to – if conscience can stand those words – get even. But I thought some of it was for us, too.

And so I wanted to say that, to see if all of this means anything to you or makes any difference.'

I am finished at last, and feel strangely satisfied. I have done as well with this as I ever could have imagined. Barbara, my wife, is crying, very hard, and silently. She is looking downward while the tears simply fall. She heaves and catches her breath.

'Rusty, I don't think there is anything worth saying, except I'm sorry. I hope you believe me someday. I really am so sorry.'

'I understand,' I tell her. 'I believe you now.'

'And I was prepared to tell the truth. At any time. Right up to the end. If I was called as a witness, I would have told what happened.'

'I understand that, too. But I didn't want that. Frankly, Barbara, it wouldn't have done a bit of good. It would have sounded like some desperate excuse. Like you were making a bizarre effort to save me. Nobody ever would have believed that you were the one who killed her.'

These words bring fresh tears, and then, finally, control. It has been said and she is, in a measure, relieved. Barbara wipes each eye with the back of her hands. She breathes deeply. She speaks, looking down at the table.

'Do you know what it feels like to be crazy, Rusty? Really crazy? To not be able to get any hold of who you are? You never feel safe. I feel like every step I take, the ground is soft. That I'm going to fall through it. And I can't go on that way. I don't think that I can be a normal person again if I'm living with you. I know how horrible that is. But it's horrible for me, too. No matter what I thought, nobody goes back to the way things used to be after something like this. All I can say, Rusty, is that nothing turned out the way I expected. I never understood the reality of any of it until the trial. Until I sat there. Until I saw what was happening to you, and finally felt how much I didn't want that to be happening. But that's part of what I can't get over. I have no life here, except being sorry. And afraid. And, of course – "ashamed" is not the word. "Guilty"?' She shakes her head slowly, looking down at the table. 'There isn't a word.'

'We could try to share that, you know. The blame,' I say.

Somehow, in spite of myself, this remark has a whimsical quality. Barbara gasps a bit. She bites her lip suddenly. She looks the other way for a second, and, in a momentary exhalation, cries. Then she shakes her head again.

'I don't think that's right,' she says. 'The trial came out the way it should have, Rusty.'

That's all she says. I might have hoped for more, but it's enough. She starts to leave the room, but stops and lets me hold her for a moment, actually a long moment as she lingers with me, but finally she breaks away. I hear her go upstairs. I know Barbara. She will lie on our bed and weep a while longer. And then she is going to get back on her feet. And begin packing to leave.

39

One day, right after Thanksgiving, when I've come to town for Christmas shopping, I see Nico Della Guardia walking down Kindle Boulevard. He holds his raincoat drawn closed around the collar and he has a worried brow. He seems to be looking up and down the street. He is coming in my direction, but I am quite certain he has not seen me yet. I think of ducking into a building, not because I am afraid of his response, or mine, but simply because I think it might be easier for both of us to avoid this meeting. By then, however, he has caught sight of me and he is heading deliberately my way. He does not smile, but he offers his hand first, and I take it. For that instant only, I am rifled by a shot of terrible emotion – hot pain and grief – but it quickly passes and I stand there, looking affably at the man who, in any practical sense, tried to take my life from me. One person, a man in a felt hat, apparently aware of the momentousness of this meeting, turns to stare as he continues on his way, but otherwise the pedestrian traffic merely divides about us.

Nico asks me how I am. He has the earnest tone people lately have tended to adopt, so I know that he has heard. I tell him anyway.

'Barbara and I split up,' I say.

'I heard that,' he says. 'I'm sorry. I really am. Divorce is a bitch. Well, you know. You had me crying on your shoulder. And I didn't have the kid. Maybe you guys can work it out.'

'I doubt that. Nat's with me for the time being, but only until Barbara gets settled in Detroit.'

'Too bad,' he says, 'Really. Too bad.' Old Nico, I think, still repeating everything.

I turn to let him go on his way. I offer my hand first this time. And when he takes it, he steps closer and squeezes up his face so that I know that what he is about to say is something he finds painful.

'I didn't set you up,' he says. 'I know what people think. But I didn't have anybody screw with the evidence. Not Tommy. Not Kumagai.' I almost wince at the thought of Painless. He has resigned now from the police department. He had no refuge. He could only claim collusion or incompetence, and so he chose the lesser – and I believe more apt – of the two evils. He did not botch the semen specimen, of course, but I've come to believe that no one would have been indicted if he'd looked back at his autopsy notes. Nobody could have put it all together. Maybe Tommy's also to blame for pushing too hard to bring a marginal case. I suppose he thought my hide would still his grief – or envy – whatever state it was that Carolyn had left him in which so riled his passions.

Nico in the meantime continues, sincere as ever. 'I really didn't,' he says. 'I know what you think. But I have to tell you that. I didn't do that.'

'I know you didn't, Delay,' I say. And then I tell him what I think is the truth. 'You did your job the way you thought you were supposed to. You just relied on the wrong people.'

He watches me.

'Well, it's probably not going to be my job much longer. You've heard about this recall thing?' he asks. He is looking up and down the street again. 'Of course you have. Everybody has. Well, what's the difference? They all tell me my career is over.'

He is not looking for sympathy. He just wants me to know that the waves of calamity have spread and washed over him as well. Carolyn has pulled all of us down in her black wake. I find myself encouraging him.

'You can't tell, Delay. You never know how things'll turn out.'

He shakes his head.

'No, no,' he says. 'No, you're the hero, I'm the goat. It's great.' Nico smiles, in a sudden way, so that you know he finds his own thoughts weird, inappropriate. 'A year ago, you could have beat me in the election, and you could do it today. Isn't that great?' Nico Della Guardia laughs out loud, pinched by his own ironies, the peculiar readings from his own terms of reference. He spreads his arms here in the middle of Kindle Boulevard. 'Nothing,' he says, 'has changed.'

40

In the front room of the home in which I have lived for better than eight years there is complete disorder. Open boxes, half packed, are everywhere, and items removed from shelves and drawers are strewn in all directions. The furniture is gone. I never cared much for the sofa or the love seat, and Barbara wanted them for her condo outside Detroit. I'll move 2 January to an apartment in the city. Not a bad place. The realtor said I was lucky to get it. The house is up for rent. I've decided that each step should be slow.

Now that Nat has left, the job of packing seems to take forever. I move from room to room. Every item reminds me of something. Each corner seems to contain its quotient of pain and melancholy. When I reach my limit, I start working somewhere else. I think often of my father and that scene I recalled for Marty Polhemus, in which I found my old man, the week after my mother's death, packing up the apartment he had abandoned a few years before. He worked in a sleeveless undervest, and he had a brazen manner as he pitched the remains of his adult life into crates and boxes. He kicked the cartons from his path as he moved about the rooms.

I heard from Marty just last week. He sent a Christmas card. 'Glad to hear everything worked out for you.' I laughed aloud when I read his message. Lord, that kid really has the knack. I threw the card away. But the toll of loneliness is greater than I imagined. A couple of hours ago, I went rummaging through the boxes of trash in the living room, looking for the envelope. I need the address to write him back.

I never wrote my father. After he left for Arizona, I did not see him again. I called on occasion, but only because Barbara dialed the number and put the receiver in my hand. He was so deliberately uncommunicative, so chary with the details of his life, that it was never worth the effort. I knew he was living with a woman by then, that he worked three days a week in a local bakery. He found Arizona hot.

The woman, Wanda, called to tell me he was dead. That was more than eight years ago now, but the shock of it, in a way, is with me every day. He was strong and fit; I had taken it for granted that he would live to be a hundred, that there would always be this far-off target for my bitterness. He had already been cremated. Wanda only found my number as she was cleaning out the trailer and she insisted I come West to settle the rest of his affairs. Barbara was eight months pregnant then and we both regarded this trip West as my father's final imposition. Wanda, it turned out, was from New York City, in her late fifties, tall, not bad-looking. She did not hesitate to speak ill of the dead. Actually, she told me when I arrived, she had moved out on him six months before. They called her from the bakery, where he collapsed with the coronary, because they knew no one else. 'I don't know why I do these things. Really, I have to tell you,' she said, after a couple of drinks, 'he was mostly a prick.'

She did not think it was funny when I suggested her phrase was what should be carved on the stone.

She left me alone to pick through the trailer. On his bed were red socks. In the chifforobe, I found another six or seven dozen pairs of men's hose. Red and yellow. Striped. Dotted. Argyles. In his last years, my father had finally found an indulgence.

The doorbell rings. I feel the faintest surge of anticipation. I look forward to a moment's conversation with the postal carrier or the man from UPS.

'Lip,' I say through the storm door. He enters and stomps the snow off his feet.

'Nice and homey,' Lip says, surveying the disaster in the living room. As he stands on the doormat, he hands me a small package, not much wider than the satin bow on top.

'Christmas present,' he says.

'That's awfully nice,' I say. We've never done this before.

'I figured you could use a pick-me-up. Nat get off okay?'

I nod. I took him to the airport yesterday. They allowed him to be seated first. I wanted to go with him onto the plane, but Nat would not permit it. From the doorway, I watched him go down the jetway in his dark blue NFL parka, alone and already lost in dreams. He is his father's son. He did not turn to wave. I want, I thought quite distinctly, I want the life I had.

Lip and I spend a moment looking at each other. I still have not taken his coat. God, it is awkward, and it is like this with everyone, people on the street or people I know well. So much has happened to me that I never counted on. And how are people to respond? Somehow it does not fit into any recognized conversational patter to say, It's tough about your wife, but at least they didn't get you for that murder.

I finally offer him a beer.

'If you're drinkin,' he answers, and follows me to the kitchen. Here, too, half the housewares are in boxes.

As I'm taking a glass out of the cabinet, Lipranzer points to the package he brought, which I've set down on the table.

'I wanna see you open that. I been savin it a while.'

He had done a careful job with the paper.

'I never saw a gift wrapped before,' I say, 'with hospital corners.'

Crumpled inside a small white box is a manila envelope ribboned with red-and-white evidence tape. I tear through that and find the glass that turned up missing during the trial, the tumbler from Carolyn's bar. I put it all down on the table and take a step away. This is one guess where I would never have been close.

Lip fishes in his pocket and comes out with his lighter. He holds a corner of the evidence envelope in the flame until he's sure it's burning, then flips it into the sink. The glass he hands to me. The blue ninhydrin powder is still all over it, the three partial prints etched there, a kind of surrealistic delft. I hold the glass up to the window light for a moment, trying for reasons I cannot discern to figure which of the tiny networks of lines are the marks of my right thumb and my third right middle finger, the former telltale

409

signs. I am still looking at the glass when I start talking to Lipranzer.

'There's a genuine question here, whether I should be touched,' I say, and now finally catch his eye, 'or *real* pissed off.'

'How's that?'

'It's a felony in this state to secrete evidence of a crime. You hung your ass out a good long way on this one, Lipper.'

'No one around who'll ever know.' Lip pours the beer that I've just opened. 'Besides, I didn't do a goddamn thing. It was them that fucked up. Remember they got Schmidt to come grab all the evidence? The glass wasn't there. I'd took the thing down to Dickerman. Next day I get a call from the lab, the test is done, I can come pick up my glass. When I get down there somebody's signed the receipt "Returned to Evidence." You know, the idea is that I'll put it back in. Only I don't got any way to put it anywhere, since it's not my goddamn case anymore. So I tossed it in a drawer. Figured sooner or later somebody's gotta ask me. Nobody did. In the meantime, Molto's like every other half-ass deputy. Signs off on all the receipts without matchin em against the evidence. Three months later he's got himself a bucket of shit. But that's his problem.' Lip lifts his glass and drains most of it. 'None of them ever had the most screwed-up idea where the thing went. They tell stories about the way Nico tore his office apart. He had them pick up the tacked-down carpet, I hear.'

We laugh, both of us, knowing Nico. When he gets very excited you can see his scalp redden where the hair has thinned. His freckles seem to stand out more as well. After the laughter is done, we wait through a little hollow moment of silence.

'You know why I'm pissed, don't you?' I finally ask.

Lip shrugs and raises his beer.

'You thought I killed her,' I say.

He's prepared for this and does not even flinch. He belches before he answers.

'Lady was bad news.'

'Which makes it okay if I killed her?'

'Did you?' asks Lip.

That, of course, is what he's come to find out. If he just wanted

410

to be a soul brother, he'd have taken the glass with him the last time he went fishing and dropped it in the Crown Falls, which rages so magnificently up there near Skageon. But it must be eating at him. That's why he's offered the glass, so I know that we're in it together.

'You think I did, don't you?'

He drinks his beer.

'It's possible.'

'Screw off. You're gonna stick your neck out like that cause it's just a little possibility, like life on Mars?'

Lip looks straight at me, his eyes clear and gray.

'I'm not wearin a wire, you know.'

'I wouldn't care if you were. I've been tried and acquitted. Double-jeopardy clause says that's all she wrote. I could publish my confession in the *Trib* tomorrow and nobody could try me again for murder. Only we both know, Lip' – I take a slug of the beer I've opened for myself – 'they never do admit it, do they?'

Lip looks across the kitchen toward something that isn't there.

'Forget it,' he says.

'I'm not going to forget it. Just tell me what you think, okay? You think I cooled her. That's not just for the sporting life that a fifteen-year copper hikes the evidence in the biggest case in town. Right?'

'Right. It ain't just sportin life.' My friend Dan Lipranzer looks at me. 'I think you killed her.'

'How? I mean, you must have worked it out in your head.'

He does not hesitate as long as I would have thought.

'I figure you cracked her in anger. The rest was just to make it look good. There wouldn't be much point in sayin you were sorry once she was dead.'

'And why was I so pissed off?'

'I don't know. Who knows? She dumped you, right? For Raymond. That's enough to be pissed about.'

Slowly, I remove the beer glass from Lipranzer's hand. I can see his apprehension when I do that. He is prepared for me to fling it. Instead, I put it on the kitchen table next to the one he brought, the one they found on Carolyn's bar, the one with my prints. They are identical. Then I go to the cabinet and take down the rest of the set, until there are a dozen glasses standing there in two rows, one sudsed with beer foam at the head on the left, one dusted with blue powder at the front of the line next to it. It is a rare moment, in which Lipranzer wears none of his hipped-up wise-guy look.

I run the water in the sink, washing down the ashes, then fill the basin with suds. I start talking while I do that.

'Imagine a woman, Lip, a strange woman, with a very precise mathematical mind. Very internal. To herself. Angry and depressed. Most of the time she is volcanically pissed. With life. With her husband. With the miserable, sad affair he had in which he gave away everything she wanted. She wanted to be his obsession and instead he's hung up on this manipulative slut, who anyone but he could see regarded him as sport. This woman, Lip, the wife, is sick in spirit and in the heart, and maybe in the head, if we're going to be laying all the cards out on the table.

'She's mixed up. She is seriously on the fence about this marriage. Some days she's sure she's going to leave him. Some days she wants to stay. Either way she has to do something. The whole thing's eating at her, destroying her. And either way, she has a wish, a wild secret hope that the woman he was sleeping with could end up dead. When the wife's rage is at a peak, she's ready to abandon her husband, head for open spaces. But there would be no satisfaction in that if the other women is alive, because the husband, helpless slob that he is, will just go crawling back to her and end up with what his wife thinks he wants. The wife can get even only if the other woman is gone.

'But, of course, you always hurt the one you love. And in her down moods, she longs for everything they had, to find some way to bring them back to old times. But even in these moods, it seems that life would be better if the other woman were dead. With no choice, he will finally give up his obsession. Maybe then they can recycle things, build on the wreckage.'

The sink by now is full of suds. The ninhydrin comes off the glass easily, although there is a sulfurous stink when it hits the water. Then I take down a towel and wipe the glass clean. When I am finished, I get a box and begin wrapping up the set. Lip helps.

He separates the sheets of newsprint that the movers have provided. He is not talking yet.

'And so the idea is there. Day after day. All the wife thinks about is killing the other woman. Whether she is in the peak of rage or the dungeons of self-pity, there is that thrilling notion.

'And, of course, as the idea takes hold, there is another twist. The husband must know. When she is raging, when she's on the way out the door, it is a kind of delicious vengeance to think of him bereft and knowing just who left him in that condition. And in her softer moods, when the thought is of somehow saving this marriage, she wants him to appreciate this monumental act of commitment and devotion, her effort at finding the miracle cure. It will have no meaning to him if he thinks it's just an accident.

'So that becomes part of the compulsion. To kill. And to let him know that she has done it. How is that to be accomplished? It is a magnificent puzzle to a woman capable of the most intricate levels of complex thought. Obviously she can't just tell him. For one thing, half the time she's planning to be gone. And, of course, on the basic level, there is a risk that – to put it mildly – her husband might not approve. He may go tattling. She has to take that option from him. And how best to do that? Fortunately, it is predictable that the husband will investigate this crime. The head of the Homicide Section has taken a powder. The acting head is a person no one trusts. And the husband is the PA's favorite son. He will be the one collecting evidence, him and his pal, the all-star homicide dick Lipranzer. And as the husband proceeds, detail by detail, he will discover that the culprit for all the world appears to be him. He'll know of course that it was not. And he'll know who it was, because there is only one person in the world who has access to this glass, or to his seed. But he'll never convince anybody else of that. He will suffer in lonely silence when she leaves him. Or kiss her bloody hand with new devotion when she stays. In the act itself, there will be purification and discovery. With the other woman gone, she will be able to find just what it is she wants to do.

'But it must be a crime that the rest of the world can reasonably regard as unsolved, when hubby declares that to be the case. It must be a crime in which he alone will realize what has occurred. That's why she decides to make it look like a rape. And so the plan proceeds. Something that must be utilized is one of these glasses.'

I show the tumbler I am wrapping to Lip. He is seated on one of the kitchen chairs now, listening with an open look that mediates between rough horror and a kind of wonder.

'It was a glass just like this one that her husband picked up and wept over, the night he told her of his affair. The self-centered sap sat there and devastated her with the truth and cried because their glasses were just like the other woman's. That will be the perfect calling card, the perfect way to tell him. You know who. He drinks a beer one night while he watches the ball game. She hides the glass away. Now she has his fingerprints.

'And then on a few mornings she saves the gooey mess that comes out when she removes her diaphragm. Puts it in a plastic bag, I figure, which probably sat a while in the basement freezer.

'And that's how it's done. April first. Ha ha. That's to help him get it. She makes a phone call from the residence an hour before the event. Hubby is at home, babysitting, but, as Nico would have argued if Stern had ever pointed out that Barbara might have been here when I made that call, you can use the phone in Barbara's study without being heard downstairs.'

Lip's chair makes a sudden screech as it jerks back across the floor.

'Whoa,' he says. 'Run that by again. Who called? Really. Not what Delay was thinkin. Her?'

'Her,' I say. 'That time.'

'That time?'

'That time. Not before.'

'You before?'

'Me before.'

'Hmmm,' says Lip, and his eyes dull as he reflects, no doubt, on that day in April when I asked him for what surely seemed a harmless favor, a trivial indiscretion, to skip retrieving my home tolls. 'Hmm,' he says again, and actually laughs out loud. I do not understand at first, but when I see his somewhat cheerful look I realize he is satisfied. We can only be who we can be. Detective Lipranzer is pleased to know that he was not completely wrong to judge me guilty of some margin of bad faith. 'So she called that night?'

'Right.'

'Knowin you'd done it before?'

'I'm not sure of that. She couldn't have overheard me, because there was nothing to hear. But if you want a guess, I think she knew. That was my sense. I probably left the phone directory from the PA's office open to the page one time when I called Carolyn. That's the kind of thing Barbara would notice. You know how fixated she is with details, especially around the house. That may even have been what kicked her over the edge. But I don't know for sure. It could have been a coincidence. She had to get in touch with Carolyn somehow. She couldn't just show up.'

'What'd she tell her on the phone?'

'Who knows? Something. Bullshit. She asked to drop by.'

'And killed her dead,' says Lip.

'And killed her dead,' say I. 'But not without a stop first at the U. She logged into the computer. Nobody ever checked, but I'll bet she loaded on some brainbusting program. I'd guarantee that machine was churning out paper for two hours. Every clever killer needs an alibi, and Barbara, you might say, has considered a detail or two. Then she drives over to Carolyn's, who by now is waiting for her to arrive. Carolyn lets her in. And when she turns her head, Barbara serenely bashes it in with a little item called a Whatchamacallit, which is just small enough to fit inside a lady's purse. Then she gets out the cord she's brought along and does some tying. Leaves the calling-card glass on the bar. And then takes a syringe and the knowledge gained from her readings in artificial insemination and injects the contents of her little Ziploc bag, full of male fluid. She unlocks the doors and windows before she leaves.

'Of course, criminal detection is a little more complicated than Barbara knew. There are entire fields of inquiry unknown to her. Like fiber analysis. She leaves traces she never counted on. The fibers from the carpets in her home, which are clinging to the hem of her skirt. Or a few hairs of her own. Remember how Hair and Fiber didn't bother with the female hair they picked up at the scene? I'm sure she never figured anybody was going to do so detailed an analysis of the sperm specimen. And I would bet that Barbara had no idea about MUD records, and was astonished when it turned out that her call was traced back to our phone. She drew more of an arrow toward herself than she intended. Same thing with that third fingerprint on the glass – probably a moment of carelessness. And of course none of us ever figured that Carolyn had tied her tubes.

'There's the rub, of course. Life, it seems, does not follow the invariable rules of mathematics. Things do not turn out as she had planned. Molto is shadowing the investigation. He picks up on everything she never meant to leave behind, and items like the fingerprints that she had probably figured I could shove under the rug. Things turn very dark for hubby. The world falls in around him. He seems completely fuddled. Maybe he doesn't even know who set him up. And now she finds herself in the one place she never counted on being: she feels sorry for him. He has suffered in ways she never intended, and in the cold light of reality, she is full of shame. She nurses him through his ordeal. She is ready at any moment to save him with the truth, until it fortunately proves unnecessary. But of course there are no happy endings. This story is a tragedy. Things are better now between the husband and the wife. Passion and feeling have been rediscovered. But now The Act stands between them. There are things he cannot say to her. Things she cannot say to him. And worst of all, she cannot stand her own guilt – or the recollection of her insanity.'

When I am done, I look at Lip. And Lip looks at me. I ask him if he wants another beer.

'No, sir,' he says. 'I need whiskey.' He stands up to wash his glass. Then he puts it in the box with the other eleven. He holds the box closed while I apply the tape.

I pour him his shot and he stands, drinking.

'When'd you figure all this out?' he asks.

'The big picture? I think I pick up pieces of it every day. There have been days, Lip, while Nat was at school when I've done

416

nothing but sit in the dark and work over the details. Again and again.'

'I mean, when did you know what happened?'

'When did I know she did Carolyn? It crossed my mind when I heard there was a phone call from here the night she was murdered. But I thought Tommy must have diddled the phone records. I didn't really know until I saw the glasses again in Carolyn's apartment and realized all of hers were there.'

Lip makes a noise, a little too ironic to be called a groan.

'How'd that one make you feel?'

'Weird.' I shake my head. 'You know, I'd look at her. Here she is – cooking dinner for me. For Nat. *Touching* me, for Chrissake. Then, you know, it would all come clear to me: I was out of my fucking mind. I wouldn't believe it at all. For days, I wouldn't believe it. Sometimes I was positive that Tommy set me up. Making me think it was Barbara was part of his scam. I thought that a lot. I would have loved to hear Leon lay it all on Molto. But, you know, at the end, when I knew what it was, I wasn't surprised at all.'

'Don't you wanna see her burn?'

I pout my lip. Slowly, I shake my head.

'I couldn't do it, Lip. I couldn't do it to Nat. We've all had more than enough. *I* couldn't take it. I don't owe anybody that much.'

'And you don't worry about the kid? With her?'

'No,' I say. 'Not that. That's one thing I don't worry about. She's in better shape with him. It pulls her back. Barbara needs someone around who really cares about her. And Nat does. I always knew I couldn't split them up – it would be the worst thing I could do to either one of them.'

'Least I don't gotta wonder why you threw her out.' Lip makes that noise again. 'Whew,' he says.

I've sat down now in the kitchen chair Lip formerly occupied. I am thus in the middle of the room alone as I speak.

'I'll tell you something that will blow your mind: she's the one who took the powder. I didn't ask her to leave. I suppose six months from now I could have woken up and strangled her in her sleep. But I was willing to try it. I really wanted to try. Crazy as she is, wild and nuts, no matter how many times you turn it upside down, you still have to say she did it because of me. Certainly not out of love. But for it. I wouldn't call it even, but we'd have both had our share to make up for.'

Lip laughs at that.

'Boy,' he says. 'You really got a way with the ladies.'

'You think I'd have been out of my mind to stay with her?'

'You askin my opinion?'

'I seem to be.'

'You're better off without her. You're givin her way too much credit. You're believin in a whole lot of accidents.'

'How's that?'

'The way you're looking at this whole thing.'

'For instance?'

'Your prints. They're on the glass, right?'

'Right.'

'And only you would know? You can't make an i.d. yourself. Gotta get the lab to do it. That means somebody else comes up with your name.'

'Yeah, but I'm a big dummy. I was supposed to recognize the glass – not ask for prints.'

'In a major murder case you ain't gonna ask for prints?'

I take a moment. 'Maybe she didn't know they could make a laser match. My prints are there just to keep me from dropping a dime on her.'

'Sure,' says Lip. 'And in the meantime the lab is lookin at the gism, figurin things out. And they got your carpet fibers.'

'Nobody ties those things to me.'

'What about your phone records, if somebody should think to look? You said yourself she probably knew you'd been usin this phone to call Carolyn. Why's she dial from here, while you're around the house? Why take that chance instead of goin to a pay phone? You don't think that lady knows from M U Ds? Or fibers? Or whose prints are on file? After twelve years of listenin to your stories?' Lip chucks down the rest of his whiskey. 'Champ, you don't got this figured right.'

418

'No? What do you figure?'

'I figure she wanted Carolyn dead and you in the slammer for doin it. I'd say the only thing that happened that she never counted on was that you beat it. Maybe two things.'

Lipranzer grabs one of the kitchen chairs and sits down astride it. We are now face to face.

'I bet she was world-class pissed when you ended up with this case. She'd have never guessed that on the front end. You're the chief deputy. You don't horse around these days with homicides. You don't have the time. You got a fuckin office to run while Horgan's tryin to save his butt. The only thing she'd know is Raymond would be tear-ass – he'd want to keep this thing in-house, right under his thumb. Anybody'd know Raymond would make damn certain the police assignment was Special Command. I think she figured that some smart homicide dick was gonna nail you. Somebody who'd look at too many doors and windows open, who'd get a report about what was in the wad and see it was all a setup – somebody who'd go lookin for a real bright guy who'd know just how to do it. That's what she was countin on – somebody who knows you real good. Somebody who goes with you to the Red Cross drive and knows your blood type. Maybe even knows you well enough to think you were keepin company with a certain dead lady. Knows what color carpet you got at home.' Lip suddenly, and inappropriately, yawns as he looks out to the living room. 'Yeah,' he says, 'when I come for you with the cuffs, that'd put the knife in pretty deep. That's what I figure.'

Lipranzer eyes me sagely. Then he nods, convincing himself.

'That's possible,' I say, after a moment. 'I've thought of that. But she said things didn't go the way she'd expected.'

'Meanin what?' he asks. 'They didn't fry your ass? I mean, what else you gonna hear but hearts and flowers: Honey, I'da saved you if I had to. What would you do? Say, Go head and turn me in?'

'I don't know, Lip.' I look at him, then I slug him softly in the shoulder. 'Fifteen minutes ago you thought I was the one who killed her.'

In response he makes his sound.

'I don't know,' I say again. 'I believe two things. She did it. And

419

she was sorry. I'll always believe she was sorry.' I straighten up. 'And anyway, it never would have done me any good to tell.'

'Speakin of tellin, did you let your lawyers know, at least?'

'Nope. Neither one. Right at the end I had this idea Sandy might have figured it out. He talked to me one night about putting Barbara on the stand – and I got a clear feeling he didn't have the slightest interest in really doing it. And the kid, Kemp, had some notion, too. He knew something was out of whack with the phone records. But I'd never have put either one of them in that position, having to choose between my wife and me. I didn't want to be defended that way. Like I said, I couldn't see taking his mother from my son. And besides, it would never wash. If Barbara really figured all this out, Lip, then she knew that, too. Nico had a beautiful argument if I got up there and accused her. He would have said this was the perfect crime. An unhappy marriage. A prosecutor who knows the system inside out. A guy who's become a misogynist. He despises Carolyn. He hates his wife. But he loves the boy. If he and his wife split, he'll never get custody. He'd have said I planned it this way. Made it look like her set-up. Right down to getting her fingerprint on the glass or injecting the spermicide. Maybe he'd say I was using Barbara as a fail-safe, the person I'd like to see nabbed in case the whole house of cards fell in on me. There are plenty of juries that might buy that.'

'But it isn't true,' says Lip.

I look at him. I can tell that I have left him out there again, floating uneasily in the ether regions of disbelief.

'No,' I tell him, 'that isn't true.'

But there is that flicker there, the brief light of an idle doubt. What is harder? Knowing the truth or finding it, telling it or being believed?

CLOSING
ARGUMENT

When Raymond called, I told him the idea was absurd.

'Instant rehabilitation,' he said.

'It is impossible,' I answered.

'Rusty,' he said, 'give a guilty conscience a chance.' I was not sure if he was referring to himself or everyone in Kindle County. But he insisted it could happen, and at last I told him that if everything could be arranged I would think seriously about it.

In January, as a result of the petition drive the City Council authorized a recall election. Bolcarro could have prevented it, but he displayed a marked neutrality toward Della Guardia. Nico campaigned actively to retain his office and he nearly pulled it out. He fired Tommy Molto with about two weeks left, but various civic leaders, including Raymond, Larren, and Judge Mumphrey, came out against him, and Della Guardia was recalled with a margin of about 2,000 votes. He has not given up. he is going to run for City Council from the South End, and I expect him to win.

Bolcarro formed a citizens' commission to make recommendations on the new P A. Raymond was a member. That was what led him to call me. Rumor has it that Mac was the first choice, but she refused to leave the bench. Raymond promised me that the papers had been sounded and that I would receive universal support. I could not think of a good reason to say no. On 28 March, four days short of the anniversary of Carolyn Polhemus's murder, I became the acting Kindle County prosecuting attorney.

I took the position with the understanding that I will not run for re-election. The mayor has told me a couple of times he thinks I'll make a fine judge, but he has not put that on paper. Right now I enjoy the job I have. The news stories refer to me as 'the caretaker P A.' My relations with lots of people have all kinds of peculiar strains and edges, but it is no worse at work than when I walk down from my apartment to buy a dozen eggs. I accepted that this would be the case when I did not leave Kindle County. It is not that I am brave, or even stubborn. I just don't think the problems of a new life somewhere else would be any easier than dealing with what is here. I will always be a kind of museum piece. Rusty Sabich. The biggest bullshit thing you've ever seen. Set up, no question about it, and then Della Guardia covered Molto. Really pathetic, the whole business. The guy is not quite the same.

The murder of Carolyn Polhemus, of course, remains unsolved. No one talks about pursuing it, surely not with me, and it's a practical impossibility anyway to try two people for the same crime. A few months ago they had some jailhouse crank who was trying to confess. I sent Lipranzer over to take his statement. Lip quickly reported to the department his judgment that it was a bunch of crap.

I go to Detroit on many weekends. With this job, it is harder than I planned, but when I cannot make it, Barbara sends Nathaniel down. On my second trip up there, Barbara suggested I stay with them. One thing led to another and we have, in a sort of half-ass way, been reconciled. She is not likely to come back here. Her job has worked out well, and the truth, I think, is that she enjoys the distance from me and the reminders. Neither of us expects the present arrangement to last. Sooner or later the swelling will recede and one of us will meet somebody else. When I think about that, I hope it's a woman a few years younger. I would like to have another child. But that's the kind of thing no one can plan. For the present, Nat seems to take comfort from the fact that his mother and I are still married, not divorced.

At times, I admit, I still think of Carolyn. There is none of that crazy longing left, none of the bizarre fixation. I guess she has finally found her place of rest for me. But I puzzle on the experience now and then. What was it, I still think. What was it I wanted with her? What seemed so imperative about it all? In the end, it must have had something to do with my sense of the torment, the agonies which drove her. That legacy of pain was openly displayed in her hard-shell manner, her hipped-up weariness, her ardent courtroom spokesmanship for the likes of Wendell McGaffen, the assailed and woebegone. She was herself someone who had suffered vastly – and who claimed in every visible aspect of her being to have triumphed over it all. That was not true. She could no more leave the horrible weight of her past behind than those Greek heroes could fly close to the sun. But does that mean it is impossible for all of us?

I reached for Carolyn. In a part of me, I knew my gesture was ill-fated. I must have recognized her troubled vanity, the poverty of feeling that reduced her soul. I must have known that what she offered was only the grandest of illusions. But still I fell for that legend she had made up about herself. The glory. The glamour. The courage. All her determined grace. To fly about this obscure world of anguish, this black universe of pain! For me there will always be that struggle to escape the darkness. I reached for Carolyn. I adored her, as the faith healer is adored by the halt and lame. But I wanted with wild, wild abandon, with a surging, defiant, emboldened desire, I wanted the extreme – the exultation, the passion and the moment, the fire, the light. I reached for Carolyn. In hope. Hope. Everlasting hope.

FOR THE BEST IN PAPERBACKS, LOOK FOR THE

In every corner of the world, on every subject under the sun, Penguin represents quality and variety – the very best in publishing today.

For complete information about books available from Penguin – including Puffins, Penguin Classics and Arkana – and how to order them, write to us at the appropriate address below. Please note that for copyright reasons the selection of books varies from country to country.

In the United Kingdom: Please write to *Dept E.P., Penguin Books Ltd, Harmondsworth, Middlesex, UB7 0DA.*

If you have any difficulty in obtaining a title, please send your order with the correct money, plus ten per cent for postage and packaging, to *PO Box No 11, West Drayton, Middlesex*

In the United States: Please write to *Dept BA, Penguin, 299 Murray Hill Parkway, East Rutherford, New Jersey 07073*

In Canada: Please write to *Penguin Books Canada Ltd, 2801 John Street, Markham, Ontario L3R 1B4*

In Australia: Please write to the *Marketing Department, Penguin Books Australia Ltd, P.O. Box 257, Ringwood, Victoria 3134*

In New Zealand: Please write to the *Marketing Department, Penguin Books (NZ) Ltd, Private Bag, Takapuna, Auckland 9*

In India: Please write to *Penguin Overseas Ltd, 706 Eros Apartments, 56 Nehru Place, New Delhi, 110019*

In the Netherlands: Please write to *Penguin Books Netherlands B.V., Postbus 195, NL–1380AD Weesp*

In West Germany: Please write to *Penguin Books Ltd, Friedrichstrasse 10–12, D–6000 Frankfurt/Main 1*

In Spain: Please write to *Longman Penguin España, Calle San Nicolas 15, E–28013 Madrid*

In Italy: Please write to *Penguin Italia s.r.l., Via Como 4, I-20096 Pioltello (Milano)*

In France: Please write to *Penguin Books Ltd, 39 Rue de Montmorency, F-75003 Paris*

In Japan: Please write to *Longman Penguin Japan Co Ltd, Yamaguchi Building, 2–12–9 Kanda Jimbocho, Chiyoda-Ku, Tokyo 101*

FOR THE BEST IN PAPERBACKS, LOOK FOR THE

PENGUIN BESTSELLERS

Riding the Iron Rooster Paul Theroux

An eye-opening and entertaining account of travels in old and new China, from the author of *The Great Railway Bazaar*. 'Mr Theroux cannot write badly ... in the course of a year there was almost no train in the vast Chinese rail network on which he did not travel' – Ludovic Kennedy

Touched by Angels Derek Jameson

His greatest story yet – his own. 'My story is simple enough. I grew up poor and hungry on the streets of London's East End and decided at an early age it was better to be rich and successful.'

The Rich are Different Susan Howatch

Wealth is power – and all power corrupts. 'A superb saga, with all the bestselling ingredients – love, hate, death, murder, and a hell of a lot of passion' – *Daily Mirror*

The Cold Moons Aeron Clement

For a hundred generations the badgers of Cilgwyn had lived in harmony with nature – until a dying stranger limped into their midst, warning of the coming of men. Men whose scent had inexplicably terrified him, men armed with rifles and poison gas...

The Return of Heroic Failures Stephen Pile

The runaway success of *The Book of Heroic Failures* was a severe embarrassment to its author. From the song-free Korean version of *The Sound of Music* to the least successful attempt to tranquillize an animal, his hilarious sequel plumbs new depths of human incompetence.

PENGUIN BESTSELLERS

A Sense of Guilt Andrea Newman

The sensational new novel by the author of *A Bouquet of Barbed Wire*. 'How pleasant life would be, he reflected, if he could have all three of them ... the virgin, the mother and the whore.' 'From the first toe-tingling sentence ... I couldn't put this bulky, breathless beanfeast of a novel down' – *Daily Mail*

Nice Work David Lodge

'The campus novel meets the industrial novel ... compulsive reading' – David Profumo in the *Daily Telegraph*. 'A work of immense intelligence, informative, disturbing and diverting ... one of the best novelists of his generation' – Anthony Burgess in the *Observer*

Difficulties With Girls Kingsley Amis

Last seen in *Take a Girl Like You*, Patrick Standish and Jenny, née Bunn, are now married and up-and-coming south of the Thames. Unfortunately, like his neighbours, Patrick continues to have difficulties with girls ... 'Very funny ... vintage Amis' – *Guardian*

The Looney Spike Milligan

Would Mick Looney's father lie on his HP deathbed? Well, he had to lie somewhere. When he told Mick that they are the descendants of the Kings of Ireland, was he telling the truth? If he was, why is Mick mixing cement in the rain in Kilburn? 'Hysterical' – *Time Out*

In the Midday Sun Guy Bellamy

On the sun-soaked Costa del Sol three fugitive brothers from England – bank robber, tax evader and layabout – contemplate the female form and the shape of things to come. But Matthew, Mark and Daniel have spent far too long in the midday sun ... 'The blue skies blacken very funnily indeed' – *Mail on Sunday*

FOR THE BEST IN PAPERBACKS, LOOK FOR THE

PENGUIN BESTSELLERS

Tomorrow is Too Late Ray Moore

With the wit and irreverence that made him famous, Ray Moore recalls
the ups and downs of his broadcasting career and tells the heartwarming
and intensely personal story of his fight for life – a story that is both an
inspiration and a tribute to his immense courage.

Bad Girls, Good Women Rosie Thomas

In London, on the brink of the sixties, two runaways plunged into the
whirl of Soho nightlife. They were raw and vulnerable – but both of them
knew what they wanted from life. Mattie Banner and Julia Smith: together
they broke all the rules.

Winner Maureen O'Donoghue

At fourteen, Macha Sheridan has nothing but her wagon, three unsaleable
nags and one burning ambition – to breed a champion horse. It is an
obsession that will take her from life among the Irish gypsies to the height
of English society.

A Time and a Place Laura Gilmour Bennett

Cotton Castello, Prospero Vallone and Chiara Galla – the journalist, the
magnate and the film star. Three lives enmeshed – at different times and in
different places – in a web of passion, guilt and betrayal. Only now, at the
Villa Robbiano, can the web be broken – and two lovers set free…

Unforgettable Fire: The Story of U2 Eamon Dunphy

The inside story of the rock phenomenon of the eighties. '*Unforgettable
Fire* is a beacon … in a cynical world' – *Time Out*

FOR THE BEST IN PAPERBACKS, LOOK FOR THE 🐧

PENGUIN BESTSELLERS

Cashelmara Susan Howatch

The road to hell is paved with good intentions, as this spellbinding story of three generations divided by love and hatred so clearly shows. By the bestselling author of *Penmarric* and *The Rich are Different*, '*Cashelmara* is a cracker' – *Daily Mirror*

Backcloth Dirk Bogarde

The final volume of Dirk Bogarde's highly acclaimed autobiography, *Backcloth* highlights the people, emotions and experiences that forged the man from the child. 'Prodigiously gifted' – *Daily Mail*

A Time of Gifts Patrick Leigh Fermor

'Nothing short of a masterpiece' – Jan Morris in the *Spectator*. 'More than just a Super-travel book ... it is a reminder that the English language is still a superb instrument in the hands of a writer who has a virtuoso skill with words' – Philip Toynbee in the *Observer*

Runaway Lucy Irvine

The story of Lucy Irvine's life *before* she became a castaway. It's a story you won't forget. 'A searing account ... raw and unflinching honesty' – *Daily Express*. 'A genuine and courageous work of autobiography' – *Today*

Love in the Time of Cholera Gabriel García Márquez

The Number One international bestseller. 'Admirers of *One Hundred Years of Solitude* may find it hard to believe that García Márquez can have written an ever better novel. But that's what he's done' – *Newsweek*

PENGUIN BESTSELLERS

A Fatal Inversion   Barbara Vine

Ten years after the young people camped at Wyvis Hall, the bodies of a woman and child are found in the animal cemetery. But which woman? And whose child? 'Impossible to put down' – Anita Brookner. 'I defy anyone to guess the conclusion' – *Daily Telegraph*

The Favoured Child   Philippa Gregory

The gripping new bestseller from the author of *Wideacre*. Wideacre Hall is a smoke-blackened ruin, but in the Dower House two children are being raised in protected innocence – equal claimants to the Wideacre inheritance. Only one can be the favoured child. Only one can be Beatrice Lacey's true heir...

Crimson Joy   Robert B. Parker

Just because all the victims are black women doesn't necessarily make the killer racist or sexist. Just because he sends Quirk a letter saying he's a cop doesn't mean it's true. *Crimson Joy* pits Frank Spenser against a psychopath.

Oscar Wilde   Richard Ellmann

'Exquisite critical sense, wide and deep learning, and profound humanity ... a great subject and a great book' – Anthony Burgess in the *Observer*. 'The witty subject has found a witty biographer' – Claire Tomalin in the *Independent*

O-Zone   Paul Theroux

It's New Year in paranoid, computer-rich New York, and a group of Owners has jet-rotored out to party in O-Zone, the radioactive wasteland where the people do not officially exist. 'Extremely exciting ... as ferocious and as well-written as *The Mosquito Coast*, and that's saying something' – *The Times*